THE GARDEN GIRLS

JESSICA R. PATCH

LOVE INSPIRED

Stories to uplift and inspire

If you purchased this book without a cover you should be aware that this book is stolen property. It was reported as "unsold and destroyed" to the publisher, and neither the author nor the publisher has received any payment for this "stripped book."

LOVE INSPIRED®

Stories to uplift and inspire

Recycling programs
for this product may
not exist in your area.

ISBN-13: 978-1-335-46307-4

The Garden Girls

Copyright © 2024 by Jessica R. Patch

All rights reserved. No part of this book may be used or reproduced in any manner whatsoever without written permission except in the case of brief quotations embodied in critical articles and reviews.

This is a work of fiction. Names, characters, places and incidents are either the product of the author's imagination or are used fictitiously. Any resemblance to actual persons, living or dead, businesses, companies, events or locales is entirely coincidental.

For questions and comments about the quality of this book, please contact us at CustomerService@Harlequin.com.

® is a trademark of Harlequin Enterprises ULC.

Love Inspired
22 Adelaide St. West, 41st Floor
Toronto, Ontario M5H 4E3, Canada
www.LoveInspired.com

Printed in U.S.A.

Advance praise for *The Garden Girls*

"In *The Garden Girls*, Jessica R. Patch creates a perfect storm of thrilling suspense and intricate plot twists that will leave readers breathless!"
—Nancy Mehl, author of the Ryland and St. Clair series

"Chilling! *The Garden Girls* is a story I won't be forgetting anytime soon. Jessica R. Patch knows how to deliver a gripping plot with dynamic characters that left me unable to sleep until that final page!"
—Natalie Walters, bestselling and award-winning author of the Harbored Secrets series

"In a word, WOW! The story caught me up and didn't let go to the final page. Tight action, beautiful pacing. Highly recommended."
—Carrie Stuart Parks, bestselling and award-winning author

"Riveting! Jessica R. Patch has created an immaculate psychological thriller. Well-written characters and a plot that sizzles and crackles with danger made this story impossible for me to put down, and yet I didn't want it to end… It's that good. *The Garden Girls* will leave you breathless."
—Mary Alford, *USA TODAY* bestselling author of *Among the Innocent*

"Buckle your seatbelt! Jessica R. Patch is about to blow you off the road with *The Garden Girls*. The story will grab you on the first page and won't let go until *The End*!"
—Patricia Bradley, *USA TODAY* bestselling romantic suspense author of *Counter Attack*, book one in the Pearl River series

"Jessica R. Patch weaves a story that is full of creepy twists and turns and fully fleshed characters. Her atmospheric tale spans the suspense, thriller and romance genres in a way that will satisfy lovers of all three. Buy yourself a copy, but don't read it before bed!"
—Dana Mentink, *USA TODAY* and *Publishers Weekly* bestselling author

"Jessica R. Patch has presented a story of truth that overcomes horror, grace that is born out of love, and redemption that is forged in sacrifice. Terrifying yet beautiful, *The Garden Girls* is everything you expect from Patch and so much more."
—Jodie Bailey, *USA TODAY* and *Publishers Weekly* bestselling author

Also by Jessica R. Patch

Love Inspired Trade

Her Darkest Secret
A Cry in the Dark

Love Inspired Suspense

Texas Crime Scene Cleaners

Crime Scene Conspiracy
Cold Case Target

Quantico Profilers

Texas Cold Case Threat
Cold Case Killer Profile
Texas Smoke Screen

Cold Case Investigators

Cold Case Takedown
Cold Case Double Cross
Yuletide Cold Case Cover-Up

For additional books by Jessica R. Patch,
visit her website, www.jessicarpatch.com.

To the late and great Susan Snodgrass.
This will be the first book I've ever written that you haven't read and reviewed, and I know how much you anticipated Ty's story. I hope I've done it justice.
You're a garden girl of another kind now, walking in paradise.
No more sorrow. No more tears. See you someday. Much love.

Prologue

Friday, August 24

Sharp claws scrape along my neck.

Back and forth.

Back and forth.

Zzzzt…zzzzzzz…zzzt…

Buzzing fills the room, and I strain to open my eyes but they're like molasses, thick and sticky and slow-moving. My stomach jumps and the room shifts as my blurred vision registers red walls and coffee-colored concrete. I inhale a hint of bleach and incense with a spicy note as I shift to survey the rest of the room, but my muscles ripple like languid water.

The air conditioner kicks on, and the cold air raises chills across my naked body.

I'm…*naked*. A fist squeezes my lungs as panic rips through my system. My memories are disjointed.

Where am I? How did I arrive here?

What is happening to me? What has already happened? Shoe soles click on the floor and silence my questions.

I am not alone. Or... I wasn't. The door closes with a quiet click.

Get up. Move. Run!

Gripping the sides of a massage table, I roll off, and my bare feet hit cool flooring. The walls close in and shift, and my stomach roils. Something is wrong. Off.

Floor-to-ceiling mirrors cover an entire wall, and my breath catches as reality comes into view.

Pink flower buds wend through a vine of black along my neck and upper back.

Confusion clouds my senses, and I stand cemented in place gawking at the angry red skin, sore and tender and smeared with glossy petroleum jelly.

A tight knot grows in my throat, and tears stab with heated force against the backs of my eyes.

I have to get out of here.

Behind me, I spot a twin bed with luxurious sheets and a thick white comforter as well as tattooing equipment. My hands tremble. Am I in a tattoo parlor? *Why* is a bed in here?

Lying on the floor next to the bed is an old iron cuff attached to a thick, heavy chain that is anchored to the wall.

Why is that in here and where are my clothes?

I snatch the downy comforter and drape it over my exposed body.

Run. Run. Run!

I open the door but have no clue which way to go or where he is or how long until he finds and cuffs me to that bed.

I've been trapped before at the hands of a vicious predator. Old memories surface and spur me across the carpeted flooring. The hall veers left. My eyes begin to adjust to the darkness as I flee to safety—no.

To a dead end.

Defeat leaches like muddy water into my soul, and my chest aches. The only choice is to turn around.

But *he's* in that direction.

Sweat slicks down my temples and spine, springing up through my pores like an underground fountain as I return the way I came.

I see what might be a crack in the wall. Light seeps through from the other side. As I approach, I discover it's a door made to look like part of the wall. I swallow hard and guide my fingers along the smooth wood until I feel a lever. I push it and the door releases, but it takes some grit to open it enough for me to slide through.

I expect some kind of lair or dungeon or God knows what— a wall with torture devices and cages—but it's not.

It's a living room with wall-to-wall windows overlooking dark water.

Where is he?

I suck in a breath as creaking registers on the stairs. There's nowhere to hide, and the comforter is bulky and will easily give me away. I have no option but to ditch it in the corner. I can't dwell on modesty.

Outside.

I dart toward the sliding glass door, silently slide it open and slip out into the warm night air before scrambling to the edge of the balcony. I crouch to make myself small, like when I was a child and needed to obscure myself.

Maybe he doesn't realize I'm gone, but then it hits me.

I didn't shut the secret door concealing the other rooms.

A sob bubbles to the surface as I shake uncontrollably like I've woken from anesthesia. The ground is far below me. I'd die or break my legs, maybe my spine. But I'd rather die than go back to that room.

To that chain.

To more tattoo needles.

To him.

I draw up my knees and wait, pray. Hope.

When the door doesn't open, I scoot across the deck, the raw wood digging into tender flesh, but I need to see if the coast is clear.

What if he's standing at the door, waiting? Watching?

I hear something and freeze.

One Mississippi. Two Mississippi... I count silently until I reach Twenty Mississippi and scoot again.

I can't be sure if he's nearby. If he is, deep in the marrow of my bones, I know the kinds of things that await me. I know what evil men can do. I've seen it. Experienced it.

Finally, I muster the courage to peep through the door. The room is empty and dimly lit from the one glowing lamp. I creep inside; my brain is fuzzy and spins.

No footsteps. Only bulging shadows in the corners.

I slither across the Berber carpet and inhale the newness. A set of stairs is on the other side of the open living concept. About ten feet of space isn't occupied with furniture, which means when I make a run for it, and he enters the room, I'll have no cover.

If he doesn't and I make it downstairs, he could still be waiting for me.

I try to form a defense plan, but my brain might as well be sludge. Making my move, more out of my flight response than logic, I army-crawl across the open space to the stairs.

Two sets of six. I practically roll down the first set and pause.

He's not there at the small landing.

Six more to go.

This time I move slower, ignoring the adrenaline shouting *sprint*. I can't. He could be waiting and I need to listen.

One...two...three...four...five...six. I pause again at the bottom of the stairs.

No light befriends me on the ground floor. Only darkness—

and darkness is never a friend. Darkness is deceptive, offering false security. Nothing good transpires in darkness. It's not a refuge to hide. But a place to be found. In the dark, I can't see my predator, but I know he's lurking.

The door is five feet away to freedom, and I sprint for it.

Hope blooms in my chest.

I mutter a prayer as I run. Three feet left.

Two.

Thank God, I'm here. I twist the knob.

It's locked.

A cry cracks loose inside me, but I hold it down and fumble with the dead bolt.

Shuffling sounds across tile.

Closer. Closer.

I manage to turn the dead bolt and pull on the door, but it sticks.

He's coming. The clicks are methodic, slow and measured as if he's in no hurry. Like he knows I can't escape. It's a game.

Please. Please. Come on!

The door opens and I slip out, forcing myself to stay calm in case my mind is playing tricks on me and it's not him. This time, I make sure to close the door behind me. The air is balmy and the wind rustles through the grass.

The briny sea air washes over my tongue and the marsh grass swishes as I dart down a private boardwalk that leads… I don't know where. I only know to run and eat up the ground and create distance between me and the house of horror. Between me and *him*.

Thick walls of clouds block the moonlight.

A door slams. Then I hear something.

Thwupt. Thwupt. Thwupt.

He's dragging something across the boardwalk. I dare not turn to look.

He's coming.

Slow and methodical. Silent. Only the awful dragging noise.

Nothing comes into view but marshland and water surrounded by clusters of trees. Alligators lie in wait. I can't remember how I know this. There are snakes and snapping turtles
too.

But *he's* behind me.

Plopping noises in the water draw my attention, and I freeze.
What is it? Will it approach me or prey on me if I enter too?

I can't risk staying on the boardwalk. I ease myself into the
icy depths and it steals my breath. Slime oozes over my feet,
and I sink into mire. Murky water reaches my waist, sending
a shock along my abdomen, but I can't gasp. Instead, I push
through the grass and hope the stirring due to my movement
won't alert him of my location.

Sharp twigs and rocks gouge into the bottom of my feet,
and I crunch my bottom lip to keep from crying. Marsh grass
appears soft at a glance, but it's strong and sharp like knitting
needles and stabs into my flesh and tender places where I've
been tattooed in flowers.

Ahead is a patch of dense trees that would conceal me even
in daylight. A huge splash sends ripples only a few feet away,
startling resting birds to flight. Now I know what's been causing the dragging noise.

A canoe.

He's cutting through the narrow channels and at an advantage.

I can't stop now. I push through the mud, which tries to hold
me captive, and toward the dense thicket of trees. I finagle my
way inside, but it's like camping in a thorn bush, and nettles rip
my flesh. A quiet cry escapes my throat, and I cover my mouth.

Did he hear me? Does he know I'm here?

I shiver in the water, my teeth chattering as something light-
weight drops onto the crown of my head and skitters into the
thick layers before I can catch it.

I squeeze my eyes shut and clench my jaw to muffle a scream. What hideous legged creature is creeping through my hair?

What swims unseen below my waist?

Plop. Plop. Plop.

Fish, alligators, snakes…him?

"Daaaah, daaaah, dah daaaah," his rich buttery tone sings. It echoes through the wetland and sweeps over my skin like icy talons. "I've got all night," he continues singing. "I'll take my time." I cup my hands over my mouth to silence my chattering teeth. He's close. So close. "I'll find you. There's nowhere to hide," he belts out as if we're in a Broadway show. His voice is magical and terrifying. "You belong to meeeee… You want only meee…"

I can't stay here. He'll find me. I work as silently as possible out of the thicket and away from the concentration of his voice. I hoist myself onto the wooden boardwalk because he believes I'm in the water. Rushing is out of the question. He'll hear my footfalls. Slow and steady is about all I can muster anyway. My legs might as well be licorice sticks.

He's still singing and slicing an oar through the water as I forge ahead, quickening my steps by a small measure until I finally reach the end of the boardwalk and am on dry ground. In the woods.

The woods mean I'll find a road at the clearing. Help will drive by, and I'll flag it down to freedom.

I wait a beat while my eyes adjust to greater darkness. The trees loom overhead, and the ground is mushy and mixed with sand. I stub my toe, tripping over roots jutting out, but press on. There's a path and I follow it. Bike path maybe?

My feet are cut and bleeding and my head pounds. The path curves, then straightens out, and I halt.

Not a road.

Not freedom.

Before me is a long stretch of beach littered with driftwood and shells that cut into my feet. Beyond the beach is the end-less sea. No homes. Only wetland to my back and the sea ev-erywhere else.

I have no boat. No canoe. Nothing to propel me to freedom. I'm on a private island, and I finally remember how I arrived.

Defeat injects into my veins, and I collapse to my knees, hot tears streaming down my cheeks.

Heavy footfalls clomp along the dock but not rushed. He has no reason to hurry. I'm out of places to run, to hide.

I'm out of time.

He's humming now instead of singing as if he's simply tak-ing a nighttime stroll. "I won't be thrilled if you've ruined my masterful work, darling." I smell his expensive cologne before I feel his presence looming over me. His silky pants blow in the breeze and brush my skin. He sighs as if I've been a petu-lant child and squats beside me, his warm, smooth hand knead-ing my lower back. "Have you gotten it all out of your system now?" he murmurs.

"Please let me go."

He lifts my chin like a lover, almost reverent. "Let you go?" he asks, and it's rife with confusion. "Why would I do that? You belong to me. You gave yourself to me." He reaches into his pocket and retrieves a small roll of thin rope. "To keep us from brawling again. Not exactly civilized behavior, now, is it?" He might as well be a gorilla and me a kitten. "I love nights like this—our scuffle aside of course. Nights when the moon hides and the clouds smother the stars. Night is beautiful. Ro-mantic. Don't you think?"

"You have to let me go."

He sighs and retrieves a thin scarf—my scarf—and shoves it into my mouth. I can't breathe, and vomit hits the back of my throat. "My father always taught me that if you can't say anything nice you shouldn't say anything at all." His voice is frighteningly calm, even sultry.

He hauls me up.

I may be defeated, but I'm not destroyed. Not yet. After he canoes us through the narrow channels of water, he leads me in the side door of the first floor into a mudroom with a large shower and forces me into it after removing my gag. Then he washes away the sand, dirt and debris while inspecting his tattoo work to make sure it's not been damaged.

He dries me off, and doesn't offer me covering. I can't stop shaking. What is he going to do to me now? I picture the chain on the wall in that small square room, but he doesn't take me there. Instead, he leads me to the second floor living room, takes a remote and clicks it. The entertainment system slides open, revealing a hidden room. It's tall and round like a tower with a heavily tinted glass dome. Inside the room is tiled and full of potted plants and flowers. The sound of bubbling water snags my attention; a large seven-tier fountain sits dead center.

It's like an English garden indoors. Beautiful. Exquisite. Masterfully done.

How could someone so vile create such beauty? My thought withers when I see seven large wrought iron birdcages painted white surrounding the glorious fountain.

No birds reside in the cages.

Women do.

Women exactly like me.

Naked and tattooed in flowers. Some more than others. Not one woman looks at me. Their knees are drawn up and their heads rest on them. They're unmoving like statues.

"Come, my little flower. Up you go." He opens the door to an empty cage, and I refuse to enter. I know if I do, I'm trapped forever. "In easy or we approach it the hard way. Your choice of course." He waits, and I peer into his dark eyes with long lashes blinking patiently. His skin is baby-smooth and his face symmetrically perfect. There isn't a single flaw. "You need to make a decision."

I don't want to go inside, but if I refuse, I don't know the level of pain he'll inflict. I only know he will. Reluctantly, I step inside the prison.

His grin is wide and his teeth are straight and white. "You're part of my private garden now. I'm going to teach you how to bloom."

I have no idea what he's talking about, but I want no part of it. "Please," I beg as I grip the bars and lean forward. "I have a family."

His dimples reveal an innocent face, and he reaches inside and caresses my cheek with a feather's touch. "I'm your family. Your maker. You're being reborn."

His voice is rich and infused with sweetness, but it's saccharine. Lying behind the surface of his eyes is a spark of red-hot fury burning. If I kindle it through disobedience it'll ignite. I'm not dealing with sanity. I've been misled. Duped. My memory is returning now—our previous conversations for starters. Underneath the fear, I'm angry at myself. "Just so you know, you've made a grave mistake. I'll be searched for, and I assure you I will be found. He'll come for me."

His laugh is low and rich and full of malevolence. "Oh, my lovely garden girl." He leans in farther until we're nose to nose and his breath smells like cool mint. "I'm counting on it."

Chapter One

Memphis, Tennessee
FBI Field Office, Strange Crimes Unit
Friday, August 31
8:25 a.m.

"Who drank the last of the coffee?" Agent Tiberius Granger barked, holding up the empty coffeepot and waving it around the Strange Crimes Unit office. "I thought we had a rule. Whoever drinks the last cup makes the next pot. It's a sound rule. I'm an FBI agent, people. I'll find the culprit."

His colleague and the SCU division psychologist, Violet Rainwater, glanced up from her desk. Maybe irritated. Maybe not. Violet always appeared annoyed. "Ty, you drank the last cup. An hour ago. Idiot," she mumbled, and his ride-or-die, Owen Barkley, chuckled.

Well, maybe he had. "In my defense, I'm out of my mind in paperwork. I hate this job."

That earned him another eye roll from Violet until her phone rang and her face softened. "Hey, John." She stood and left the office for privacy. Ty made kissy sounds on her way out the door to get under her skin. She and the Memphis Missing Persons detective had been all about each other since last October when they'd worked a case together in an east Kentucky holler. So much so she now wore a big fat engagement ring, and Ty wondered if she'd shot and killed someone to get it. That was one big rock. And Violet was one good shot.

Owen met him at the coffee bar that their admin assistant, Cami, had put together, calling it Pinterest-worthy. All Ty cared about was that he had hot caffeine to keep him awake when he was out of Monster energy drinks. Owen dumped the filter in the trash. "Your coffee tastes terrible and your tie is ridiculous." He poured distilled water in the coffee tank and scooped grounds into a new filter.

Ty smoothed his new tie. "I'll have you know this tie says I'm a fall guy."

"It's a chalk outline mixed in between fall leaves."

"I know." Ty grinned. "Fall. Guy. Get it?"

"I wish I didn't." He pressed Start and the machine gurgled. "You think serial killers are taking autumn off? Less psychotic since summer is over? It was a scorcher. Even I wanted to kill someone."

Ty leaned on the counter. Early in June, a sick-wad called The Priest had crucified men, leaving a trail across the Louisiana bayou. But nothing since then, except paperwork and phone calls. Well, they had helped Violent Crimes on two cases that weren't considered strange—no religious undertones. Those crazies belonged to the SCU. Nope, it'd been entirely too silent since then. Ty never liked the quiet before the storm. Didn't like storms in general since he'd been caught in a cat 1 hurricane in Barbados. And yet he'd still remembered to bring back gifts to the team, though he'd noted not one of them had ever worn the tropical shirts.

"I'm not sure serial killers take too much time off. Just enough to plot their next murder." He glanced toward the big kahuna's door. "Hey, you bringing a plus-one to Asa and Fiona's wedding?"

Owen frowned. "That's over a month away, bruh. I barely know who I'm taking out this weekend." His sight traveled to the small cubicle at the back of the room where their computer analyst, Selah Jones, sat with thick black frames on the tip of her nose. Ty had a sneaking suspicion they weren't even prescription lenses. Selah and Owen flirted and hung out on occasion, but O didn't date colleagues, and like Ty, he wasn't interested in serious relationships.

Bexley Hemmingway had ruined Ty for other women, or maybe she'd ruined other women for him. Either way, she was the last person he wanted on his mind and the only one on a constant loop since last year when he discovered she hadn't actually been dead for the past seventeen years. He had a million questions, but not enough nerve to call and ask them. Besides, if she'd wanted, she could have found him. He'd been on the national news on more than one occasion, and where serial killers were concerned, everyone had a fetish tuning in to interviews, podcasts and press conferences to mine any perverted nugget they could, so she'd more than likely seen him at least once.

"Who are your weekend options?" Ty asked, redirecting his thoughts away from Bexley and anywhere else, even Owen's dates.

"No one," came the grisly voice from behind. Asa Kodiak, their Papa Bear and SAC, wore a grim expression. Fiona followed with the same narrowed eyes and scrunched brow. They'd been married and divorced, but they'd reconciled after catching the Nursery Rhyme Killer last summer. Since then he'd proposed again, and the next wedding was set for this October. Both Owen and Ty were Asa's best men. Violet was going to be Fiona's maid of honor. Violet in a fancy dress.

This would be fun to watch, record and all-around enjoy. He hoped for John's sake she at least smiled for the photos or their own wedding photos would look like something straight out of the 1800s.

"We're leaving for the Outer Banks at noon," Asa said. "Blue Harbor Island, a little place near Roanoke."

"What nightmare has presented there?" Violet stood by the door to the office, already texting. Probably to let John know she was about to fly to sandy shores for a few days, two weeks tops. That's the longest they stayed on a site, though they often returned if needed.

"Last month they found a woman, Amy-Rose Rydell. She'd been missing six months. They discovered her propped at the door to the Currituck Beach Lighthouse in Corolla. She'd been tattooed in roses from her neck to her mid-thighs. Local sheriff thought it might be one gruesome, but isolated, incident."

"That didn't pan out, huh?" Owen asked.

"No. Forty-five minutes ago, another missing woman from five months ago was discovered in the same manner at the Cape Hatteras Lighthouse entrance." He glanced at his phone. "A Lily Hayes. Both late twenties. Neither woman had the tattoos before they went missing. Her tattoos were of lilies."

"It's bizarre," Violet said, "but you know what I'm going to ask. What brings it to our door? The Manteo resident agency unable to assist?"

Asa pocketed his phone. "They're on site now, but it has a religious undertone."

Almost all of their cases had twisted religious ritualistic behavior, which is why Ty had a job with the SCU. His expertise as a religious behavioral analyst kept him busier than he wanted to be, but people to some extent were predictable if they had some kind of religious faith. Their beliefs motivated not only day-to-day behavior, but their killings as well, and that belief manifested in their signatures, aka their homicidal calling cards.

Ty knew firsthand about warped religious views; he'd been born into a cult and was thankful every day he'd left. Religions boiled down to two things—money and power. Dark purposes and greedy gain. Grubby paws that swiped at the objects they lusted over. From preachers peddling healing handkerchiefs to poor desperate souls riddled with sickness to gurus who ensured people who did good things could come back in the next life more prosperous than the one before. It was all a long con. A scam. A joke.

Ty wasn't falling for any of that nonsense ever again.

Asa rubbed the back of his neck. "They each had a solid white index card nailed into their right palm that read in black print, 'Bloom where you are planted.' That's a phrase used in Christian circles. Right, Ty?"

The Christians—his favorite group of twisted fanatics. How anyone could be duped into believing that a higher power loved a human enough to die for them so they could spend eternity together was ludicrous.

Every soul had a god—self. And no self would die for another human being. End of story. But millions had fallen into the trap, including three of his SCU members. To each his own as long as they didn't push it on him.

"It's a Christian phrase, yes?" Asa asked again.

"It was said by Bishop of Geneva, Saint Francis de Sales, but later made famous by an illustrator. I can't remember her name. It's often seen on bumper stickers with the Jesus fish as well as on home decor signs and stuff. Pretty self-explanatory." He shrugged. "You may not like where you are, but make the most of it. You know, like me and paperwork."

Fiona frowned, and Asa ignored him and turned to Violet. Violet had a superpower. She could slide into the brain of a serial killer and was rarely wrong. It was terrifying, but it came in handy for them. "Violet?" Asa asked.

She blinked a couple of times and cocked her head. "I need

to see photos of the tattoos. Are they good? Hack job? Did he tattoo them and dump them, or did he keep them for a period of time after the tattooing?"

"I don't know," Asa said. "I wouldn't think it would take four months to tattoo someone's body."

Violet closed her eyes again, her telltale sign she was becoming a killer. "I want them for myself. I enjoy seeing my ink, my brand, on them." She opened her eyes. "Sexual assault?"

"I don't know yet," Asa said.

Violet returned to that dark place and Ty studied her, icy fingers scraping down his spine until he inwardly shuddered.

"I want them for myself but it's not enough. I need the world to see them, see what I did. I want them under a spotlight— the lighthouse. It's not about them, though. It's about me. My handiwork."

"We're looking for a narcissist," Fiona said.

Ty grinned. "Owen, did you do it?"

Owen gave him a you're-not-as-funny-as-you-think look. "Ha ha. I'll check the distance between the lighthouses." Owen was a great geopattern theorist, and his work helped them triangulate where killers might live or work and where they hunted based on geographical patterns. Total old school when he had software that would accomplish the same task.

Asa handed Violet an iPad with preliminary photos of the bodies. Ty stood behind her to check out the artwork. "Professional and intricate."

The flowers were identical to each other and the stems were perfectly straight.

"Ty, I rarely say it because it's rarely sayable," Violet said, "but you're right. No way a captive woman would hold still for this. He's meticulous and precise. Moving would cause a mistake, and he doesn't make mistakes. Mistakes enrage him." Violet handed the iPad back to Fiona. "It's more than narcissism.

I need to see the bodies, and I need to know if they've been sexually assaulted. Either way, it's about power and control."

"That'll affect the profile," Fiona said. Being in the SCU meant having access to the Behavioral Analyst Unit in Quantico, but Fiona had gone through the lengthy training early on, and she and Violet often worked up the profiles on their unidentified subjects, or UNSUBS, without calling for a BAU consult.

Owen clapped his hands together. "Well, let's go get him."

Ty made a fist, and Owen bumped it.

Asa's gaze landed on Ty. "Can I see you in my office a minute?"

That was never good. "Sure, Bear." He looked to Fiona for some inkling of what Asa might want, but she offered no help. Definitely not good. Ty followed Asa into his office and closed the door. "What's going on? Am I in trouble?" It'd been a while since he was in the official hot seat.

Asa eased into his leather chair and pointed to the other one across the desk.

Yeah, he was in trouble. But he'd pretty much been toeing the line and keeping his cake hole in check. Ty plopped in the chair. "I've been using a filter in public, Bear. Honest." He'd gotten himself in deep trouble when he'd made some snide comments about a killer in Virginia they'd been tracking. Someone with a cell phone had recorded it, and it had gone viral due to his humorous remarks. Could have been worse. He could've talked trash about a colleague or something. Still, it had been unprofessional, and he'd been careful since then about what he said. In public.

Asa smirked. "I'm not talking about that viral video, though Fiona thinks you deserve a medal to celebrate not ending up on someone else's TikTok or YouTube."

"I kinda concur." Although that case involving the Fire & Ice Killer had gone cold three Septembers ago, he had nagged Ty the most. Ty still wanted him. But there hadn't been a murder since the TikTok and YouTube video released. No new evidence. All Ty was left with was his own blunder. "You're not suspending me again, are you?" His punishment had been fair, and he'd taken that week to gain some clarity in Barbados, only to be trapped in the middle of a hurricane. That had been a suck year.

Asa tented his hands. "No. Have you been paying attention to the news?"

"Like politics and stuff? 'Cause no." He had enough sociopaths to deal with in his job. The last thing he wanted to do was come home and turn them on his TV as background noise.

"This case is in the Outer Banks, and the weather team is keeping an eye on a storm gathering in the southeastern Caribbean Sea. Right now, the probability is low that it'll generate into a hurricane, but they're watching it, and I know how you feel about bad storms and about North Carolina in general."

He held Ty's gaze. Ty did hate storms, but it was highly unlikely they'd be in the Outer Banks when one hit. They'd exit before it was too wild. Being in North Carolina altogether was a whole other ball game—where curveballs were thrown and heavy hitters struck out.

It's where he was born and raised in the Family of Glory. "That's more about Asheville, Asa. Are we going to Asheville?"

"I don't know the answer to that, Tiberius. We never know where a case will lead. You know this. But…since Cami is on vacation, I thought I'd give you the option of staying here and helping Selah answer phones and do the paperwork you love so much."

He scratched his scruffy chin—he hadn't had time to shave for oversleeping. "Paperwork and phones over catching a killer. Hmm…tough choice." He didn't necessarily love going back to his home state. Too many tragic memories and pain. The night he'd been disfellowshipped from the Family, it had been storming. Maybe that was the genesis of his fear and hatred of storms. But this was an assignment. A chance to catch a sicko.

"I'm not paralyzed by my past, and I've worked other cases in North Carolina." Which had been few and far between. "I'll be fine." He stood. "But thanks, man. I appreciate you looking out for me."

"If you're good, I'm good."

"I'm good. This case has nothing to do with me. And I'll be on my best behavior." He saluted.

Asa raised an eyebrow. "That's really not saying much."

"That's valid." He left the office with a grin, then spotted Violet poring over a file with pursed lips. "What's up?"

She tapped her index finger to the cleft in her chin. "This case reminds me of one of our cold ones. I couldn't place it, but when Asa called you in his office, it jogged my memory."

If Ty's possibility of getting into trouble jogged her memory of a cold case, then it had to be the Fire & Ice Killer. "Which one?" he asked anyway, his stomach churning.

Her face said it all. Yep. The Fire & Ice Killer.

"It's similar," she said. "He staged his victims, naked, at doors of historical churches—beacons of hope."

"Not the same at all. No tattoos."

Violet arched an eyebrow. "Lighthouses are also beacons of hope—bringing ships to shore. Symbolically it fits. Both sets of women in Virginia and North Carolina were in their mid- to late twenties."

"But the Fire & Ice Killer painted his victims' lips red." He'd used Revlon's Fire & Ice lipstick, which is how he earned his nickname. But he only used the lipstick and matching polish on their lips, fingernails and toenails. "No tats. And no flowers in their names."

Violet eyed him until he squirmed inside. "No, but he went silent in Virginia. North Carolina isn't that far away. Maybe he was evolving. From lipstick and polish to a more permanent brand. It's possible he spent the past three years working on his craft. I'll run the signatures through ViCAP. Might take some time, though."

The Violent Crime Apprehension Program would tell them if there had been other similar murders around the country and give them patterns and timelines. Was this possible? "He didn't leave notes that said 'Bloom where you are planted.'"

"But he did leave notes with the same kind of note cards nailed into their palms. Same color of ink."

The sadistic freak had left a message from the King James Version of the Bible. Isaiah 1:18. *"…though your sins be as scarlet, they shall be as white as snow; though they be red like crimson, they shall be as wool."*

Ty wasn't sure how that note had evolved into flowers and notes about blooming. "I'm not buying it."

She folded her arms over her chest. "I'm not trying to sell you. I'm simply saying he could have progressed."

"I wish you wouldn't have said *anything*," he muttered.

He didn't need this looming over him, eating at his gut lining and forcing him to take stock in antacids.

Violet nonchalantly lifted a shoulder as she collected her badge, gun and purse. "If I were the Fire & Ice Killer, I'd bide my time, perfect my game, get *more intricate* and seek revenge on you. He's already in your home state."

A shudder ripped through him. "Don't say stuff like that!"

Because she was rarely wrong. And if it was true, then these murders might be on his head for foolish jesting that some guy caught on a cell video. Yeah, Ty had been made out to be the hero and was hilarious, but the killer wouldn't think it was funny. He'd feel emasculated, challenged and insulted on every level.

Ty waltzed from the office into the hallway and found the YouTube video since he didn't have a TikTok app. He pressed Play. In the video, Ty sat next to Asa and Fiona at an outdoor café, fiddling with his straw and leaning back with his arm casually over the chair.

Dude, it's not going to take us long to find this guy, Ty said. *He's an idiot. I've seen more intricate murders from twelve-year-olds using cats. And…he colored out of the lip lines. That's kindergarten level.* He laughed, and Asa smirked.

No one had known they'd been caught on camera, using humor to deflect the gravity of what they'd seen earlier that day. Not until the next morning when it was trending on Tik-Tok and uploaded to YouTube.

No more bodies surfaced, and the case went ice cold.

But Violet thought otherwise. And she might be right. Maybe he was on fire again and just getting started.

Near Kipos Island, North Carolina
Friday, August 31
7:15 p.m.

The horizon was dipped in magenta, gold, turquoise and purple. The perfect backdrop to the evening as the Artist reclined in the boat at the dock near his island—Kipos Island, meaning *garden*. Every part of this evening was enchanting and planned down to the type of grapes and wine and cheese.

He gazed at Catherine. Exquisite, tall and lithe with virgin skin—his favorite canvas to work with. Not that he couldn't work with marred flesh—he could and he had, but there was something special about skin that had been untouched. Unpainted.

Catherine was on her second glass of merlot and her eyes sparkled and glazed with desire. He'd met her when he'd been on a walking trail at Nags Head. She'd been with a friend. He'd noticed her and she had noticed him, but it wasn't until the friend called her name that he recognized it was a flower, and then he'd expressed more interest.

"The sunset is perfection, don't you think?" she asked through a dreamy sigh.

"It is." He peered at the horizon, wishing for that kind of power—to create something the world would marvel over and post to their social media accounts, making him famous.

He would be famous. His work would be seen all over the world.

Patience was the key, and he'd perfected the virtue.

"You were right about the view from out here," she said in her sweet soprano voice. "It's truly breathtaking."

Blue Harbor was nestled on the Croatan inlet that connected the Pamlico Sound with the Albemarle Sound, and from his island in the center of an archipelago, the scenery was magnificent.

"I didn't even know there were houses out here," she continued.

Ten miles south of Roanoke Island. He'd spent years hunting the perfect place for his garden. His masterpiece.

Patience. Patience. Patience.

That was the problem with most men. Impatience. They rushed and hurried and made messes. Life was about waiting. Right opportunities. Right moments. Perfect storms. That soured his mood. A storm was churning in the Caribbean, and while he anticipated storms, he wasn't thrilled about one possibly hitting. But he wouldn't rush things in a panic. He never panicked.

"Just mine. I like my privacy."

Batting her lashes, she ran her index finger around the lip of the wineglass. "What do you like to do in the privacy of your own home and island?"

"Well, to be honest, whatever I want. It's my island. My home. My…kingdom." He winked, and her cheeks bloomed a lovely shade of crimson. "How's the wine?"

"Delicious. Want a taste?" Her eyes darkened and her pupils dilated.

"I do." He reached for her wineglass, and she pulled it away and leaned forward.

"It might taste better on my tongue." She brushed her lips to his and let him explore the fruity flavor.

"You're right. It does," he murmured against her lips, tasting the fruit and fermentation.

He carefully brushed a strand of her long blond hair behind her ear and pulled back. After all, he was a gentleman. He never took what wasn't offered. If she said no, then it would be no.

But they never said no. Not to him. He never had to beg or force himself.

She set the glass on the deck and slid nearer to him. "You don't have to be shy, Art."

"Catherine, I am far from shy. But I'm on your timetable. Whatever you want or don't want."

She ran her hand through his wavy hair and kissed his neck below his earlobe. "I want," she whispered. "You smell so good." She wrapped her body around his like a snake, her arms around his neck as she faced him.

"What do you want?" he asked. "You must be clear. No mixed signals."

Leaning into his ear, she told him exactly what she wanted, and she was not shy about it.

"Are you sure?"

"I've never been more sure."

"Because you'll belong to me if you do," he breathed as he ran his lips along her jawline. "Do you want to belong to me?"

She leaned back, giving him access to her neck. "Yes."

That was all he needed to hear.

Permission granted.

Catherine wheels. He would remake her with the rare intricate white flowers that bloomed in clusters. Rough textured stems and petals that gave the appearance of wheels. Oh, he owned the perfect shade of green for the centers. She would be a gorgeous addition to his garden.

Chapter Two

Blue Harbor, North Carolina
Saturday, September 1
9:10 a.m.

Last night, once the team arrived, they'd wasted no time. The Dare County sheriff's office had been accommodating. Sheriff Hanover was more than happy to pass the buck as well as the agents in the resident agency, also located in Manteo. They'd all helped, and would aid them if needed, but from here on out, the SCU team had jurisdiction and Asa called the shots. Period.

After, they'd gone back to the beach house that Selah had booked for them in Blue Harbor. Ty made sure to text Cami and let her know that Selah had way better booking skills than her. He'd never forget the B and B in Night Hollow. The thought of that place and that case in Kentucky still freaked him out.

But Asa preferred to stay close to the crimes when they traveled, which wasn't quite as orthodox as other divisions, but this unit wasn't exactly an orthodox unit to begin with. Blue Harbor appeared to be the link between the victims, not the lighthouses, which were spaced throughout the islands of the Outer Banks.

Amy-Rose Rydell lived on Roanoke but worked at a boutique here on the main strip, and Lily Hayes resided at the edge of Blue Harbor and worked at a gift shop three doors down from the boutique where Amy-Rose had been employed. If Blue Harbor was the epicenter of this killer's hunting ground, they wanted to remain close to their predator.

"I could get used to this view," Owen said as he walked out on the second-story deck with a cup of coffee.

The sky was blue and clear like the world was full of sunshine and good days, but the meteorologists were watching the storm in the tropical waters and discussing possible trajectories. It was like a shark, prowling the ocean and scouting out where it wanted to pounce. Unnoticed by its prey that frolicked without a care in the world. Then it made its attack, and once it did, nothing could stop it. Blue Harbor—the Outer Banks. Coastal towns would be powerless against it. Ty wasn't sure which scared him more—the unstoppable hurricane or the possibility that someone might be killing people as part of a revenge scheme against him.

"It is a beautiful view. For now. Won't lie, though. It's bringing up some memories I'd rather forget." Dad had brought him and his two brothers out here for fishing trips, which had been a ton of fun, but there were times Dad wasn't fun at all.

"We could always go back to Miami. That was a trip."

"Bruh," Ty said, and pounded his heart with his fist. "Nothing but love for that weekend."

"You get the list yet?" Owen asked, sipping his coffee. He'd already cleaned up and shaved. Ty noticed the new purple tie. Dude loved purple.

Ty had been tasked with acquiring a list of women who had

gone missing from Blue Harbor and neighboring islands within the past year. He'd asked Selah to put the women with flower names at the top of the list. "Waiting on an email, and then I'll get started. You want some help while I wait?"

"You putting pushpins in my map? Pass." Owen hated anyone messing with his maps. Once Ty had spelled out *LOSER* in orange pushpins, and in retaliation Owen had mixed vinegar with the water in the coffeepot when it brewed. Fortunately, Fiona had gone for a cup before Ty.

"What do you think about Violet's theory? About the Fire & Ice Killer?" The idea had needled him since she said it in her creepy, nonchalant way.

Owen set his cup on the railing and then leaned over it, gazing out at the still waters. "It's possible. But I know you. If it's true, it ain't on you." He smacked Ty's back in a brotherly gesture. And Owen was most definitely his brother—by choice, not by blood. It had been almost twenty years since he'd even spoken with either of his full biological brothers. Truth be told, there was no love lost between him and the eldest of them, Garrick. The younger, Lysander, had only been fourteen when Ty had been disfellowshipped and led out of the gates of his community in Asheville.

"You hearing me, Ty?" Owen asked. "If it is this guy, you can't take blame."

Ty wasn't so sure. "It'll feel like it's on me."

"Violet's stretching based on the locale being North Carolina. I'm not saying he hasn't evolved and moved locations, but it's a serious stretch as far as I'm concerned." Owen finished his coffee and brushed his lavender dress shirt.

Ty's phone dinged with an email notification. "Got the list of missing women, concentrating on those with flowers in their names only—for now. Selah said eight women with flower names have gone missing in the past year." He scanned the list. "Amy-Rose Rydell from Roanoke, but worked in Blue Har-

bor. Dahlia Anderson—a travel agent from Nags Head. Ivy
Leech, a schoolteacher at Cape Hatteras and Lily Hayes, sou-
venir shop employee from Blue Harbor. Iris Benington was a
nurse in Nags Head, Heather Wade was a barista in Ocracoke.
Susan Mayer lived and worked in Blue Harbor and went missing
eight months ago." He paused on the last name and location.

"What is it?" Owen asked.

He read it again. Two times, then three to be sure he wasn't
misreading the name. He unbuttoned his top button, which
was choking him, and swiped at the sweat gathering above his
lip. "I know the most recent woman who's gone missing. She
lives here. In Blue Harbor." His mind wouldn't process the information. How was this possible? "Owen, I'm not sure Violet
is stretching about the Fire & Ice Killer." Not now.

"Who is it? How do you know her?" Owen leaned in to
read the email.

He didn't have a clue where to begin. His past was complicated, unbelievable and disturbing. Not to mention shameful
and humiliating, especially the events that occurred the night
he was disfellowshipped. "I grew up in the Family of Glory.
A cult. The missing woman—Ahnah—is the little sister of the
girl I wanted to someday marry. To make a long story short, a
lot of crazy things went down when I was eighteen. Bex was
only seventeen, and we were going to sneak away since she
was a minor."

"Why? You realize it was a cult?"

"No. We one hundred percent believed we were condemning
ourselves from heaven for leaving, but we loved each other, and
Bex's hand had been asked for by my older brother, Garrick."

Owen frowned. "So?"

"In the Family, the eldest son of each wife—it's not bigamy
to have many wives in the Family—marries first, then the next
is allowed to be married, and so on. My eldest brother from

our mom asked for her, and it was granted by the Prophet." He still wasn't sure why when he knew how much Ty loved her.

"You were running away and breaking all the rules for love," Owen said.

"Yes, and we were taking Ahnah with us. She was only twelve at the time. The Family wasn't a safe place for girls or women. Bex wouldn't leave her, and neither would I. I went to Atlanta to find an apartment for us and a job—hoping to lose ourselves in a big city so they couldn't find us and haul her and Ahnah back to Asheville. In the end it didn't matter how many miles we put between us."

"Why?" Owen asked.

"When I returned, I found out that Bex had been taken into the Prophet's marriage circle—or harem, if you want to get technical. I broke the greatest law."

"Which is?"

"I slept with her outside of the marriage bed, and it was brought to the Prophet's attention. See, in the Family, if a woman is engaged to a man and he finds out she's not a virgin, then the proposal is forfeited. She's ruined for any other man...except for the Prophet, who takes her into his home as mercy. She'll marry him and bear him more children." Ty paused at Owen's shocked expression. "I know. It's archaic and sick, and honestly, the Prophet's way of adding to his collection of young brides."

"Did she admit to it?"

"I don't know. Probably not, but the wives examine her to prove it."

"You are kidding me."

Ty's neck flushed hot. "I wish I were. I didn't see her. I was promptly escorted to the Prophet's office and rebuked and disfellowshipped, then escorted to the gates and out of the commune."

"Which is where?"

"A community in the mountains on the outskirts of Asheville. But only the leadership lived in the gated community. The Family has tens of thousands of followers all over North Carolina, and they attend church by satellite, and there are monthly gatherings in the mountains for everyone."

Owen inhaled deeply. "You never saw her again?"

"No," Tiberius answered quietly. Now Ahnah was among the missing women. Vanished on August 23.

"You think the Fire & Ice Killer discovered this information and targeted Ahnah? Why not Bex?" Owen asked.

"For one, Ahnah's middle name is Oleander, and it's a flower. I already knew that, but it's on the full-name list sent to me. Bexley doesn't have a flower in her name."

"And for two?" Owen asked.

Ty had no idea. He was positioned behind a thick veil, unable to see the killer's motives. "Asa still in the house?" Ty ignored Owen's question, trying to make sense of this new information while being flooded with old, sour memories.

"Yeah. He's flying to Raleigh to the ME's office in an hour. I think Fiona is going with him. Maybe Violet." Owen followed Ty inside. "They should be back by lunchtime or right after."

Everyone was in the living room with laptops, coffee and sober expressions.

"PSA…" Ty blurted as he entered. "I was engaged when I was eighteen." Might as well lay it out sooner rather than later.

Asa popped his head up; Fiona followed suit.

Violet cautiously closed her laptop. "This isn't an episode of *Dr. Phil*, Tiberius. And some of us already know it." Ty had revealed this tidbit to her when they were working the Blind Eye Killer case in Night Hollow. He'd overheard a conversation of hers and thought she'd needed to hear something personal from him. He'd been right. They'd bonded—as much as one could bond with Violet at that time. Even now, her personal life with John and his preschool-aged daughter, Stella, was guarded.

"*She* knows that?" Owen asked, his eyes wide as he gawked at Ty. "How does she get to know that and I'm just now finding out?"

Some subjects were too difficult to discuss, even with his best friend. Ty repeated what he'd already told Owen.

"Bexley Hemmingway?" Fiona asked. "That's why you snatched the business card from me that night I gave it to Ruby Boyd back in Night Hollow."

"And why you told me to vet her first," Violet said.

"What does that have to do with the rando declaration?" Selah, their tech analyst, asked through Asa's computer monitor. He kept her on video call most of the day.

"Ahnah is on the list of missing women, and Oleander is her middle name. Vanished a week ago. Lives here. The address is registered to Bexley Hemmingway." He tugged at his collar again. "Vi, you might be right about the Fire & Ice Killer." He turned to Asa. "I—uh—don't want to recuse myself. But if you think I should…"

Asa tapped a pen on the table. "We don't know that it's the killer out of Virginia. But I don't want to rule out the fact that whoever is doing this might be personal to you since a victim is personally connected. It's interesting to note, but possibly coincidental."

Yet doubtful, and the turmoil in Asa's steely gray eyes said as much.

"I can go with Ty to interview the families of the missing women," Violet said. "I need to work the victimology, and you don't need me at the ME's office. We can reinterview the victims' families while we're out if we have time." Violet holstered her weapon, then slipped on a black blazer. She wasn't one for wasting time.

"Asa?" Ty asked, waiting to see if he wanted him actively working the case. He almost hoped he'd tell him to pack it up and go home. If not, he would have to visit Bexley, and he wasn't ready for that. Wasn't sure he could. The easy way out was hopping a plane for home. Not to mention the possible hurricane brewing over the ocean that could decimate the whole coast.

"Go ahead. We'll take it one day at a time."

Sounded about right. Asa had let Fiona actively work a personal case, concerning the Nursery Rhyme Killer. Well, *let* was a loose term. Fiona was going to do what Fiona was going to do. Ty nodded, then followed Violet to the Suburban. They'd rented two of them. Most times local law would give them a cruiser, but in these small unincorporated island communities, there weren't any to spare. "You familiar with the Outer Banks?" Ty asked.

"Is this your way of asking to drive?" Violet asked.

"Yes."

"Just ask, you buffoon." She tossed him the keys and climbed in the passenger side.

"You do a lot of name-calling since you and John got together. Is this some kind of aggression aimed at him you're transferring onto me?" He cranked the ignition, then ran a hand through his wind-whipped hair. It was vicious coming off the surf.

Violet buckled her seat belt. "Is this your way of avoiding the Bexley Hemmingway conversation?"

"Maybe. Probably. Yeah." He punched in Bexley's address— a beach house six minutes away.

Violet remained silent, sipping coffee from a thermal cup as Ty listened to the GPS and drove to Bexley's. The house was a small bungalow painted a salmon color with white trim. A long dock coming from the side of the house and rounding to the back stretched out to the sound, where a small private beach held two blue-and-white-striped chairs with umbrellas.

He parked, noticing no cars were in the driveway.

"You going to get out of the vehicle and approach the house

or just call her name from here and see if she comes out?" Violet asked.

He was working up the courage. "You should know, when I said she married the Prophet, there's more to it."

"How much more?"

"The Prophet—he's my father."

Violet remained stoic, but she'd understand having a monster for a father better than anyone on the team, and maybe that's why it was easier to confide in her.

"I wasn't raised only as a cult member, Violet. I was the son of the First Wife, making me, and my two full-blooded brothers, heirs."

Violet didn't appear shocked or appalled. But then, nothing seemed to ruffle her feathers other than Ty's nonsense. "You're saying the woman you wanted to marry was forced to marry your father."

His stomach pitched, and he could barely even bring himself to envision it. "That's what I'm saying. Bertrand Granger. He goes by B and Granger outside the cult. Inside people call him Father Granger or the Prophet. Even his wives. So that's gross." But it had been completely normal until he'd left and seen what the real world was like. "When I was disfellowshipped from the Family, he had twenty wives, and I can't count how many children."

"Is it more complicated than *that*?" Violet asked, and opened the car door.

"Don't you think that's enough?" He walked up to the front door and banged on it, then rang the doorbell, his insides trying to claw their way out.

No one answered.

A woman hollered from next door, catching his attention. "She's not home, hon. She's at work. If you're looking for Bexley Hemmingway."

"I am," Ty said and held up his credentials. "Do you know Ahnah Hemmingway?"

The woman with a short blond bob nodded emphatically and closed the distance between them. She was probably in her early sixties with bright blue eyes and an easy smile. "Oh yes. She's a sweet girl. Used to help me weed my herb garden when I was down in the back. Terrible thing that happened to her. She wouldn't up and leave like that."

Ty didn't believe it either. Ahnah and Bex had been closer than close. Bex had protected Ahnah, sometimes at a cost— the last one pretty steep for him and Bex. "Where does Bexley Hemmingway work?"

"Little counseling center near Blue Harbor Baptist Church."

He nodded. "Thanks." After searching and entering the address in the GPS, he and Violet traveled in silence the mile and a half to a little slate-gray facility built on stilts and framed by palm trees. A sign outside read Ruth's Refuge Counseling Services.

Ty turned off the engine and unbuckled, but didn't budge. Seventeen—almost eighteen—years since he'd laid eyes on Bex. He wasn't sure he could face her and under these circumstances—to tell her some sadistic killer who might very well have a vendetta against Ty had targeted her sister. That couldn't be random, and yet who on earth would know that he, Bexley and Ahnah were connected—or alive? Someone who knew how to dig for information like their own analyst, Selah Jones. She could have found the information if she wanted. She might even know already and was sitting on it.

But to go in and face Bexley. It was deeply personal, and he wasn't sure he could do it.

He needed to, though.

"Vi," he choked out. He needed to be alone with no one else privy. The uncertainty of how it would go down was nauseating. If Bex never died, then why not contact him? She had a counseling center in Memphis. She had to know he was part of the SCU South Division located in Memphis. Why not reach out? He had so many questions, but he feared the answers.

Violet wrapped her hand over his, a shocking gesture for her. "I'll be here. Go in. Do what you have to in order to get the job done."

He shifted in his seat. "I like you better since John came into your life. No telling me to pull it together and get over it—even though you're a psychologist and should never say that."

"John isn't who came into my life who made the change, Tiberius. But he's definitely made an impression."

Ty couldn't deny a change in Violet or Asa and Fiona. But he had a hard time coming to grips with the idea that a higher power did some kind of internal supernatural sanctification. If Ty wanted to quit eating donuts, he quit eating donuts. If he wanted to be nicer, he chose to be. No help from above, just good old-fashioned willpower.

"John's a good dude. I like him." He couldn't speak to the other. Smelled like rot to him. He got out, his intestines knotting and his palms clammy. He climbed the five wooden steps and opened the door. The smell of lavender hit his senses, and soft instrumental music filtered through a speaker. A young woman with short, spiky red hair smiled. "Help ya?"

"I need to speak with Bexley Hemmingway." He held up his FBI credentials, and her eyes watered.

"Is Ahnah...?"

"Still missing." He put her at ease—as much as one could be when a loved one was unaccounted for. As of now, they couldn't say she was deceased. "Do you know her well?" he asked.

"As well as one can know Ahnah. She's private. Loves to paint with watercolors. She made me that." She pointed to a painting of a sunset over the water.

"It's very nice." Ahnah had loved to color as a child, and Ty had shown her how to do what he'd called doodling. He was pretty good with a pencil and a blank canvas. He'd taught her how to make flowers. They were pretty easy. A circle for the middle, then loops all around. Guess she'd kept up with the hobby.

"Bexley is straight back on the right. I'll let her know a federal agent is here."

"Thank you." He trudged down the hall, his feet heavy and stalling out on him. Standing in front of her door, he debated texting Violet to switch places with him. He could recuse himself for being close to the case, but that was the coward's way out, and Ty wasn't yellow. He raised his fist to knock when the door opened, his hand in midair.

Ty lost his faculties. His breath.

Dark eyes met his. Her long curly black hair was still thick, massive and uncontrollable.

"Tiberius," Bexley breathed, wide-eyed. Her cheeks paled, and she blinked a few times as if she wasn't sure that what stood before her was actual flesh and blood.

His name on her lips retrieved a tsunami of good memories. Hopes and dreams and promises of a future with one another, which included a big family and no one ordering them around or deciding their futures without their consent.

Little lines had sprouted around her eyes and she was curvier than at seventeen, but he couldn't deny she was still beautiful with eyes a little too big for her face, overshadowing her pert nose and thin lips.

He had to speak. Form a word. Anything.

"Hey Bex."

Bexley Hemmingway stood frozen. Seeing Tiberius in person was the moment she'd dreamed about and dreaded. She stood dumbfounded for what seemed forever, then her brain finally kicked in, and the biggest fear concerning Tiberius being here became a reality.

"Ahnah." He was here about her sister. Had they found her? Was she alive? Bexley had been going out of her mind for a week.

"She hasn't been found yet." He held up his credentials and spoke with cool professionalism, but his green eyes were windows into his soul, and he was uncomfortable and confused with every right to be. She'd disappeared as dead and never once contacted him, and then there was the awkwardness of the fact she'd been forced to marry his father.

She had her reasons even if over the years she'd warred with them. Had she made the right call, or was forging ahead without him the biggest mistake she'd ever made? She wasn't sure. "I've seen you on TV before—a few years back. Press conference." She didn't bring up she'd seen a viral video of him in regards to a killer they didn't catch in Virginia. No point kicking him while he was down, and seeing her would be a big low spot for him.

His gaze was searching, angry and heartbreaking, but she couldn't look away. Bexley had to own up to her choices—all of them. And she didn't want to look away from him. He'd always been a handsome boy, but now he was a striking man. Muscular, his face chiseled and strong with a lawn of scruff shading his lower face. A possibly defiant act, if even subconscious. Men in the Family of Glory were to be clean-shaven at all times. This look fit Tiberius in his well-tailored suit and shiny red tie, and it clued her in to the fact he'd probably not gone back to the Family had the Prophet been forgiving. Sometimes he was when it came to Tiberius. Ty had always been his father's favorite.

If he was here to investigate, that meant he'd be on the island and in her business for more than a few moments. Days maybe. Weeks even. "How long will you be here?"

"Am I bothering you? Am I an inconvenience?"

No and yes. "Of course not. I… I didn't realize the FBI would be involved and especially not the SCU."

"I'm not at liberty to discuss intimate details of the case. I'm here to talk about Ahnah. Can I come in?"

Bexley was all but barricading her office. "I'm sorry." She swung her arm and motioned him inside. "Yes, of course. I don't have a client for another fifteen minutes."

He sidestepped her, and she caught a whiff of understated cologne and body wash. She stood at the threshold while he nonchalantly perused her office, but she knew him well. He was going far deeper than the casual observer. Tiberius had a keen eye for detail. She'd always admired that in his drawings. She'd saved every single one he'd given her. Some things couldn't be tossed out and forgotten. Couldn't be left behind.

Pointing to a blue club chair, she asked him to have a seat. Then she sat behind her modest oak desk. Sea colors were her favorite, and she'd set up her office in coastal shades that evoked a sense of peace and tranquility. But not even the soft robin's-egg-blue walls could calm her nerves now. To hide her trembling hands, she balled them into fists and tucked them into her lap under the desk.

Tiberius lowered his frame into the chair, his jaw ticking. He removed a notepad and pen from his inner suit coat pocket and laid the notebook on his lap; he clicked the pen, retracting the point several times.

"I have no idea where to start." Did he want to talk about Ahnah? The fact that Bexley and she were alive? How far back would he go, and how much would she tell him? She owed him one hundred percent of the story from that night he was disfellowshipped to today, but she wasn't sure she could trust him with the whole truth. She'd need more facts about his life and where he stood regarding the Family before she loosened her lips too much. Just him being here, knowing she was still alive, could put her in danger.

His jaw pulsed again. "Well, we can start with the fact you're a liar."

She wasn't expecting the barbs so quickly. But that was Tiberius. Flying off the handle before collecting facts. No wonder he had a viral video out there about a serial killer. "I see you're still quick to jump to conclusions and impulsivity."

He slung his hand in the air toward her. "I see you still can't do anything with your hair."

Her...hair? She lightly touched it and then laughed through her nose. No filter. How did he even do this job? It required patience and waiting and a whole lot of filter.

Ty waved off his remark. "Sorry. I didn't mean that."

"To call me a liar?" She hadn't ever lied to him or to Ahnah. She hadn't wanted to lie to anyone. It went against everything she believed, and she'd taught Ahnah to be honest as well. Honest and a free-thinking woman who was strong and independent. Something the Family men didn't allow. They were—for the most part—cruel with the belief that women were nothing more than sex objects and baby incubators to give them a strong posterity. They were better to be seen than heard and to look pretty while at it.

"No. I meant that. You can control whether you lie or not. The hair..." His eyes widened as he gave her untamed hair the no-hope-for-you expression, but she caught a glimmer of amusement. Ty always did use humor to deflect or lighten tension or to escape conflict.

"So, are we going to have this talk now?" She braced herself. Time to rehash the past, and she wasn't sure what she was going to say about the present. She wasn't expecting him to show up out of thin air. But over the years, she had been rehearsing what she'd say if the day ever came. Now all her words vanished and she was at a loss.

"No. Because I'm not here about you or us or our past, or even your lies." He ran his tongue across the inside of his

cheek. "I'm here about Ahnah's disappearance and the murdered women at the lighthouses. That's it. Then I'm out of your
hair—pardon the pun—for the next seventeen or so years. Not
here on a white horse, Bex."

His words shouldn't sting, but they did. "I never asked for a
knight or a white horse. I can saddle my own, but clearly, you're
in shock that I'm alive. I imagine you want some answers."

"Bexley I've known you were alive since last October when
I saw the business card you gave to my colleague Fiona Kelly.
You spoke at her church. I've gotten over the shock you're alive.
Not really over the shock you went from one cult to another.
Maybe all the hair's tangled your brain," he mumbled.

Well, this was clearing some cobwebs on where he stood
about the Family, and God. A year, though. He'd known a
whole year and didn't reach out. She couldn't fault him. She
hadn't reached out in almost eighteen. Didn't mean she hadn't
thought of him every single day, because she had. "I see. Well,
I'll tell you all I can about Ahnah, then."

He clicked the pen again and picked up the notepad from
his lap. "Does Ahnah take off often without telling anyone? Is
it possible she's out doing something on her own?"

"She's a grown adult and doesn't need permission, but she
does live in my home. If she plans to be gone for an extended
time, she lets me know so I don't worry. You know I help broken women who have come out of domestic abuse and trafficking. Ahnah has seen what can happen to women, so she's good
about telling me and we have shared locations on our phones to
track one another, but her phone has been off since she's been
missing. I've already spoken to the sheriff numerous times."

"She's…twenty-nine now. Wow," he murmured. "I remember when she was a little squirt following us around as if we
didn't know it."

Bexley smiled. "She loved you very much."

"I loved her," he whispered. "And I am going to find her, Bexley."

"I believe you." She had no reason not to. Tiberius had never been a liar.

"Did she know Lily Hayes and Amy-Rose Rydell?"

"She knew Amy-Rose better. They worked together at Blue Boutique and hung out often. Lily was more of someone she knew in passing. I don't think they spent personal time together, but they did work on the same strip. Most everyone knows each other or of one another."

"Boyfriend?"

"No. She'd dated some but… Ahnah didn't trust most men. You can guess why." Tiberius had witnessed the atrocities that were inflicted upon her sister. Upon many of the young girls in the Family.

Tiberius glanced up from his notepad, compassion in his eyes. That was one thing that had separated him from his father—the Prophet, aka Rand Granger. Her blood boiled at the thought of that vile man and the community he'd created that had warped and twisted everyone who came in contact with him, but he'd won them with great looks and charisma. Then he'd bound them to him and the way of life he'd declared God had given him.

"I do know, and I'm sorry it stunted her growth for relationships." He cast a quick glance at her left ring finger as if checking to see if her growth had been stunted as well. It had, but not for the same reasons. "Were the two of you still close? Did she confide anything in you that might give you pause or anything that would appear abnormal?"

Were they close? It had been a rocky road with Ahnah. At twelve, after they'd escaped, she'd missed Mom and Dad and didn't understand why they couldn't call or visit. She had no concept that what they'd been brainwashed to believe was a lie from the pit. Even Bexley hadn't realized they'd been fed lies until Renee Helton, the woman who'd found them after they'd run and who'd become her mentor, had showed her real truth. It had taken a long time to untangle the false beliefs.

"It was off and on with us. She had some resentment over me taking her away from her life and family, but she later understood I was saving her from your brother. From lies. From a lifetime of subservience to men like him. I put her through counseling—with someone else. Made her take self-defense classes and did anything I could to promote self-awareness and confidence. I wanted her to be her own woman. Make her own choices. Sometimes she thought I was too hard on her, and maybe I was." Bexley had made mistakes. She was human.

"She's had no contact with the Family, including your parents?" he asked, scribbling notes as he spoke.

Seemed like they were getting personal without actually saying it. "No. That was the hardest—not speaking to our mother. But they thought we were dead too. The only person who knew we were alive was Mother Mae. She passed four months ago. I kept in contact with her over the years. She helped us escape from the inside."

"Mother Mae?" He frowned. "Really?"

"Yes. She wanted to leave the cult, after awaking to its barbaric nature, but wouldn't because she knew Rand wouldn't allow her to take the children, and she had four daughters. She stayed to protect them and others the best she could."

"I had no idea," he murmured.

"I called her once, though."

"Mother Mae?"

"No. My mom." Emotion clogged her throat. "I wanted to hear her voice. I never revealed it was me. Never even spoke, but it was like she knew. She said my name, and it was all I could bear. I hung up and never called again. Mother Mae called when Mom died two years ago. Cancer. My dad has remarried. I believe he's up to five wives now."

"I'm sorry. I didn't know about your mom. I always liked her."

Bexley grabbed a tissue and dabbed at her eyes. "Do you see your mom? Since she's out?"

"I do. I found her when I was given the boot. She was living in Greensboro. She moved to Memphis when I got transferred to the SCU. I love her, but she's wacky in new ways." He shrugged.

At least he still had her.

"Did Ahnah help you with Ruth's Refuge? Could one of the men have a vendetta? Any of them threaten her?" he asked.

"No. She's familiar with the work I've done and has seen some of the pain up close, but she never wanted to volunteer or work for the ministry. I suppose it was all too close to home for her. When Renee, the original owner of Ruth's Refuge, passed, I spent a lot of time working and opening new locations across the South. We have eight now. Our most recent one is Memphis. I think Ahnah resented me being away—at first. She was pretty young."

"Good for you, Bexley. Way to entrepreneur it," he said without hiding the cutting sarcasm.

"You made a life. Why shouldn't I?"

He laid the notepad on his lap. "The difference is, Bexley, I made a life because I felt like I had no choice. You were married to my father. I went pretty much mad and hatched all sorts of plans to break in and whisk you and Ahnah away. And I tried."

Bexley drew her hand to the hollow of her throat. "What do you mean you tried?"

Ty raked a hand through his hair. "Six months after I was kicked out and you were..." He shook his head. "I came to beg Father's forgiveness. I hoped he'd show me grace and I could coax you to run again. I didn't care that you'd been with my dad. But when I arrived at the gates, Dalen pulled in behind me. We had a conversation—"

"Couldn't be a good one." His half-brother never cared much for Ty.

"No. He told me you and Ahnah had died in a boating accident about three months after marrying Rand. I didn't believe him, so he brought me to the house. Mother Mae was outside with the children, and she confirmed it. She'd have no reason to lie. Except now, knowing it was her who helped you... I kicked myself for not returning for you three months earlier. I told myself if I had, you might not have been out on the water that day. Might not have died."

Bexley's heart splintered. "If she thought you were returning for grace, she'd have never told you the truth. And she sure wouldn't have shared that information in front of Dalen."

"I'm seeing the whole story now."

A rotten devastating story.

"All these years I've carried your death and my guilt because I felt to blame," Ty said. "It's my fault you had to marry him at seventeen. My fault for everything, and yet you weren't dead at all. And no wonder Ahnah resented you. You left her behind for your career."

"You make it sound like I abandoned her."

"Maybe it's a pattern."

She sucked in a deep breath. "I think we're done here." He was becoming belligerent, which meant he wasn't going to talk like an adult, and he wasn't going to obtain what he needed professionally. Not today.

He stood. "I guess so." He walked to the door. "Though we've been done a lot longer than this."

A lump lodged in her throat. "The night she went missing, she closed at the boutique. Her shift was up at ten p.m. She'd texted me at nine to say she was going to the Blue Marlin for a few drinks and should be home about midnight. I went to bed, and the next morning when I woke—around six—her car wasn't under the carport. I didn't think much of it. She'd drunk too much and stayed with friends before, but when work called after she didn't arrive for her nine a.m. shift, I called around. No one had seen her. The bar manager—Jeff Malone—said she left sober around eleven thirty. In case you needed to know that. Save yourself a second trip."

His hand reached the doorknob. "Thanks. That's all I need from you." He paused, and his eyes softened. "I am sorry about Ahnah. She didn't deserve this. None of them did."

"No, they didn't, but Ahnah is a fighter—you know this better than anyone. She's strong and resourceful. I'm believing the qualities that shaped her and gave her strength will keep her alive long enough for us to find her. I… I debated calling you myself. Maybe I should have."

"Maybe you should have years ago. I wouldn't have been sick daily about the fact you'd died."

The door blew open, nearly knocking Ty into the wall.

Bexley's heart stopped. She froze, mouth agape.

No. No. No. No.

Bexley wasn't ready for this. Not now. Not under these circumstances.

"Hey, sorry, man."

Ty saluted. "No worries, kiddo. Maybe knock before an appointment."

Bexley's pulse spiked.

"Dude, like I'd take counseling…"

Don't say it.

"…from my *mom*."

Ty's smirk turned somber. "What's that?"

Bexley couldn't hide it. Didn't want it to play out like this.

"This is Josiah. My son."

Chapter Three

My son.

Those two words echoed through Tiberius's brain.

Time froze and the room slanted as Ty scrutinized the gangly teenager. About six foot. Two inches shorter than Ty. Dark curly hair like his mother's. Completely untamed too.

But his eyes.

Like green diamonds. Tiberius's eyes.

"How...how old are you?" he managed to ask, but his mouth had turned into a massive wad of cotton.

"I think it's time for you to go, Agent Granger." Bexley's bottom lip trembled, and her eyes were shifty. This truth could not be masked, and she wore it like a neon sign across her pale face.

Ty was staring at his son.

He had a son.

A *son*.

His entire world shifted, and he ran a damp palm over his mouth and nose. This kid belonged to him, and he had never known. Might not have ever if their case hadn't brought them to North Carolina.

Another chilling thought forced its way into his mind. What if he wasn't his? What if he was… No. He refused to let himself go there. The possibility punched his gag reflex. It was too much. Like a double-edged sword being thrust through his middle, taking its time entering and exiting.

But he had to know either way.

"I don't think it is," he said.

Josiah frowned. "Mom, you didn't answer your cell phone, again. Thought I'd come by to clue you in that I'm alive and to remind you that if you want me to answer my phone, you might want to lead by example."

Bex's lips pursed, and she darted a glance at Ty. "I'm with someone right now."

"Yeah, story of my life. You work on weekends and holidays. Whatever," he muttered, then started for the door.

Apparently, the kid needed a class in manners. Did she always allow him to talk this way to her?

Josiah paused at the door. "Wait." He eyed Ty. "Dude, who are you again?"

"I um…" He cleared his throat and shook his head, running a hand through his hair and trying to gain composure. He retrieved his credentials. Couldn't say he was his father. Maybe his brother. "I'm Agent Granger with the FBI."

"Aunt Ahnah?" he whispered, and his hand fell from the doorknob. Even his voice sounded like Ty's. Did the kid notice?

"She's still missing, but yes, I'm here about her. Do you know anything that might help me?"

"You think those girls they found at the lighthouses might have something to do with her abduction?" Josiah asked. "I've thought it. I mean, she was friends with Amy-Rose and kind of knew Lily. I've been shook for days. Ahnah's middle name is Oleander. Doesn't he tattoo the flowers of their names on them?"

"He does. And we're looking into every possible connection."

Josiah's jaw hardened, and he shot a furious glance toward Bexley. "Since you're FBI, weird stuff has been going on at our place."

"Josiah!"

"What?" He splayed his hands, bowing up as if he dared her to deny it. "The photo of us on the sofa table is gone. And you also said the blanket you crocheted was missing. That's weird right?" he asked, pleading with his eyes for Ty to back him up.

"It's odd, yes." A photo and a blanket she handcrafted were personal. "Anything else missing?" he asked Bexley.

Blushing, she said, "Um…a box of mementos I kept in the top of my closet."

"What was in it?"

"Mementos," she stressed, and it dawned on him. She kept a box of photos or things that reminded her of them. It would have solidified they'd been an item, but the killer would have to have been knowledgeable about their relationship prior to finding the box.

Unless the killer was someone Bexley or Ahnah knew. Someone they'd confided in who could also be the Fire & Ice Killer. He'd worked dozens of cases where a killer inserted himself into the lives of his prey not only to play head games but to keep up with them. It was sick. But plausible.

"Okay. Was Ahnah missing anything?"

"I don't know," Bexley said as Josiah shrugged. "She didn't mention anything."

Had the other victims mentioned missing anything prior to their abductions? Ty would follow up with that when they visited the homes of the missing women and talked with their families.

"Why haven't you answered your phone?" Josiah asked. "Is *it* missing?"

"No. It's in my drawer," Bexley said to Josiah. "You know I can't be on my phone during sessions."

"I could be dead in the road, but let's not interrupt someone else's dying moments." He graced her with an eye roll. "Whatever. I'll be home later. Me and Abe's game might go long."

"You be home for dinner. Five." Bexley gritted her teeth and averted her gaze from Tiberius. This kid might be his, but regardless, he was a disrespectful brat.

"If you think of anything else, let me know," Ty said, as Josiah started out the door.

"I will."

After the door closed, Ty crossed his arms over his chest, waiting for answers, but Bexley didn't budge. Didn't offer a single word. He let time tick by. Finally he couldn't stand it any longer. "I have a million questions, here, Bex. But first off, is he mine?"

She nodded.

"Are you sure? You married my father. Dalen said you'd died three months after the ceremony so..."

Bexley sniffed. "I did marry Rand. But after the wedding... I couldn't go through with the consummation, Ty. Mother Mae helped me and Ahnah escape and fake our deaths. I'm sure Dalen spun the story that we were out on the lake having a great day and a tragic accident took place—and that the tragedy occurred later than it actually did, which was the wedding night. Mother Mae made it appear we drowned escaping."

Dalen had spun it exactly like that. Ty had no reason not to believe him.

The Family would never have reported two minors running away. They would have looked into it privately, using any law enforcement who was in the cult to hunt for them on the down-low. Bringing in authorities meant the possibility of uncovering the fact Ty's father—and other members—were bigamists and that he'd been taking minors as brides.

Bexley hadn't been with his father. Eons worth of nausea lifted from his shoulders.

She wiped her wet cheeks with the back of her hand. Inhaling deeply, she squared her shoulders. "Josiah doesn't know who his father is, and Tiberius, you can't tell him."

Couldn't tell him?

"You have kept *my* son from me for seventeen years with zero intention of telling me. No wonder you were so shocked to see me. I rained on your secret baby parade. What do you think this is, a bad made-for-TV movie?" He tried to contain his feelings, but they crept out in his raised voice.

Bexley's office phone rang, and she answered. Her brow furrowed. "Okay." She looked at Ty. "I have an emergency phone call." She pressed a red button on her phone. "Bexley Hemmingway." She frowned. Then her mouth hung open, and she slowly met his gaze. "It's for you." She held out the phone receiver to Ty.

"For me?" Who would be calling for him? Only his team knew he was here, and they could call his cell phone. "Who is it?"

"I don't know. He sounds funny."

He accepted the phone. "Agent Granger," he said.

"Hello, Agent Granger. I suspect you're not having a good day." The caller's voice was modulated. Because Ty would recognize it or because Bexley might?

"Who is this?"

"Someone who knows far more about you than you think you know about me. I'm looking at your son right now. Kinda looks like you. Oh yes, I know you have a son. I know all kinds of things, and I'm going to use them to my advantage. I'm not nearly as stupid as you suspect. Bye for now. But see you soon." The line clicked.

Ty's heart thudded in his chest. He checked his watch. The call hadn't lasted long enough to triangulate a location, and if the UNSUB was smart, he'd have used a burner.

"Who was it, Tiberius? What did he say?" Bexley's bottom lip trembled.

"I don't know, but he knows I have a son. Where was Josiah going?" The caller had been following Ty and must have spotted Josiah leaving the building. Violet was outside. That gave him some comfort.

"Probably the arcade at the boardwalk. Is he in danger?"

Somehow, he knew about him and Bexley. How? "I don't know." He knew nothing. His life had been tossed a grenade and was exploding into pieces. He had a son. Bexley didn't want Josiah to know. But this killer also knew, and he had Ahnah.

"I don't have time to further discuss our personal life. But know this much—it isn't over. Josiah is going to know he has a father, and I'm going to be a part of his life. And if I have to drag your sorry self into court, then that's what I'll do. I am not leaving North Carolina without me knowing my son and my son knowing me."

Bexley raised her chin. "I did it to protect him. I'm still protecting him, Tiberius. You don't know him."

"You haven't let me! And now I have a killer to catch who might target him," he boomed, and the door opened again.

Another young man entered, dark hair and eyes.

"Tell me that's not a twin or something." He was hanging by a thread.

She shot him a look.

"Miss Hemmingway, are you okay? You need anything?" the young man asked, giving Ty a once-over.

"No, Milo. You know the rules. You can't interrupt or walk in without being let in by me or my assistant. Sometimes sessions get heated. I'm safe."

Milo studied Ty once more. "I'm sorry. I heard yelling, and I was afraid for you."

"She's good," Ty said.

Milo—the client—hesitated, then backed up and closed the door.

"I need you to go straight home after work," Ty said. "Walk out with your assistant. Do not talk to strangers. Maybe don't even talk to someone you know."

"Fine. Quit talking to me."

"You know what I mean, Bexley." The woman had never been lax in the wit department. It had been one of the things he'd loved about her. But she needed to take this seriously.

Could the UNSUB have extracted this kind of information from Ahnah? Either by force or grooming? She might have gone with him willingly because she knew him. He'd invaded her life. Tricked her.

"And call Josiah now. I want to know he's okay. Tell him to go home."

Bexley retrieved her cell phone. "You're scaring me, Tiberius."

"Just do it."

She made the call. "Where are you?" she asked Josiah. "Okay, I need you to go straight home and text me when you get there. I won't be too far behind... Yes, it's about the case." She listened and then sighed. "Just go home, Josiah. Lock the doors." She ended the call. "Well, I've terrified my kid into going home versus the arcade."

"Maybe you should go on home too."

"I have two clients and then I will. I promise. Is this person coming after me and Josiah?"

"I don't know. But he's definitely out to give me grief." Ty blew out of the office and the building with a whirlwind of thoughts and no time to process. Outside, he scanned the area for the unknown caller. Then he stopped dead in his tracks.

Josiah sat on the wooden stairs with his phone in his lap.

"Hey." He wasn't sure how to act. This was his son. "Aren't you supposed to be heading home instead of the arcade?" Did he lie concerning his whereabouts often? Ty let his gaze circle the area again. Nothing out of place. A blue car zipped past, and someone walked across the street toward a coffee shop.

Josiah stood. "I didn't want my mom to know I needed to talk to you." He rubbed his hands on his back pockets. "You said if I thought of something to let you know, and I did."

"Okay, you can tell me." He held up a finger. "But give me one second." He bounded down the stairs, and Violet opened her window.

"What's going on?" she asked, before returning her sights to Josiah on the stairs, his dark curls whipping in the wind, reminding Ty of one of those blow-up creatures used at car dealerships.

Ty gave her the CliffsNotes version of the phone call, omitting anything personal. "Have you seen anyone suspicious or a vehicle?"

She shook her head. "A few cars passed but nothing to give me pause." She glanced across the street. "He could be in any of those shops."

Ty didn't see anyone, but an icy sensation gripped his ribs and raised hairs on his neck. His gut warned they were being watched. "The kid wants to talk to me. Give me a second." He raced to the stairs. "Okay, what is it you didn't want your mom to know?"

"My mom doesn't know this because she gets all up in our grill—me and Ahnah—when she's not traveling. Although she's gone pretty much all the time."

"She's probably in your business because that's what moms do."

"Whatever, man." He rolled his eyes. "There was a guy that dated Ahnah's friend. Amy-Rose. His name is Skipper. I mean,

I doubt that's his real name, but no one calls him by anything else. I was hanging out at the arcade waiting on Ahnah to get off work one night and ran out of money, so I was in the store killing time. He came in, but Amy-Rose had dumped him. He was being all stalkerish. The manager asked him to leave, and at first he wouldn't, but then Ahnah told him if he didn't, she'd call the cops. He pretty much cussed her out, then told her she better watch her back and Amy-Rose too."

Skipper. Shouldn't be hard to track down someone with a nickname like that in this small town. If he was from here. He'd talk to the manager, who might know more.

"You seen him around since Amy-Rose or Ahnah disappeared?" Ty asked.

"No. But I could draw him for you. I'm pretty good at portraits."

Ty smiled, but it hurt. One more thing Josiah had inherited. Ty could draw, but portraits were never his strong suit. His early plans had been to study architecture, then go into the family business of construction and real estate development and marry Bex. But plans changed when Garrick pulled his cruel stunt by asking for Bexley's hand in marriage. And their plans to run failed. Everything swirled down the can. "Yeah? You want to be an artist?"

"Nah." He tossed him a crooked grin that mirrored Ty's. "I want to play video games on YouTube and get rich. But I'll probably do something with the art. Maybe…teach, or like, I don't know. My mom says I'd make a great architect. I have the talent, and they make good money."

"She said that, huh?" She'd encouraged their son to follow in the footsteps of his father yet withheld his existence.

"Yeah." He shrugged. "Anyway, I'll draw him. My sketch pad is at home right now, though. My mom says I need to go home due to the case. Are we in trouble?"

Ty needed the boy to be alert but not afraid. Right now,

he knew little to nothing. The man on the phone said he was watching Josiah. Ty saw no one. Not a single person even in their car. He'd lied to scare him. Hadn't he? He never actually said where Josiah was to prove his claim.

"Be cautious. Be careful. I'll be by later to get it. Okay?"

"You got a card or something? My mom is blowing off the stuff at the house as her forgetting, but after Ahnah, I don't know. My gut says something else."

"Go with the gut." He laid a hand on Josiah's bony shoulder. Moisture burned in his eyes, and he rushed to conceal his emotion with his sunglasses. "It's usually right." He gave him a solid pat, then handed him the card. "I'll be by around dinnertime."

"Cool." He strolled toward an old Honda, then turned, walking backwards. "Hey, is that, like, your partner in that Suburban?"

"Yeah," Ty said warily. What had Violet done to him? She was unpredictable.

"She's hot." He grinned as he hopped inside his car.

Ty found he could chuckle. "That hot one would burn you alive, bruh."

"Hey, I wouldn't mind going down in flames."

This kid was a chip off the old block—not necessarily a good thing.

Josiah reversed from the parking spot without a glance, nearly taking out a minivan. Ty winced. He was going to get into a fender bender sooner rather than later, but Ty hadn't been able to teach him to drive or how to use shading techniques. He hadn't even been able to purchase Josiah's first sketch pad.

"Well?" Violet asked, once he was inside the vehicle and situated.

"You may be dead-on, Violet. It's personal, and he made sure to let me know he's not stupid like I implied on the video. It's the Fire & Ice Killer."

"And what else couldn't you tell me with ears around?"

Ty leaned back and sighed. "He's my son…and the killer knows it. I'm not ready to divulge that information further. I might be recused if Asa knows, and I was down with that initially—before coming to meet with Bexley. Now there's no way I can walk away from this case, this place."

"At some point he needs to know."

"I know. Let me process it all first. I can't even think."

Violet's eyebrows twitched. "Alright. Your call. I disagree with it."

"You don't keep secrets? You do. You have. Don't judge."

"I'm not judging. I'm disagreeing. You say it was less than thirty seconds—the call?"

"Less than ten seconds. We'll get nothing." Ty gripped the wheel and entered the address of Amy-Rose's family into the GPS. "What's up with the missing personal items?"

"I don't know. Mementos. Could be items in there to get to know you better. Recon, so to speak. You really made this guy angry. So angry he brooded and hatched a plan. We have no idea what his goal is, but what we do already know about him is he's calculated, intelligent and hard to track or trace. This won't be easy."

Violet never had anything good to say. But she was truthful. And nothing about this case was good. "We'll see if the other victims had personal items removed. Could be connected."

"Could be, or could be specific to you. I'd like to have her catalog what exactly was in that box."

"Okay."

"One last little mention," Violet said. "I've had the radio on, and that tropical storm is gaining some muscle off the West African coast and heading for the Bahamas. We both know how unpredictable hurricanes are. It could die down or it could ramp up. Either way, we need to pay close attention."

He was already in a hurricane of his own and his gut projected the case was going to escalate to a Cat 5 if they didn't get ahead of it.

The Artist casually stood to the side of the counter in the local coffee shop, awaiting his latte and a spinach quiche while concealing a grin. Everything he'd ordained was falling into place like perfect little puzzle pieces, forming a big picture. A picture he had created, spun and been meticulous to bring to fruition. Guiding a human life took a considerable amount of time and study. Arranging the women at lighthouses and hinting at Agent Granger's past indiscretions were all he'd needed. These bread crumbs had brought him right to the Artist's door.

Each coordinated detail was another crushing blow for Tiberius Granger. He'd mapped out his destruction and couldn't be outmatched. Granger would pay for his sins—pride at the top of the list. When he finally fell to his face, he would be humbled, humiliated and held accountable.

He'd been in the shadows as the agent went inside the counselor's office. Seen him come out in angst and turmoil. But he'd also been enamored with the brunette beauty who'd remained inside the vehicle. Long, dark hair with a sun-kissed glow on her skin. She'd turned in his direction as if sensing his presence, challenge in her eyes, and he wondered about folding her into his plan. He'd think on that later. For now, he savored the game.

The barista batted her lashes while he waited near the counter. Her desperation radiated like the Carolina noon heat. Smothering and sticky. She wasn't the woman who'd caught his interest. No, the woman who had his undivided attention had lovely hazel eyes, though one was a little lazy, but they were sharp. She was several inches shorter than his six-foot-two height, but her legs were long, and underneath her clothing, he imagined she was toned and sleek.

She presented an aura that hummed red, a warning to steer

clear, and confidence oozed from her pores—another layer of defense if one ignored the first signal to keep away. From his side view, he studied her short hair—not his preference, but it revealed a slender, delicate neck. From a few feet away, he caught her coconutty scent. He also caught her quick glances at him. Not lusty but aware of his presence. Most women paid little attention to their surroundings, and when a man had his physique and face—not pride but fact—they dropped their wary guard, which inevitably worked against them.

Women were the lesser sex and shallow creatures.

She ordered an Americano black and backed up next to him. They were about two feet apart while she waited.

He caught her eye. "Afternoon."

Bucking her chin, she acknowledged his greeting.

Oh, he liked her quite a lot. Wary. Sly. A challenge.

"You don't look like a local."

She shifted, her hand lightly swatting her black fitted blazer in a gesture to unveil smooth steel in a side holster. Another warning signal. Interesting she didn't flash the bling on her left ring finger instead. No, the gun instantly disclosed she was independent. Strong on her own two feet. But he already knew that about her.

He entered his passcode and opened his phone. He had things to check on.

"I'm not." Her tone was no-nonsense but not necessarily irritated.

"Me neither. I mean, to the Outer Banks. I'm from North Carolina, though. Moved with my wife—she got a transfer." Her hard-edged glare softened at his disarming lie.

"Not a terrible place to transfer," she commented.

"Fiona?" the barista called, and lightly placed her drink on the counter.

He cocked his head. "Fiona. That Irish? My wife's Irish. On her mom's side. Kiera."

She retrieved her cup and eyed him again. "Enjoy your day."

"You too," he said, and held out his phone a measure as he studied his garden girls. All beautiful and right under Agent Fiona Kelly's nose. Oh yes, he knew all about her and the entire SCU team. While they had a solid track record of catching killers, they'd never been up against a man like the Artist. He was unrivaled. Unmatched.

They were completely in the dark, but he planned to bring himself into the light.

In due time.

All she had to do was cast one tiny peek at his phone and she'd see his girls. She could use that gun to subdue him, force him to his knees in surrender. No one else would need to die.

She didn't give the phone a single glance.

In real time, his next-to-newest flower huddled in a heap weeping in her room. She'd been like that all morning too, bringing down his mood. As if her condition was his fault. He'd made it clear what giving herself to him entailed, like he'd made it abundantly clear with all the others and his newest garden girl to replace Lily Hayes.

They chose him. They gave themselves to him.

Now she was nothing but a whiny mess he'd have to fix later.

"Art," the barista called.

He received his drink, glancing at Agent Kelly and the big guy, Asa Kodiak, who thought he was large and in charge. He wasn't.

The Artist was.

And he was coming for Tiberius Granger.

Passing the counter, he plucked a napkin from the holder and purposely dropped his phone, the camera on and his lovely garden girls in their hanging baskets awaiting him to come and command them to bloom.

Agent Kodiak bent and swiped his phone from the floor. A thrill zinged through the Artist's middle, goading him to shout, dance, do a victory pump in the air. The girls were in the agent's hands; he only had to ignore politeness and peek.

"Here, man," Agent Kodiak said and handed him his phone. Idiot. Yet one more layer of proof that he could not be touched or outsmarted.

"Thanks. Clumsy me." Lies. "Y'all have a nice day. Enjoy the Outer Banks."

"You too," Agent Kodiak mumbled, not looking up from his own phone. Agent Kelly raised her eyebrows when he turned back and caught her eye. As he neared the door, he heard Agent Kodiak say, "Stop gawking at Orlando Bloom, Fi."

"I am not gawking, and he is not Orlando Bloom. Orlando *wishes*," she muttered.

"I heard that," Agent Kodiak replied. "Drink your coffee and look at the dead bodies instead."

To their detriment, there would be many more dead bodies.

Chapter Four

Blue Harbor
Saturday, September 1
4:25 p.m.

A charcuterie board had been set out on the kitchen counter. Fiona snagged a black olive and laid out paper plates.

They'd visited Amy-Rose Rydell's family's home and then Lily Hayes's. Amy-Rose's family didn't think anything was missing, but they weren't as close as they used to be and had no idea about anyone named Skipper. They did say she was a bit wild and they thought she partied too much. Lily Hayes's family said nothing was missing as Lily still lived at home. She'd finally been coming into some money from a side job that she said was delivering groceries, but they didn't believe her. When asked what they thought she might be doing on the side, they answered with silence and shrugs.

If both women were into partying and maybe even stripping or escort service work, that might be how the killer found them. Ty ignored the food. The interviews had been hard to conduct because he kept losing his train of thought, and eventually Violet took the baton. His focus was on Josiah, and the fact he had a son. A son the killer knew about.

Would Josiah even want to know Ty was his father? Would he want a relationship with him? Questions fired in his brain like a semiautomatic. Tonight, he hoped for some answers—the kind that required more than head nods and one-word responses.

"Who put this together?" Ty asked. "Looks like the froufrou stuff Cami feeds us when we work through lunches." Looked pretty. A grown-up Lunchable minus the chocolate sandwich cookie. She'd never found his comments amusing.

"Yeah, and they're delicious without putting forth a lot of effort." Fiona pointed to a large to-go sack that read Blue Fin Grill. The adult lunch-meat board had been catered.

"What'd that cost?"

"Me less time," Fiona shot back, popped another whole black olive in her mouth and snagged a cube of cheese.

"That's all processed," Violet added, and dropped her purse on the kitchen counter by the fridge.

Fiona made a display of shoving a piece of pepperoni in her mouth and going gaga over it. "So did you catch the killer?" she asked to annoy Violet.

Ty chuckled.

"You know we didn't." Violet didn't always understand jokes. Or maybe she didn't find them all that funny. At least not Fiona's.

Asa raised his head from the dining room table turned into conference table. They'd set up an official command post at the sheriff's office ten minutes away in Manteo, but were using the beach house too. The view was amazing and breathed some hope into a vicious case.

They'd borrowed a whiteboard from the Manteo FBI resident agency and had already taped the photos of Amy-Rose

Rydell and Lily Hayes on the board along with pertinent information and the photos of the missing women with flowers in their names.

"What did the Rydell and Hayes families have to say?" Owen asked. He had his laptop out in front of him with the high-tech geopattern software open, but he'd also tacked a map onto the living room wall and placed pins marking the locations where the women lived, worked and often visited.

"Let the man eat. He gets hangry," Fiona said.

Under normal circumstances, Fi would be right, but not today. Today he'd pretty much lost his appetite even though his stomach was so empty he'd felt his last swig of water slide down, leaving a cold wake from his gullet to his gut. "I'm not hungry."

Asa and Fiona both snapped to attention.

"How bad was it at Bexley Hemmingway's?" Fiona asked.

Violet sat poker-faced and silent, leaving the conversation to Ty's discretion.

"This killer might have targeted a woman I cared about when she was a child and he might target Bexley." He explained about the guy named Skipper—a possible lead. Their only possible lead right now. "I feel responsible, but I'll go by the house later to pick up the sketch her son said he'd draw." He nearly choked on the words *her son*.

"I can have him in five minutes," Selah said through the computer screen, pushing her chunky black glasses back up on her nose.

Ty didn't protest or it'd stir up questions he had no intention of answering and instead walked to the whiteboard and added information about the women's partying, a mysterious side hustle, and the possibility things had gone missing. "What did you find out at the ME's office this morning?"

"No signs or evidence of sexual assault on either victim. They'd been fed—and not shabbily either. Medical examiner found remains of steak in Amy-Rose's stomach," Asa said. "She died not long after eating. Cause of death is overdose. High levels of Xanax in her system. We won't know if Lily Hayes is the same until the tox screen comes back."

Four to six weeks. Unlike cool criminal TV shows.

"But," Asa continued, "we can make an educated guess it's the same. These women who've gone missing are overlapping in time, so I believe he's keeping them all at once. Working on them individually. We're talking at least eight, maybe more. He'd need a place to keep them."

"Any evidence of physical abuse?" Violet asked. "He feeds them well and he keeps them alive for a period of time. I have to wonder if Amy-Rose and Lily Hayes were casualties in a much bigger plan. To do that much work on them—Amy-Rose more than Lily—and then to kill them? No. He wants every inch of their bodies and then to collect them like a garden of flowers. One murder does nothing. Two, with a religious calling card, brings us out here." Her gaze connected with Ty's. "This guy was willing to give up two of his victims in order to snag our attention—Ty's attention. He knew there had to be some kind of overt religious undertone. Thus the note card."

Fiona strode to the whiteboard to add updated information. "The medical examiner did find evidence of torture. Amy-Rose had several broken fingers that hadn't healed properly, a broken wrist, and a few burn scars on her armpits, the bottoms of her feet, and her groin."

"He's hurting them in places that won't affect the tattoo work, which tells me he wants perfection on the visible skin," Violet said.

Fiona pushed her plate away. This was the kind of conversation that chased away appetites or any hope in humanity. "We think he's using physical torture to keep them under control or to submit to his wishes—not the inking. He overdosed Amy-Rose—and probably Lily Hayes—with Xanax, so he's likely using it to put them under for periods of time to do the ink work."

"The nice meals," Asa continued, "could be rewards if they obey or submit. You act right, you are taken care of. You do not, you incur pain. After a lengthy period of time, he'd get them to submit and obey his every whim, which is exactly what he wants. Control. Power. Ownership of them. But what does he do with them when he's not tattooing them? Where do they stay, and what do they do if it's not of a sexual nature? He's perfected his tattooing method too much for these to be his first victims. Has anything similar popped in ViCAP?"

"Three sex workers in Raleigh went missing and were found dead and tattooed with flowers about three years ago, but it's noted they can't be sure if the tats had been inked in captivity or not. Two more were discovered in Charlotte eighteen months ago. One definitely did not have the tattoos before, according to an undercover cop who knew her."

"He's been practicing," Violet added. "Did the prostitutes have flower names or go by flower names?"

"No," Selah said.

"We can't be sure if it's the same guy, but it could be, which means he may have been practicing for the real flowers. The women didn't matter to him. He'd consider them to be throwaways."

Ty pressed the heels of his hands to his eyes. The kidnapping and killing of all these girls wasn't Ty's fault. This guy wanted them and had already been abducting and murdering women prior to this new insane plan. Taking Ahnah and planting the two most recent victims—that was on Ty. "The Fire & Ice Killer also tortured his victims. He knows how I insulted his intelligence. Violet is right. He could have evolved, and while doing so, created this scheme to get revenge. It took a while, but it's no different than a long con. We need to dig back into those old cases and search for something new, something we didn't notice before but would now due to the newest case."

"I'm already on that," Selah said.

Violet nibbled on her thumbnail. "We know the Fire & Ice Killer abducted the women and kept them for a week before killing them. He strangled them, though. Wasn't a sexual deviant either—which makes me lean toward him evolving. Sexual predators are always sexual predators even if targets or locations change, and if this UNSUB is holding them even longer than a week—months—there would be evidence indicating rape. Torture seems consistent in both cases."

Asa blew out a heavy breath, then sipped his sweet tea. "Lily Hayes had no broken bones or burn marks, which indicates not all the women were tortured. They found sand and bits of American beach grass on her, but that doesn't really give us anything detailed. You can find that all over the Outer Banks."

Ty picked up the photos they'd returned with from the ME's office. The roses were perfect and expertly placed on Amy-Rose Rydell.

Bloom where you are planted.

Not all the roses inked along her body had been blooming roses, though. Several on her upper neck and back were rosebuds. "How many broken fingers did Amy-Rose have?"

"Uh…" Asa studied the autopsy report. "Seven."

Ty carefully counted the number of rosebuds.

Seven. Interesting. When she bloomed where she was planted—obeyed or acquiesced to whatever he requested—she received blooming roses. When she did not submit, she didn't bloom and was punished. "Which wrist had been broken?" he asked Asa.

"Left."

Ty found a photo of her left arm and studied it. A nice long sleeve of roses in multiple colors. Each one blooming, except for the circle of red rosebuds around her wrist. He quickly began laying out the photos in a horizontal line and watched in horror as his theory materialized into reality.

"What do you see?" Violet sidled up beside him.

"Look at her left wrist."

Violet hummed low, seeing the looming picture. She pointed to the victim's neck. "Closed buds...they start opening around the middle of her back."

Exactly. "Give me Lily's photos."

Asa passed them over, and he laid them out. "Closed buds beginning at her neck and opening further down on her back." She wasn't as tattooed as Amy-Rose Rydell. She'd gone missing one month later. "He starts at the neck with closed-up flowers because they're fighting him—being disobedient—but as he brings the pain, they begin to cooperate with him—whatever that entails." What was this man making them do?

"Y'all, I can't see." Selah popped up on-screen, and Asa shifted the laptop to face the photos.

"Lily Hayes's blooms open and stay open. But Amy-Rose is littered with rosebuds," Ty said. "I think she fought harder and longer than Lily."

Way to go, Amy-Rose.

"That means he's not picking a type—a passive personality—but is choosing women solely based on flower names," Asa said.

Except Ty didn't believe Ahnah was chosen just for her flower middle name.

Violet leaned her hip on the table. "Amy-Rose's family said she was outgoing, star of the show wherever she went, which was a lot of places. Her mom even mentioned she'd been headstrong. She knew she'd have fought to the bitter end, and that gave her some comfort. Lily's family said she was home early most nights, was always a good girl and—"

"A rule-follower," Ty said. "She'd have far fewer closed blooms." He tapped his index finger on the open blooms located on her back. "Bloom where you are planted. When it's not in a place you'd choose to be or want to be, you bloom despite the hardship and turmoil. The phrase is derived from a verse in the Bible. Well, several verses about being planted by streams of water and yielding fruit in season. There's also a verse in the New Testament—I can't remember where, but I'll google it—about flowers withering and fading."

"Got it," Selah said. "According to the King James Version, the New Testament verse is James 1:11 and Peter 1:24. Three more in the Old Testament. Two from the book of Isaiah, though it appears they go together in context, and one from the book of Job. You want me to read them?"

"Yes," Ty said as he concentrated on the photos. They were close to a profile, and once they had it, they could compare it with the one on the Fire & Ice Killer. Rule him in or out.

Selah read them. "Isaiah forty, verses six through eight, says, *'The voice said, Cry. And he said, What shall I cry? All flesh is grass, and all the goodliness thereof is as the flower of the field: The grass withereth, the flower fadeth: because the spirit of the Lord bloweth upon it: surely the people is grass. The grass withereth, the flower fadeth: but the word of our God shall stand for ever.'*"

Hmm… "Read the one in Job."

"Job fourteen, verse two, reads, *'He cometh forth like a flower, and is cut down: he fleeth also as a shadow, and continueth not.'*"

"Interesting. Job is a book about intense suffering. Maybe he's plucking them to test their ability to stand up to suffering—submit despite the pain." This wasn't his area of expertise, but Violet's.

He'd rather not know or be able to sink into a devious mind. Except for now.

Now he needed to know. Because it was personal.

"We need to give a press conference," Asa said.

"Ty needs to give it," Violet said. "The Fire & Ice Killer will hate it. I'll coach you on what to say. You give it and he'll make a mistake. He won't expect it to be you. Asa hasn't let you give a press conference since the viral video. Now it's time to take away some of his limelight by making you the face of this investigation."

Ty wasn't sure about the idea. What if it made the killer angry enough to kill another woman—to kill Ahnah or take his son?

Kipos Island
Saturday, September 1
5:30 p.m.

I've been fed pills twice since he brought me back the other night from my escape attempt. He says they're Xanax, and I've seen them before, so he's not lying. I welcomed them after the first night when he broke my pinky finger for running. It throbs with a sharp ache, and it's black and blue and swollen.

He told me if I obey, he wouldn't have to do these things. I've heard the same garbage before. I know it's gaslighting. All abusers use it to make their victims believe they're crazy and that it's their fault they were abused.

I will not be one of his garden girls.

He outweighs me by over a hundred pounds, and when I flee again—and I intend to—I'll need brains over brawn.

I sit on the cold concrete floor in the room he calls mine. I will never take ownership of this prison no matter how well he feeds me or whether he gives me a luxury bed. A bed he has yet to enter himself. I'm relieved, but my heart stays in a constant stutter that in the middle of the night when the door creaks open, he won't enter to tattoo my body, but he'll violate me in other ways. No, he's not been in my bed.

But I have been in his.

I remember it all now that the initial drugs—not Xanax— have worn off. I came of my own volition.

I trusted him.

I had no reason not to.

I can't think about the events that led me here to this mansion on an island I can't escape without a boat. We'd taken one from the marina. Then, from a private dock, we switched to a canoe to manage the narrow channels of water that lead to the house. I know it's out there, bobbing in the water, and I will find a way to get to it. He never leaves me alone with the other women—his garden girls. When he can't be with all of us, I'm confined here. I'm okay with that. I do not want to be in that cage. I don't know what happens in there, but I know it's something sinister and sick. Maybe my nice comfy bed is a teaser. The violation doesn't happen in here where I expect it to, but in that room, in a cage…in front of those other women.

My belly hiccups at the thought. I have a small bathroom with a toilet and a sink. No shower. I've thought a thousand times about drowning myself. Cupping water and inhaling it. It's my last resort. I'm going to find a way out of this place unless help comes first, and I know people are looking and contacting resources who can find me. Aren't they? The days and nights have blurred and I'm not exactly sure how long I've been here.

But he's hoping for my rescue, and I'm not sure why. It sends little caterpillars inching along under my skin. Was I some kind of decoy? I don't know. There are other women. Women who have been here longer than me.

They didn't speak or even look up when we were together, which has only been that one night. He forced me in the cage and sat in a chaise only to stare at us in silence. At least I now know these women sleep in those rooms behind the other six black doors, but there are not seven women in the cages. Two are empty, so two rooms might also be empty. I'm not sure if he's killed them or if he's hunting new prey.

He's not the man I knew before. But knowing him doesn't bring me any comfort. Having slept with him brings me no comfort either. He's an evil monster hiding behind an attractive face, money and culture. The man I knew is gone. He's flipped a switch or snapped. Either way. This man... This man I fear.

I hear the secret door creak open as I'm sitting on the bare floor. His footfalls come toward my door, and my hands tremble. I jump up, the chain clinking on the concrete, and pounce on my bed, drawing up the covers to hide my body.

We have no clothing. Not even a robe.

The door opens, and his frame looms in the doorway. He's dressed in black silky pants and a matching button-up shirt. It's open, revealing his muscular chest. But it's not his perfect body that draws my attention. It's the fact it's heaving and his jaw is hard. His eyes are cold pools of fury.

I haven't tried escaping today. Has someone else? He's fuming, but it's quiet, except for his eyes, and I stare at the floor because the eyes—dark and devouring—are too much to bear. I shrink farther into the covers, but the truth is I know there's no hiding from him.

"I need my girls. All my girls," he says, with that sultry tone that had once sent delicious shivers coursing through me. It's so strange how one voice—the same voice—can make me feel safe and loved and then hours later fill me with dread and terror.

His approach to my bed is calm and measured. Even angry, he's not bursting into flames. It's a quiet cold that permeates the room as if someone has poured dry ice over his bones and created an unseen fog. He unlocks my chain. "Did you enjoy your dinner last night?"

I remain silent. I will not give him the satisfaction of knowing he's my master and I'm a slave. As if a nice meal is something I should be grateful for. Maybe it is. But I'm not.

"Cat got your tongue, lovely?"

He waits a beat and sighs through his nose, then removes the heavy iron cuff. My wrist feels like a feather, but it's tender and bruised. My finger throbs and is crooked. I know it'll never be straight again.

"How long are you going to keep me?" I ask, my voice raw and hoarse from endless yelling.

He gently turns down my covers, and the cool air raises chill bumps across my body. He grins at the sight. "That's a good question, and one I honestly can't answer. I do apologize."

Does that mean he plans to kill me? Surely he's not going to let me go. I'm some kind of pawn in a sick game he's playing, but I'm not sure why.

He uses my good hand to draw me up, gripping me like a vise, but I don't howl. He guides me down the hall I ran through before, only to reach the dead end, but there's another secret door. I know it's going to lead into the solarium garden thingy he's built into the house.

Inside, the room is bright with sunlight, and warm but not uncomfortable. The other girls are in their hanging baskets with heads on their knees and arms wrapped around their shins. Their hair is pulled into tight ballerina buns. Mine is not.

"I've had some irritating news. I need to relax. Release."

I swallow hard and take a stab. "What kind of news?" If I can befriend him—again—he might let his guard down. Because I really don't care what disturbs him.

"The kind only arrogant fools dish out. You'd think he'd have learned his lesson not to open his mouth in public. But he did. For all the viewing area, giving a false sense of security to locals. As if he can control me. Me!" He raises his voice on the last word, but not in a burst of uncontrollable rage. An emphasis. As if that word meant something more powerful than one person. "One or one hundred press conferences won't save you."

He commands me to lower myself on the chaise. His chaise. Is that where it's going to happen? The violation. My intestines protest, and I need to go to the bathroom.

"Why?" I ask because I need an answer. I need five seconds to prepare. Five seconds to go to another place and block it out.

He cocks his head and lifts my chin. "When I tell you to

do something, you don't ask why. You simply abide by my request. It's called obedience, my dear." He makes a quick sweep of my pinky finger. My broken pinky finger. A silent warning of what's to come if I utter another word.

Defeated, I sit on the chaise, awaiting him to push me back. To have his way with me. I already know it won't be like the first time. Nothing special or romantic about it. He straddles the chaise from behind me and I go into that same kind of shaking when you come out of anesthesia. It's induced by anxiety. Unwanted tears leak down my cheeks. Inside, I beg and plead and pray he won't touch me.

His fingers gently comb through my hair. "You have lovely hair. It needs washing. Maybe later." He smells like money and power and temptation, and I wish I'd never succumbed. I wouldn't be here if I hadn't, and I cry harder now. I'm furious at myself. People I know and love would tell me it's not my fault. I did nothing wrong. But that's not true. It is my fault. I made my choices. I should have… I don't even know. He's gathering my hair and lifting it off my neck. His breath is warm and minty, and I cringe as a memory invades of how sweet he'd tasted. Now I want to vomit.

I feel a brush go through my hair. One stroke. Two. Over and over he brushes my hair like I used to with my dolls when I was a little girl. When my innocence hadn't been stolen.

He's pulling up my hair and twisting it into a bun. Then an elastic band twines around the knot, holding it in place. I now look like all the other garden girls in cages, only with a different flower.

One leg swings over the chaise, then the other, until he's kneeling in front of me. I wrap my arms around my chest as a shield and covering.

"Oh yes, yes, yes, yes," he coos. His finger trails down my cheek and neck, then traces my collarbone, and I flinch. "Shy girl now, are you? You were quite lively before." His chuckle is breathy and full of flirtation. Everything that had roped me in. "Now, up you go," he says like a father putting his child on a bike for the first time.

My pinky finger is throbbing and I don't want another one broken, so I stand on wobbly legs and follow him to the wrought iron barred cage. He opens the massive door, and I step inside. The other girls have yet to glance up or express any interest. It's like they're mannequins of flesh. His bare feet pad across the room back to the chaise, and he picks up a remote control and presses a button.

I don't know what to expect and lurch as loud classical music filters through unseen speakers. Stringed instruments bring hairs to attention on my neck. The deep thrum of the cello bumps in my chest, a sense of foreboding, and the violins screech like wailing victims. I cringe and crouch. What is he going to do? The others never move position. They're used to this. But what is *this*?

He lowers the remote to the table and claps his hands twice as he glides across the tile, his dark hair falling into his eyes. He's in the center of the cages, which are positioned in a circle around the fountain. "Bloom for me, girls."

What does he mean? What are they going to do? What does he expect me to do?

I watch in horror, my heart slamming against my ribs, as these women rise to their bare feet and perfectly plié in unison like ballerinas in a private performance.

He throws his head back and his arms stretch to his sides as if the dancing has empowered him. I do not rise to my feet. I do not dance. I can't. I'm frozen in place at the chilling display.

The music grows faster, more intense, like someone threw blood in the ocean and has created a frenzy. "Yes!" he cries out again in that velvety tone as he waltzes in and around the human birdcages. He's keeping time to the beat, bowing an air violin. One arm crossing over the other as new waves of chills are birthed along my arms and my scalp tingles.

Is this my fate?

As the crescendo begins, he bows with more vigor, weaving in and out and around the dancing garden girls. A sheen of moisture forms on his brow, and his eyes are drunk with lust. But the women are silent. Faces expressionless. Eyes hollow like open graves.

"Bloom! Twirl! Yes! Yes! *Yeeeesss!*" His words are loud but in breathy pants.

His blooming flowers obey him and twirl counter clockwise, arms over their heads in a perfect arc, their naked inked bodies swaying at his command. To bloom. To dance. To bring him pleasure.

My brain refuses to register this nightmare. I want to go home. I want my family even though we've been having some turmoil lately. Like Dorothy in Oz if Oz were hell. I want to get back to Kansas to someone who loves me even if we fight.

He's gliding around the bubbling fountain. This man is mad. How did I not see it before? I should be able to recognize the signs. I've seen madness, stared it down and even cowered to it. I did not see this.

I am trapped.

I am broken.

He's furiously bowing in the air to the climactic moment, savoring every sick second. Suddenly, he drops to his knees, completely spent as the music softens, and then he rests on his back, his chest heaving and his eyes closed.

His cheeks are flushed, and he blows a satisfied, satiated breath from his lungs.

I think it's over. This perversion. This sickness. But my heart continues to pound, and my throat feels parched and achy. A sharp stab throbs behind my right eye.

The naked dancers stay in standing position, their arms arcing over their heads.

What have I witnessed?

His smile sends a wintry shiver into my bones. It's over for now. Or is an encore performance awaiting me? When did he teach them this synchronized dance? My pinky aches and reminds me if I do not comply to this twisted ballet, the next thing he breaks might be something bigger like a leg, an arm or elbow.

Maybe my neck.

Heat surges through my body, leaving me dizzy and jittery.

A humming begins in his lower register, and then he breaks into song. A rich, melodious voice that could rival Josh Groban's. His arms rise up as if he's trying to grab the sky as he sings.

Oh, so lovely garden girls
unfolding flowers
bloom for me in these dark hours
then you shall dance, and twirl and twirl
Look how lovely my garden girls.

Peace flushes his face.

Deafening silence permeates the room as the dancing girls resume their former pose: knees drawn into the chest, arms wrapped around their legs and heads bowed on the tops of their knees.

I realize then the greater, more frightening picture. These women, these flowers, are closing for dusk. Limbs are petals. Their faces the center bud.

A balloon deflates in my chest, leaving me breathless. I gasp and pant, but a deep breath eludes me. I hang my head between my knees and force myself to breathe. If he hears, he'll come near, and the last thing I want is the master of the garden to frown upon me.

Even those bring pain and destruction.

But beyond these walls and this island, I'm being searched for. I continue to tell myself this, and my chest loosens. My breaths even out.

I will be found.

I just don't know if it will be alive.

Or dead.

Chapter Five

Blue Harbor
Bexley Hemmingway's office
Saturday, September 1
6:05 p.m.

Bexley checked her watch. After seeing Tiberius this morning, the rest of the day went to pot until she saw him less than an hour ago on TV giving a press conference. His confidence was professional and assured, not arrogant. If Ahnah wasn't missing, Bex might find solace in his words to the community that they would put in their best efforts to catch this killer. The promise in that statement made its mark. But Ahnah was missing, and there was a possibility that they wouldn't find her before he killed her.

They'd been through a rough patch lately—the whole family. Josiah was sullen and angry all the time. She was to blame for sure. A boy needed a father, and he'd been bringing it up more often. The hostility was new, which she'd been passing off as teenage boy hormones with a side of "I need a dad."

Milo's session had been a debacle earlier due to her lack of undivided attention and had resulted in agitation, but the man who had Ahnah had called her place of business and knew her name, talked with Tiberius. He knew where they were, and she worried Josiah and she might be in danger. She grabbed her voice recorder and pressed Record, forcing herself to concentrate on the job. "Patient exhibits positive parental transference due to a core belief that it's his job to protect. This stems from guilt associated with domestic violence in his own home." Milo obviously believed Bexley was meeting his emotional needs that his own mother, who had been terribly abused, couldn't at the time. Bexley had helped his mother and as a favor agreed to help him work through the trauma.

"Earlier today he interrupted me in my office with someone. Loud voices triggered the deep-seated need to protect. I'll continue to monitor him and work through the transference through cognitive recognition. If it escalates, I'll reevaluate and assign him to a new counselor." She clicked the stop button and leaned her head against the chair headrest, rubbing her temples.

After three minutes of breathing exercises and prayer, Bexley collected her purse and keys, then left the office with her admin assistant, locking the door before walking outside. Exhaustion weighted her limbs, and a sharp pain hammered against the side of her head like a woodpecker to a tree.

Seeing Tiberius brought up her own past trauma, and she'd taken fifteen minutes earlier to call her own therapist. After fleeing that night, she'd felt this same kind of exhaustion and anxiety, which had resulted in her passing out at a bus station. Renee Helton, a therapist who rescued girls like Bexley in all kinds of situations from trafficking to domestic abuse, found her and Ahnah and brought them here to the island and to this home. She missed Renee terribly and wished she was still with them.

Bexley unlocked her car door and all but collapsed inside. How was she going to tell Josiah about Ty? What would he do? Terror that her son would contact the Family to find his roots had kept her silent so far. The Family of Glory was a sick, twisted institution using a real and good God as a front to wield male authority over subservient women and abuse them however they saw fit. Women were born to be wives and mothers and to pleasure their men. If they succeeded in complete submission, they were awarded great honors in heaven and the assurance their children would be with them—if they abided by the rules and laws and weren't disfellowshipped or left willingly. Leaving or disfellowship resulted in eternal condemnation in darkness and torment. Isolated and burning with the shame of failing their families.

Renee had worked tirelessly for months helping to deprogram Bexley and Ahnah from these wicked beliefs. Rand Granger was nothing more than a charismatic, rich pervert. A narcissist and immoral predator seeking greater wealth and pleasure at the expense of broken men and women. The therapist deserved many crowns for that alone. Bexley wanted to give back in the way Renee had given to her. But it had cost her by consuming her. Desperation to see other women set free had fueled her ambition to open up further facilities across the South.

The terrors that she and Ahnah endured should never be faced by anyone else.

She pushed her ignition button and inhaled deeply before buckling her seat belt. "We were gonna risk it all," she murmured. But not at first. At first, they believed that eventually Garrick would marry. Then Tiberius could officially propose to Bexley, and their lives would be perfect. But Garrick's torment of Ahnah increased, and Bexley had divulged the things he'd done and made Ahnah do. Tiberius had taken that information to his father, which kicked off Garrick's heinous plan of asking for Bexley's hand himself.

They'd had to decide: stay and be miserable now. Or go and be miserable in eternity. Their love for one another and desire to keep Ahnah safe had won. They had planned to leave.

From day one, Renee had drilled into Bexley that she could never return to the cult or to Tiberius. He was the son of the Prophet, and it was always a possibility that Rand would find favor with him and have him reinstated. Rand carried all the power, and that meant making new rules and changing rules that benefited him under the pretense that God had spoken to him through his meditation.

No way Bexley was going to let her child be raised by a monster like that. Renee made good points to a seventeen-year-old girl. What did Renee know about Tiberius other than those facts? And Bexley would have and did counsel other young women to do the same—cut ties with members. Clean slate. New chapter. Grace to move forward.

Turning left, she wiped her wet cheeks. She had made mistakes, but she'd only wanted to protect herself, Ahnah and Josiah.

Now Tiberius was in her life, busted right in like a hurricane. Which she also had to think about. Most of her neighbors said it wasn't going to be as rough as they'd predicted and planned to hunker down. Meteorologists had to say the worst to cover their behinds.

She couldn't leave Ahnah, but she needed to keep Josiah safe. If it actually swept through the coastline. Right now she was more worried about Tiberius sweeping through her life, leaving a serious disaster in his wake. How could she help him understand her reasoning behind not contacting him about his son?

She glanced at the time on her car clock. Late. Josiah would be angry. He wasn't one hundred percent wrong to be. She hadn't put her job above him intentionally. She was working to provide for him through traveling to raise awareness and funds for the non-profit on top of researching and writing grants. It took time to help those who were alone and destitute. Or maybe he wouldn't care if she was gone. Lately he'd been holing up in his room, online gaming with friends.

As she rounded the corner, a big black SUV was parked on the side of the road. Blood drained from her head, leaving her light-headed.

Bexley's stomach coiled tighter than a rattler. She pulled under the carport, breathed a prayer, then checked her hair in the rearview mirror. It was as curled as her stomach. Even when she had it thinned out, it was still a massive amount of hair. Like Medusa's.

Yanking her purse and laptop off the passenger seat, she stomped inside her galley kitchen, which needed an update. The savory scent of roast permeated the house, and her stomach rumbled.

The sounds of gunfire and grenades exploding on the Xbox in the living room drew her attention away from the slow cooker. Josiah and Tiberius were locked into a war game.

What had Tiberius revealed? Had he gone against her wishes?

"Dude, you should have had that!" Josiah hollered. "You're an FBI agent. You're supposed to be handy with a gun. Remind me to never ask you to protect me in a gunfight." He laughed at his burn.

Tiberius snorted. "How many guns you handled in real life? If any, you'd know this is not the same."

Josiah shared Tiberius's mischievous grin. "Whatever, dude. You suck."

Tiberius's laugh was deep and genuine. Guilt leaked like acid in her lungs. He did deserve to know his child.

"Hey," Bexley said, drawing their attention and unable to continue watching them bond; it was too heart-shattering and reminded her of so much she'd lost. So much they'd all lost. Even so she'd made the right decision in the end.

Hadn't she?

"Mom, don't expect much out of Agent Granger. He sucks at gun battle."

"What did I tell you about saying 'sucks'?" she reminded him. Josiah's mouth had slowly been creeping into lewd territory, and he had a bigger brain with more creativity.

"Not to," he said with a roll of his eyes. "I could say a lot worse, you know."

Tiberius's eyebrows rose. What did he think a child he fathered would be like? Obedient and always polite? *Pfft*. Josiah was Ty's mini-me when it came to the mischief department. The disrespect was new and all his own, but that snark came from Tiberius.

"Except you won't." She gave him the perfected mom-eye.

He sighed but didn't argue. "I sketched Skipper for Agent Granger. He says I totally have a career in art. So maybe I won't do architecture like you suggested."

Bexley's cheeks heated. Great. Wait… "Who's Skipper?"

"A man who Ahnah knew. We can talk about it later," Tiberius offered.

Okay. "Josiah, Agent Granger and I need to leave." She stressed the words for Tiberius to pick up on. He was here uninvited by her, and she most certainly didn't want to discuss their son with him in the next room. They needed to take this somewhere far away. "Dinner's in the slow cooker. You can—"

"Eat alone. Par for the course." He tossed his controller on the couch and stomped down the narrow hallway before slamming his bedroom door so hard the artwork on the walls rattled.

Tiberius gave her a reprimanding wide-eye. "If he knew who I was, and I was a figure in his life, I'd say something about his lack of respect. Is this a habit of his? And do you let him do this often?"

Bexley rubbed her temples again as the ache became sharper. "He's a good boy and usually sweet-natured, but lately he's been...well...the opposite. I'm sure Ahnah's disappearance has him frazzled and on edge. I know it has me on edge." She wished she could go to bed. Crawl under the down comforter and bury herself in her pain, pity and pride. "I am sorry for all of this. I know it's my fault. You deserve an explanation."

"You think?" He resumed his seat on her worn cream leather sofa, toying with Josiah's controller. "He's good at this game, though. Does he do anything else? Sports? Fishing? Books?"

She snorted, snatched Josiah's shoes by the couch and placed them near the front door. "Drawing. He played basketball for a while, and he was on the swim team in junior high. Now it's drawing and video games and hating me."

Tiberius didn't respond. He hated her too. Couldn't blame him.

"Girlfriend?"

"No. He's always been a loner, and his closest friend was Ahnah. She's been more like a sister than an aunt."

"Can I see Ahnah's room?" Tiberius asked. Guess she'd given a good segue into it.

"Sure." She motioned for him to follow her down the hall; Ahnah's room was across from Josiah's. Music filtered from underneath his door. She'd talk to him later about his disrespect, but she'd have to tread lightly. He'd know if she was shrinking him. He hated when she got inside his head.

Ahnah's room embodied who she was as a person. Neat. Tidy. Colorful.

"Nothing appears to be missing?"

Bexley shook her head. Tiberius perused the room, her photos of them from trips to Nags Head and Disney World. He grunted but said nothing. A vacation like many he'd missed out on. He opened her closet and sorted through her hanging clothes. "No empty hangers. Her luggage bags are in here." Everything pointed to an abduction, not a vanishing of her own making, but she prayed it was the latter.

"She ever mention a Skipper to you?" he asked.

"The guy Josiah sketched? No. Should she have? Is he someone you're looking at? Why does Josiah know?"

He raised a hand to halt her. "Slow down. His name came up in connection to Amy-Rose. How long did Ahnah know her?"

"Couple years when Amy-Rose was hired at the boutique. She was a bit of a wild child, I think. But then maybe Ahnah was too. I feel like I didn't truly know her at all."

After combing through Ahnah's possessions, Tiberius walked into the living room and perched in the rocking recliner that matched her couch.

"Now that work is out of the way, let's talk other things, like you not telling me I have son. And make it good, Bex. Because it better be good."

"I don't want to discuss this where he might hear."

"He's not going to hear anything. Not over the music going in his room, and he's probably wearing headphones to game online. You know it, and I'm a guy who games online so I know it too."

"Fine." Bexley huffed but sat on the couch and tucked her bare feet underneath her, leaning on the edge of the sofa and praying her headache away. "I don't know if it's good, but it's the truth. You were kicked out and gone. I had no one, nothing. When my mom came to approve of the wedding, I stole her sedatives, and Mother Mae caught me about to take the whole bottle."

"You were going to kill yourself?"

That night was the darkest of her soul. She nodded. "But Mother Mae told me that if I would go through with the ceremony, she'd make sure afterward I could leave. She needed time to pull it together."

Tiberius shook his head, his mouth slack. "What did she do? I had no clue she wasn't happy in the Family or being married to my father."

"Neither did I. But your half sisters were minors, and she wouldn't leave them behind. Instead, she helped me. While our families were at the chapel, she packed us each a bag but not from our own closets, and gave me a thousand dollars. Told me to get on a bus and go to Johnson City, Tennessee, and to a church where someone she'd known from her high school days—before she joined the Family—was the pastor. She gave me an address and his name. She said he would help us. But we met Renee first, and I never made it to Tennessee."

She shuddered, remembering the wedding ceremony. Her white dress and the flowers in her hair. Rand at the bottom of the stairs as she descended. He was quite attractive, but he was old to a seventeen-year-old girl, and he was Tiberius's father. After their nuptials, he'd bent and given her a chaste kiss, but she'd never forget his whispered words.

You've only been with a boy. You'll like being with a man so much better.

She inhaled deeply and pushed through. "After the ceremony, I was to go to my bridal chamber to prepare. Mother Mae was with me with Ahnah—she knew I'd never leave without her. Ahnah didn't protest. She was frightened and confused. Mother Mae had placed a ladder at the window, and we climbed down and ran."

"But how does that come to dying in a boating accident?"

"I'm not sure how Mother Mae worked out all the details. She was clearly crafty, but she did say that we had to be dead. Or they'd coming looking for us both since we were minors. She said to take the boat across the lake but not to dock it. It would float downstream. Leave the life vests inside. She'd tell Rand we ran with the clothes on our backs in a rush to escape and stole the boat, and Ahnah must have fallen out—unable to swim. In our hurry, we didn't wear life vests. I must have died trying to save her. For good measure, I tossed one of my shoes near the shore so it would appear it drifted from the water."

"She is clever. My father would have no reason not to believe her. She was devoted—outwardly. They probably combed the lake and hospitals. The lake pours out into the river. The fish and turtles could have eaten you."

"Ew."

"I'm just saying. If you had run out of fear with no clothing, no bags, then it made sense to not think to put on life vests. You would have been unskilled at driving a boat and could have hit something, tossing out Ahnah. At night in the pitch black, you legit could have died from exhaustion trying to find her in the murky waters."

Bexley had wondered about all the details, the conversations, the combing of lakes and her mother's tears. "Renee often visited bus stations looking for transient girls before some sicko found them first. If she hadn't found me, we'd have made it to East Tennessee."

"Why not try to find me? You knew I was going to Atlanta."

"At first, I was afraid and didn't know how to contact you. Your phone would have been cut off, and I had no phone. I didn't know what apartment you secured for us because when you returned, we were separated. Later, when I didn't believe the Family doctrine anymore, I couldn't be sure if you still did. If Rand found out we had a son, he might offer you forgiveness simply to secure Josiah in his clutches. I wouldn't allow him to grow up in that nightmare. I didn't know I was pregnant until Renee took me to the doctor and had me checked out a couple of weeks after giving us sanctuary."

Tiberius rocked back and forth in the chair until she squirmed. What was he thinking? Did he believe her? Did it matter? Finally, he spoke. "I understand that fear, but you knew

I never wanted to go back, and for the record, I don't believe that junk anymore."

"What do you believe these days?"

Ty's laugh was hard and cynical. "I believe in me, myself and I. How's that for a trinity?"

She brushed wayward curls from her eyes. She'd say it was pretty blasphemous. "You must be disappointed on the daily, then." No person could rely or depend on themselves alone without failed expectations. She didn't have the strength or power to fight her battles, which were many, and sometimes more than she could bear.

"Mom." Josiah stomped down the hall. "I thought you were leaving."

"We changed our minds."

He folded his arms over his chest and glared. "Whatever." He proceeded to stomp with equal force into the kitchen. "Where's the ciabatta bread?" he called from the kitchen.

"It's—" She paused. Palming her forehead, she groaned. "Sorry. I thought I bought it, but I forgot," she called.

More murmurings.

Tiberius stood and stretched nonchalantly. "How about we grab pizza or a burger? You can be privy to the case, dude. You earned it." He put an index finger to his lips before Bexley could protest. "I won't relay gritty details," he whispered, "though it's already in the news. You clearly need a win, and I want time with my son."

Lord, help her, she did need a victory. "Sound good?" she reluctantly asked.

"Yeah," Josiah said with more inflection. "I'll put this slow cooker on Warm unless you're still freaked out about it since watching *This Is Us*."

Bexley laughed and enjoyed the millisecond of Josiah acting more like himself. "No, it'll be fine." It wasn't a slow cooker catching fire she worried about. It was some deranged killer who might be toying with Bexley.

The items that had been stolen had been taken after Ahnah vanished.

Blue Harbor
Sea Scape Pizza
Saturday, September 1
7:36 p.m.

Ty sat on one side of the booth in the small local pizzeria specializing in seafood pizzas. Josiah and his mom on the other. Dim lighting screwed with his eyesight. Fishing nets and photos of generations of fishermen holding their catches lined the rustic walls—croaker, striped bass, speckled trout, drum, flounder and spot. Garlic, basil and oregano wafted through the cozy eatery, reminding Ty he was starved.

Out the window, the Pamlico Sound stretched before them. Not even a hint that a terrible storm might be hurtling through these parts in a matter of days. Residents could take precautions, but it wouldn't necessarily save them if Hurricane Jodie— Why did they give hurricanes mostly women's names? Was there something to that? Most of the evil storms he chased materialized in the form of men. But if she chose to exert her power and destroy everything in her path, none of their efforts would save them. They would be rendered powerless. Helpless. At her mercy if she chose to show any.

Hurricanes, like killers, never did.

Bexley sipped her diet drink while Josiah gulped down two-thirds of his sweet tea as they waited on a large pepperoni with mushrooms and a lobster pizza that Josiah promised they'd die over.

"Do you take all your missing persons' families out to eat?" Josiah asked, through chewing on his straw. He was a ball of fidgety energy, and Ty wondered if he'd passed on his ADHD too along with his keen observation skills.

"No," Ty said, fumbling for the right words. He looked to Bexley for help. She was the one demanding the cat stayed in the bag, and the local pizza joint wasn't the prime place to drop the Dad bomb. Keeping his yap shut was one of the hardest challenges of his life, but he'd learned how to appear impassive and even chill in the most insidious moments. He'd interviewed dozens of killers, forced to hear the grimy details of how they committed heinous acts on innocent men, women and children. Attempting to treat this situation as one of those wasn't panning out as well as he he'd hoped. Josiah wasn't a serial killer. He was Ty's son. After only a few moments, Ty recognized he was a fidgeter and had an impulsive streak.

Bexley twirled the beat-up napkin tighter with each twist. "We, uh. We actually went to the same school in Asheville."

Truth, but a stretch. They lived in Asheville and were home-schooled.

"Cool." Josiah leaned in, mischief pulling at the corners of his mouth. "What was my mom like in school? She never talks about growing up, and Ahnah doesn't remember much before they moved to the Outer Banks."

The atrocities Ahnah likely remembered were nothing she would want to share. No, those were things that poor girl would want to forget, which would be a sweet mercy if she could.

Time to have a little fun at Bexley's expense. She had it coming. "What *does* she say?"

Bexley dropped the napkin. "I say that I was quiet and followed the rules and made good grades, which is what I expect out of my son." She gave him the eye to tread lightly. When had Tiberius ever tread lightly?

My son.

Our son.

"Well, she was quiet in class, but she only followed the rules when authority figures were watching." He grinned. "But when they weren't, your mom was a wildcat."

Josiah's eyes lit up, and his mouth made the perfect O shape. "Dude, Mom. No way." He laughed. "Mom doing anything wrong? I can't imagine it."

"I probably have a list somewhere of all her wrongs." They were written on his heart in glass. Bex's cheeks had turned a nice little shade of red, and Ty felt zero shame.

"Let me tell you something," Ty added.

"Oh yay. Life lessons from Tiberius," Bex muttered before sipping her diet drink again.

He swiped his hand in the air, waving her off. "I know some things. Some rules are meant to be followed, but not all rules."

Bexley snorted. "Do not listen to that advice."

"*Do* listen to that advice," Ty countered. No one should have followed the rules of the Family. Each one was archaic and abusive.

Josiah chuckled as the server approached with their pizzas, disintegrating the rule-following conversation. Ty dove into the lobster pizza. The kid wasn't kidding. In his words, it was bussin'.

"So, how'd you get into the FBI?" Josiah asked through a big bite of pepperoni, cheese stringing from his lips down his chin.

"When I left Asheville, I was on my own." He cut a glare at Bexley. "I had some skills but I decided to attend school. I majored in religious studies and minored in psychology. I guess I was trying to figure out the world. What makes religious people tick—all religions. That degree won me a trip to Quantico to the FBI Academy, and the rest is religious history."

"Your degree had the FBI calling you?" Josiah asked.

"Not exactly. I got a job working with the university doing some case studies for the chair of the department. Then the Harbinger of Death cropped up in Charlotte."

"That serial killer. I saw a documentary on him once."

"Yep. I helped the SCU South division solve that case and was recruited for my specialty, but for fieldwork, you have to go to Academy."

Josiah took his third piece of pizza. Had he even tasted a single bite the way he was wolfing it down? "That's cool. Who's the craziest killer you've caught?"

If Ty had a dollar for every time someone asked him that. People were fascinated with serial killers, and he understood it. The psyche of that brand of monster was impossible for a normal human brain to grasp. What made sickos tick? What or who shaped them? But in his opinion, they were far too glorified and the victims and their hurting loved ones far too forgotten.

"I don't know, man. They've all got their screws loose. Last year we worked a case in a Kentucky holler. Guy was taking his victims' eyes and sewing their lids shut, then leaving those women in a cave for a period of time before strangling them. That was pretty bizarre to say the least, but we got him."

"Who's the *scariest* killer you *never* caught?" he asked, and wiped his mouth on a napkin, swiping the string of cheese that had been there this whole time.

Easy enough. "The Fire & Ice Killer." If they'd caught him, Ahnah might not have vanished and Ty wouldn't be sitting here. But if Ty wasn't sitting here, then he wouldn't know he had a son.

"In Virginia?" Bexley asked.

He nodded.

"The one where your mouthing off about him went viral?" she asked, then froze. She'd made a boo-boo. The Fire & Ice case was three years ago, before Bexley came to Memphis and spoke at Fiona's church, giving her the ministry's business card.

She'd known all along where he was and she was never going to tell him about Josiah. He swigged his sweet tea in an attempt to swallow that bitter pill. "Saw that, did ya?"

"Everyone saw that," she muttered.

"I didn't. I'm gonna look it up." Josiah snagged his phone as Bexley's dinged with a notification. She frowned and began moving her thumbs across the screen.

"What's wrong?" Ty asked.

"Nothing. A patient not following rules." She emphasized the *not following rules*.

"So," Ty said to Josiah as he watched the video and hooted at Ty's remarks. "Do you have a girlfriend?" Bexley had told him earlier that he didn't, but sometimes boys hid things like this from their moms. But not their dads—or guys in general. Not that he'd fess up in front of her.

"No." He smirked. "But I got options." He laid the phone down. "That was epic. I wonder if he saw that video."

Pretty sure he had.

"Options, huh?" He put out a fist. Josiah bumped it. "Nice."

"What about you? You see a lot of action?"

"Josiah!" Bexley squawked. "Inappropriate table talk—or talk in general. Women aren't action. They are people who deserve respect."

Josiah's cheeks reddened. "I meant dating action. Now whose mind is in the gutter?"

Not so much the gutter as reliving the past.

Bexley shoved a mass of hair behind her ear. "Well, either way. His personal life is private."

Ty picked a piece of lobster from a slice of pizza on the pan. "I haven't been serious about anyone in decades."

Bexley met his searching gaze. The air grew thick with tension.

"Yeah, Mom don't date either. Like ever." Josiah didn't seem to notice the clogged atmosphere, and grabbed his fourth piece of pizza.

Ty continued to hold her gaze. "Never?" Ty cycled women like a revolving door, but he had always been up front with them. He was not looking for a committed relationship. Dating was easier than falling in love and then having his beating heart shoved out a fifty-story building only to be run over by a party bus. Pass.

"Okay, enough about my private business." Bexley laid her napkin over her plate and pushed it away.

Josiah opened his mouth, but his phone dinged. "Hey, do you care if I cut out early? Abe wants to game awhile at the arcade."

"How do you plan to get there?" she asked.

"I'm gonna meet him at the arcade at the end of the board-walk. Cool?"

Bexley let out a tired mama sigh. "Not a great idea."

Josiah rolled his eyes. "The arcade is literally down the strip and public. Abe can drop me right off on the porch. You can track my location!"

Bexley looked to Ty, and he slightly nodded.

"Fine. Be home by nine. We have church tomorrow."

Ty bristled. Out of one cult and into another, forcing it on their child. He had a mouthful to say on that subject as soon as Josiah left the table.

He snagged one more slice and waved it as his goodbye. "I hope that sketch of Skipper helps. It was cool meeting you." He paused, his expression sobering. "And I really hope you find Ahnah soon."

"I'm gonna do my best."

Josiah tilted his head as if measuring him up. "How good is that?"

Ty smirked. "Pretty good."

With that, Josiah nodded, shoved half the slice in his pie hole and rushed out of the restaurant.

"Do you not feed him often? He inhaled half the pizza in thirty seconds."

"He's seventeen, Tiberius." Bexley rubbed her brow bone. "Can you really find Ahnah, or are you giving Josiah a pat FBI answer?"

Ty wiped pizza grease from his hands. "I'm gonna do my best, and my best is pretty good." He tossed his napkin on the table. "Now, when are we telling him the truth? Because *never* is off the table, Bex."

She rubbed her hands together. "He's worried about Ahnah. They're like siblings. Throwing in more stressful news wouldn't be good for him emotionally or mentally. He's impulsive, Tiberius. Like you. I'm not sure what he'd do, and I'm not sure how to tell him because he cannot go looking for Family members. He's been without for so long, he'll want the connection, and if for no other reason, he'll do it because I tell him not to."

"What have you told him about me?"

Bexley rolled a straw paper between her fingers. "That you come from a bad family, a criminal family, and neither of us are getting involved with them."

"So you didn't say I was but you all but implied it, Bexley. Why would you do that?" The kid thought he was in some kind of mafia. Great.

"He doesn't believe half of what I say, and if he knows you're not a criminal, he might not believe your family is either."

"And whose fault is that, Liar, Liar Pants on Fire?"

She grimaced. "Mine. It's my fault. I'm taking ownership. I'm not perfect, Tiberius. I was his age when I had him. Remember how seventeen-year-olds think? They don't."

"'Kay, but you aren't seventeen now. You can't blame bad decisions after seventeen on your seventeen self, and you absolutely knew how to contact me. You didn't want to. Whatever the reason, you can't keep coming back to the teenage mom blame game." Harsh words? Yes. True? To the core.

"I'm in agreement we tell him. But can we hold off long enough to find Ahnah? It's a lot for him to take, and he's clearly going through something right now."

"How did you get Ahnah to comply?"

She huffed. "She remembered Garrick and didn't want to

go back or see Josiah get sucked into the Family. It wasn't that hard."

Garrick had been untouchable.

Touch not thy Lord's anointed.

He'd done things like block her path and not let her get to the head mistress's house for school. Sometimes he pinned her against trees and told her things a twelve-year-old girl should never know, but he was "training her to be a good wife" for some man someday.

Ty wasn't sure what else Garrick did that Ahnah never confessed, but the last straw had been one afternoon when she'd been in the woods with friends and Garrick had found her. He'd forced her to kneel in front of him with all the other girls watching and commanded she lick the mud off his boots.

All of it.

Slowly.

She had no other choice but to drop down and do it. Garrick was God's future prophet and to question Rand or his heir—or any man for that matter in the Family—was complaining against God Himself. Questioning, rebuking or refusing was strictly forbidden. One could be disfellowshipped for it, and that meant eternity burning alone and miserable in outer darkness.

Ty had taken a chance anyway.

"The best I can offer," he said, "is two weeks. I hope she's found by then. But I'm not leaving here without him knowing."

She nodded once.

"I guess what's done is done, Bexley. I don't think I'll ever forgive you for robbing me of being a father. But what happens from here on out, I'm involved in, and that begins with why you're keeping him from one cult but forcing him into another. Christian church? Really? Let's count how many pastors and leaders abuse women and molest children. Immorality abounds. I can't believe you were duped twice!"

Bexley sat up straight. Resolute. "I am not duped. And you're right, there are a few bad apples in the bunch. That doesn't make the rest of the apples bad. They're what apples should be. As far as Josiah, he's never been forced to believe anything. He has to make his own decision."

He rolled his eyes. "You make him get baptized or handle snakes or something?"

Bexley snorted. "Tiberius, don't be an idiot. We don't handle snakes."

"I don't like it."

"Noted."

A server asked if they needed anything else. Her way of letting them know she wanted to turn the table. "No, thanks. Just the check." A crowd gathered at the front, taking up the benches and standing around.

Suddenly, an alarm blared, and people began to chatter and hop up from their tables.

"Fire!" someone shouted.

Ty stood to assess the situation. Had a fire started in the kitchen? A manager came running, calling out that it was a false alarm. A kid pulled it. Panicked people ignored him while many others sat idly by as if nothing had transpired.

"Tiberius, what's going on?" Bexley stood and grabbed her purse.

"Stay put, Bexley. The manager says it's a false alarm."

Hardly anyone showed Southern charm now; it was every man and woman for themselves.

"It's a false alarm!" the manager hollered again. "You have to pay your bills!"

Ty stepped into the aisle, and a man bumped into him. "Oh, my apologies, sir," the man said.

"Yeah, no worries," Ty muttered, but the man had already disappeared into the crowd.

"Tiberius," Bex said. "What's this?"

She held up a white letter-sized envelope.

"I don't know." The pizza churned in his gut, sending fiery reflux into his esophagus. He searched for the man who had moseyed by with no reason to bump into him other than to distract him and Bexley.

"Should I open it?" she asked, concern raising her voice a few notches.

"No. Let's get out of the frenzy first." After dropping a fifty on the table, he snatched the envelope in one hand and Bexley's in the other, then led her through the throng of people and outside onto the deck overlooking the water. He sat on a bench, wishing he had a pair of gloves.

His nerves hummed as he cautiously opened the envelope. Inside was a solid white note card identical to the ones nailed to the victims' palms. He turned it over to see the same black lettering as well.

Don't be so sure in your confidence, Agent Granger. I got you here, didn't I? I plan to keep you here until I'm finished with you. Plan to suffer.

PS My work's a step up from painted lips and nails, don't you think?

Chapter Six

Blue Harbor
SCU beach house
Saturday, September 1
8:55 p.m.

"It's him. The Fire & Ice Killer." Ty paced the floor and threw up his hands.

Asa cut off his worn path. "We don't know that. He said his work was a step up from painted nails and lips. Implication, not fact, Ty. We focus on facts."

Ty didn't buy it. It was him. Who else could it be? "I shouldn't have given the press conference earlier." He shot a glare at Violet. It had been her brilliant idea. "I know it was him who bumped me and left that envelope. He probably tossed some cash to a kid to pull the alarm and cause the panic, which kept me distracted. Exactly what he wanted." He pounded his fist into his palm. "I could have had him. He was right there."

"I stand by my assessment," Violet said, sipping herbal tea

that smelled like lemon and freshly mowed lawns. "The killer has targeted you. He wants to make you suffer. I said seeing you confident in a press conference would infuriate him and cause him to play his hand. He did."

Fiona and Asa sat on the love seat with laptops resting on their legs. Owen sat at the breakfast bar, tapping an ink pen against his chin.

Would Asa make him recuse himself from the case now that it was even more personal? He couldn't leave. He had Josiah now. He'd quit his job before he'd go home without revealing to Josiah he did have a father who loved him.

Violet cupped her mug and held his gaze. "It appears he might be targeting people you love from your past, starting at the beginning with Ahnah. She's an easier mark, and she has a flower in her name. The question is how long he'll keep her alive and when will he escalate, because rest assured, Tiberius, he will."

How long did he have until this killer plucked another loved one from Ty's grip? Bex. Josiah.

Violet. No one had mentioned she had a flower name, and they were close—as close as one could be with Violet.

Ty had no clue what kind of research the killer did to discover he'd once loved Bexley and knew and cared about Ahnah too. "Where's he keeping them?"

"Somewhere they can't escape while he's working on them," Owen said. "I've found three tattoo salons in Blue Harbor alone. He's a tattoo artist or he was. He can't keep them in his own shop. Too many risks. But he could be hiding them in his home. I asked Selah to do a search across the Outer Banks and as far as Wilmington and Charlotte for abandoned tattoo shops. In case they go with him willingly. Know him. Travel that far with him."

Ty nodded. "Good. Good. What about this Skipper?" He'd given Asa the sketch as soon as he'd blown through the door after dropping off Bexley. He'd asked her to stay here, but she refused with the excuse she needed to be home when Josiah arrived or if Ahnah returned. She was holding on to hope, but the letter had thrown her into a tailspin, and Ty wasn't able to answer her endless questions. He had questions of his own.

"Skipper," Asa said, "is a nickname for an Ethan Lantrip. He's a boat captain with a legit business license. Lives in Blue Harbor. Thirty-four. No rap sheet on him. A few speeding tickets." Asa held up a photo they'd printed, stood and walked toward the whiteboard to place it and the sketch Josiah had done— which was a remarkable likeness. "Found this on his website. I think the amount of tattoos on his body is interesting." He had an ink sleeve of nautical tattoos on his right arm, snaking up the side of his neck. Skipper, aka Ethan Lantrip, looked like a fisherman with weathered, tan skin. Dark eyes. Brown hair that was a little long and pulled back in a short ponytail. Decent-looking for a dude, he guessed.

"Any photos of him with Amy-Rose Rydell on his social media accounts or hers?"

Asa shook his head. "No. If they were dating, they kept it private."

"What twentysomething woman doesn't shout to the internet when she's in a relationship?" Ty asked, frowning. Didn't make sense.

"Maybe he wanted her to keep it private. No record doesn't mean he isn't nefarious. It means he hasn't been caught." Violet stood and carried her empty tea mug to the kitchen, rinsing it and setting it in the sink.

"Where is he? You've had all day to find him," Ty barked.

Asa arched a lone eyebrow.

"Sorry. That's the stress talking." Between the case and his present personal life mixed with the past, his insides were like a volcano erupting.

"He was closed for business. Maybe he's taking a long weekend with Labor Day approaching. I don't know. We have his address and visited his residence, but he wasn't home either. We'll try again tomorrow after FedEx picks up the evidence to be taken to the lab in Quantico."

"Yeah, well, last time we used FedEx, the evidence was stolen by a third party." Not that it was the driver's fault, but it had still happened.

"You want to fly your personal plane out?" Asa's sarcasm was a clear indicator Ty was on thin ice. If he was still in the Family, he'd have access to two personal jets, but he refrained from voicing the remark.

"I'm going to bed," Ty said, spent and not wanting to brawl. His nerves were frayed, and he knew he was being a jerk. He climbed the stairs to the top floor, then marched onto his private deck and leaned over the railing, staring out at the sound.

As the water lapped at the beach, he let his mind wander to the past and pick up the random memories. Making mud pies with Bexley. Climbing trees. Swimming in the creek. The first time he told her he loved her. He was eleven. He'd meant it even then. He'd never wanted to be with any other girl. At seventeen, he'd told her again he loved her. On her sixteenth birthday. Sealed it with a kiss under the stars.

He'd never meant it to go too far. Never imagined their secret would be uncovered, and to this day he wasn't sure who saw or how anyone knew. He never dreamed Garrick would ask Father for Bexley's hand in marriage, or that his father, who knew Tiberius loved her, would allow a union with Garrick.

Garrick's laugh as he came downstairs still scraped against his spine like needles. Marrying Bexley was nothing more than a dig at Ty, who was the favorite son, and a way to get his hands on Ahnah more often.

But he didn't get what he wanted. Neither did Ty.

And then there was Dalen. His oldest half-brother, laughing

at the news right in Ty's face and rubbing in the fact that the golden child wasn't going to get Bexley after all.

His youngest brother, Lysander, had only been fourteen and thought Ty was mad because he got caught setting off firecrackers in John Marlin's carport. *That* his dad overlooked. But the eldest son rule was the rule, and Ty still didn't have a clue why he didn't change it. Maybe Rand had always wanted Bexley for himself and saw Garrick's accusation of her defilement as a way to have her as his own bride. She was beautiful, and he had often leered at her when she visited the house. Rand had made a point to bless her before leaving their home when she came over to hang out, which involved touching her hair and pronouncing a blessing before kissing each cheek. At the time, Ty never thought anything about it. Now? Rand was a perv.

"Hey man," Owen said as he opened the squeaky screen door. "I knocked but you must have been in deep thought. Cool if I'm out here?"

"Sure."

Owen took the Adirondack chair next to the small end table, and Ty eased onto the other one. For a while they sat in silence, listening to marsh grass rustle and the water lap in a calming rhythm.

"What's going on, bruh? Ain't like you to unload on Asa. Not unless he's the one acting like a total behind."

"People are dying because of me. Fire & Ice Killer or someone else. Doesn't really matter. I'm the cause, and the woman I loved…she could be next. Ahnah could die. I gotta find this nut job. Quick. And we have one lame lead. It ain't Ethan Lantrip or Skipper or whatever his name is. Can't be." Could it?

"Who's got a vendetta against you?" he asked.

"Fire & Ice Killer. The MO is too similar. I want to look at the old case files myself."

"Violet has them."

Of course she did.

"You may be too fixated on the Fire & Ice Killer. Violet isn't always right."

"She's mostly right, and again—the MO. Plus no one had a vendetta against me that I know about."

"What about someone from your past? From the Family. Your brother—the one that wanted to marry Bexley and was cruel."

"He got what he wanted in the end. Rid of me. I'm not a threat anymore—never was. I never wanted to take the office of Prophet. He knew that."

"Anything I don't know about? I feel like you've been keeping a lot from me when I've been forthright with you. You were there for me when things went south with Jasmin. That one stung, man."

O was right. They'd been through a lot together. He owed him the truth, but he held back Josiah. For now. "No."

Owen cocked his head and narrowed his eyes. "Walk me through your past again. Garrick to the inner workings of the cult. Close your eyes and go back to that place. Before you left to rent an apartment in Atlanta and take Bexley and Ahnah away. Tell me about the women and the girls in the Family. What were the beliefs, and how did they affect the two of you?"

"The Family of Glory honored pure marriages. Women were to remain virgins until after the wedding ceremony. If it was discovered that they weren't prior to the wedding, they automatically went into the Prophet's harem as another wife. Gave the man the chance to marry a virgin."

"Okaaaay, keep going."

"Everyone knew I wanted to marry Bexley, but I couldn't until Garrick was married or at least engaged. But Garrick had zero intention of settling down."

"But he asked for Bexley's hand in marriage, and it was granted."

Ty's eyes were still closed and he nodded. "Yeah. Felt out of the blue at first, but later I suspected it was retaliation. I went to Rand about his behavior specifically toward Ahnah, and just the accusation could have gotten me disfellowshipped. No one, including siblings, were to report negative behavior. It was considered verbal abuse against a man of God, and in our Family, the men of God were never wrong and were above reproach. Complaining against them—even if warranted—could cost a member everything. Rand talked with him, though. Garrick denied any wrongdoing. I was severely reprimanded instead of kicked out, and I think the proposal was Garrick's retaliation."

"So for some reason—that you don't know—your father granted him permission."

"Yes. By the time I heard, it was a done deal. Signed in a contract with her family. Arranged marriages are standard."

"Women—girls—had to marry any old man?"

He opened his eyes and looked at Owen. "Young. Old. If the Prophet said it was ordained by God then it was."

Owen shook his head, his jaw tight. "You set the plan to run in motion. But while you were gone, something happened. Somehow Garrick caught wind that Bexley and you had been intimate."

"Yeah. The elder wives would examine her to see if she'd, and I quote, been 'deflowered.' Obviously, she had been."

Owen winced. "What, is this biblical times? It's archaic."

"Yeah," he said through a huff. "Upon my arrival, I was brought before my father and the elders to be questioned. I couldn't deny it. And after feeling the wrath of my father's words, I was escorted out of the community and disfellowshipped. Bex was taken into the wives' circle—aka a harem—to await the wedding ceremony. Usually within two to three days. But Bexley said it happened that night." It had been storming that night. Dark. Cold.

"Dude, I don't even know what to say."

What could anyone say? Depravity and hypocrisy abounded

in that place. He pinched the bridge of his nose, working to stave off a headache, but it was no use.

Owen reached over and gripped his shoulder. "I can't imagine, but I'm seeing red flags, Ty. Flags you should be seeing, but it's personal to you. Your mind is fuzzy. The note implies that it's the Fire & Ice Killer, but it's public knowledge what he did to those women with the polish and lipstick. So while we assume it's Fire & Ice, it could be a copycat who has a vendetta against you. Someone who knows the past. Next, did you hear the words you used about your sick cult?"

Ty shook his head. Owen was right, he was fuzzy, completely unfocused. His arrows weren't shooting straight, but he couldn't let Asa know. He had to stay and stick this out.

As long as they had to stick it out. Hurricane Jodie was picking up velocity as it barreled toward Elbow Cay, Bahamas. If she didn't slow, she could head straight for them.

"*Deflowered*—we gonna come back to that nasty term later—but our guy is tattooing flowers on his victims. One possible victim is Ahnah, who was in the cult with you and who also has a flower for a middle name."

The deck slanted and his blood froze. How had he not already connected the dots? "We had a signature logo of pretty flowering dogwood blooms on a cross…"

"You have any enemies that were in the Family of Glory with you or who left?" Owen asked, leaning his forearms on his knees.

"I was eighteen. I mean, I never got along with my oldest half-brother, Dalen, but I never did anything deserving of this, and he wasn't cruel like Garrick. Just a jerk."

"Was he already married?"

"No, but in our home it was the eldest son based on the wives. Garrick was firstborn of my mother. Dalen was firstborn of Mother Anne."

"That is so messed up. How many half-siblings do you have?"

"I have no idea. Hundreds maybe by now."

"Could it be him? He didn't like you. He was jealous."

Dalen? His jealousy was no secret, but once Ty was disfellowshipped and lost his favorite son status, Dalen would have no reason to give him another thought. "No."

"What about Garrick?"

Ty shook his head and batted a mosquito away. "What would be the point? His motive? Once my dad dies, Garrick will be the new Prophet. He was vile, but he never hated me." Or had he?

Owen gave him the get-real look. "He asked for your woman's hand in marriage. Sounds like hatred."

"He thinks Ahnah and Bex are dead."

"If Bexley helps cult girls escape, what's to say he doesn't know she's alive? What if this is still about you and Bexley and Ahnah?"

Violet had vetted Bexley and Ruth's Refuge. Her website had no pictures, and when Dexley visited churches, recordings weren't allowed. She protected her own identity from the cult. Although now there was nothing they could do since she and Ahnah were of age. No forcing them to return, and it wasn't like they murdered former members.

At least not that he was aware of.

But she wouldn't want them sniffing around. Wouldn't want her parents to get wind they had a grandchild. And if his own father knew... Bexley was right. They might try to contact him if Josiah didn't reach out first. "I don't know what to think."

"We need to bring this to the team and let Fiona and Violet do their wiggy-jiggy on it."

Ty laughed. He and Owen had all kinds of names for the way Fi and Violet profiled. *Wiggy-jiggy, hu-du, ju-ju.* The *jeeper-creeper*—that was his favorite. "Yeah. I guess so."

Could someone who had once been in the Family of Glory be the Lighthouse Killer and/or the Fire & Ice Killer?

Kipos Island
Saturday, September 1

Infernal classical music filters from unseen speakers in my cell. If I survive this I will never listen to instrumental music again. We're let out of our cages sometime after dark. Time and days have disappeared. I can't keep up. But I know we're led one by one to our prisons with nice beds. Sometime after light, he repeats the leading, and we enter the cages again. He calls them hanging baskets, but they don't actually hang. We can't dance in swinging cages.

I've refused to dance altogether.

And I have paid the price. My left ring finger is now a throbbing, aching mess. He'll have to break all of my fingers, because I'm not going to bend. I can't. I'm surely being looked for, and I am holding on to hope.

Yesterday, he entered my room with Xanax and made me take it. I don't want to, but he's going to tattoo me anyway, and it's a few hours that I don't feel like I'm going to come out of my skin and lose my mind. And if he does anything else to me, I don't want to be awake for it.

He wasn't prepared for my quick outburst after swallowing it, though, which had been strategic. When he rolls in the tattooing cart with all his gadgets, I've been eyeing the needles with hopes it'll pick my iron cuff and maybe the door. I knocked over the trays and, in our scuffle, he broke another finger, and I managed to slide a needle under my bed. It's long and hooks like a noose at one end. I'm sure it has a name. I don't know it but it fit the bill.

I'm not sure how long I've been working it into the cuff, but it's not budging and I kick a bare foot at the wall and let out a cry. This has to work. God, let it work. I flex my aching good hand, which cramps from holding the thin, long needle, then inhale deeply. Frustration only robs me of focus. I must focus.

After a few deep meditative breaths, I insert the needle into the lock again and find a little groove. Sweat forms above my lip but I'm cold. Never can get warm. I feel the needle in the groove and begin to twist and turn until it moves, and the click sounds like freedom.

I can't control the dam of tears that breaks, and the heaviness resting on my shoulders dissipates. I. Am. Free. I'm getting out of here.

Preparing to the pick the lock on the door, I'm in shock when I turn the knob to test it and find it unlocked.

Another wave of joy rides my tears, but it's short-lived as I halt.

Why would he leave the door unlocked?

My breath trembles, and I jerk my hand from the knob. Is he expecting me to try again so he can punish me for lack of submission? Is he out there waiting to catch me? Is this a game? I glance upward, searching for a camera, a blinking light, anything to indicate I'm on-screen.

Nothing.

I play the what-if game, and with each scenario, my pulse increases until my chest aches and I can't inhale a full breath. If I don't attempt to break free, I know at some point I'm a dead woman. And if do break out and get got, I'm only deader faster.

I ball a fist and inwardly scream. What choice do I make? What is he up to? Will a sensor signal an alarm and my escape attempt?

The walls close in on me, and spots form in front of my eyes. With no more thought, I yank open the door and pause, waiting for the blaring of a bell or buzz of an alarm, but only silence fills the hallway.

One beat. Two.

No one comes.

Maybe he's not here. Maybe he simply forgot to lock the door because I was dead out from the drugs. Maybe he's overly confident and underestimates me. Two broken fingers will not keep me from trying.

I dart into the hallway and instinctively cover my chest with my arms.

Should I open the other doors and free the remaining garden girls? Would they come with me? No. Too many of them. I have a better shot escaping alone and sending help. I clutch the needle in my hand; it's the only weapon I have for now.

If I can make it to a phone—a landline if he has one or a cell phone or laptop—I could call or message someone for help, but most cell phones and computers have passwords, and landlines are practically obsolete. No, that's too risky. My best bet is to find that canoe at the private dock. I dread returning to the marsh, but I'm going to die if I stay. But I could die out there too. By an alligator. Do I want ripped to shreds by an ancient water monster or ripped to shreds by a wicked human monster?

I take my chances on the alligator. At least the beast will show me mercy as he forces me down into the murky water for the death roll, drowning me and shoving me in a log for later.

I'll never be found. No closure for my family.

But I may never be found otherwise. I head for the stairs. I know where they are and can move fast. One flight. Two. I pause and listen. Nothing but the low hum of the TV he's left on the news channel.

The newscaster warns an approaching hurricane could hit the Eastern Seaboard. She's called Jodie. If I don't make this attempt to freedom, then I hope she comes with all her untamable force. I've been in a hurricane before. You're powerless to stop it coming. You cannot beg, bargain or bolt from something that unrivaled, unmatched.

I hope she comes in with severe judgment and sweeps the entire island under and never vomits it up again. We'll be casualties, but our deaths will be sweet relief. Underwater it's quiet and still and peaceful. I'd open my mouth and inhale death, letting it consume me whole like the alligator but without the sting.

The door beckons me to come. To find my escape. To take refuge in the marsh. I won't make the same mistake twice. I'll hide for hours in one of the thickets until he has to give up.

But then…what if he takes the canoe? What if I make it to the dock and it's gone? Then what?

My throat is tight and my stomach lurches, but I dash to the door.

I unlock the sliding dead bolt.

Turn the lock on the actual knob.

And I freeze, losing my bladder at his voice.

"Where are you off to this time of night, darling?" It's a quiet before the storm kind of tone. I turn but he's not there, and it dawns on me his voice is coming through a hidden speaker.

He sees me. From where I do not know. A camera system. Has he been watching the whole time from working to unlock the fetter that held me to right now in this moment?

A buzzing at the door draws my attention and I gawk in horror as the sliding lock clicks back into place.

With trembling hands, I unlock it again.

But the buzzing repeats and the lock returns to its place.

"I can do this all night if it's the game you want to play," he says. "I do enjoy your determination."

It's a smart house. He can run anything including lights and appliances with the touch of a finger.

I know now he left the door unlocked the last time on purpose to prove I have no power. He's been in control the entire time.

I don't think. My flight-or-fight mode has kicked in and I run. My brain won't process rationally; it screams *hide. Run. Get as far away as I can.* I slide the bolt once more and reach for the knob, hoping this time I can wrench open the door before it relocks.

I'm not that fast.

"Ah, ah, ah," he singsongs through the speakers. "Outside is a no-no. If you need me to talk to you as a small child, I'll indulge you. But I'd rather treat you like a woman."

"A woman? You're holding me prisoner!" I scream and rotate in a circle, looking upward though I don't know where the hidden cameras are located.

"You gave yourself to me. We're one flesh. You belong to me. You are me."

I run through the living area to the other door, but it's locked too, so I scramble up the stairs to the second floor. My gaze roams over this living area as my blood pressure rises to dangerous heights, pounding in my ears and giving me a sharp pain through the back of my skull.

I know I have nowhere to go. No way out. Nowhere to hide.

I collapse in a heap and pound the floor through my guttural sobs. "Let me out! Let us go. Please, let us go."

He says nothing for a long time. I know he's watching me in a crumpled heap, losing my mind. I feel the shift inside me. The breaking point. It cracks along my rib cage and seeps into my blood, which runs thick and cold through my veins. Buzzing zings in my ears.

Suddenly I'm numb.

"You can march yourself to your room like a good girl or we can do this the hard way. I'll let you have the freewill choice." His voice is soft and slow like a dad reading his child a bedtime story. But I'm not a child, and this is a horror novel. One I don't have a pen to change the chapter ending for. I am powerless. Voiceless.

Hopeless.

Deep below the marrow, a voice calls to fight. To be brave. To hold on and hang in. Not to quit. It's not over yet.

A hurricane is coming.

And people are tracking me. He's seen the press conference.

I push myself up off the floor and shove hair matted from tears away from my face, straightening my spine.

"That's a good girl. Well done."

I lift my chin to the ceiling and my fist too. "You come down here, you son of—" I swallow. "I'm not going anywhere."

And I know I've unleashed a cold fury.

Chapter Seven

Blue Harbor
Bexley Hemmingway's home
Sunday, September 2
12:46 a.m.

A noise startled Bexley awake and her eyes flew open. Her pulse pounded in the darkness. Something or someone was outside. Once her eyes acclimated to the pitch black, she swung her gaze toward the window. A shadow moved, and her body went rigid. Ahnah's abductor? Tiberius had admitted that whoever was doing this was personal to him—a killer who wanted revenge for that viral video. Was he coming for the rest of those Ty once loved?

Would he know about Josiah and come for him too?

She quaked and sweated simultaneously. Whoever was out there was watching, and she didn't want to tip him off that she was awake and alert. Crawling her fingers up the side of her nightstand like a spindly-legged spider, she found her cell phone and inched it to her, tucking it under the covers and wishing she'd closed the blinds. But after the fright night at the restaurant and that terrifying letter, she came home, took a hot shower before crawling under the covers for sanctuary, and fell sound asleep.

Gently, she rolled over and nestled into the blankets, sneaking another peek outside the window. The figure was still there. Now that she was under the covers, she entered her passcode and scrolled to Tiberius's name. After he'd left his business card, she'd programmed him into the phone. Agent Granger. If he had news on Ahnah, she wanted to answer and not let it go to voice mail like many unknown numbers she received.

God, don't let him sleep like the dead anymore.

On the second ring, his groggy, rough voice punched through the line. "Agent Granger."

"It's me," she whispered. "Someone's outside my window and has been for a while I think. Watching me."

"Bex?" His voice was more alert. Concern replaced annoyance.

"Yes. I'm in bed. Under the covers. I don't think he knows I'm awake or if he does, it's not scaring him off. But I'm scared."

The sound of a zipper and keys being scraped across a table filtered through the line.

"Stay where you are and on the line with me. I'm on my way. Josiah okay?"

"As far I know," she whispered. "Should I go check on him?"

"No. Whoever's out there probably assumes you're asleep, which means he might stick around long enough for me to arrive and grab him. If he thinks you're awake, he'll bolt."

A door closed and the beeping of a car unlocking let her know he was entering his vehicle.

"What if he tries to break in?" What would she do? She had no gun, only a lone baseball bat by the side of the bed.

"If he tries to enter, you jump up and let him know you've

called the police. He doesn't want to be caught, and he'll likely run. But if he doesn't move, you don't either. I'd like to catch him myself."

"Are you using me as bait, Tiberius Lee Granger?" she hissed. "I have a son inside. *We* have a son inside!"

"Now he's my son." His tone was tight.

"Really? You're going there. Now?"

"Sorry. I'm worked up. What's he doing?"

She dared a small glance toward the window and gasped. "He's got his hands on the window, peering in." Panic rippled down her back, and she prayed for help holding still. If she could hold still, Tiberius could catch him.

"Can you see his face?" he asked after a stretch of silence.

"No. It's too dark." She white-knuckled her comforter.

"I'm on your street. I'm going to park and come to the house on foot. Surprise him. If you see a second shadow, it's me. Okay?"

"Okay. But don't kill him. If he knows where Ahnah is, we need him alive."

"One of us does this for a living," he said, with amusement. "I'm putting you in my shirt pocket on Speaker. I can hear you, but maybe don't say anything in case he can hear you too."

"Okay." She paused. "Tiberius?"

"Yep," he whispered.

"Please be careful and don't die."

"Do my best," he murmured and went silent.

She squinted, keeping an eye on the peeper, when his head suddenly swiveled to the right. Then he vanished.

"He ran away. You spooked him."

"I'm not even to the house. Can't be me. Wait. I see headlights in your drive!"

Had he parked in front of her house, or was someone else here? If so, who would it be? Could it be about Ahnah?

Bexley sprang from bed, snagging her ratty blue robe and

sliding into it as she ran down the hall. Pausing at Josiah's room, she cracked open his door and startled as the front door swung wide open. Shrieking, she clutched her robe lapels.

Josiah blew in like a storm cloud with Tiberius on his heels.

"Josiah? What are you doing outside?" Had he heard the noise too?

"He's the headlights, Bex." Tiberius scowled, his hair disheveled from sleep and his scruff looking more like a beard. His T-shirt and jeans were rumpled, and he held his gun in his right hand.

"What is going on? He almost tackled me!" Josiah said, ripping away from Tiberius and putting distance between them.

Tiberius sniffed and his eyes narrowed. "Have you been drinking?"

Josiah raised his chin and bowed his chest. "No. And even if I had, what's it to you? You're not my dad!" He stomped down the hall, almost bumping Bexley. Had it been Josiah outside? What was happening? Drinking?

Tiberius's jaw ticked and his nostrils flared. He thrust out his hand. "I'd call him back, but why should he listen?" He pointed a finger to his chest. "I'm not his *dad*."

The room swirled around her, and she gripped the side table by the wall to hold herself upright. Nothing was holding her up inside. Any minute someone would show up and cart her off to the asylum, and she'd welcome it.

She slunk to the floor and rested her head on her knees, willing herself not to have a panic attack. Instead, she cried.

Being a single mom was her choice, but she was messing up at every turn. Being gone was being a bad mom. Sticking close smothered him. Bexley had tried to give him independence, but she was unsure how much leash to give. Mistakes had been made. Grave ones. Now Ahnah was gone, and she might not have the chance to make things right between them. And a vicious killer was prowling around her house, all while Josiah was out…drinking?

Tiberius's shoulders slumped, and he sighed as he slid down the wall beside her, draping an arm around her shaking body. His hold was warm and his body solid. He smelled of lingering cologne and cinnamon mints.

This was the grace she needed but didn't deserve.

"Yell at me or something." Screaming and accusation would be so much easier to handle. She deserved every hateful and hurtful word he might release from his lips. And yet, she leaned into him for his strength because she flat-out had none of her own.

"I will," he said. "Later. Once you're done crying. I'll lay into you good, and you can start the waterworks all over again. Sound like a plan?"

Sounded like Tiberius. She laughed through a sniff. "I thought I was doing the right thing."

"I know—that you were scared." He rested his head on top of hers. "I know you were."

"Can you forgive me?"

Tiberius inhaled. "I don't know. I want to hate you, Bexley. And to be honest, on some level, I do hate you. I hate you for leaving me. I hate you for lying to me." He paused, then murmured, "I hate you for loving me once."

Bexley felt the dam breach. New tears flowed. "I thought you were gonna make me cry later."

"No time like the present I guess." He laid his head against the wall. "The peeper got away. Josiah's friend's headlights scared him off before I got here."

"The killer is coming for me—us—isn't he?" What else could it be?

"Maybe. But at the moment, I'm more worried about our son. Who is this Abe person he went to meet at the arcade earlier? What if he'd been drinking too?"

Bexley wiped her nose on her robe sleeve. "He's a local friend. I honestly don't know much about him other than they game online often and meet up at the arcade on weekends." She hugged herself. "Josiah's a good kid, Tiberius. He's going through a hard time. He needs—"

"A father?"

The hurt in his voice was a piercing sword cutting into her and ripping at her decades-old wounds. "Independence and guidance. I'm doing a terrible job balancing. And yes, yes, he needs a father, and yes, it's my fault he hasn't had one."

"He needs to better understand the danger, Bex. This killer targets women, but this is personal, and anyone I care about is in the crosshairs. I don't know that it's only women who aren't safe."

Who would want to wreak this kind of torture on Tiberius? "Who is doing this?"

"I don't know."

"The blanket and photo taken from my house...they were taken after Ahnah vanished. I'm not sure what that means."

"What about the box of mementos?"

"I can't say for sure. They weren't something I often looked at or used. Could be before. Maybe after." She shrugged.

"I'll run it by Violet. In the meantime, you should know that there might be a more personal connection to me in this case. One that leads...to the Family."

Acid sprang in her throat, and she clutched her chest. "No," she whispered.

"Possibly. I need Rand to give me a list of members who left or were disfellowshipped."

This was a terrible idea.

Tiberius enveloped her clammy hands. "I won't reveal the truth about you, but someone already knows you and Ahnah are both alive. I don't want them to know about Josiah either.

But I need to know who's left the Family in the past five to ten years. It's a thin link at best, I know."

"Rand will never give you what you want."

"All I need is information on Garrick and if he was disfellowshipped or remains in the Family." He held her gaze as she processed what he was saying. She shuddered at the implications.

"You think it's Garrick."

Tiberius shrugged. "No, not really."

"I'm afraid."

"I know." He rubbed the scruff on his chin. "How would you feel about me staying here at night until we find the killer?"

She didn't want Tiberius here every night. It was hard enough seeing him only a little, but she wasn't stupid. She needed him. Needed protection for herself and Josiah.

"You would be willing to do that?"

Tiberius stood. "Bexley, that's my son in there. And I don't want to see you hurt. So yeah, I'll do it. And we need to tell Josiah enough to get it through his thick head that he needs to be more careful and stick to curfew."

"Not to mention the possible hurricane coming. It's growing. Have you seen the news?"

"It's eating through the waters and targeting land. Targeting us and we can't stop it. We have to find Ahnah, the other women, and who's behind this before it makes landfall. Or... I don't know what will happen."

"My neighbors don't think it's going to hit us, and if it does, it won't be that bad. We've braved hurricanes before. I know how to prepare. But yes. Yes, you can stay with us. Let me talk to Josiah about the danger and curfew, and the drinking. Are you sure you smelled alcohol on his breath?"

"I know that smell well. I'm sure."

She rubbed her aching temples. "Okay. I'll talk to him."

He nodded. "I'll bunk on the couch the rest of the night and call my SAC. Let him know."

"I'll get you pillows and a blanket." She headed for Josiah's room. "And thank you," she said, pausing. "You don't have to make things soft or easy."

"No, I don't." He combed his hand through his hair. "And after this is all said and done and he's caught, it won't be soft. I won't make it easy then. Truce while a killer is out there. Then things are gonna be real different."

She feared that more than a hurricane threat and almost as much as a twisted killer.

Blue Harbor
SCU beach house
Sunday, September 2
8:12 a.m.

Ty stumbled into the beach house, massaging the crick in his neck from sleeping on the couch. Freshly brewed coffee wafted in the air and drew him straight to the pot.

"Bruh, you look rough," Owen said, sipping a cup at the kitchen island.

"Yeah, well. I'm pushing forty. I can't do late nights and couches anymore." He poured a cup of coffee—black as a killer's soul—and sipped. "Where is everyone? I know Fiona's up and moving. No one else makes coffee this strong."

Owen clicked and clacked on his laptop. "She's up and in full form. Violet was outside on the deck talking to John and Stella." He took another drink. "I wonder how long after she marries John she'll resign. The travel is a lot. Stella's almost five."

Violet as a mom. "That kid doesn't have a fighting chance. Ain't gettin' away with diddly-squat." He closed his eyes, mimicking Violet's procedure of slipping into a sicko's head. "I would wait for Dad to go to bed and then slowly open the window, but earlier that day I'd have greased it so no one will hear it open or close. I can't leave it open. Mosquitos and stuff."

Owen snorted at Ty's representation of Violet at work.

"Then," Ty said, in whispery voice like Violet's, "I leave the yard and push the car down the road. No lights. Can't be seen. I want to meet him. I've been planning it. Covering my tracks and using a burner phone I learned all about from my detective dad."

He opened his eyes, and his grin died a sudden death. Violet stood three feet in front of him, hands on her skinny hips and drilling a hole in him with her icy blue-green eyes. He gave her his best apologetic shrug while Owen covered his mouth, his shoulders shaking with his silent laughs.

"No, no. Go on," Violet said.

"You wrecked my mojo." He sipped his coffee instead.

"You have no mojo." Her right eyebrow tweaked upward and she folded her arms over her chest. "You think the guy stalking Bexley's place is your killer?"

"Asa filled us in this morning," Owen said. "Otherwise, I'd be grilling you about why you didn't come home last night."

Ty rolled his eyes. "I don't know. Josiah said a picture of them and a blanket she made were missing. The picture and blanket after Ahnah was taken, and she can't be certain when the memento box disappeared. Amy-Rose's and Lily's families weren't sure if anything had been lifted. Amy-Rose hadn't lived with her parents in a few years. It's possible our guy toys with them before striking. Or he's known to them and was taking things when he was there visiting. What do you think, Violet?"

"Let me close my eyes a minute and get a feel," she said, dryly. Bumping him out of the way, she maneuvered to the coffeepot and poured a cup, her long dark hair hanging over one shoulder.

"Mimicking is a form of flattery," he jested.

"Flatter someone else, then."

Voices on the third floor and footsteps on the stairs redirected their attention.

"I'm capable of going alone, Asa. Get a grip," Fiona said.

"I'm only saying he can go with you."

"No. We talked about this," she countered as they entered the room. She was toting a small carry-on bag.

"What's happening?" Ty asked.

"Four female bodies were found in Natchez Trace Park. Mass grave. One's fresh, and two girls hiking last week arc missing. I'm meeting with the Investigative Branch Services of National Parks this afternoon. Asa's taking me to the airport."

"Why SCU?" Violet asked. The same question she asked every time they were handed a case or consult.

"The bodies are wearing identical rosaries around their wrists. And...they're dressed in habits."

"Bad ones? Bad ones get you killed every time." Ty grinned over his coffee mug. "I'm kidding. Nuns being targeted?"

"No." Fiona poured a travel mug of coffee while Asa scrolled through his phone and glanced at his watch. Seemed he always had, always was and always would be waiting on Fiona. "They were costumes. So...there ya have it."

"You mean, there you habit," Ty said. Owen nearly spit out his coffee, then raised his fist. Ty bumped it with his own.

Fiona shot him a glare, screwed on the lid and pointed at Asa. "We're not gonna be late. Stop looking at me like that." She breezed past him toward the door. "I should be back by the end of the week."

"Ty, walk with us." Asa motioned him to follow.

Great. "Now am I in trouble?"

"No." Asa paused at the bottom stair. "Hurricane Jodie became a category 5 and made landfall at Elbow Cay, Bahamas. If their new projections are right, the Outer Banks is going to take more than a hit. It could be decimated." At the moment the sky was blue like Texas bluebonnets. Not a cloud to be seen. "I could send you with Fiona. This UNSUB isn't expecting you to leave the island. If he finds out you've gone, he'll make a mistake."

"He'll kill Ahnah."

"You don't know for certain he has her."

Except his gut screamed otherwise, and he would not leave his son.

"If I leave, he'll make a mistake, but it'll be at a life's expense. He has a process, which means they're probably all alive for now. We have time."

"Short window if what they say about the hurricane proves true."

"Now who's making us late?" Fiona called. "You in or out, Tiberius?"

"Out. Besides, I don't have time to pack."

"You never unpack. We all know this." Fiona stepped inside the rental and closed the door. She had a point. Ty never unpacked his suitcase no matter where they went. Never knew when he'd have to roll out quickly, but the truth was he didn't like unpacking because it felt like putting down roots. Even after all these years living in Memphis, his apartment was simply a place where he crawled into bed at night.

Wouldn't call it home.

His last home had gates. Guess he never wanted to be chained. Wanted to be able to escape at any moment. That's how he felt inside. Like he was always scaling walls but never reaching the top, never reaching freedom. At some point he might need to simply give up and quit climbing. Because once he scaled it, where was he supposed to go? What was beyond the wall? What was freedom?

"I'll behave," Ty said to Asa.

"That's bunk and we know it." Asa clapped him on the back. "I'll see you in a couple of hours."

Ty watched them drive away and went inside. "Who's in charge while they're gone?"

"Obviously me," Violet said. "I'm the boss."

Ty struck a Bruce Springsteen pose, his arm up overhead, one foot kicked behind him. "Fine," he conceded.

"Come on. They have Skipper at the sheriff's office in Manteo. After we question him, we can chat with the boutique manager, Leslie McDonald." She pointed at Owen's laptop. "Anything at all to help us pinpoint where our UNSUB might work or live?"

"Not so far. But I'd say he's on Blue Harbor Island. Maybe Nags Head area. Or he's here on the island often for business. Knows the locals. He's not taking tourists." He handed Ty the list of missing women from the past year.

"Thanks."

"Everything cool?" Owen asked in a low voice.

"Yeah. He thought if I went with Fiona, I'd tick off the killer and he'd make a mistake. And he might, but I said no."

"Bexley Hemmingway holding you here?"

No. His son was. And a killer.

Kipos Island
The Garden
Sunday, September 2

I can hardly walk to my small bathroom for the searing pain. Hot angry tears blur my vision as I relive last night. No more broken fingers. The cracked bones clearly don't work on me. Last night after my great brave—or stupid—stand, he did come for me. He came in deliberate steps and a velvety voice, but the frigid fury behind his eyes revealed I was in more trouble than anticipated.

One never acclimates to pain. I can't say I'm used to it. I'm not. I never was. I expected it, though, in the past—and last night—but expecting it and enduring inflicted torture are two different things.

He'd used the flicker of fire to my groin. The tender area between my thighs and pelvis is now riddled with angry red puckers. This is how he's going to break me. Not with fractures but fire.

I don't cry over the suffering but over the fact it's only a matter of time before I succumb and rise when he demands I bloom. Before I arc my arms over my head and dance like all the other garden girls.

I'm better than this. They are better than this.

But I'll end in submission. I can't endure the fire. Can't walk through it. Can't pace in the midst of it. No one is in the flames with me. Only the enemy holding me in, and through the affliction, his true nature manifests. He is not the angel masquerading as light, teasing me with lust and a delusional fantasy of living happily ever after. Lies drip from his forked tongue and flattery from his fangs. Feeding me false hope to ensnare me in his trap I can't escape.

An hour ago, he brought me a breakfast tray as if he hadn't strapped me down spread-eagle and tortured me through quiet lulls to accept the punishment, bloom where I'm planted, resign myself to the fact that this is my fault and I gave myself to him. I'm being reborn and remade, which takes time. I must be patient. And all I could think about was poking his eyes out with the plastic fork. One gorgeous eye, then the other. Marring his mask of beauty. Slicing through the facade to reveal the serpent he truly was inside. His organs black as night and rotted with maggots. He is walking death, decay and destruction.

His footsteps clack down the hall and he reaches my door, unlocking it and then entering. His masculine cologne might as well be decomp smeared on his smooth skin. Nothing about him is appealing, and the thought of being with him sours my stomach. How did I ever willingly walk into this psychotic freak show?

He eyes my full tray of eggs, bacon and toast and my untouched orange juice and water. I roll onto my side, facing the wall, and wince at the soreness. Any movement is searing. I'm exhausted and can barely lift my head. My mouth is like cotton saturated in molasses, but I will not drink.

"You must eat, but it's your choice."

I almost laugh at his words. I have no choice in any matter. He's a liar. The father of lies.

"I brought you an ice pack. You can take it with you to your basket. It's time to bloom." His presence grows closer to me. I know this because the atmosphere that swirls around him is bitter cold, and the hairs on my arms and neck rise to attention. His weight jostles the bed as he sits, and his hand runs through my hair. "I need my garden girls this morning. I need you to dance for me. Open up and bloom. I need the company and companionship. I need the release. Come now. Please don't make me ask again." His slight Southern accent is rich, buttery, and calm as usual, and it sends a wave of chills through me. "I'll have to find new places of pain so the beauty of your sweet pink flowers won't be overshadowed. So many buds. Aren't you ready for gorgeous blooms? You'd be so pretty with them."

He's talking to me as if he's coaxing a lover to dinner. His tender touch is like porcupine needles across my exposed flesh. I don't welcome or want it. But I lie silent and unmoving. I'm not sure how much fight is left.

"What do you decide?"

I remember the red-and-black gas lighter clicker. The same kind I use to light my vanilla cookie crunch candle. I rise, and he brushes my hair, then pins it in a bun on top of my head.

I walk like one of his minions to his secret garden of horrors and step inside the cage without so much as a pause. I glance over and notice a new garden girl today. She is as naked as the rest of us. Her hair isn't pulled into a bun. Not yet.

But there is a breaking point for everyone. That moment when your soul rips until there's nothing but numbness and the light slowly dims and your eyes become hollow wastes of space because you see nothing. No future. No happiness. Nothing but gray, bitter cold.

She has a few tattoos but not many. If I had to guess, I'd say she's only days into her living hell. I wonder which room he's confined her to. This could work to my advantage. She might be beaten down, but she's not broken. If she has some fight, I might have an ally.

"I'm in the mood for Beethoven's *Moonlight Sonata*, first movement. Oh yes, that will do." He walks to the table and grabs the remote. The new girl gapes but says nothing. She mirrors my first glimpse at this terror—questions, fear, dread. He morphed from a tender and passionate lover to a psychotic monster getting his jollies on girls dancing to classical compositions. Yeah. It's a shock to the system.

Anger cracks like a whip up my sagging spine, snapping me to attention. Maybe I have some fight left yet. "You know he's conditioning us, right? We're nothing short of Pavlov's dogs. Dancing at the music. You...new girl. You don't want to be here, do you? Good beds, obedience and good food. It's Stockholm's you're feeling, ladies. Believe me, I know this. I know battered woman syndrome when I see it. We're stronger than him together. We can get out, and I can get you help. I know a place you can go. My—"

"Silence!" he commands. His tongue lashes like a cat-'o-nine-tails. The new flower fades, turning inward on herself and assuming the same position as the other women.

"This is why I don't leave you alone together. You present as such a delicate flower, but you've been nothing but a thorn in my side." His body begins to shake, and I realize I've struck a nerve. I've put a crack in his armor. It doesn't scare me; it invigorates me.

"Shut. Your. Mouth," he says through gritted teeth and a

hardened jaw. "Or the pain you felt last night will be nothing in comparison to what I'll do next."

Haunting piano music begins. One little note and then the next like raindrops pitter-pattering, building steps to his castle of torture. It evokes heavy black clouds and bloodthirsty bats circling his den of iniquity. I know what comes next.

The choice I have to make.

"Garden Girls...*bloom* for me." His words are breathy and full of anticipation.

Pliés and pirouettes begin in a room that reeks of defeat and hopelessness.

The new girl rises to her bare feet, taking in the other garden girls' positions and mimicking them, but it's messy and clumsy.

He praises her with clapping, a wide mouth full of perfectly straight white teeth grinning with pleasure.

Then he casts his wicked gaze on me, awaiting my choice.

I swallow hard. I feel the burn in my groin. My pulse quickens and my chest constricts. Sweat breaks forth all over my body.

But I do not bloom.

I cannot bloom.

I fear I've sealed my fate.

Chapter Eight

*Manteo
Sheriff's Office
Sunday, September 2
9:45 a.m.*

Ty shifted in the uncomfortable metal chair in the sheriff's office where he was interviewing Ethan Lantrip, aka Skipper. Ty tossed a look behind him knowing Violet was there scrutinizing the entire shebang.

Next to him sat Deputy Grady Dorn, who prided himself on his metaphorical guns as much as his shiny sidepiece. Ty strained to hold in a sneeze, but Dorn's cologne was overpowering. Was the guy speed dating or conducting an interview? Dude.

"Who are you again?" Skipper asked.

"Strange Crimes Unit. FBI."

"What exactly is that?"

"They hunt down sickos who kill people based on their religious beliefs," Deputy Dorn said.

"Well, not—" Ty blew off Dorn's explanation. No time to correct him about the cases the SCU investigated or aid Skipper, who was obviously stalling for time until he requested an attorney. "How long did you date Amy-Rose?"

Skipper tucked a lock of dark hair behind his ear. In person, the weathered look fit the cool fisherman vibe he was putting down. Like Florida Georgia Line pioneering a new cool face to country music. Skipper was all sea captain, down to the captain's hat, wrapped into some kind of retro look. Whatever worked for the guy. Ty wasn't going to knock it.

"I wouldn't say we dated. We hooked up a few months. She liked the boat rockin'."

Please let that be legit and not metaphorical. "When was the last time you saw her?"

He scrunched his nose. "Man, five, six months maybe?"

"We heard you came to her place of employment, caused problems and were asked to leave. What was that about?"

Skipper removed his hat, swiping a thick swatch of hair back, then returned it to his head. "Amy-Rose was a wildcat. Loved everything forbidden. I didn't go in there causing trouble. We'd gotten into an argument because my boat had been taken out the night before. Gas was low and I found an empty hard ale bottle. I knew it was hers. I clean my boat every night to prep for fishing tours, and the ale was her brand with her ruby-red lipstick on the mouth of the bottle. I confronted her, and she didn't want to admit she'd lifted my keys and taken her girls out joyriding. She blew me off, so I questioned one of her gal pals. She got buck with me and I got booted. End of story."

But was it? "Who was the friend?"

"Ahnah Hemmingway."

"What did she have to say? Did you suspect she was in on the joyriding?"

"Ahnah was pretty quiet. I didn't take her for a liar, but she was Amy-Rose's friend, so who knows? That chick lied like her tongue was forked. Either way, I let her know we were done and if she ever took my boat out again, she'd pay."

"You threatened her," Ty said.

Skipper gave Ty a you're-an-idiot look. "Yeah. I did. That's my boat. My baby. My livelihood. I should have turned her in for it. I didn't kill her. I didn't tattoo her and toss her on a lighthouse doorstep. And I didn't do the same to that other one either."

Ty wasn't so sure. "Where were you the night she went missing?"

"I don't know where I was last weekend. Months ago?" He paused. "What night did she go missing?"

"A Saturday night."

"I don't do night tours. Visiting my grandma in Wilmington probably. She's in an assisted living home."

Ty held back his laughter. Yeah. Right.

"Don't look at me like that. My grandma raised me. I owe her, man."

Guess his face hadn't hidden the skepticism. "I'm going to check that. Not only with Grandma but nurses and staff."

"Whatever, man. Check it." He leaned back and pointed at Deputy Dorn. "You can check it too, Grady."

Deputy Dorn shifted in his seat and then stood. "I think we're done here."

Ty wasn't. "You two know each other?"

"School. He was a jackwagon then too," Deputy Dorn said.

Ty watched him swagger from the room. "That true?"

Skipper grinned. "That we went to school together or I'm a jackwagon?"

"I already know one of those answers." He crossed his arms over his chest.

Skipper sighed and tented his hands on the table. "Amy-Rose was cool. Completely crazy but cool. I didn't kill her. I don't know who would, but if she was willing to steal my boat, then she might have done something to someone else to tick them off. Or maybe she was named the wrong name and in the wrong place at the wrong time. I mean, this guy is picking girls with flower names, right? Amy-Rose didn't even go by Rose until she came back from a year of college. Reinvented herself. She was upper-crust, rich girl Amy in school."

Maybe they were all in the wrong place at the wrong time with a flower name. "Did you know Lily Hayes?"

"Nope." His answer came fast—too fast—and his eyes shifted to the floor. Why would he lie about Lily Hayes but not Amy-Rose or Ahnah?

"You sure about that? If I check—and I will—and it comes back you knew her, then I'll have to go through this all over again. Last chance."

Skipper sat silent. Ty didn't have anything hard enough to keep him on. For now. "You're free to go."

After he exited, Violet entered. "I'm not saying it's him. But he's hiding something, and his first-naming Deputy Dorn felt like a warning. Maybe a threat. I'd like to do some further digging into Grady Dorn too."

"He sure did end his part fast after that, didn't he?"

Violet nodded. "Likely bad blood between them, and he left before Skipper could air his dirty laundry in front of us. But it could be something else. I'll have Selah run a check on Dorn. See how deep their connection is. But it's probably teenage rivalry that neither got over."

Violet was probably right.

"Asa texted," she said. "He's back at the beach house, and Fiona's in Natchez. He wants to walk through everything we've found on the missing women with a flower in their name."

"Can we go by and talk to the boutique manager first? Leslie McDonald. I want to ask her about Ahnah too." Ty stood and slipped into his suit coat.

"Sure. I saw a little shop over there I want to go in."

"What kind of shop?" he asked as they left the interview room.

"The kind where I buy a Kitty Hawk kite for Stella."

Ty nudged her with his shoulder. "Aw. Will it be pink and pretty?" Ty loved giving Vi a hard time, but it was cool seeing her soften up as she became a mom to John's preschool-age daughter.

"She wants to be a sheriff. I saw one with a gun on it. And yes, it was pink. Let it go."

"Let it go...let it go." He sang the Disney song and threw his arm around her only to be shrugged off.

"I hate when you do that."

"I know." But he couldn't help it. He had songs on shuffle in his brain. Music had been his escape as a kid. Not that his father ever physically abused him, but there had been a fear of his father deep down. A voice had warned him Father was an evil man and his teachings false, but Ty wasn't sure where that voice had come from. He'd obeyed blindly, but that didn't mean he never doubted.

"Hey Violet, remember after you made it through the woods, looking all gnarly and rough?"

"I'd almost been murdered, so I get a pass, but yeah."

"Remember what you told me? That God was real. You didn't believe, and then after that night you did."

"Yeah," she said, striding through the bullpen to the front lobby doors.

"You still on that bandwagon?"

Violet paused. "Yes. Are you curious?"

He sighed and opened the door for her. "I'm curious why you believe it, but not enough I want to talk about it with you."

She frowned, pushing open the lobby door. "Except you are talking about it."

"I changed my mind." He got inside the SUV and cranked

the engine. He shouldn't have even brought it up. He wasn't sure why he had. Maybe because of that voice warning him the doctrine was false. It wasn't coming from his own thoughts. Or maybe he was losing it. As he pulled out of the parking lot, he thought he saw someone in a car watching him.

Nah. His mind was playing paranoid tricks on him. This killer wasn't stupid enough to sit smack dab in the sheriff's office parking lot.

Unless the killer was a cop or welcomed by law enforcement.

Blue Harbor
SCU beach house
Sunday, September 2
1:04 p.m.

Ty wadded up his sub sandwich paper and shot it into the trash from his chair in the dining area. According to the news, Jodie had picked up more velocity after becoming a category 5 and making landfall at Elbow Cay, Great Abaco, in the northwestern Bahamas, decimating it. They reported that Jodie was the strongest hurricane in modern records to make landfall in the Bahamas. After crawling westward and west-northwestward toward Grand Bahama Island, it weakened but then picked up again, the eye of the hurricane east of Florida. They weren't out of the woods yet. Anything could happen when it came to unpredictable storms.

Barbados flooded his memory. Being caught in the hurricane and hunkering down. And things that he'd never spoken about before.

Owen perched next to him with AirPods stuck in each ear and maps laid out, his laptop in front of him. Asa, at the head of the table, perused the list of girls gone missing in the past year.

Out of the eight women, only two had been found—Amy-

Rose and Lily Hayes. Would he kill all the women and position them at lighthouses? Did he have all the missing women?

Violet sat at the opposite end of the table with her laptop open and a bottle of sparkling water. At least once, he wanted to see her drink something sugary or bad for her, prove she was human. She must have noticed him staring. "What?" she said, dry but sharp.

"Who do you think is doing this? An evolved Fire & Ice Killer or someone formerly involved in the Family of Glory?" he asked. "It can't be Garrick." His research late last night proved Garrick still belonged in the Family. His photo was on the Granger Construction and Real Estate website as CFO. He'd seen photos of him and his father at ribbon cuttings, shaking hands with the mayor. They had members at every social and financial level. But the events occurred over a year ago, and they may have simply not updated the website. Could he have left within the past year? Possibly. The earliest missing woman was a little over a year ago.

"Why not? If he travels often, he has time. Maybe they did a real estate development in Virginia, and he went silent because it was finished," Violet offered. "But anyone could have hinted at being the Fire & Ice Killer. Like Asa said, the note didn't offer specifics that weren't public knowledge."

"Let's work on what we do know," Asa said. "Four women went missing from Blue Harbor within the past year, even though Amy-Rose lived in Roanoke. Lily Hayes five months ago, and Amy-Rose six months ago. Susan Mayer went missing eight months ago. And Ahnah was reported missing last week."

Ty nodded.

"Dahlia Anderson went missing a year ago last week, and she's never been found. Why not kill these women? Why kill the ones who had been taken more recently?"

"Did too much work to let them go," Owen offered. "He'd want to keep and savor it."

Asa tipped his head to the right in thought. "Maybe. But we also have Ivy Leech, who went missing three months ago from Hatteras. She'd have the least tattoos. Why not kill her? And Iris Benington—the nurse from Nags Head—went missing ten months ago."

Violet tapped her ink pen and went deathly still. "Amy-Rose and Lily Hayes are the only ones we know of at this point with a connection to Ahnah Hemmingway, who directly connects with Tiberius."

"This isn't the Kevin Bacon game, Violet," Ty said, but she was right.

"No, but it's a game to him. He's having fun with this. Bringing you here. Those were the words he used. Keeping you here. Making you suffer. Those are God-complex buzz words. He's sovereign over you."

"Let me tell you right now. No one is sovereign over me. This UNSUB isn't controlling me. He's delusional if he thinks so. I'm going to find him. Then we'll see who's ranting about suffering." Unfortunately, time was thin with an impending hurricane.

Asa grabbed his empty coffee cup. "I'm leaning toward cult ties. You mentioned serious rules about premarital sex, but they called it *deflowering*—"

Owen cringed. "I hate that term so much."

"Me too!" Selah's voice registered from Asa's laptop. "Ew."

Violet tapped a manicured nail on the table. "No signs of sexual assault in the autopsy reports, but I wonder if they're consensually sleeping with him prior to the abduction. If he's testing them in some form to see if they'll...you know...give up the bloom."

"Ew, Violet," Selah screeched. "Like, that's so nasty."

"Grow up, Selah," she said calmly and quietly. "We have to think like killers, and it's never not nasty. Now, back to what

I was saying. If it's a test and they flunk, then maybe tattooing the flowers is his way of purifying them of—"

"Do not say that word," Owen said.

Violet sighed. "Can we be adults here and talk about this? This is his twisted tale, and we have no choice but to climb inside for the ride. If you're not willing to hear or use the terminology, then you can't be objective in discovering who he is at heart."

Violet was right. The terminology didn't affect Ty adversely, but he'd grown up with that exact word. *Deflowering.* "He's choosing flowers. Vi is on to something. He sees sex outside of marriage as a sin, one that someone can be purified from. But he's having sex too, so why is he not sinning?"

"He's a god in this scenario and a god gets to do what a god wants to do. He's the tester. The purifier," Violet said. "He's supreme and doesn't have to adhere to their rules."

"This guy is one of the absolute worst we've dealt with as far as his ideas and twisted religious beliefs," Owen said.

Ty agreed. He was pretty sick in the head. "Why has he only killed two women? Not that I'm complaining."

"One kill won't bring us. It takes two to four kills for us to catch his scent. He has a plan. That's undeniable. We need to figure it out before it goes another step." Violet closed her laptop. "I'm going to call the assisted living center in Wilmington and talk to the grandma of Ethan Lantrip, aka Skipper."

"I've been going through the missing women's social media accounts," Selah said. "I'm trying to see if I can connect them other than through flower names. Friends of friends, preferably a man who is friends with all of them. It's a good place to start. So far two of them were at the same Morgan Wallen concert in Charlotte. Nothing else connects other than they all work jobs that require name tags. I think that's interesting. Easy to spot and notice. Retail and food industry leads the charge, except for Dahlia Anderson, who went missing a year ago. She worked for a travel agency in Nags Head."

Asa perked up. "Shopping and eating, easy. But travel agency? You go in there with an intent, same as a hospital, unless he saw Iris Benington wearing her badge on a break, eating at restaurant or café. If he's noticing name tags, we need to see a client list from the travel agency going back fifteen to eighteen months. Not only her clients, but all clients."

"I'll call now," Selah said. "Going to mute myself."

"I can't get a read on the locations," Owen said. "I've triangulated the lighthouses and where the victims lived and worked, and it's scattered. It's almost like he knows geographic pattern theory and is scrambling the system. There's no pattern emerging. He's literally all over the map, which makes no sense when he's calculated and orderly." Owen massaged his eyes with the heels of his hands.

"Take a break," Asa said. "Go with Ty to the neighboring tattoo parlors and circulate the work. Every artist's work has a signature or stamp. Maybe someone will recognize it."

Violet's eyes widened as she suddenly focused on her laptop screen.

"What?" Ty asked. "You don't think Owen and I can investigate without supervision?" Ty was known to go rogue at times—like Fiona. And Owen was always down to get sideways if necessary. They weren't line crossers, but none of them minded blurred lines except Asa.

"Not without wisecracks and complaints."

"Found you when you went AWOL."

"John found me."

"*We* found you."

She smirked, a sparkle in her eyes—which was new of late.

Owen slid on his tailored gray suit coat over a turquoise shirt and silver-and-turquoise tie. Ty gave him a hard time for dressing for church instead of the job. One could see their reflection in his dress shoes. All he was missing was a pocket square. His midnight eyes met Ty's. "We got this."

"Yeah, we do."

Owen's confidence happened to be genuine. Ty's bravado was nothing short of false. Truth be told, this killer was under his skin and already doing exactly what he wanted—making Ty suffer.

Owen snagged the keys from the counter. "I'll drive."

"'Cause you specialize in geography?" Ty asked on the way downstairs to the ground level.

"No. Your driving makes me carsick. You're all over the place."

Ty snorted. "Whatever. I'm practicing for the job I actually want. NASCAR driver."

Owen brayed like a donkey and unlocked the SUV's doors with the fob. "Keep the day job. And I say that as your friend." Owen entered the first address into the navigation system. "There are three tattoo parlors—do they still call them parlors?—in Blue Harbor."

"I don't know. I've heard studio. Or shop. Does it matter?" Owen and his random need for useless knowledge. Ty should download some knowledge that wasn't useless. "O, I gotta tell you something. You asked if I was keeping anything from you, and I lied."

"High time you come clean. I knew you were withholding information."

Said like a justice seeker to a criminal. "I have a son."

"What?" Owen did a double take. "I knew you been keeping something under your hat. Wasn't expecting it to be a kid."

"I didn't know until I went to Bexley's for the initial interview. He's seventeen and doesn't know about me. A son, Owen."

Owen blew out a heavy breath. "Wow." He beamed as he came to the stop sign. "So your mama *does* have a grandchild you didn't know about. Remember that time she asked you about any kids? I remember because it made Asa laugh when he really needed one."

Ty scoffed. "Shut up. For real though." He told him everything he knew about Josiah, including his recent behavior. "I don't think he was drunk, but I smelled beer on his breath when he got home. I had to stand there and say nothing."

"Who else knows this?"

"Violet. Because, well, she's Violet. I don't want Asa to recuse me. I have to stick this out. Even with the stupid hurricane looming. I need you to know because… I'm gonna do whatever it takes to find this guy."

Owen's cheeks twitched. "I hear you. I feel you." Reaching over, he clasped his shoulder. "Whatever it takes." He tapped his chest with his fist, and Ty nodded. Owen would have his back no matter what. "What does Bexley say about his new behavior?"

"Teenage junk, but I don't know. Something feels off. He's overly angry, and I think it has to do with not knowing his father and feelings of abandonment. I sound like Violet."

"You sound like you have a dad's gut. If you think it's more than teenage hormones, it probably is. Go with your gut. What do you think he'll do when he finds out?"

"I don't know. Bexley thinks he'll try to find my family or if they discover him, they'll track him down, which is true. But I've been in that house and talked with him and haven't said a word. Me? I'd be fit to be tied and unleash some serious rage. Compounded with his already simmering anger…who knows what he'll do? I don't even know how to tell him."

"You'll know when the time is right. The words will come. They always do."

Ty hoped so, but Josiah was a ticking time bomb. Every day Ty was in his life not telling him he was his father was another day he could blow. The GPS signaled to turn right in two hundred fifty feet. "You think they'll recognize the artistry and style of these tattoos?" Ty asked.

"I guess we'll see."

Ty hoped for a break, a lead that would get him ahead of this killer. But he was so advanced and prepared that it had Ty in a state of perpetual dread and anxiety. He wanted Ty. What was his next move toward the end game?

Chapter Nine

Blue Harbor
Bexley Hemmingway's home
Monday, September 3
7.36 a.m.

Bexley woke from a disturbing sleep, the weather channel playing on low volume. Elbow Cay, Bahamas, had over two hundred lives destroyed. The hurricane had finally lost some steam but was now moving northward toward an environment of high shear and cooler waters, re-strengthening to a Cat 3 as it flowed over the Gulf Stream. It was now offshore of the Georgia and South Carolina coasts. Jodie was expected to hit the Outer Banks soon. Officials were warning them to prepare for a Cat 4 hurricane if it increased in velocity.

What about Ahnah? Would she be safe wherever she was being held? Bexley's mind wouldn't let her believe that Ahnah was dead. Her sister was resilient and tough and smart. Bexley had trained her well in cults, manipulation, narcissistic men and any other form of psychology that would help keep her from becoming a victim.

Ahnah was not a victim, but a survivor. All Bexley could do was pray Ahnah would survive whatever was happening to her right now. Ahnah knew Bexley would scour the earth and enlist every resource she had, which were many, when dealing with rescuing women. Ahnah also knew Tiberius was FBI, and if push came to shove Bexley would call him. But it looked like the killer called him first. Bexley had picked up the phone half a dozen times but never called. Did that make her a terrible sister?

As far as Hurricane Jodie, Bexley would give it a few more days to decide on hunkering down or evacuating, and in the meantime, she'd make sure they had plenty of bread, junk food and water. Ty had camped out on her couch again last night. He'd come in about ten o' clock, looking weathered and wearied. He hadn't said much, but when Josiah had come into the living room, Ty's eyes brightened, and they spent an hour playing video games. She'd been surprised Josiah had even come out of his crypt after the conversation she'd had with him about drinking and friends who might be a bad influence.

Maybe she'd given him too much independence. How was a parent supposed to know how long to let out the leash? Seemed like every choice she made concerning her son was the wrong one. Josiah had taken the lecture mostly in silence, with a few eye rolls and a couple of huffs. When she'd brought up his new behavior, he'd commented he didn't need a psychiatrist and that he was working through some junk that was personal and was none of her business.

Children. She'd die for him and wanted to kill him simultaneously.

She swung her feet over the bed and slid her glasses onto her face, then proceeded to her bathroom. After brushing her teeth and running a brush through her mass of uncooperative hair, she padded into the living room, passing Josiah's closed door. It was Labor Day. He'd likely sleep all day. Teenagers. Oh well, tomorrow he'd return to school until the weather amped up and then they'd cancel.

But today wasn't a holiday for Tiberius or Bexley. When she entered the kitchen, he greeted her with a chin lift. The smell of coffee and frying eggs wafted through the room, and he stood over the stove with a spatula in one hand. He wore athletic pants and a Panthers T-shirt. His hair stuck up on one side, and his eyes were a little red.

The toaster popped, and four slices of toast sprang up. "Hope you don't mind," he said.

"No, no, it's fine."

"I gotta eat when I can. Who knows what the day will bring. Figured you'd be hungry. You still eat first thing when you wake or is that going away with age?"

"You calling me old?" She snagged a piece of toast and began buttering it.

"I'm calling you older." His grin was smug, and he flipped over the eggs without breaking a yolk.

"When did you learn to cook?"

"When my mama wasn't around to do it." He put the eggs on two plates. "I figured the boy won't be up for hours."

"Good call."

"That kid can eat, Bex. He went through an entire family-sized bag of Doritos and a two-liter last night. How do you afford him?"

"I go hungry," she teased, but caught his serious eye. "What?"

"I need to give you money. Seventeen years' worth."

She gingerly laid a hand on his shoulder. "Tiberius, if I wanted your money, I'd have made sure to get it. God has been good to us. We've always managed."

His right shoulder lifted. "Still. I feel like I've shirked my duties. Granted, I didn't know I had duties."

"I am sorry."

He handed her a plate of steaming eggs over medium. She put two pieces of the buttered toast on his plate, and they sat at the bar eating quietly.

Finally, Tiberius spoke. "We've been thinking about this killer. It's possible he's infiltrated your life. Any new clients lately or within the past year?"

"If he's a former cult member, I'd know him." She tore off a piece of toast and swiped it through the yolk.

"Not necessarily. Only if he lived in the gated community, and maybe not even then." He sipped his coffee. "We have to think of every possibility."

"I always have new clients, but the lion's share are women. No one is on my radar, but I'll go through and look. Thanks for breakfast, by the way, and spending time with Josiah. He kick your butt in *Call of Duty* again?"

"Well, of course. You talk to him about the drinking?" He mimicked her toast-dipping action.

"I did. It wasn't a pretty confrontation, but what teenager wants to be reprimanded? I think he'll adhere to the rules." At least, she hoped he would. A roaring out front caught her attention, and she frowned and headed for the front door.

Seemed a little early for mowing, especially small lawns with very little grass. She peeked out the front door. "You've got to be kidding me."

"What is it?"

"Not *it*. Who. Milo Brandywine. My client who walked in on us the other day. He's out here trying to mow my yard." She threw open the door and waved him down. He wore a faded blue Charlotte Hornets T-shirt, jeans with the knees worn, and grass-stained tennis shoes. His push mower was ancient, and he wore earbuds in his ears.

With a boyish grin, he shut down the mower and removed his earbuds. "Hey Miss Hemmingway. I drove by the other day and noticed your yard needed mowing. Thought I'd help you out."

Milo had no reason to be driving by her house when he lived on the other side of the island. "That's kind of you, but I can mow my own yard." After he burst into her office the other day, she had a feeling something like this might happen. "Really. It's Labor Day. Go home and relax. I'll see you in a few days for your appointment."

He pulled a face and held his hands out. "I wanted to do something nice for you, Miss Hemmingway. You've been good to me. You deserve to be taken care of, you know?"

Tiberius stepped up behind her, and his chest grazed the back of her head, his body heat radiating. "Problem out here?" he asked. She elbowed him in the gut.

"No. Milo was being kind, but it's unnecessary, right, Milo?"

"I guess." He leaned on the mower. "You're that guy yelling at Miss Hemmingway the other day, aren't you?"

"Milo, that's none of your concern. I'm completely safe. I'll see you at your appointment, okay?" Bexley said again with more insistence.

Reluctantly, Milo pushed his mower toward his beat-up truck. "Fine. But I don't think anyone should be yelling at you."

"I agree and appreciate that. See you soon." She closed her door as Milo clambered into his truck. Inside, she spun on Tiberius. "You're here about Ahnah and the person who abducted her. Not my personal life. Milo is sensitive and needs to be handled with care. He's no threat."

Tiberius shot her a warning look. "Everyone, until they're ruled out, is a threat. My job is to deal with threats." His phone rang. "Hold on, I'm not done."

"I am."

"Finish your eggs, Bex, and quit being bratty." He answered. "Hey, Bear, what's up?" His face paled and his jaw hardened. "Okay. I'm coming to you." He ended the call.

"What is it? What's happened?" She clutched the counter, her heart beating wildly out of control, and her muscles turned to lead, so heavy. Every limb of her body tugged her down as if the floor would open and suck her in.

"Another woman has been found. At Bodie Island Lighthouse. We don't know who she is."

"That's the north end of Cape Hatteras island. Nags Head. Can I come? What if it's—" She couldn't bring herself to say Ahnah's name. But it could be her. It might be her.

What if it was her?

Cape Hatteras, North Carolina
Bodie Island Lighthouse
Monday, September 3
8:16 a.m.

Tall pines, marshland and small ponds surrounded Bodie Island Lighthouse. While a sight to behold, it wasn't the most well-known lighthouse on the island. At one hundred fifty-six feet tall, its beams shone for miles at night. Ty had visited here before. He'd visited all the lighthouses growing up through fishing trips with his father. They always reminded him of massive black-and-white-striped candy canes.

Today, it was nothing more than a beacon of death. He'd forbidden Bexley to come. If this latest victim was Ahnah, Ty didn't want her to see her this way. Ty didn't want to see her this way either. A cold burn filled his body as he ingested the sight. The crime scene tape drew a crowd, and he, along with the team, was already scanning the area. The killer might be here in the throng of people, watching with giddiness and awaiting a reaction from Ty. He would give him nothing and braced himself to see the sweet little girl—now a woman— Ahnah Hemmingway.

No one would be allowed in except for the SCU, the medical examiner and the FBI's Emergency Response Team, and anyone Asa said could cross the threshold. Increased foot traffic meant increased chances of compromising the scene.

Marsh grass rustled and the pines swayed as Ty gulped in the salty air with a hint of musk. White farming fence surrounded the lighthouse, visitor center and museum—which gave off farmhouse vibes.

But there, propped up at the entrance to the imposing light-house, was a naked woman. From here, her facial features were difficult to see. Her head rested against the door and her deli-cate left hand had been placed on her thigh, one ankle crossed over the other.

Brunette hair was piled in a tight bun on the top of her head. Milky eyes stared lifelessly. Her pale skin had been tattooed in multicolored flowers except her soles, palms and face.

Owen murmured a prayer, and Asa heaved a sigh. Violet moved closer to the body and knelt, staring at her from eye level. The wind picked up as if protesting this death, and the murmurs of the media floated on the increased force.

As Ty approached, he realized it wasn't Ahnah. A weight lifted from his shoulders, and he let out a breath. While he was relieved it wasn't the little girl he'd loved, the stark reality that this was someone's loved one and they would receive no relief like Ty pressed against his rib cage. He had to get justice for these families. To at least give them closure.

"Any identification?" he asked.

Big Guns, as Ty had dubbed him, was on the scene.

Deputy Grady Dorn shook his head. "Not yet."

"These tattoos are dahlias," Violet said.

The name rang a bell. "Dahlia Anderson went missing over a year ago in Nags Head." Explained the full-body coverage of tattoos. She'd been missing the longest. "She was on the list. Hold on." He brought up the list with photos of each missing woman. There she was. Alphabetical order. "It's her. It's Dahlia

Anderson." He showed the team her photo. They'd still have a family member ID her.

Her flowers ranged from pink to orange to blue. Intricate and looking almost 3-D. Some had double blooms. Others were smaller—the ones by the neck like on Amy-Rose and Lily Hayes. "Not as many closed blooms on her as Lily Hayes but far less than on Amy-Rose."

"I stand by my theory," Violet said. "Open blooms mean she obeyed or acquiesced. Closed blooms reveal her rebellion." She pointed to the note card nailed into her palm. "You want to do the honors?"

Not particularly, but Ty knelt and read the black lettering aloud for the team and Deputy Dorn, who was squinting, his head cocked, studying Ty.

I can only imagine how your heart thrummed in your chest as you approached my sweet Dahlia. It's not Ahnah. That doesn't mean the next one won't be. I hold the power of life and death in my hands. That includes yours, Agent Granger. It also includes those you love. I know each and every one you hold dear. Get ready for more pain.

A reply wouldn't form. His tongue was glued to the roof of his mouth. Bexley. Josiah. Ahnah. "This cements what we suspected. He has Ahnah. He's toying with us. With me." He slammed a fist into his palm after promising himself he'd show no emotion in case the killer was watching, but the fury and fear were equal, hot and cold driving his reaction.

"We'll get him. We will," Owen insisted.

"She isn't crudely posed," Violet said, "which reiterates this wasn't sexual in nature—at least not the posing. Her nudity is about exposing his art. Like Michelangelo's *David*. She has calluses on her big toes. Was she a dancer?"

"Nothing in the report to indicate so, but we can find out," Asa replied. "Did the other women have calluses?"

"I'll need to check the photos again. If they do, I missed it." Violet continued to inspect the body. "Ty, do you remember anything else about her other than that she was a travel agent?"

"Twenty-seven. Specialized in trips to the Outer Banks, in particular Blue Harbor and Nags Head. Lived alone. One cat. Family lives in the Charlotte area—we called and talked to them two days ago. No boyfriend. Selah hasn't said anything yet about her social media accounts other than she can't find connections or a singular man who could link to all the victims."

Ty texted Bexley to inform her it wasn't Ahnah. She was probably climbing the walls about now.

"What happens when he runs out of lighthouses?" Owen asked.

"Good question," Violet said. "They're his shining light, his shining moment. What I want to know is, how long will he keep these women? Not all of these women are linked to Ty. He's killed two to bring us to his doorstep. One to toy with Tiberius—and all of us—and to let him know he's got Ahnah and at any time could kill her. He's screwing with you at their expense."

Would the next body be this evil man's toy or would it be Ahnah?

Ty's eggs and toast threatened to come back up. The fact his name was being used in nearly every sentence regarding this killer sickened him. Ty was no one's pawn. Under no one's authority, especially a deranged ink master who clearly knew his past.

Ty couldn't put it off any longer. He should have made the call two days ago. But he'd wanted to be absolutely certain before interjecting himself back into that world for even thirty seconds.

"Excuse me," he said.

As he walked away, he heard Owen say to Violet, "Was that foreboding display necessary, Violet? Sometimes you don't think."

"All I do is think, Owen, and it's a big part of the reason we catch these killers." No braggadocios in her voice. Simply facts.

Once Ty was out of earshot, he texted Selah for the number. Didn't even have it anymore. Had never wanted it again. Had no intention of ever hearing that low, thundering voice.

Selah returned his text with a shamrock emoji next to the word *good* and the number.

With a trembling finger, he pressed the number and let it ring.

Once...twice...

"Rand Granger," his father's voice said, transporting Ty back seventeen years. He'd been the favorite who could do no wrong. The only son to bear the Prophet's middle name.

Did he call him Father or Rand?

"It's Tiberius." He decided to let Father take the lead on the titles and position.

Silence stretched like a taut rope awaiting a fool to test it over an abyss.

"Tiberius," he said softly. "What can I do for you?" No *son*. No *Agent*. Did he even know he was a special agent with the FBI? Ty had been on the national news, which Father watched. Only leadership were allowed TV privileges. Other members were barred from watching propaganda and wickedness that would rot their souls.

"I'm with the FBI now. We're investigating three murders in the Outer Banks and missing women who potentially connect."

"Yes, I heard that. Saw the press coverage."

Rand had watched him on TV. Did he have any positive thoughts about him? Should it matter? It sickened Ty to realize he still clung to the hope his father would approve of him—this vile man. "We have evidence that leads us to believe it might be a former member of the Family of Glory. I wanted to ask if you'd be courteous and send us a list of members who have left or been disfellowshipped within the past ten years."

A hissing of breath releasing filtered across the line. "Our Family has enough false rumors circulating. I do not want a serial killer getting any kind of connection to us in the press. Besides, it's highly unlikely."

"Anyone who may have been disfellowshipped for deflowering a young woman? Can you at least tell me that?"

"Other than you, Ty?" His accusation landed with a one-two punch to the kidney.

He swallowed the jagged pill. "Besides me. Garrick hasn't left in the past year, has he?"

"Of course not. He's taking my Office when I go to rest in peace. But these days, I'm believing I may live to the millennium."

Ty rolled his eyes.

"And to insinuate that the Lord's anointed would have anything to do with murder—"

"I want a list, Rand." This man fathered him but he was no father, and Ty would never call him by that term again. "That's all."

"Well, you can't have one without a warrant. Good day, Agent." The line went dead. He white-knuckled the phone, knowing this was the projected outcome but irritated anyway. Nothing had changed.

He returned to the scene and relayed the phone call with the team.

Asa frowned. "For now, Ty and I will go to the morgue with the medical examiner," Asa said. "You good to fly out?"

Ty nodded.

"Violet, you and Owen follow up here."

"We'll make sure no one gets through the tape," Deputy Dorn said.

"Thanks." Asa motioned Ty to follow him.

Once they were boarded on the plane to Raleigh, Ty asked, "How are we going to get ahead of this one, Bear? We have nothing concrete for a warrant, but we need that list."

"I don't know. I'm going to pray for a break."

At this point, Ty would take that prayer. He needed anything he could get.

This monster was coming for him full force and willing to extinguish anyone in his path. But unlike a hurricane, this killer was flesh and blood. He could be stopped. He could be put in the ground, and Ty was going to see to it that it happened. He only hoped it was before another person died.

Chapter Ten

Blue Harbor
Bexley Hemmingway's office
Monday, September 3
10:46 a.m.

The body was not Ahnah.

Bexley's relief tasted like fresh water from a bubbling brook. For now, Ahnah was alive—or so she hoped. She had to be. Bexley trusted that Ty and the SCU team would be able to solve this case and bring Ahnah home safely. Somewhere out there, though, another family was going through their worst nightmare, and she prayed they'd find comfort in God within the midst of their fiery trial. He was the only hope keeping her afloat.

"Fight, baby sis, fight," she half muttered, half prayed, and checked her watch. Her client was late. Sometimes after a few sessions, patients refused to show up due to the stress of dealing with the open wound. She hoped that wasn't the case here, but her client had been wrestling with some past abuse in relationships that went all the way back to an uncle during childhood. If she didn't show in the next fifteen minutes, she'd call her.

A knock pulled her from her thoughts, and Drew Monroe's head popped inside. He worked one street over and was a top-notch counselor. He was also her therapist.

"I got your voice mail about a male patient exhibiting parental transference onto you. You want me to assess him and take over his counseling?" he asked, and entered as she motioned him. Having his presence in the room comforted her. After Renee had passed, Drew had helped her work through her trauma.

"I do. I have his file though I haven't spoken with him about it. He's not going to like it, and I'm not sure if it's better or worse passing him on." She leaned her head back on her office chair and released a pent-up breath.

"How are you doing?" He eased his well-built frame into the chair. His dark eyes matched his dark, thick hair that was pulled back in a man bun. Not many men could pull off the man bun in their mid forties, but Drew wasn't like most therapists.

"I'm not paying for a session, Drew."

"I'm not here as a therapist, Bexley." He cocked his head and crossed one leg over his knee. "I heard they found a new victim this morning. News says her name is Dahlia Anderson."

She nodded. "Tiberius texted me earlier that it wasn't Ahnah, but he didn't go into any other details."

"And how are you processing him being in your life, on your couch, and knowing that Josiah is his son?" His arms rested lightly on the arms of the chair as he studied her facial expressions and body language.

"It's surreal. I don't know how Josiah is going to respond. He's been so angry lately. Dropping this on him now would wreck his mental state, but putting it off will too. I'm not sure any timing is good. As far as Tiberius, he's the same and also different. More mature, though he masks it with sarcasm and joking—that's not anything new. I think he's more worried than he lets on."

"You don't think he believes he can find Ahnah?" A dark eyebrow rose.

"He appears confident, but it's taking a toll. Seeing his vulnerability makes me want to run to him and help, but he's not been open about his fears. Probably not to worry me. He never wanted to see me afraid or fretting. He's a fixer at heart. I dumped what Ahnah was going through on him, and his solution was to fix it, but..."

"It only made things worse, and you think he harbors guilt over that."

"We both do."

Drew checked his watch. "I have somewhere I need to be, but why don't you schedule an hour with me for real? No charge."

Bexley shook her head. "If it's a session, I'm paying. End of story." She handed him Milo's file. "Let me know if you'd be willing to take him on and we'll get the ball rolling."

"Will do. Be careful, Bexley. You've made such good progress. I don't want to see you have a setback because Agent Granger is here unraveling your emotions. Take care of yourself."

"I will. Thanks for coming by." She walked him to the door, catching a scent of his aftershave. She peeked into the waiting area, but her ten thirty was still a no-show. Once she closed the door, she pulled Catherine's file and called the primary number.

Voice mail.

She called the secondary number.

It rang twice before she heard a woman on the other end. "Hello? Catherine, is that you?"

"No, this is Bexley Hemmingway. I'm calling about Catherine. Is this Mrs. Overly?"

"Yes. How do you know my daughter?"

"I'm her therapist. She hasn't shown up for her appointment or answered her phone. I wanted to check in with her, and this number was an emergency contact."

Catherine's mother sniffed. "Catherine hasn't been home in two days. Hasn't shown up to work or answered any of my calls or texts. It's not like her. I called the police twenty minutes ago and filed a missing persons report. I've been watching the news. I know what's happening, and Catherine is a flower name." Her last words came out garbled.

"It is?"

"Catherine wheels. Are you sure her appointment was today?" Mrs. Overly asked.

"I am. I'm so sorry. Maybe she went off for a few days for a breather. Some of what we're working on in therapy is tough, but you know this. She's mentioned you know all about her problems and were the one to suggest a therapist." Deep in her bones, she didn't believe Catherine took a breather. Not with a flower for a name.

"I don't think so," she said through a shaky whisper. "The police say they'll look for her, but…" She left the words hanging. The words of finality. "If she does show up or call, will you let me know?"

"Of course. And will you do the same?"

"Absolutely. Is there anything the police should know? From her appointments with you?"

Nothing Bexley could confide in them. "I'm happy to talk to them. And I have connections with the FBI who are in town. My—my younger sister went missing a week ago. I understand."

The woman remained silent, then broke down into tears. "I want her back."

"I know. Me too." Every day she had to get up, get dressed and go through the day-to-day activities and routines. See clients. Deal with Ruth's Refuge homes and finances. Be a mom.

Buy groceries. And all with Ahnah and what might be happening to her on a constant loop in her mind. She ended the call, scrolled to Tiberius's name and tapped.

He answered on the second ring. "Bexley, everything okay? Is it Josiah?"

"No. Josiah's fine. It's about a client. She's been missing for two days and her name is a flower."

Kipos Island
Monday, September 3

Sunlight dances in the solarium, casting shadows on the tile, and the heat warms my naked body. I'm in the cage. I'm done tallying the broken fingers and burns. I have new ones since my stand against blooming.

I've been under twice. The little yellow school buses baptize me into sweet darkness, and I hope with each time he'll have given me too much and I'll stay immersed in that unaware bliss. My sister tells me when we breathe our last breath, angels come to usher us into the arms of Jesus.

Any arms are better than those of the man who sits on his chaise with a folder open. I can't tell what he's looking at, but he's invested in it as he no longer pays attention to his garden girls. The newest one sleeps in the room next to mine. I hear her crying in there right now. At some point it'll stop or simply become dry tears and sobs no one but God can hear.

Classical music plays. I know this one. *Für Elise* by Beethoven. I played it at a recital when I was ten and butchered it, but the audience clapped anyway. He doesn't command us to bloom. No one speaks.

The strong smell of his espresso reminds me how much I miss good coffee. He doesn't bring us coffee. We are allowed water and orange juice and for dinner sweet tea. A breeze sweeps through the room from the open door and I all but salivate. Open doors are freedom.

He closes the file and frowns, then catches my eye. I am not in a seated position like the others, though I wear the bun he put in place before escorting me to my thirty minutes of sunshine. Just. Like. Prison.

"Why flowers?" I ask, my throat hoarse from not using my voice today. There's no one to talk to. But I'm curious, and if he was once logical and reasonable and seemingly sane, I might be able to appeal to that person. Get on that level. Connect. Sitting on his green chaise, reading while sipping espresso and listening to music make him seem absolutely normal. No one would suspect he's locked women in cages. Three are empty. One has been empty all along. One is for the newest victim who I know is in her room. I heard the buzzing of the tattoo gun late into the night and early morning.

Where is the other one who was inked the most? Where could he possibly find another inch of skin to create a flower?

He sips his espresso and puts the tiny cup on a saucer with a quiet clink. "You do not speak unless spoken to first. You know that." He swings his legs over the chaise, and my blood pumps so hard it hurts. I flinch and cower in my cage, hating myself for becoming this, but the pain he inflicts is becoming impossible to stand up against.

I've done my best.

But he doesn't rip me from the cage. Instead he grips the bars and smirks. He knows he's wearing me down, getting me right where he wants me. And I know that in only a short time, I'll be twirling and dancing.

"My mom was a master gardener. I helped her often. It was a labor of love. Much like what I'm cultivating here." He leans in farther. "You will bloom," he murmurs. "We both know it, and the open blooms I'm going to create, remaking you, will sing."

I say nothing. He's not wrong.

"Storm's coming," he says louder so the others can hear. "Hurricane Jodie. She decimated the Bahamas."

One of the flowers—one I actually recognize, Ivy—raises her head, eyes wide. He snaps his fingers, and she immediately resumes her resting position.

"Where is the other garden girl?" I ask.

His eyes darken, and dread fills my belly with churning acid.

I know she's dead. I don't know why or what purpose that served and I dare not ask.

"No worries," he says to us all. "The hurricane can't stop me. I always get what I want. Now it's time to make my next move."

"What move?"

"The one that gets me what I want and sets in motion the next act." As he says this, the song crescendos and comes to an end.

And I know that I am coming to an end too.

Chapter Eleven

Blue Harbor
SCU beach house
Monday, September 3
12:05 p.m.

"Catherine Overly worked the day shift as a server at the Blue Crab," Ty told Owen. "Her last shift was Friday and ended at three o' clock. Coworkers said she talked about a spicy date that night. She didn't show up to work Saturday or Sunday. Manager called and left voice mails and texts. Said it wasn't like Catherine."

They'd searched online for Catherine wheels, a white spidery-legged flower. Asa and Violet hadn't returned from interviewing the Overly family. Selah was combing social media accounts.

"Did she say who the hot date was? Name? Description?" Owen asked as he entered new information into the geopattern location system.

"He was the epitome of tall, dark and handsome. According

to the staff, she had been talking to him for a little while, and noted he was a mystery she wanted to solve."

Owen opened a box of pushpins. "I'm not a fan of the mystery."

"O, that's literally your job description. You solve mysteries." Tiberius took a long pull from his bottle of water.

"I mean in relationships. I don't want a woman of mystery. I want someone to tell me what they're thinking, where they want to eat, and not to use cryptic words like 'I'm fine.' Because they never are fine."

"Women are cold cases. We ain't ever gonna solve 'em." Ty massaged his temples. "I have a perpetual headache. I had to buy a roll of antacids yesterday. Popping chalky pills to help with emotional heartburn ain't working."

"We gonna solve this one, though." Owen's somberness echoed Ty's. "You got a son, man. A son. What's that feel like?"

The emotion was hard to describe for someone who didn't have a lot of good words. "Like I'm having the best dream after living in a nightmare. Except I can't act on it. Can't do anything but play video games and try to steal glimpses of him. He looks like me. It's weird. I made this little being who's lanky and kind of disrespectful, but funny."

"So he takes after you in all areas." Owen grinned. "I want to meet him. Meet the little Granger. God help us all." He shoved a pin where the Blue Crab was located.

"We gotta find this guy before the hurricane. I won't leave without my son knowing he has a father. Who..." His throat tightened. "Who loves him. I've known about him for a hot second, but I do, man. I love him. Like...it's crazy and weird and how does that even happen?"

"It's called being a dad—a good one. You'll make a good father, Ty. For real. My dad was never around. My uncles stepped up though."

"I don't know how to be a dad," Ty admitted. "My dad was sick in the head. He never harmed me physically, but he had weird ideas about God and life and women. He was all into control—controlling his church, his people and his family. I will never be controlled again, and I'm not gonna control what my kid believes either."

Owen remained silent.

"You'd think that Bexley would run far from organized control, and yet she's got that boy in church, teaching him another patriarchal system that exploits women and steals your money in the form of tithes."

Owen raised his eyebrows. "You actually think that?"

"You know I do."

"It's not true. What you think about God." Owen sighed. "I gave my life to Jesus at church camp when I was fifteen."

"Every teenager gives their life to Jesus at church camp. They condition you to do that."

"No one conditions them." He laughed. "I'm not one to preach even though my maternal grandfather was a pastor. Little Missionary Baptist Church in Greenwood, Mississippi, where I was born and raised."

Ty peeled the paper from his water bottle. "I never knew that about you—the church thing, not the delta."

"I don't share it. Because...there's some shame there. I think, I think maybe I was supposed to be a preacher. Ran from it. I get geographical locations down pat, but my heart is a bit directionally challenged, and I think yours is too, bruh. You've been given a compass. Maybe pay attention to where it's pointing."

Owen's words burned in his heart, drilling into deep shadowy places, exposing what he'd hidden. Pain. Disappointment. Fear.

"Maybe I will. We ain't gettin' younger."

Ty had a seventeen-, almost eighteen-year-old son. Life had changed overnight. His running around and vacations alone— gone. Not that he did much running around these days. O had been his weekend party pal, but he'd dialed his late-night activities way down, and now Ty understood why. He was in some kind of crisis of faith. Ty was having another kind of crisis. One that pitted him against a killer who had time working for him.

"I'm gonna tell you right now, I'll risk everything because I have to find Ahnah and protect my son—and Bexley. She pulled some crummy stunts, but neither of us is innocent. And once this is over, I'm taking my son fishing."

"After you tell him you're his dad, that is. And hope he doesn't lose his mind on you." Owen picked up his coffee cup and stood.

"Well, I imagine he'll be madder at his mother for keeping a secret. I didn't know. I thought she was dead. That's my saving grace." Truth? He had no clue how Josiah would respond to the news. Could they make up for time lost? Would Josiah want to? Could Ty return to Memphis without him?

Owen grunted as a group text from Asa came through.

Ethan Lantrip has returned to the police station with new information. Meet me and Violet there ASAP.

"Guess he had a change of heart about cooperating," Owen said.

"Maybe." Ty wasn't so sure. Ethan Lantrip gave him the selfish-piece-of-trash-who-wouldn't-come-forward-with-squat-unless-it-was-advantageous-to-him vibe. "Guess we'll find out."

Manteo
Sheriff's Office
Monday, September 3
12:23 p.m.

"Let me talk to him," Ty said to Asa, who stood outside the interview room with Deputy Dorn. "I have a less intimidating approach than you."

Asa rubbed the silvery scruff on his chin and cheeks, same silver streaking his dark hair and temples. Then his gunmetal-gray eyes met Ty's. "Anything you want to tell me?"

Did Violet rat him out?

"No. But if this is the Fire & Ice Killer, I want lead. If it's not, it's someone using him, and it's personal to me. I can't stand behind the glass and watch."

Asa finally nodded. "Okay. I'm going in with you though."

"Fine." He glanced back, and Violet and Owen headed for the room behind the glass to observe. Inside the small interview room, Ethan Lantrip perched on a metal chair with a can of Coke, a white captain's hat on his head.

"Skipper," Ty said, calling him by the personal nickname and trying to gain camaraderie. "What brings you in today?"

Removing the cap, he brushed back his long dark hair that touched his collarbone, then laid his hat on the table. "I may not have been forthright with ya last time."

"May not or weren't?" Ty asked, removing his sports coat and draping it on the back of his chair. Asa remained in his stiff suit coat.

"Wasn't." He batted his gaze between him and Asa, his body language screaming discomfort. "First off, nothing was illegal. It was all consensual," Ethan said.

That's what most sexual deviants claimed. "Alright." Ty opened his notepad and put the pen to the paper. "Go on."

"I do fishing excursions, but I got a side hustle for real good cash money."

"You're a male prostitute?"

"No. Why would you think that?"

"Because you said it was consensual and I assumed you meant sex. Then you said you got paid for it."

His cheeks turned red, and a bright blue vein popped on his forehead. "Well, that wasn't what I meant. My part is simple. I give the girls a boat ride from the marina to their job."

"What job is that? Be specific so I don't have to assume."

Ethan ran his finger on the inside of the neck of his Skipper Fishing T-shirt. "For a price, men—and women—can fulfill their fantasies. I give the girls a ride to fantasy island."

Ty exchanged a look with Asa. "*Fantasy Island* like the show?"

Ethan shrugged one shoulder. "That's how I met Amy-Rose. I picked her up and shuttled her to a stretch of the island that's secluded. When I'm texted, I return and pick them up. I make money, and they make a killing. End of job. What goes on in the house, I don't know. Amy-Rose and I hooked up after one night. Can't be in a real relationship with a woman who does what she does for a living."

"Prostituting?" Ty asked. "I thought we were being specific."

Ethan's face reddened again. "Sometimes, but...it's weird stuff. One time...she said all she had to do was dress like a schoolgirl and paddle a bad schoolboy." He scrunched his nose. "Some people have dark and dumb fantasies, and there's a guy who makes it happen for a steep price."

Ty had seen far sicker things than that in his career. "You think whoever is behind making these fantasies happen killed Amy-Rose and Lily Hayes?"

Sweat popped along Ethan's brow and upper lip. "I need a deal."

"We can't offer you a deal. We can put in a good word, though. If what you say gets us somewhere," Asa said.

Skipper picked up his hat and forced it on his head. "Deal or I don't say another word and walk."

TV was wrecking interviews for them. Bad guys demanded deals. Actors playing cops and district attorneys handed them over. Why not use the TV shows to his advantage? "We'll talk to the DA. Tell us what you have first."

"Three months ago, I boated a girl named Jenny Davis out to the house. I have no idea what the fantasy was. But about two hours in, I get a text to come ASAP. When I get to the house, I think I'm taking Jenny back to Blue Harbor. But I'm not. Whatever went down in there went sideways. Jenny died, and I was paid four grand to dump her body. And I did."

Okay, he was not expecting that. Did Jenny have a flower for a middle name?

"Who gave the order? Who is in charge of this freak show?" Ty asked.

"Patrick Swain. Real rich dude. Lives on the southern tip of the island."

"Where did he ask you to dump the body?"

"The water." His lip quivered. "I dumped her in the water."

Ty itched to talk to this Patrick Swain. Sounded like he could be their guy, or maybe the killer was one of his clients. "Did you know any of the other girls besides Amy-Rose?"

He nodded. "Not all of 'em. But I knew two other girls. I lied last time you asked. I did know Lily Hayes."

"And the other woman's name?"

"Ahnah Hemmingway."

Chapter Twelve

Patrick Swain's beach home on the southern tip of Blue Harbor was pale blue and four stories tall. Beyond were miles of blue water and a small archipelago. It wasn't exactly a private island, but an underdeveloped and secluded area of beachfront property. If Hurricane Jodie was as strong as they were predicting, this place was toast.

Palm trees framed the home, and it resembled a place for family reunions and vacations, not a den of dark and wicked dreams. Ty stood next to Violet as they surveyed the house. Asa had gone back to their beach house to brief Selah and get her going on anything she could find about Patrick Swain and this lucrative business.

Right now all they had was Ethan Lantrip's word against Patrick Swain's, and he wasn't going to confess. Not when there was no proof and Ethan hadn't had any proof. He might be lying, and if he was lying about Patrick then he might also be lying about Ahnah.

Ahnah involved in men's dark fantasies after what she went through as a child? Maybe. But Ty didn't want to believe it, and until he had concrete proof, he wasn't sharing her alleged side hustle with Bexley. One more devastation might send her over the edge. He was on the precipice himself.

"Think Selah will find anything?" he asked.

"I doubt it. These kinds of businesses are run through the dark web, and you know how untraceable that is."

"I was thinking the same thought. He's smart, and smart people don't Google or put their nefarious acts online where anyone like us can see it." No single person about to commit a crime had any excuse, other than idiocy, to Google how to murder or search poisons or best places to hide a body. Not when they had free access to private browsers where search histories were nonexistent. But those idiots did make law enforcement's job catching diabolical criminals like this UNSUB easier.

Why was he leaving Ty cryptic notes? What was he setting up? The anticipation of knowing he had twisted plans coming down the pike on top of the ticking time and a hurricane that wasn't ebbing or shrinking was enough to send Ty into a spiral. Rand Granger wouldn't give them what they needed, and they had no probable cause for a warrant. Nothing was going their way, and this new information given by Skipper didn't sit right in his gut. What did he have to gain by confessing to a crime he was an accomplice to after the fact?

Violet leaned on the SUV. "You going in or are you just going to enjoy the view?"

He shot her a scowl. "I'm thinking."

"Can't multitask? Is that a man thing?"

"That's sexist."

"I've noticed it's a man thing." She punctuated the air with her index finger.

"Whatever. I'm thinking, why would Skipper incriminate himself to give up Patrick Swain? The only goodness in his heart is directed toward his ailing granny, and I'm not even sure that's true." When Violet had called the assisted living center, she'd discovered Grandma had dementia, making her no valid use to them, which may be why he gave her as an alibi. Ole Skippy might be smarter than he looked. Maybe that was the point. To appear stupid and unable to pull off this elaborate revenge scheme. By offering information, he would appear to be cooperating, all while having Ty right where he wanted and inserting himself into the investigation. Killers had done it many times before. And no body meant no crime. He might be counting on that.

Violet pulled her credentials from her blazer pocket. "I agree that's odd. He wasn't remorseful. He seemed agitated, to be honest. As if he didn't want to be there at all. But we need to follow the lead, though I don't like interviewing this guy blind. I wish we had Selah's findings. Something we knew concretely so we could establish a baseline. Is he a liar? Is he not? Discover any tells."

"Well, if he's a psycho, you'll know it better than anyone."

She snorted and headed for the door under the carport. A newer navy blue Audi glimmered. Sweet ride.

Violet rang the doorbell. "You want this one? He might respond to a man better. Women are likely nothing but objects of pleasure to him. I'll get no respect."

"R-E-S-P-E-C-T—"

"Shut it."

Aretha's song died on his lips as a good-looking dude about six-two with dark hair and eyes, wearing a tailored suit, cracked open the door.

Ty showed his creds, and the man's casual perusing of Violet vanished. "Patrick Swain?"

"Yes," he said, his tone buttery and baritone.

Ty introduced them. "Could we ask you a few questions?"

"Regarding?"

"Lily Hayes and Amy-Rose Rydell." He studied Swain's face, but he showed no recognition, no shock or fear. His early-forties face was smooth, calm and confident. But Ty hadn't mentioned Jenny Davis yet. He was saving her.

"I recognize the names from the news. You've got a vicious killer to contend with, Agent Granger."

"Can we come in?" he asked.

"No. No, I see no reason for that, and I have an appointment to which I'm going to be late."

"Would it be to set up a dark fantasy?" Violet asked in her sultry yet cool tone. "The kind where women dress as young girls so sick pedophiles can get their thrills? Maybe an old man needs a good spanking for being bad. I can go on."

Please don't.

"It's vivid," he said with smugness. "I'll give you that. But I run a commercial real estate business. I specialize in beach properties. Not fantasy land. I pay my taxes and give to the poor. So good luck finding anything revolving around niche fetishes and myself."

Interesting way to interpret the business. Swain wasn't going to give them squat. Time to change tactics before Violet went all wiggy-jiggy.

"Here's the deal. We don't care about your side business. It's consensual for both parties. But Lily Hayes and Amy-Rose Rydell have been brutalized and murdered. One of your clients might be a serial killer who wanted more than a night of role-playing. He could have taken it too far. He's going to do it again. Do you want a man like that for a client?" Would Swain take the bait, admit to the dark business so they could start building a case and possibly get a warrant to search his house based on Ethan Lantrip's confession?

Swain's jaw ticked. "I wish I could help you. You have a real conundrum here."

"Yes, I'll admit murder is a conundrum," Ty said.

Swain checked his watch as if bored with the conversation. "I don't know those women. I don't dabble in the dark affairs of men. Where are you getting this rubbish from?"

"Ethan Lantrip. You may know him as Skipper. He gives rides from the mainland to your beach house. And he tells a tale about a woman named Jenny Davis. Know her?"

"I can't say that I do."

Can't or won't? Cunning flashed behind his eyes. Ty's gut screamed Swain was dirty up to his cow-patty-colored eyeballs. "Well, Ethan says you do. So you see how we have a new... conundrum."

"*You* certainly do."

Ty ground his jaw. He didn't want to lose his grip and say something he and the team would regret later. "You're saying that Jenny Davis never darkened the door of your home?"

He brushed the fancy lapels on his suit. "She did not. I have no idea why this Skipper person would come to you with lies, but if you need anything further, you'll need to contact my attorneys. Yes, *attorneys*, plural. Good day." He locked his door and sliced between them to his sports car. Revved the engine and backed out without casting them a single glance.

Ty and Violet climbed inside the SUV. "I hate him. Also his voice sounds like Crunk from that Disney movie about the groovy emperor."

"It's *The Emperor's New Groove*, and his name is Kronk. Why can't you get your Disney movie names together? Remember the *humpback* of Notre Dame?" Violet rolled her eyes, then batted an invisible mosquito—or maybe she was attempting to bat away Ty. A metaphor for his annoyance. "Let Selah do her thing. He knows we know. He's going to react. Probably need to see about extra protection on Ethan Lantrip. He knows we only have Ethan's word. No hard proof or we'd have arrested him."

"We could get a dive team out to see if they can recover remains."

"By now she's been washed out to sea and deteriorated. We can check if she's been reported missing. That's a good start."

Patrick Swain was a rich entitled tool and reminded him of his father or any other high-ranking member of the Family. "What's your first impression of him?"

"Past his striking good looks, he believes he's untouchable, and that means he's covered his tracks well. But he's never met Selah, and if there's a speck of dirt, she'll uncover it. I also think he's a sexual deviant. I don't believe everything that transpires in this house is consensual, which is how Jenny Davis may have ended up dead."

Ty leaned in that direction too. Patrick Swain felt familiar to him. Could be the resemblance in personality to Rand Granger. Could be something else. He pulled onto the main road.

Violet's phone rang. "It's Selah." She answered. "You're on Speaker, Selah. Ty's with me."

"Hey. So yeah. Okay."

"Are you trying to tell us something, or are you having a stroke?" Violet asked in her dry, unamused way. She wasn't one to waste time or mince words.

"I found something on Lily Hayes."

"Nothing on Patrick Swain to connect him to the allegations Skipper made?" Violet asked.

"Nothing yet, but give me two full hours already, Violet. Lily didn't have any tattoos in the photos on her social media accounts, but I've been combing the iCloud for photos taken of her that were set to public."

If anyone took a photo and the picture was set to public and synced with the iCloud, it was fair game to anyone, including law enforcement. All they had to do was set up a geofence, which was a virtual geographic boundary, defined by GPS or radio frequency identification technology, that enabled software to trigger a response when a mobile device entered or left a particular area.

"I have one, y'all. It's a good one. I'm sending it now."

Their phones *dinged*, and Violet opened up her texts. "That's a tattoo."

Ty pulled to the shoulder of the road and leaned over to see the photo. Lily Hayes had been inked on her upper left hip with a tasteful lily. "This tat wasn't noted in the autopsy report."

Violet exited the email. "Let me look at the autopsy photos again." She pulled them up digitally. "Ah. Our sicko ink specialist covered it up with his own lilies. It's good too. You can't even tell it was there. No wonder it wasn't noted in the report." She showed the photos to Ty.

They'd canvassed tattoo studios in the area, showing the killer's work, but no one had been able to pinpoint the ink master. However, they'd hadn't shown around this tattoo because they didn't even know it existed. Someone might recognize this one. The last upscale and reputable tattoo shop in town, Pure Thirteen, said the work was incredible. Straight lines and excellent shading techniques. The owner, Paul, recommended checking shops in more urban areas. "I guess we need to go back to the shops we visited before."

"Inky Octopus in Wilmington is the parlor you're looking for," Selah said. "As if I'd only present y'all with half the info." The sound of nails on computer keys clicked. "I'm looking through the iCloud now for Amy-Rose Rydell and the newest victim, Dahlia Anderson. It might take a little time—hold up. Wait a minute. Sending a photo through now of Dahlia Anderson. It's on her social media account. She has a tat. Small hearts hooked by a blue dahlia on her left upper shoulder."

"I don't have her autopsy photos yet," Violet said. "It was probably inked over as well."

The line was quiet except for Selah's quick fingers. "Don't see where she had it done, but guess what? I found a public photo taken by one Ethan Lantrip. It's of Amy-Rose Rydell receiving a tattoo of a unicorn blowing roses from its mouth. Hold on…same place, y'all. Inky Octopus."

Two victims with tats from the same shop. Interesting to say the least when Blue Harbor alone hosted three tattoo shops. Why travel to Wilmington? Unless it was popular and trendy to have one done there. "You up for a ride to this place?"

"It's a solid start. Thanks, Selah. Keep us posted." Violet ended the call. "I'll let Asa know where we're going." She made the call, and he answered on the second ring.

"Glad you called. Have either of you listened to the news in the past hour or two?" he asked.

"No, why?" Blood drained from his head. Ty wasn't sure he could handle another blow.

"Hurricane Jodie's large eye passed right over a National Oceanic and Atmospheric Administration buoy just offshore of the South Carolina coast and is continuing its northeastward motion."

"What's that mean?" Ty asked, dreading the answer.

"They say its eye is going to pass near the Outer Banks, making landfall right over Blue Harbor."

They needed more time. Days weren't enough without solid leads, only more pieces to a puzzle they couldn't sort out. Exactly what this unpredictable killer wanted.

"Everyone might have to evacuate, including the killer. Owen believes he's either on Blue Harbor or on an island nearby like Nags Head or even Roanoke. He won't be taking his victims with him. If we don't find them before Jodie hits, we'll lose all of them."

Talk about the worst timing for a hurricane. Ty glanced out

his window. Again, nothing but sunshine and blue skies. The calm before the storm.

"We need to charter a plane out of Kitty Hawk to take us to Wilmington," Ty said. "We have victims who received tats from the Inky Octopus. Our killer tattooed over them. We don't have time to make the five-hour drive. Not now. But the killer might also be our tattoo artist. That would be epic." But nothing was ever that easy.

Asa okayed the flight, agreeing they needed to check out the place and people in person rather than over the phone, but it would have to wait until tomorrow if the shops were closed for Labor Day. Violet did a check.

Closed.

Ty balled his fist. "What do you want us to do in the meantime?"

"Come on back and help Owen. Violet and I can continue interviewing family members of the missing girls, and hopefully Selah can dig up some dirt on Patrick Swain and find connections to him and our vics as well as Jenny Davis."

If she could make those connections, they'd have enough to get a search warrant for Swain's house, and Ty was sure that searching his home would result in a break in the case. "How were the girls contacted for jobs or even knew this house and this business existed?"

"Good question. Ethan Lantrip is going nowhere for now. He's admitted to accessory after the fact. I'll have Deputy Dorn talk to him. But we can only hold him forty-eight hours since we have no proof a murder has been committed. We do know that Jenny Davis was reported missing the day after this alleged event transpired."

"We can talk to him since we're stalled until tomorrow."

"Go ahead."

Ty ended the call and headed back to Manteo to the sheriff's office with Violet. "If you were the killer, would you live and work five hours away from where you imprisoned and murdered the women? That's risky."

Violet was moving her thumbs across the keyboard of her phone, texting. Probably to John to keep him in the know. His late wife had been undercover DEA and ended up murdered. Violet's job was far from safe, and she often kept him updated, but he'd never once asked her to quit—as far as Ty knew.

Her phone chimed, and she read the text and grinned. After she pocketed her device, she shifted in her seat. "Our killer believes he's invincible, so I think it's possible for him to work at a tattoo shop in Wilmington and keep the victims out here. He'd find it thrilling. But I'm not sure he's doing that. How does one have two homes on a tattoo artist's salary? He could be the owner, though. That's a different story and would make his schedule flexible."

"It's our only connection either way. We have to chase it." He turned right. "So, subject change. When is the big day? You set a date yet for the wedding?"

"January 25. Friends and family—his family. Nothing outrageous. I don't want it and he's already had it."

"Ruby going to be your maid of honor?"

"Yes. Lula and Stella will be flower girls."

Lula was her niece, and she and Stella were both around the same age. "I don't know if I can ever hear 'flower girl' and not think of this case, but they'll be cute. They gonna dump violets on the ground?"

"Maybe." She half smiled.

"No one has brought up the fact that your name is a flower, Violet. And you're close to me."

"Only by proximity," she deadpanned, and adjusted the air-conditioning vent away from her. "You think I haven't already thought about that, Tiberius? He might make a go at me at some point. It'd be a mistake."

Ty would have laughed if Violet was making a joke, but she

wasn't. Still, it was a possibility she could become a target for both her name and her connection with Ty.

Violet's cell phone rang again. "It's Selah." She answered. "You're on Speaker with me and Ty."

"I got something on Patrick Swain. A photo in the iCloud with him and Ahnah Hemmingway at his beach house. You said Skipper told you she was one of the girls he ran to the fantasy island house, right?"

"Right." Ty had hoped that Skipper had been lying. "That all?"

"No," she drew out with an edge of excitement.

"I have enough suspense going on in real life, Selah. I don't need any on your end," he said. "Get there faster."

"Dude," she said. "Jenny Davis and Amy-Rose Rydell are also in that photo. And you've ruined the climactic moment for me. I'm over it now." She ended the call.

Ty looked at Violet. "We got him."

Manteo
Sheriff's Office
Monday, September 3
2:43 p.m.

Patrick Swain still wore his fancy suit, but the smugness wasn't quite as strong sitting in an uncomfortable metal chair in the Manteo Sheriff's Office interview room. Finally, Ty was getting somewhere. He'd pulled his history, and Patrick traveled often due to his line of work in commercial property.

"Well, hey again, Mr. Swain. Or can I call you Patrick? Pat? Patty?"

Swain's glare was enough to send Ty six feet under. Violet sat beside him silently, her arms folded on the table.

Swain's chin lifted, and pride rolled in sheets from his skin. "I have nothing to say."

"No worries. You don't need to speak to us. We'll let the photos do all the talking." Ty laid out the printed photos Selah had snagged from the iCloud public domain and put them in a nice neat row. "You said you didn't know any of these girls, but here's Amy-Rose Rydell, Ahnah Hemmingway and Jenny Davis—she's the one you had dumped. In case you're getting dementia or selective amnesia. They're right here with you, smiling, and if I'm not mistaken—and I rarely am—that's your beach house."

Finally, Swain's entitled face fell.

Now to the gem Selah discovered. "Also I noticed that over the past several years, you've taken business trips to Virginia. Smithfield, Richmond, Fredericksburg. You know what's in those places besides historic churches?"

"No."

"Dead girls on their doorsteps."

Swain held Ty's gaze, then smirked. "I was born in Virginia and have family there. It's not a crime to visit."

"No, but it is a crime to murder women. Poor taste to paint them in Fire & Ice red."

Swain laughed, but there was zero humor involved. "You think I'm a serial killer."

"I think you're slimy."

Swain eyed the photos. "I see photos of me and women smiling without being coerced, and nothing indicates criminality. As far as Virginia, many men were in those vicinities besides me. And as for this Skipper. It's his word against mine. Amy-Rose Rydell and Lily Hayes are dead, and according to him, Jenny Davis is dead. And as for Ahnah Hemmingway...she's missing." Swain had him by the throat, and he knew it. The sparkle behind his cool but menacing glint declared the fact.

"Why did you lie about knowing these women?" Violet asked.

"You seem like the smarter of the two here. Why do you think?"

"I think it doesn't matter what I think."

The corner of his lips quirked. "I like you. These women are dead or missing. I'm not an idiot."

Ty would beg to differ.

Swain stood and straightened his tie. "Now, if you're not charging me, you have to let me go. I'm done talking."

Ty's blood heated. "Don't leave town, Mr. Swain. This isn't over."

Swain swaggered to the door. "Oh, I believe it is, Agent." Ty's phone chimed with a text to keep Swain in place. Asa and Owen were five minutes out.

"I have a few more questions. Two. That's it."

Swain sighed and folded his arms over his chest but refused to return to his seat.

What was going on? Asa must have something solid if he wanted Ty to keep him here.

"You need a drink or anything?" he said, stalling.

"No."

"Snack? Chips…a cookie? You look hungry." He continued asking stupid questions and even offered to share a knock-knock joke to stall him. Finally, Violet had enough and paused the investigation by leaving the room.

A few minutes later, the door opened and Asa, Owen, Violet and Deputy Dorn stood in the hall. Dorn carried a laptop in hand. "Give me a minute." Ty entered the hall, closing the door behind him.

"This thumb drive arrived at the beach house from a FedEx in Charlotte," Asa said. "And a note that it's Jenny Davis. We used our printing kit. Nothing. I'll send it off to the lab in Quantico after we watch it."

"You haven't already?" Ty asked.

"No. We came straight here, and Dorn grabbed a laptop. You can't stall that long believably."

Ty elbowed Violet. "No need to reveal I was reduced to knock-knock jokes, Vi."

Asa arched an eyebrow. "She didn't. I just know you." He shook his head. "Let's watch this while we have him in custody and see what's what."

"The killer sent this, didn't he?" Deputy Dorn asked.

"Most likely," Asa said.

But how did the killer procure it, and what would Jenny Davis have to do with the current case? They entered a second interview room and put the laptop on the table. Dorn plugged the drive into the USB port and hit Play.

The team crowded around the laptop, with full view to the fantasy night unfolding. "I wonder if he films every party without the guests knowing. It's obvious they have no idea the camera is there. They haven't looked at it once."

"I told you what he was," Violet said.

Ty pinched the bridge of his nose. The killer must believe that one of the participants was Jenny Davis, but it was dark and the people wore costumes with masks. "This is flimsy. Unless she takes off her mask before it's over, and I really want it to be over."

Furries weren't his jam.

"Brings a whole new meaning to warm and fuzzy, am I right?" Ty asked, and his comment was met with a punch to his shoulder from Owen. He rubbed it as he stared at the man in his skunk costume with a woman who allegedly was Jenny Davis. Her pink cat head was pretty big. It added height, and according to the missing persons report she was only five foot three. This person looked to be much taller, and there was no way to figure out her weight inside the bulky costume. Nothing proved it was actually Jenny.

Owen shivered and tapped out. "I've seen more than I want to."

But not enough to prove the participant was Jenny Davis. They had no body. No definitive proof that she'd been killed or dumped, only that she'd been reported missing.

Asa fast-forwarded past the frenzied animal action to the end when the man who was masked wrapped his fur-covered hands around her neck.

"Skipper said it was an accident." Ty cringed as the woman allowed the man to strangle her. She clearly thought he wasn't going to kill her, but as she needed air, fight-or-flight kicked in and she frantically pawed at him, but he hung on, enjoying the role-playing.

"Maybe Swain told him that," Asa said. "If Skipper wasn't there and hasn't seen this video, he'd only know what he'd been told."

"Or this is part of the fantasy. Strangling is the fetish but only to make them pass out." Violet pointed to the screen. "He's letting up now, and she was consensual at first."

The woman lay utterly motionless. The man shook her. Shook her again. But she didn't move. His shaking became more intense, and he hollered, "Wake up. Wake up!" His voice was panicked and his breath ragged as he cursed and undid a paw of his costume, revealing a meaty hand. The man felt for a pulse, then cursed again.

"Oh, this can't be happening," he said, and began pacing the floor. He rushed to the wall and hit a button. Then the feed went blank.

Swain had been watching, the sick voyeur, then cut off the feed when the button had been pressed, an emergency button or something to let Swain know the fantasy was over. Either way they didn't have Swain on camera, and he'd know it. And they couldn't prove this wasn't part of the fantasy—pretending to accidentally murder someone. No definitive proof the man had actually murdered her, but Ty knew it. The panic in the man's voice was real. But other than him being white, due to seeing his hand, they had no idea who he was. And no idea why the killer would send this. Was he in the costume? Was he Patrick Swain? Would this be a fun thrill? To get them so close but not close enough to arrest anyone or find that woman—if she was Jenny Davis?

"We still have nothing," Asa said. "Unless we can trace who mailed the thumb drive. We can get a warrant for Swain's security footage, which is recording this, but my guess is if it wasn't destroyed after you two visited him earlier today, it's gone now. And without a body, we don't have a murder. Without Swain on camera, we can't prove he was even in the house. And we can't prove that this guy in the skunk costume actually killed anyone. For all we know she got up and walked away after the camera went black. And if he did kill her, all we have is a skunk."

Ty kicked at the table leg. "We can secure a warrant for the footage if there is any and to search the house or at least this room. Let's do it. Question him. Maybe he'll slip up. We can hold him a little longer but not much. We gotta find something. This guy...he's involved. I know it."

"You don't know it," Asa said.

"He took pictures with Ahnah and Amy-Rose and Jenny Davis."

"It's a relatively small island, and they were smiling and not being confined," Asa said. "We can't arrest every person who took photos with them. He's lied about knowing them. But that's not necessarily a crime, and he's not been arrested."

"He's impeding an investigation."

"That's Blue Harbor SO business. But I'll let you have a crack at him one more time."

Ty huffed. "Okay. Give me a few minutes to pull it together." He walked outside into the hall, headed for the drink machine and bought a bottle of water. As he was gulping it down, Owen approached.

"Don't let this guy burrow under your skin. I know you got a lot riding on it, but you have to keep a cool head." He put two dollars into the machine and punched a Coke button. It rattled and clanked into the bin. "Do you think it's Swain?"

"I don't know. If he is, then he inserted himself into our investigation with enough information that throws us for a frustrating loop while he walks away. Our killer is that clever. On the other hand, if our killer is giving us this guy—without concrete evidence of any crime—what's his motive? What does it have to do with the women he's tattooing and murdering? What does it have to do with me specifically?"

"I don't know, but if he is the killer and literally gave himself to us like this… I'll be honest, my gut's in knots. Who does that?"

Someone who knows they can't be caught. A voyeur enjoying law enforcement's frustration. Ty wiped drops of water off his chin. "Let's see if he'll crack."

"He doesn't seem to be that kind of egg, Ty."

Ty didn't have a choice but to try. Was this a wild-goose chase? Was he lying? Had Ahnah been involved with this kind of activity? She was in the photo. Why would Skipper come forward, and who sent the thumb drive? Ty's nerves pulled taut. Any moment he was going to explode.

How was he going to get a step ahead of this guy?

If he didn't, people he cared about were going to die.

Chapter Thirteen

Wilmington, North Carolina
Inky Octopus
Tuesday, September 4
10:21 a.m.

Wilmington was more vibrant with tourists than Blue Harbor, which—barring gruesome murders—was a quiet, charming seaside town. One Tiberius could imagine settling down in, if he wasn't doing this gig.

The wind off the Cape Fear river blew his hair. Next to him, Owen gawked at seagulls skulking around the Riverwalk Landing near South Water Street. A string of shops, restaurants and boutiques lined the river, but mostly it was rows of condos. At night it was probably hoppin' with nightlife. The smell of beef grilling, funnel cakes and the brine from the river infused him with memories of vacations and leisure days.

Nothing about this morning was leisure.

"I can't believe we're going to have to cut Skipper and Patrick Swain loose. I'm telling you, Swain is dirty." Ty shucked his suit jacket as they made their way down the boardwalk to the Inky Octopus, a tattoo shop that might give them some answers about the original tattoos on two of their vics. The killer might have inked them, then talked them into another, only to trap them and tattoo the flowers.

"You think Selah and Asa will find anything?" Ty asked.

"In the home or the location perimeter?" Owen sniffed and paused. "Let's eat lunch here after. It smells good. I could go for red meat."

Ty could care less where they ate. "Geofence." Geofencing was the frontier of investigation these days, thanks to technology. They could get a warrant for a certain geographical perimeter, then sift the iCloud for photos and videos within that perimeter, if they'd been set to public. Or it would also give them phone user names so they could reach out and personally speak to the person who posted the image.

Now they'd been given a warrant to search the night the photos were taken of Patrick Swain, their two victims and the missing Jenny Davis. Somebody took that photo, and they needed to know who so they could talk to him or her. With a warrant, they could search that date with the geographic location and find anyone who had used their phones within those parameters. It was also something Selah could do—or any good hacker—without a warrant, but if they wanted an arrest, they had to go through proper channels.

"I don't know." Owen shoved his hands in his pockets and nodded at the two brunettes walking toward them. The woman on the left held Owen's gaze until she passed.

"Let me guess, you want to find her afterward too." Ty remembered when he could still have a little fun on cases. Joke around while getting the job done. But not this case. He was bound to this one. Like quicksand pulling him under faster than he could catch his breath.

"Nah. I want to find this killer and get my friend back."

"You got a friend in me…" he sang half-heartedly to prove he was still himself, but the upbeat song fell flat.

Owen shook his head. "Lame." He pointed. "That's the place." They climbed the wooden stairs and entered the Inky Octopus, a modern shop with sleek metal and black-painted open ductwork. The lingering scent of cheap marijuana couldn't be masked with the incense. While the building appeared clean and sleek, seedy vibes crawled under Ty's skin.

Behind a black half-circle desk stood two women in their mid- to late-twenties. One was clearly into the gothic look, like the actress in *NCIS*, and the other was all bohemian. "How can we help you, Suit?" She pointed to Owen's fancy get-up.

Owen went with the flow, gracing her with his signature grin that usually won him digits. "Can we talk to the manager?"

"Tarique isn't in. Won't be until Friday. Do you have an appointment?" she asked. "A name?"

"Agent Barkley." He showed his creds, and her interest dimmed. Guess she thought he was a flashy businessman. He definitely dressed the part. "We have a few photos of tattoos that we're trying to connect to the artist." The ones they had done here and also the ones the killer designed. Maybe they'd get a twofer.

The other woman's green eyes grew to the size of hubcaps. "Those women they found dead in the Outer Banks? I saw that on TV. Aniyah, they're here about the Lighthouse Killer."

"The who?" Aniyah asked, clearly not one to be into the news.

Green Eyes waved her off. "I'm Kate. We have two artists in today. Tweak and Buzz. Buzz is with a client, but Tweak's available, and he's been here since the place opened. Hold up." She left behind a gray door.

"Who did your ink?" Owen asked Aniyah.

"Everyone here pretty much, and my brother did the old-school ones. As for the piercing—" she made a grand display of her very flat midriff "—Kate did it. She does a lot of piercings." She pointed to the gold marijuana leaf jewel in her navel.

"Nice," Owen said, and then glanced up as Kate returned with a scruffy dude with more ink than skin. Long hair hung in a braid down his back and a toothpick hung from his lips.

"Kate says you're here about the ink on the women killed at the lighthouses." He extended his hand. "I'm William Tweakton, but folks call me Tweak. I do a lot of touch-ups, cover-ups and the like. Follow me back to my station."

They went through a different gray door, the sound of a tattoo gun buzzing as they passed a station, and then turned right. Standard tat equipment setup. Ty laid out the photos on the table, and Tweak winced slightly. "Can I pick 'em up?"

"Sure."

He held up a photo. Amy-Rose Rydell. Pulling down a magnifier and adjusting the lamp, he studied the tattoos more closely. "Definitely professional. I haven't seen shading and line work this good in a while. It's a serious level of talent."

"You recognize it?" Ty asked.

He studied Amy-Rose's body again, and then he looked at the photos of Lily Hayes and Dahlia Anderson. "The older work looks like Smoothy's hand. Can I show it to Buzz?"

"Sure."

"Hold on." He walked out of the room.

"Smoothy. Do these people have real names?" Ty asked. "I'm gonna start calling you something. I need to think on it."

"I'm gonna call you Windbag."

Ty grinned and tried it on for size. "Windbag. I like it."

"You have no shame." Owen laughed, and Tweak returned with a guy who was as inked as he was; even his bald head was covered in a skull. Not exactly clever, but it worked for the dude.

Buzz inspected the photos. "Smoothy left one of his albums

here. Hold up." He left, then returned. "Yeah. Check this out." He pointed to a page full of roses. "Looks the same, no doubt."

"What about this one?" Ty showed the photo of Lily's unicorn with the flowers coming out of the mouth.

"Oh yeah, that's him. His signature's on it. Barely but it's there. That's why he got fired. He was putting his brand on the tats, hidden, but one of the girls noticed it embedded and had a meltdown. He's been gone a year now maybe?"

"Name?" Ty asked.

They shrugged. "We called him Smoothy because he didn't have a single piece of work on his body. Nowhere. That's odd for an inker."

"Does anyone know his real name?"

Ty's earlier vibes were being confirmed. This was a cash-under-the-table kind of place, with who knew what all going on in back rooms. Maybe drugs changing hands. They were definitely smoking pot. And it was still illegal in North Carolina.

"Maybe Tarique does, but probably not." Tweak and Buzz exchanged a knowing look. This place was not on the up and up, which meant he likely didn't care about names or licenses to tat.

"Can you draw him?"

"I'm not a sketch artist. I don't do portraits," Tweak said.

"Neither do I. But Pimp does. I can have him do it when he comes in and text it to you. Probably be this Saturday. That work?" Buzz said.

It would have to do. "Sure. Can you show me the embedded signature on both tattoos?"

Buzz brought the magnifier down and grabbed a pencil. Using the tip, he showed them a faint little picture within a picture. It wasn't visible upon first glance. It was like focusing on a stereogram. Once it came into focus, it couldn't be unseen.

Ty recognized the signature brand.

It was a small cross with dogwood flowers in the center.

The Family of Glory's logo.

Blue Harbor
Bexley's Hemmingway's home
Tuesday, September 4
8:44 p.m.

Bexley nestled on the couch and yawned more out of emotional exhaustion than the physical need to sleep. Every day Ahnah was gone was another day Bexley feared the worst. She'd gone back through Ahnah's room and called every number that had been marked somewhere, which had turned out to only be three numbers, but no one knew a thing.

She'd driven to all Ahnah's favorite places—again—and repeated the same questions she had before, and was given the same answers. What else could she do?

By the time she'd made it back home, it was nearing dinnertime so she'd tossed together a sheet pan of chicken tenders and vegetables. Then she and Josiah had eaten in semi com fortable silence.

She'd been tempted to tell him the truth during dinner. If the root of his mood swings and abandonment issues stemmed from not knowing who his father was, telling him would pull him from the funk. But she'd choked due to fear and second-guessing. What if it didn't help him but worsened his mood? And if she were being brutally honest with herself, she was terrified he might hate her. Would he understand her need to protect him from the Family?

Instead of being brave—being the adult—she kept the truth hidden and ate her dinner on autopilot. God, help her get the nerve to tell him. If she didn't, Ty would, and soon.

The news was nothing but devastation thanks to Hurricane Jodie. Tomorrow the rain would begin. Goodbye sunshine and hello gray skies and worsening weather by the hour until it made landfall on Friday or possibly the early morning hours of Saturday as predicted.

"Mom," Josiah said, coming into the living room.

"Yeah, hon?"

"Is that agent coming back over tonight too?" he asked as he crashed on the oversize chair, his size-eleven feet stretching out on the ottoman. He was dressed in black basketball shorts and a Nike T-shirt with a black stripe, his hair a little too long on the brow and around the ears, but if that's how he liked it, Bexley let it go. His haircut wasn't a hill she was prepared to die on.

"Yes, why?"

"Just wondering. Are we legit in that much danger or…is something going on? I mean, y'all know each other and clearly have a history. I'm not blind. I see the way he looks at you. Although to be honest, he seems kinda mad at you at times. Did you like dump him?"

Bexley hadn't intended on dumping Tiberius. "Not exactly." Should she tell Josiah now that he'd gone and sort of opened Pandora's box? "The danger is real, Josiah. Agent Granger is going to keep us safe. Staying here is important."

"Why's he care so much?"

Okay, this must be God's way of saying tell the kid already. "He cares so much because—"

A knock interrupted her words, and Josiah jumped up. "It's probably him. I got it." He peered out the window to make sure it was actually him. At least he had that much sense.

"Hey," Josiah said, and let Tiberius inside.

"Hey man. How you doin'?"

"Good. You got any leads on my aunt?"

"Maybe." He spotted Bexley, and her heart thrummed like a bass drum. Big heavy booms. A mixture of sorrow and regret. "We found a tattoo artist who might have inked the victims before they were tattooed by our UNSUB. Did Ahnah have any tattoos?"

"No."

"Yes."

Bexley stared at Josiah with her mouth agape. "When did Ahnah get a tattoo? She never mentioned it to me." The Family didn't allow them, but once she'd been removed from their teachings, Bexley had nothing against them and wouldn't have reprimanded Ahnah.

"She got a tribal design on her left shoulder blade a year ago. She didn't tell you because she wasn't sure you'd approve."

"Do you know where she got the tattoo?" Tiberius asked Josiah.

"No. She didn't say and I didn't ask. Maybe I should have."

"There was no need to know. Don't beat yourself up. I'm waiting on a portrait artist to sketch the tattooist. But if you remember her tattoo, could you sketch it?"

Josiah's eyes lit up with the thrill of being useful in finding his aunt. Tiberius had clearly seen their son's need to help. Josiah was limping along in this, and now he'd been given a chance to walk—by his father. "Yeah. Yeah, it won't take long. It wasn't big. I'll do it right now." He hurried down the hall to his room and the door closed with a quiet click.

"Thank you for that. He needs to feel useful. So do I." She told him what she'd been doing for part of the day to aid in the hunt for Ahnah. "I feel guilty for going to work and cooking, eating. Sleeping—even if it is fitfully. I'm moving on with my days while Ahnah's days are uncertain. What's he doing to her? Other than tattooing her body. He's seeing her, Tiberius. He's... he's looked at her. He's stripped her. And I fear... I fear..."

Tiberius closed the distance between them and lightly gripped her shoulders. "Don't go there, Bex. You can't go there even though it feels impossible not to. We didn't find any evidence of sexual assault."

"Any...torture?"

His grim expression was enough to make her knees buckle, and his grip tightened, holding her up. "If she's obeying him then it's likely she's not being physically harmed."

"Then we're in trouble, Tiberius. She's not the submissive little girl you once knew who allowed Garrick and others to abuse, humiliate and degrade her. Once we left, I taught her how to speak up, to fight. I taught her that her voice mattered and she was to never let a man do to her what they did. What my own father did—conditioning her to be an object only. She'll fight the killer every step of the way, not giving an inch. So... I have no comfort in that." She was proud of the fighter Ahnah had become, though.

"Hey, that's not a bad thing. You taught her to be smart and strong. She'll survive this." He took her hand. "We need some fresh air. Wanna go for a walk down the beach before it's too late?"

"You seen the prediction of Hurricane Jodie?"

"Oh yeah." They slipped out the sliding glass doors and Bexley texted Josiah that they'd gone for a walk to get some air and would return shortly. "You ever been in a hurricane?"

"Once in Barbados on vacation."

"How frightening. Were you alone?"

Tiberius cleared his throat. "No. But it wasn't a romantic getaway exactly."

Bexley didn't want to picture Tiberius vacationing with another woman, and it was clear he'd been with a woman in Barbados. She'd walked away. Couldn't hold other women against him. "What are the chances this maniac doesn't have her?" she asked instead.

They walked down the private dock to the beach. Sand coating her bare feet and the breeze off the sound blowing her uncontrollable mane. Water lapped at the shore and chilled her toes.

"Slim, Bex. Pretty slim. At least we know she's probably alive if she is with him. Not much comfort there, I know, but it's better than dead."

"How did it go at the tattoo shop?"

"Three of the girls had tattoos before, and embedded in those tattoos was the Family of Glory's logo."

"The cross with dogwood blooms in the middle?"

Tiberius nodded as they walked the stretch of beach. The moonlight cast romantic shadows over the water, and the air tasted briny.

"I called Rand for a list of people who'd left the cult or had been disfellowshipped like I told you I was going to. Got squat from him. I need that list to track down who left. Then I can find out who took a job at the tattoo studio and placed the logo on unsuspecting women. I'm not sure we can get a warrant on a logo. Anyone could have done it and tattooing victims months ago with it doesn't mean he killed anyone."

"Was it a brand to show he'd targeted them? If you said it that way you might secure one."

He sighed. "It doesn't work like that." They walked quietly a few moments. "Who would have a score this big to settle with me? I need to know why I'm the cause of this. Why my life is getting people killed. I was eighteen when I left. What teen-ager makes that kind of impression?"

Bexley felt his torment and heard the guilt he carried. "This is not your fault. I don't blame you. No one does. You were the favorite, and Rand often made decisions that benefited you. Any number of people might be salty about that. Have you talked to your mom? She might know some inside stuff you don't. Have an idea."

"I haven't talked to her other than to let her know I'd made it to the Outer Banks safely. I'll talk to her, but she left before me. What would she know?"

"Maybe nothing. What's she doing now?" Bexley often wished she could talk to her mother. She missed her terribly.

"She works for a shipping container company in Memphis."

"Is she happy?"

Ty nodded. "She's never dated anyone since, but she has a

group of friends she does fun stuff with, and she's involved in a thriller book club. I told her she ought to write a novel with our lives as fodder, and she said readers would find it far-fetched. Fiction has to be more believable than reality."

Bex laughed. "I guess that's true. I like romances but I can't venture into scarier books. Too many triggers."

"I wish we'd have grown up differently."

She stooped and collected a little broken shell. "I do too, but I don't believe anything in our life is wasted. This shell is chipped and broken. Been tossed by the waves. No control and yet it's here on this beach. It's not so far destroyed that I can't recognize what it's meant to be or find the beauty in it. I think the broken shells have stronger, richer stories than those I find that are in mint condition."

Tiberius took the broken, chipped shell from her hand, his fingers brushing her sandy ones and sending a shiver through her. "That makes sense. I took my broken past and studied religions to make sense of life. To discover if anything was true. In doing that, I landed this job, and as much as I detest paperwork—and there are mountains of it—I love it. I mean, I hate that by the time we get on a scene, death has already occurred, but when we track an UNSUB and arrest him, we do save lives. For a moment we've made the world a better place to live. Justice is served, and we're able to give families closure. For so long I wanted closure. Knowing you were alive wasn't closure, Bex. Now I know why you did what you did, but I feel like we have three dots after our names."

"An ellipsis?"

Tiberius grinned. "You were always the smarter one."

"I don't know about that."

"How many perfect shells do you find out here?" He rolled the tiny pieces through his fingers.

"Not many."

"We're all broken, aren't we? We've all been chipped away

at in one form or other. Beaten up. Beaten down. Lied to. Exposed, exploited. Betrayed," he whispered. "We never arrive on sandy shores unscathed."

"No. We don't. We carry scars, little chips and cracks. They reveal our story, but there's hope, Tiberius. There's always hope that what was marred can be mended."

His eyes filled with moisture. "I could use some hope. Some mending."

Couldn't they all? Without hope, there was no meaning in life. The ocean was vast and shadowy, always reminding her that darkness lurked and was immense, terrifying and unpredictable, but when dawn peeped over the horizon it brought light to the darkness and color. Vibrant and beautiful. That was hope—light piercing the darkness, overwhelming it with its glory and majesty, bringing a new day and fresh mercy. Light chased away shadows and sparkled on the shores, beckoning one to come and stand in its presence with outstretched arms and to be wrapped in its warmth. Yielding to hope was possible. For Tiberius. For anyone who wanted to come and partake.

A gust of wind whipped her hair in her face again, and Tiberius shook his head. "That hair yields to no one." He brushed it from her face, tucking a thick lock behind her ear and holding her gaze, searching her eyes under the moonlight.

"I missed you, for what it's worth," she admitted. "I thought I'd die every day for that first year. Every milestone with Josiah was bittersweet. I truly am sorry and regretful."

"Nothing's wasted, though…right?"

What did he mean? Could they make up for the time eaten by fear and mistakes? "Right."

He leaned in, placing the shell in her palm as he grazed her lips with his.

"I finished the sketch!" Josiah's voice sliced through the moment.

Tiberius pulled away and tossed her a smirk. Then they

walked in comfortable silence toward the house. As they drew closer, hairs rose on the back of Bexley's neck. She hesitated, peering into the darkness and seeing nothing.

But a dark presence hovered. Watching. Waiting.

Inside, she locked the door and headed for her bedroom while Josiah showed Tiberius the sketch of Ahnah's tattoo. She took out her contacts and put on her glasses, then pulled her hair up into a big clip. She glanced out the window and froze, her heart jumping into her throat.

Forcing herself to calmly enter the hall, she waved her hands and caught Tiberius's attention.

"Someone's outside my bedroom window again."

Chapter Fourteen

Blue Harbor
Bexley Hemmingway's home
Tuesday, September 4
9:20 p.m.

Tiberius bolted out the front door onto the porch, his eyes straining to see in the dark. Was that movement thirty feet north of him? With his Glock drawn, he eased off the steps and carefully headed toward the shifting shadow, using houses and cars for cover.

Whoever had been lurking was gone. Vanished like vapor in the wind.

Tiberius backtracked and stumbled at the sight of a small white box on the porch beside the front door. He hadn't seen it in his chase after the lurker. "Bexley," he called from the front door. "Can you bring me my bag I brought in, please?"

A moment later, she came to the door, a bat in one hand and a bag in the other.

"Nice. You need a gun."

"I'm perfectly fine with my trusty bat." She handed him the bag, and he opened it and found a pair of latex gloves in his kit. Once he had gloves on, he brought the box inside and laid it on the kitchen table. It was light, as if it might be empty.

Nerves taut, he carefully opened it. The killer knew exactly where to find Tiberius. He started to peel back the white tissue paper, fearing a finger or toe would be inside, then hesitated. "Bexley," he said, his voice clogged. "I need you to go into the living room, and I'll call you in after I open it. Where's Josiah?"

"I sent him to his room and told him to stay there until we said it was safe."

"Good. You go too. Okay?"

Wide eyes met his, but she nodded and retreated. Ty retrieved his cell phone and used the camera to snap photos and then record a video. "This box was put on the front porch of 2122 Linden Lane, Blue Harbor, North Carolina, at 9:20 p.m." He propped up the phone and removed the white tissue paper from the box. Blood hadn't seeped through, but a postmortem body part didn't bleed.

Not a body part.

He lifted out two wooden sticks that resembled rulers attached to black fishing line. What on earth? "Bex, you can come in."

Bexley returned. "Marionette strings? What does that mean?"

He turned off the recording and studied the strings and wooden handles as the meaning settled like an arctic tundra in his bones. "He's calling me a puppet. He's pulling the strings. My strings." A taunting gift reminding Ty he was nothing more than a play toy.

Puppets' actions were controlled by the attached strings. How was he being controlled? Okay, the bodies brought his team here, but after arriving, they followed leads in the investigation. Could the killer be controlling even their investigation?

Seemed likely with the information he fed them with the flash drive and video.

This went far deeper than a killer wanting revenge. This was a killer who wanted complete dominion over Ty.

Bexley wrung her hands. "What's that mean, Tiberius? How?"

Tiberius massaged his chin. "Honestly, I'm not sure."

But it must connect with the girls Patrick Swain hired for his fantasy land beach home business. Ahnah had been one—which he still wasn't telling Bexley about. Not yet. Amy-Rose, Lily Hayes and maybe other girls who were on the missing list.

The killer had wanted them to know about Jenny Davis and Patrick Swain.

Why?

Was it someone who wanted Swain under scrutiny? He needed to see Skipper again.

Ethan Lantrip's Good Samaritan act never did sit well with Ty. But what was at play here? How was Ty being this killer's puppet?

Had Ahnah's alleged nefarious activity landed her on this killer's radar? Was the killer the person paying for the fantasy? Had he specifically asked for women with flowers in their names?

Patrick was in commercial property, which meant he had access to warehouses and abandoned buildings.

Commercial property. Just like Ty's own father.

Could Patrick Swain have ties to Rand Granger? Had he been in the Family but not lived in the gated community, which was strictly for leadership families? Other members were spread all over Asheville and Charlotte. As far as Raleigh.

Maybe even the Outer Banks.

"Ty, I can see your wheels turning. What's going on? Whatever it is, I can handle it. I need to know. I might even be able to help you." Bexley stepped into his personal space. "I know you. Seventeen years have passed, but I still know you, and you're keeping something from me. What is it?"

He hesitated. This would not be easy for her, and they had no proof. But she might be able to help somehow. "It's going to be a blow."

"I can take it."

He sighed heavily. "Ahnah might have been prostituting."

"Lie!"

The force behind the word startled Ty and Bex. Josiah stood in the hallway, his nostrils flaring.

"She would never do that!" Josiah ran back to his room.

"Let me," Ty said, and chased after him, entering his room without knocking.

"Go away," Josiah said, sprawled on his bed, his pillow covering his face.

"I said it was possible, Josiah. You weren't meant to hear that. We don't know for sure. But we do know that Skipper— the guy you told me about—he took girls out to a beach house where they did things that I can't talk about."

Josiah uncovered his face as he scooched up on his rumpled bed. Such a boy's room. Musk and old sock smells permeated the small space. Clothes littered the floor, and empty food containers and soda cans cluttered the desk and dresser. "Ahnah could be kind of wild at times. But it's Mom's fault."

"How so?"

"She's always helping other women and never giving Ahnah attention. Or me... She's a terrible mother."

"I think you might be too hard on her."

Josiah snarled. "Of course you'd stick up for her. You just want in the sack with her."

Recognized as his father or not, that was enough. "Now, hold up," he said, reining in some of his temper. "I get teenage boy rebellion, but your mom has done nothing but provide for you, putting a roof over your head and food in your stomach all by herself—"

"Because my father is a class-A piece of garbage who couldn't care less about me or my mom."

Ty gritted his teeth. "Did she tell you that?"

"No. But he is. If he wanted me, he'd come find me."

Balling a fist, he mentally counted to ten. "What if he didn't know about you? What if he's none of those things, and he's as in the dark about you as you've been about him?"

Josiah jerked his head, the motion sweeping his bangs from his eyes. "It doesn't even matter. I'm over it. I'm over him. I don't need or want him in my life. He could walk in today and I'd shut him down, kick him out and not even care."

Untrue. His emotions were fueled by affliction and suffering, but they sawed through Ty like a rusty serrated knife. Ty sat on the edge of his bed, waiting for the demand to leave the room, but Josiah covered his face with his pillow again and turned to the wall. This kid had big, valid feelings, and Bexley had bound Ty's hands.

He noticed Josiah's laptop, Discord open on the screen, and caught Bexley's name with a derogatory word for women—one Ty absolutely hated and always had—next to it. It was a message from a friend named Abe. The kid he'd gone to meet at the arcade the other night. Josiah had been griping about Bexley in typical teenage fashion. *She never lets me do this or that. She thinks I'm a child.* But Abe's words held vitriol.

"Josiah, I know you think your mom doesn't love you or give you enough freedom and that your father doesn't care about you or want you. And your aunt is missing. You have a lot to juggle on your plate, but hold tight and some of these problems will be solved. And, as far as me and your mom, you need to have greater respect for her and know that I am not staying here for illicit reasons. And if you bring that idea up again, we'll have to have more of a man-to-man talk than a man-to-boy. You feel me?"

Josiah grunted from underneath the pillow.

"I also have to wonder if this Abe guy is a good influence."

Tossing the pillow, Josiah sat up and slammed his laptop shut. "Why are you looking at my chat?"

"It was open, and profanity linked to your mom caught my eye."

"Well, it's none of your business, and maybe you don't want to sleep with my mom, but just know that dating her will never work. She'll break your heart. She has no follow-through. Dated a few decent guys but in the end dumped them." He strode toward his bathroom. "I don't see you being any different."

Ty stood, sensing his time was up. "You're short-changing her." With that, he slipped out the door and down the hall into the main living space of the home. Bexley stood at the stove, a teakettle steaming.

"He wants a dad, Bexley. He's angry and hates me and doesn't even know me. Thanks for that. Not to mention his friends are trash." He left the kitchen and went out on the porch. He had a pair of puppet strings to discuss with the team. But right now, he felt more like Bexley's Pinocchio than the killer's.

Kipos Island
Tuesday, September 4

The girl in the room next to mine has danced every single time he's asked them to. She now wears several open blooms on her upper back and arm. I have no idea what they are. Who she is. Who anyone is or how long they've been here other than the number of flowers tattooed on their flesh. More flowers, been here longer. Less tattoos, less time.

My entire back and right arm are now covered in little pink buds. They're exquisite and well-done and I hate them.

When we're alone in our rooms, I've been whispering to the new girl. I tell her we can fight him. We have the numbers. Escape isn't possible. We're on camera and the house is powered by his phone, so sneaking around will never happen. It's a crushing blow, but if we were to gang up on him, we could overpower him and kill him. It doesn't appear the new girl is on board. She never responds.

I hear doors opening and closing. He's leading us like sheep to his sick pasture. One by one escorting us to iron bars where he expects us to perform for his perverted pleasure. I rub my right wrist that's surely fractured, and the fresh throbbing pain in my groin reminds me if I do not succumb to his wishes, he'll continue to break me, to burn me.

The moment I dance it'll signal my defeat and his victory, and I've lost everything else. I've lost my clothing, my rights, my dignity. My freedom. My family. I'm losing hope now too. How much longer can I hold out, hang on?

His footsteps grow closer and I know it's my turn. The door unlocks, and he steps inside in a tailored suit, loosened tie and shiny shoes. He could be a cover model. My stomach pitches. I hold out my arm for him to unlock me.

"Will you plan to bloom today? Is this display a show of surrender, submission?" he asks, with delight in his voice and cheery surprise in his eyes. His phone is poking from his suit coat and it's now or never.

I make my move and shove him. Then, using the iron cuff, I wallop him against the side of his face, cutting his cheek. I swing again, but he blocks the blow. His fist slams into my gut so hard I lose my breath, and the grilled chicken from last night threatens to come up.

Grabbing me by my hair, he wrenches my head back. I knee him in the A frame and snag his phone. He can't lock doors without his phone. Racing from the room, I rush into the living area, down one section of stairs and then the next to the first floor.

The door is in sight.

I make it and twist the knob. It's unlocked!

Flying down the dock that stretches out and turns into a maze across the marsh, I race for the canoe. We came by boat and docked, then took a canoe through to the private beach. From there, we followed a dock to the house. It had been dark that night, and my mind had not been memorizing how to get away.

I never realized I was going to be held captive.

Waves pound the beach; the wind is fierce and the clouds are heavy with rain.

The hurricane's work—rain and storms preceding her arrival soon.

The dock breaks into a patch of what appears to be woods, and I remember walking through here, his arm holding me up when I tripped. Our laughter and stolen kisses.

I trip over the tree roots jutting from the ground and they bloody my bare feet, ripping away skin, but it's the least of my worries.

That's when I hear it. Feet pounding the dock. He's behind me. He knows my destination. My escape plan. My breath hitches and my knees buckle, but I don't fall. I keep running.

I have his phone.

I press the side button. One. Two. Three. Four... The phone falls from my hand as he shoves me forward and I crash onto the wooden dock, splinters sliding into my palm. My head smacks into the rail and warm thick blood oozes from the wound.

"I have had enough out of you," he hisses and yanks me up by my hair, the blinding pain sending me into a fit of retching. Before I can raise a hand or cry in protest, his fist connects with my face, and the world spins into darkness.

When I open my eyes, I'm in my cage. The garden girls in their assumed positions. He's changed clothes and is now wearing another pair of black silk lounging pants with a matching shirt, unbuttoned and open. Classical musical is playing, but he's not given instruction to bloom or they'd be dancing.

My palms burn and the splinters are wedged inside my skin. My entire body aches, and I'm pretty sure my fractured wrist is now completely broken. My head feels like someone has run a steel rod through it and attached it to an electrical outlet.

"I see you're awake. I didn't want to start without you." He presses the remote and the music grows louder.

My hair is down and loose and I feel the streaks left from tears, a little sticky. I touch the tender spot from where I fell, and wince. "I'm never going to dance for you. No matter what you do." I know I'm lying. My armor's cracked. I'm stripped bare to the soul.

He grips the bars. "I hoped for better and expected as much. That's fine." He leaves my cage and stalks the other prisons. "From now on, I'm not going to hurt you. I'm going to hurt one of them. But which one?" he asks, excitement lacing his tone as he strolls between the women, his arms locked behind his back.

"Eeny…" He circles a cage and a woman gasps, but he keeps moving. "Meeny…" He pauses and inspects his flower, who doesn't move, speak or breathe. He nods and makes his circles again, in and out of the cages like infinity loops, and I know that's how long I'll be here if he doesn't kill me first. "Miney…"

One of them whimpers. He strokes her hair, places an index finger to his lips. "Shh…" He loops through again and stops. "Moe." He stands at the new girl's cage and opens its door, then sticks his hand inside.

If I dance he wins. If I don't he hurts another woman. She's been obedient and doesn't deserve this. I can't be this person. I don't want to be either person. I choke down a sob and sit in position, my knees drawn up.

He yanks her out anyway, dragging her toward me. "Look at me," he quietly demands.

I raise my head from my knees, acquiescing because I do not want my punishment inflicted on anyone else. I will bear it myself. "I'm in position. I'm going to dance. She's bloomed."

The monster twists her arm behind her back and she cries out, her knees buckling and her bladder releasing.

"I'm going to bloom! I'm in position."

A pop fills the air and nausea floods my gut. She shrieks, and he releases her as she falls in a heap on the floor, her arm hanging at an angle that sickens me. Releasing a satisfied sigh, he pats her head. "You'll be fine." He holds my gaze, his eyes cold and calculating. "Or maybe you won't be," he mutters, and drags her by the good arm across the tile as she wails and pleads.

I white-knuckle the bars and beg him to stop. To fight me. Take me. Pick me.

I'm ready to die. I want to die.

But he ignores my cries.

Chapter Fifteen

Ty trudged into the SCU beach house. Violet sat at the dining table drinking coffee and staring out the window at the choppy waters. "Jodie's predicted to be worse than Dorian," Violet said as she continued to gawk outside. The wind rattled the screens on the porch. "Rain's picking up."

"Maybe it'll die out before it hits here."

"Hurricanes are unpredictable beasts. Like the ones we catch, except we can't outmatch a hurricane, can we?" she mused.

"No." Ty wasn't sure they were going to outmatch the Lighthouse Killer either. Last night after the debacle with Josiah, he'd called Asa about the marionette strings and shipped them out to the lab in Quantico before arriving here this morning. Time was slipping through his fingers. Like he was trying to hold a bucket's worth of water in his palm. Couldn't be done. No leads. No answers yet. Investigating was slower than on TV and they did a lot of waiting. But on TV they weren't up against a force of nature bent on their destruction with the power to do it.

"I tried calling Rand again last night, but he won't answer my calls now that he has my number. This smooth-shaven guy who tattoos the Family logo has to be someone who's left the cult, and I need that list. But a logo isn't enough to prove someone from the Family did it, and I don't see us getting a warrant unless the portrait ends up being of someone who is in or was in the cult."

"Lot of *if*s." Violet tucked a long bang behind her ear. "Patrick Swain and Ethan Lantrip are being cut loose today. The footage from Swain's house didn't reveal anything telling to indicate if the woman we saw on video was Jenny Davis. We can't be sure it wasn't a snuff film—other than she has been reported missing. Her family said she was a sweet girl. Lit up a room—they never do though. They might be lit up in a room."

"Look at you making jokes—or trying. I like it."

She ignored his comment. "No boyfriends at the time of her disappearance. No enemies. No notes. They had no idea about her side gig. So that was fun to divulge."

Ty winced. Nothing about this job was good except when they caught a killer and brought justice to victims and families, but for as many cases they solved they had as many—if not more—cold cases. Not everyone got their happy ending.

"Where's Asa and Owen?"

"Asa's picking up Fiona from the airport. Investigative Service Branch agents for the national parks are running with the case. She built a solid profile. Owen dipped out to get pastries. All that sugar is going to kill him. Kill all of you."

Ty ignored the health nut's criticism. "And have you given any thought to the marionette strings?"

She sipped her coffee. "It's pretty clear he thinks he's pulling your strings. He wanted you here. He got you here."

"That's not enough. Jeeper-Creeper it."

Violet sat with perfect posture, her long dark hair parted down the middle hanging well past her shoulders and her blue-green eyes suddenly cold and hollow, giving him the jeeper-creepers. "If I wanted to pull your chain, I'd pick women who matter to you. Check." She made an air-checkmark. "I thought he put them at the lighthouses to showcase his work to the world, but he only cared about you seeing his work. He wants you to see something. I think he wanted you to see the hidden tattoos on the vics. He chose them. Knew you'd investigate and knew where you'd end up. He's leading you to him."

"If he's leading me to him, he has to believe he can kill me. Right?"

"I don't know if he wants to kill you or make you live life destroyed, but he has a grand finale planned."

"Nothing like a sadistic Geppetto toying with me," Ty muttered. "But what do Patrick Swain and Jenny Davis have to do with me personally?"

Violet placed her mug on the table. "Not sure what his motives were for that. Other than to keep you running down leads he wants you to find and hiding leads he doesn't want you to know about...for now. I'm not ruling out Patrick Swain or Ethan Lantrip as our killer yet."

The idea that this sicko could orchestrate an entire investigation and had enough ammunition to force someone to admit to a crime he couldn't be charged with was overwhelming.

"He thrives on keeping me close, then."

"Absolutely. He's not a thrill-seeker but a man with a god complex. He doesn't believe he can be caught. He dropped you a note personally at the pizza place."

"But they don't have cameras, so that was a bust." The UNSUB likely knew this information.

She nodded. "I imagine we've either already encountered him or will before it's over. He'll come right under our noses to prove he can, to prove our impotence and ineptness, which will only feed his delusions of grandeur."

"He's some average Joe we wouldn't think twice about?"

"No. He's far above average in intelligence and looks. He's probably charming and charismatic. People don't mind following him or befriending him. He says all the right things, exudes confidence and false compassion."

"That sounds like a cult leader if I ever heard of one."

"He's a highly dangerous sociopath. Puppet strings are the least of your worries." She crossed one leg over the other and looked out on the water again. "I might like living on a beach."

"You just said a dangerous sociopath is after me and going to crank it up, and in the next breath discuss beach living? Maybe you're a sociopath."

"A year ago, I'd say that might be true. But I have feelings, Tiberius. Right now they involve a quiet life on a beach with people I love and far away from monsters." She sighed longingly.

How long did the SCU team have before Violet hung up her holster and gun for a baking apron and bun in the oven? "Hurricane might be coming to wreck that beach dream." His way of saying *don't go*. He grated on her nerves, and she was terrifying at times, but she was family.

Anyone leaving the South Division was too hard to imagine. Fiona had transferred divisions once, leaving a gaping hole in their team, but now they were reunited. They needed one another, supported one another. Had a rhythm and endured more than most blood kin families did in a day. But it was bound to happen. What would change when Fiona and Asa married and babies came along? As much as he wished things to remain as they were, that wasn't how life worked. Things had already shifted. Once Josiah knew the truth, could Ty up and leave for two weeks at a time with little to no notice? Someone had to clobber evil and make the world safe.

Someone had to sacrifice.

Violet tented her hands on the table. "Hurricanes are always coming, Ty. You weather them or you drown in them. Your choice. And I know what you're thinking. I'm not going anywhere. As John puts it, I have a gift, and it would be wrong not to use it. Only way you're getting rid of me is if a killer gets the jump on me, and let me tell you, he better be real good to do that."

Solid truth. "Nice to hear. I *was* wondering."

"I know." She smirked. "Now, enough sloppy gooey words. Let's catch this vile creature by his rattling tail."

"I want to talk to Skipper again, see if I can get him to crack on his motives for returning with the information on Jenny Davis. And I'm going to have to climb a mountain—literally. Rand Granger won't give me squat or answer further calls. Maybe if I'm standing in front of him in flesh and blood he'll have a change of heart—except he has no heart."

"I could shoot him and we can pilfer the place," she added dryly.

"A year ago, I would believe you. But that's against your new religion." He winked.

"That's against being a good human. Unless he gives me a reason. Twitchy fingers, hands behind his back, drawing a weapon, I'll pull the trigger."

"Who's pulling triggers?" Owen asked as he clambered up the stairs holding a box of pastries; the sweet fresh scent of vanilla, sugar and chocolate made his stomach rumble.

Owen had shaved and was dressed in a flashy gray suit with a bright orange shirt that looked good against his darker skin. Ty couldn't wear orange without looking like he'd had the flu for six weeks or had been on a weekend bender with the bottle.

"Violet says she'll off my dad so we can get a list of names of disfellowshipped members."

"Nice," he said, and dropped the box on the counter. "Can we eat a bear claw first?"

"Sure. I don't like killing people on an empty stomach," Violet said, and Owen paused mid-bite.

"I like that you joke now. They're always scary, but I appreciate them." Owen handed Ty an apple fritter—his favorite. Then he picked up a cake donut. "Woman at the shop said this is sweetened with maple syrup, not sugar, and it's gluten-free. So probably taste-free too, but I took a chance." He handed it to Violet.

She bit into it. "It's good."

"Only because you've forgotten what sugar tastes like." Owen devoured his pastry and washed his hands. "Okay, now what?"

"Selah find anything on Patrick Swain?" Ty asked. Being at Bexley's at night threw him out of the loop.

"Not since yesterday afternoon," Violet said. "She's doing double duty with Cami on vacation, but go ahead. Call her and wake her up."

"It's pushing eight o' clock. She's up," Owen said. "Double duty or not, she rarely sleeps."

Ty let the remark slip and texted her to call if she had anything. Within seconds, the phone rang and Ty answered. "You're on Speaker. Go."

"So Patrick's Swain's commercial real estate company checks out. According to the geofence information, we found he was on his cell phone around the time and location Ahnah disappeared from the Blue Marlin. And interestingly enough, he was also within the vicinity of Catherine Overly when she disappeared after leaving work for that hot date she'd talked about, but he has a home on the island and it's not huge, so it doesn't mean he abducted them—or retained them after they consented to be in his house. We're still sifting through the other missing women on the list and hunting for a connection between them. He has no record. I'll keep shoveling and dig up something. Give me time."

"We don't have a lot of that," Ty said.

"I know, but I can only find what I can find. I'm working around the clock and I'm doing more than just my job. Not all of us are enjoying time off."

Ty ignored her huffy tone.

"I'll update you when I know something."

In the meantime, it appeared after talking to Ethan Lantrip Ty was going to take a trip to Asheville.

Blue Harbor
Bexley Hemmingway's office
Wednesday, September 5
9:43 a.m.

"What do you mean *it's best*?" Milo said as a crack of thunder shook Bexley's office, reminding her that serious weather was on the way and she was going to have to make a choice—stay or evacuate. Neither would be ideal.

A divot had formed along Milo's brow, his sandy blond hair flopping to the side. "You're helping me. No one has been able to help me like you. What did I do that was so wrong? Mowing your yard was a kind gesture, wasn't it?"

Bexley tapped a nail against her teeth. "Milo. What is happening here is called positive transference. You're seeing me as a parental figure, and that's not productive for our therapy sessions. Dr. Monroe has been gracious to open up his calendar and take you on as a patient. He's nothing like your father. I think it's going to be a nice fit. He's here and wants to meet you. That's it for today. A simple meet and greet."

Milo's jaw worked, and he pinched the bridge of his nose. "You're abandoning me. Rejecting me." She'd feared it might go this way. She was right in her assessment. This morning he'd greeted her with a coffee and an offer to fix the door outside her office building.

"I'm not seeing some guy I don't know." He crossed his arms like a petulant child.

"You didn't know me at the beginning either."

"Yeah, and you're dumping me!" He flailed his arms as he jumped to his feet with such force the chair fell over and Bexley startled.

The door opened and Drew stepped in wearing a fresh suit, his eyes conveying concern. "Excuse me. I didn't mean to interrupt. Milo? I'm Dr. Monroe, but you can call me Drew."

"You can't help me."

"Milo, breathe. In deep and out slowly. You don't want to lose your temper," Bexley said.

"I have every right to lose my temper. You're abandoning me."

"Let's look at it as if she's going on vacation for a couple of weeks. I'm going to step in while she's away. And if things go well, which I believe they will, she may stay on vacation a little longer. Can we choose to see this through a different lens, Milo? Would that be possible?"

For a moment she expected him to agree. Drew had a way with words, a soothing effect with his clients. But Milo's eyes narrowed. "I doubt it." He stormed from her office, cussing a blue streak.

Could she take much more of this? Milo storming out. A literal storm pouring sheets of rain, the windows streaked and blurring the outside. This morning Josiah had stormed out on her too. What was with all the storms?

"What's going on? You're far too upset for this to be only about Milo. Talk to me."

"Josiah has a friend that's a rotten influence. Tiberius saw some chats with him and they're pretty degrading toward me and his father. I spoke to him about positive and negative influences in his life, and he all but told me where I could stick my parental pep talk. And he did use the phrase 'parental pep talk.' So yeah, I'm upset."

Drew closed the door Milo had left open and perched on the edge of Bexley's desk, his freshly showered scent a comfort. Reminded her of a familiar smell she couldn't place. "Are you going to tell him Tiberius is his father?"

"I almost did, but then the thought of dumping one more bomb on him might be too much, or maybe it's not a bomb. Maybe it'll be a gift. His behavior is stemming from this—I think. The anger—it's so new and—"

"I disagree." He laid an easy hand on her shoulder, and she covered it with her own, appreciating his friendship, tutelage and grace in her life. "It might do the opposite of what you hope. His dad is here but not for him."

"I've danced around his questions for ages. He's never asked if his dad knows about him, simply *who is my dad* and *why can't I know him*. If he knows I never told Tiberius, then he might not be so angry."

"Not with Tiberius but with you. Now is not the time for him to feel abandoned by you and Ahnah and his father—though he's here now. Do you think he can actually find your sister?" A stray curl fell into his eyes, and he slid it behind his ear in a smooth gesture.

"If anyone can, it's him and the SCU team. He only reveals what he's allowed. I can't divulge that information or I would. Right now, they have some leads but nothing definitive."

His eyebrows rose. "What do they plan to do when the hurricane hits?"

"I don't know. I don't even know what I'm going to do. I can't leave the island. Ahnah is here, I think. But I might not be able to stay if it's as rough as they predict. I have Josiah to think about. What are you going to do?"

"I don't think it'll be as bad as they say. They have to give the worst-case scenario to the public. I plan to hunker down. Why don't we get some dinner tonight? We can talk it out. Enjoy some delicious food."

"I would love that under other circumstances." She stood and wrapped her arms around him. "Thank you for all the support and your friendship, Drew."

After a quick hug, he grinned. "I'm always here for you, Bexley. I'll call Milo after he's had time to process. I can coax him into seeing me."

Of course he could. "Thank you. I hope this doesn't set him back or on some vindictive rampage."

"I can handle a tantrum or two. Be careful and stay safe." He left her office. She slumped on her couch, propping her feet up on a pillow and rubbing her temples to bat away yet another headache, but it was pointless. Stress headaches wouldn't subside until the stress did, and with each day it grew exponentially. She closed her eyes and tried to relax and pray to calm her nerves. Prayer generally brought peace to her heart.

Her cell phone rang, startling her. She must have dozed off. She checked the time. She had slept for twenty minutes.

Her phone screen read *unknown caller.*

"Bexley Hemmingway."

Silence filled the line except for soft breathing. Her heart skittered a beat, and she bolted upright. "Ahnah. Ahnah, is that you?"

"You'd like that, wouldn't you?" The same modulated voice as before slipped through the line, curling around her ribs in icy bands.

"Who is this?" she asked, her voice cracking. "Do you have Ahnah?" The phone slipped in her wet palm, but she gripped it tighter.

"I have whatever or whomever I choose."

Bexley's throat tightened. "Please, let her go. Please."

"You don't have negotiating power, Bexley. Let me tell you what I want. I want you to separate yourself from Tiberius Granger. He's no longer allowed to sleep on your couch. Oh, I know he does. I'll know if he's there or gone. You cannot hide anything from me. And if you tell him about this phone call, I'll know."

Why did he want Tiberius gone? To kidnap her and Josiah without trouble?

"You make sure he knows you don't want a romantic affair with him. And before you lie and say it's not on that trajectory, I know about the late-night beach walk."

Now it was clear—he had been stalking her home. Her entire body flushed until a cold sweat broke out across her body. "And if I do what you want?"

"Maybe I spare Ahnah. Maybe I spare you and your son too. Or maybe I spare no one."

The call dropped. Bexley let the phone fall onto her lap as she faced yet another impossible decision.

Chapter Sixteen

Blue Harbor
SCU beach house
Wednesday, September 5
12:22 p.m.

"I'm going to talk with Ethan Lantrip instead of heading to my father's. I forgot it's Wednesday and he won't be at the house. Wednesday is his time alone with God," Ty announced to the team. "Who knows where he'll be. One time it was a flight to Vegas, so..." He rolled his eyes. "As far as Lantrip, I don't believe he turned himself in of his own volition. In fact, I think the killer used him like a puppet too. I don't know why, and I want to. He might be willing to talk if I let him know we're aware of what's going down underneath the surface." This killer was a cold iceberg. His massive plan was still lingering under the water. They'd only been able to see the tip—what he intended them to view.

A bolt of lightning streaked across the hazy, rain-filled sky, and Ty frowned at the reminder that time was running out and devastation was on its way.

"You think you can crack him?" Asa asked.

"Figuratively or literally?"

"Take Fiona with you." He and Fi had returned a couple of hours ago, and he'd brought her up to speed.

Ty sighed. "Come on, Fi Fi McGee."

"I hate that," she said as she snagged her purse and holstered her Glock. "Let's go. I'll keep you from bashing skulls."

"Fiona, so you know," he said as they walked outside and he held an umbrella over her head, "if I want to crack that man's skull, you and no army can stop me. And I'm not sure you would. You blurred some lines when it came to the Nursery Rhyme Killer."

"And it nearly killed me." He opened her door and she jumped in. Then he rounded the vehicle, getting soaked when he lowered the umbrella and tucked it inside. "You're going to be one of Asa's best men. You have to survive to stand up there and witness our marriage."

"I witnessed your first one."

She laughed. "This one's gonna stick."

He believed it, and that was causing some existential issues with him. Was he here for a divine planned purpose, or was his being on earth simply chance? Ty kept waiting for Asa, Fiona and Violet to revert back to the people they once were, but their newfound faith seemed anchored down deep while Ty might as well be a kite blowing in the wind with no one manning the string.

Except for this UNSUB.

"Don't you even want to know about the case in Natchez?"

"Not to be a jerk, but I don't care about anything except this case."

"Fair enough."

The remainder of the drive was silent. Ethan was pacing the

interview room when they arrived. He'd barely been released when he'd had to turn back around.

Deputy Dorn thumbed toward Ethan. "I've already tried. He's not going to give you squat."

"But you know him, right?"

Dorn snorted. "We went to school together. I wouldn't call that knowing him well."

Selah's dig into Grady Dorn revealed very little concerning Ethan Lantrip other than they went to school together and the two had been suspended for three days for fighting each other. Lantrip had given Dorn a broken nose and two fractured ribs. Didn't appear they made nice, but nothing more nefarious than that. At least not on paper.

"Seems you knew his fist pretty well."

"Water under the bridge."

Was it?

Dorn touched his slightly crooked nose. "I went to one side of the law and clearly he chose another. You want me to come in there with you?"

"Nah. But thanks." Ty motioned Fiona to follow him inside the room. "Ethan, nice to see you again. This is my colleague Agent Kelly."

Skipper dipped his chin in greeting. "What is it you need from me now? I told you I dumped a body. I have nothing to add or offer." He ran his hands through his long hair and chewed on his already nubby fingernails.

"Why did you come forward?" Ty asked as he sat across from him. "That's sticking in my craw, man."

Ethan shrugged. "I guess I was feeling guilty about it."

"Try again."

"What? I do feel guilty. I mean, I didn't kill her, but I'm not into that stuff. I'm a boat captain and I live a pretty simple life, which is the way I like it."

"I think someone has dirt on you. No one confesses to a crime when they're not even on the law's radar for it."

"Mr. Lantrip," Fiona said, "we're not interested in the fact you dumped a body. I'm sure someone is, but it's not why we're here. We're concerned about the missing women, soon to be dead women if we don't find them. If you're not into that stuff, then help us keep them alive. You had no reason to come to us unless you have an ulterior motive to get Patrick Swain in trouble. Is that it or is it something else?"

Skipper snapped to attention with wide eyes. Then he bit down on his bottom lip.

That was it. This wasn't about Jenny Davis or Skipper's conscience. It was about Patrick Swain. "Who else knew about Jenny's death?" Ty asked. "Was there anyone else at the house that night? Any other male participants?"

Skipper shifted in the metal chair and raked a hand through his hair again, a nervous tick. "I don't know. That's above my pay grade. I give them a ride and I pick them up. Sometimes they're a little high or drunk and talk about the fantasy. Sometimes they don't. But Jenny was dead when I got there. No one was around but Patrick that I saw. Not even the guy who did her."

Fiona nodded as if she understood implicitly. "I get it. You're out there trying to make some side cash. Nothing nefarious about giving a boat ride to a consensual party. It got out of hand and you got stuck doing Mr. Swain's dirty work. But who wanted Swain's activities known to us? Who sent you to confess? We only want to find Ahnah Hemmingway, Ivy Leech, Iris Benington, Susan Mayer, Catherine Overly and Heather Wade. We want justice for Amy-Rose Rydell, Lily Hayes and Dahlia Anderson. You can make a wrong right."

He shifted in his chair, listening to Fiona catalog the women missing who had flowers in their names. They couldn't say concretely that the killer had these women, but it was a solid deduction.

"Did you ever give rides to any of these women?" She laid out the photos of the missing women. "You recognize their names or faces?"

"Just Ahnah Hemmingway."

"What else can you tell us?" she asked.

Ty remained still—Skipper wasn't responding to him like Fiona. She had a soothing way with her voice when she wanted to; when she didn't, she could use it to take someone to the grave.

"I don't think someone wanted you to get into trouble, Ethan. Someone knew you couldn't be charged with accessory after the fact because there's no proof a crime was committed, and it's clear we'll never find Jenny Davis if you dumped her in the water. Seems to me someone wanted Mr. Swain in hot water. Is that person you? Are you seeking revenge for what he made you do? Or for something else?"

"Me? No." He violently shook his head. "He paid me real good. Enough I could quit my day job if I didn't love it so much. But I love the water. Love fishin'."

"Then why did you come forward? Who are you afraid of?"

"I don't know," he whispered. "I got a message from a random number on WhatsApp. Said to go to the sheriff and tell what Swain asked me to do and to make sure the SCU team knew. And not to worry about prison or an arrest. If I did it, I'd get paid a hundred grand."

"Did you get paid?" Ty asked.

"I did. It was in a brand-new white cardboard box on my boat when I got out of this place. Crisp new bills."

"Why did you believe this random message?"

"Dude knew the details. He knew where I dumped her. Must have been out that night fishing or something. I didn't see him, but if he was in the marsh in a canoe or kayak, I wouldn't have."

WhatsApp had strict policies. They didn't store data for law enforcement and even had that information on their website. "Did you delete your account with them?"

"He told me to, so I did."

Ty swore under his breath. If the accounts had been deleted with the company and their server, then the message was gone. "Can you tell us exactly where you dumped the body?"

"About twenty miles south of the Swain property. Just weighted her down with concrete blocks and dumped her over. But if you try to arrest me again, I'll recant."

If he thought he could, then Ty would let him think it. Ty ran his palm across his face. "Would it be common for someone to be on a boat that far out at night?"

"Sure. Lots of reasons. Fishing, hanging out, being with a woman, stargazing... I can go on."

Maybe the killer had known about Patrick Swain's little side gig and had been biding his time watching, waiting for something like this to use in some grand scheme.

It wasn't out of the realm of possibility. Their killer crafted and planned this elaborate show to bring Ty to the Outer Banks. He clearly had enormous amounts of patience. What was in it for him, though? What benefit would it be to him to get Patrick Swain in trouble or on their radar? Maybe he couldn't care less. If he wanted to send Ty on a wild-goose chase simply because he could, then he'd accomplished his mission. Ty wasn't ruling out the idea Patrick Swain himself might be toying with him simply because he could. Face-to-face and Ty none the wiser.

"Thank you for being honest, Mr. Lantrip," Fi said.

Nothing more here for them.

They left the office and headed back to the beach house. Ty told Fiona his thoughts. "What do you think?"

"That you're right. This guy has been plotting for a long time. Fantasizing over it."

Ty's blood froze. "Fi, could this be his fantasy? Could Patrick Swain be orchestrating this whole thing for someone—or maybe it's *his* fantasy? To be brought in for murder with no way to be charged or tried? His fantasy is getting away with murder and revenge on me. But I don't know him."

"Doesn't mean he doesn't know and hate you."

"Maybe I'll have more information tomorrow after taking a stab at Rand Granger. He can ignore my calls but he can't ignore me."

"How do you feel about that? Seeing him?"

"In one word? Bad."

She grinned. They passed a rain-soaked teenager on a red mountain bike. Then they pulled into the drive and Asa opened the door, greeting them with a grim face. "What is it?" she asked.

Asa held up an envelope. "Teenage boy on a bike brought this by. Said a tall guy with blond hair and a beard offered him five hundred dollars to deliver it to this address. Guy wore sunglasses. Nike T-shirt and jeans. I don't think our guy is dumb enough to reveal his true identity to a kid we're going to question so I think it's a safe guess that he was disguised."

"Have you opened it?" Ty said.

"No. Just got it. I was about to but you pulled in." Asa handed him a pair of gloves. "It's addressed to you."

A chilly draft swept over him as he slid his hands into the latex and took the envelope. He carefully opened it, making sure not to tear too much in case they could get DNA, but that was a pipe dream. Inside was a solid white piece of paper written in the same handwriting as the first note to him and the cards left on the victims.

He read it aloud. "'Agent Granger, how did you like the puppet strings? Do you like dancing for me? My garden girls love to dance—no strings attached. I have a favorite flower, but she doesn't want to bloom. She's feisty and I know you care deeply for her, but Agent Granger, flowers that won't bloom, wither and die. When one flower won't bloom, I'll have to pluck another who will. Keeping your loved ones close won't save them. I know who's next. Don't you wish you did too?'"

How was he going to tell Bexley that Ahnah might not make it because he couldn't find her in time and that no one close to him, including her, was safe?

A rap on the glass door startled Ty, and he turned to see Bexley standing there, hair wet and rain slicking down her cheeks—or that might be tears.

He hadn't even had time to gather his thoughts and plan out how to tell her. He rushed to the door and opened it. "What are you doing here?"

"Probably signing someone's death warrant. Probably mine."

Chapter Seventeen

Blue Harbor
SCU beach house
Thursday, September 6
6:01 a.m.

Ty poured a cup of coffee into his mug. Exhaustion leached into his bones and weariness blurred his vision. Bexley's bomb had unnerved him in ways he couldn't begin to describe. The UNSUB had contacted her. Made demands. Expected compliance. Bexley wasn't supposed to tell him that—only for him to hit the trails and leave her alone.

He'd been prowling and preying on their moments and now wanted Bex isolated. Or he might want Ty to feel isolated, rejected. Either way Ty wasn't letting Bexley and Josiah stay in that home without him or someone for protection. After a lot of thought and consideration from the team, they all thought it was best for Bexley and Josiah to stay here with them. There was a chance someone might die, but the killer had made no promises that anyone would live if Bex obeyed.

Bexley entered the room and pointed at the coffeepot, her thick locks all over the place, and his gut tightened. She was still wildly beautiful. And in danger because of him. Retrieving a mug from the cabinet, he poured her a cup. "Morning, sunshine."

She hummed low and sipped the brew. Thunder boomed and a fresh wave of heavy rain fell. "Not gonna see sunshine for a minute," she said. "I wish I could stay in bed all day."

"I feel that. Hurricane Jodie keeps up east and Hatteras could be decimated by storm surges."

"I saw that this morning. She's moving faster than they originally predicted."

"What are you going to do?" he asked.

"I still don't know."

Asa stormed into the kitchen, as dark and gray as the rain-clouds. Fiona followed with a grim expression.

"They found a new victim. Roanoke Marshes Lighthouse. We're heading to Manteo. Owen and Violet are coming down-stairs now."

Another victim.

Ahnah. Dread pooled like thick oil in his gut.

"This is my fault, isn't it?" Bexley whispered, and her hands trembled, sloshing coffee over the side of her mug. "I went against his wishes. He knows."

"No," Ty said. "It's not your fault. It's mine."

"It's neither of your faults," Asa said. "You made the wiser decision to stay safe. This man has already laid out his plans re-gardless of any of our choices. If anything, you've put a chink in his armor by letting him know he's not calling the shots."

"But what if it's Ahnah? I won't forgive myself." Bexley set her cup on the counter. "I'm going too. I have to." She darted for the other room before Ty could protest.

"You know she shouldn't be there," Asa said.

"I know but…"

Asa nodded. "What about Josiah?"

"He won't be up until noon with school canceled for weather now—if I had to guess. I don't want him seeing this."

Asa frowned. "Not really your call, is it?"

Technically? Yes. But Ty had been keeping that doozey from him. No way was he being kicked off the investigation. "I don't see Bexley letting him, but she won't want him to be alone either."

Bexley returned, her curls up in a clip, straggling hair sticking out. No makeup and a pair of jeans and solid V-neck T-shirt. "Let's go."

"What about Josiah?"

"I woke him and told him I had an emergency. He assumed work and I didn't tell him different. Drew is coming by the beach house to pick him up in twenty minutes. I'll have him wait outside since you have sensitive material in here—not that Drew would ever divulge it to anyone."

"Now, let's go." Asa and Fiona headed to the first level and Ty followed, Bexley in step with him.

"Who is Drew?" Ty asked.

"Drew is a friend, my therapist and a good man. I trust him."

Ty's heart pumped with green ooze. "How long you known this guy?"

"Two years. But we've worked closely together. Josiah will be fine."

"Does he know about Josiah and me?"

"Of course."

Ty made a note to have Selah do a check on the therapist. She followed Ty to the SUV and paused. "I need to take my car. You'll be there longer, I imagine."

"You want me to drive?" He glanced at her shaking hands. "I know it's only a ten-minute trip, but…"

"Would you?"

He saluted the team and jumped in the driver's side of Bexley's car. "Listen to me. When we arrive, you promise to stay outside the perimeter? Let me assess the scene—you can't be on the premises anyway. You don't need to see anything. I'll let you know if…"

"If I got my sister killed." She covered her face. "I never seem to make the right decisions and it always causes someone anguish."

"Bex." He took her hand and clasped it in his. "We'll get through it. Together. We're gonna get through all of this together."

"You forgive me?"

"I understand somewhat, but I lost seventeen—almost eighteen—years of my son's life. I need more time to sort through those emotions. I'd think you'd know that." Right now he was sorting through the fact that he hadn't been sharp enough to catch this guy. Someone else was dead. More people were going to die, and it was like playing Russian roulette. It could be anyone. He'd let these women down. Let himself down.

Ty backed into a spot downtown, and from here they'd walk to the lighthouse. As they exited the car, Bexley grabbed his hand and began praying. He wasn't sure if he should pray too or say an *amen* or simply let her prayer make her feel stronger. If God was real and he prayed to Him, would He even listen to someone who didn't believe? Would He hear anyone's cries or just those who confessed Him as Lord? Ty was versed in scripture for his job, but it had never penetrated his heart.

But now, in this moment, a verse struck him with hurricane force, and yet it was gentle. How could something be both? Powerful and yet tender?

"*…the cry of the poor to come unto him, and he heareth the cry of the afflicted.*" From the book of Job. If anyone had been in a mess that couldn't be controlled, it had been Job. Everything wiped out from under him within moments, then horrible affliction. That's how Ty felt—everything was being ripped away. But did God hear the cry of the afflicted? All? Any? Would He answer? How would He answer? How would Ty even know?

Stop acting stupid. You're following your friends like a dumb sheep. Prayer cannot help you. Only you can help yourself. Quit walking blindly.

Forty yards ahead, jutting into the Roanoke Sound, was the Roanoke Marshes Lighthouse. Unlike the other white brick towers with the black stripes, it had a seaside cottage vibe with a sloped red roof and gabled windows with black shutters. The only things identifying it as a lighthouse were the fenced-in observation deck and the cupola-style lantern room.

The team slowed as they approached the Dare County sheriff and his deputies, including Grady Dorn. Asa had called in the ERT out of Charlotte. The ME was on his way.

"She's got a note stabbed into her palm, but it's not like the others," Dorn said. "We set up a perimeter to keep out media and anyone who got word this early and decided to play the vulture. She fought. Valiantly if I had to guess. Feet are bruised and cut up, abrasions on her knees and hands, along with splinters. Maybe fell on a boardwalk? She's also got a knot on her head where she might have fallen or been hit. Not a single open bloom on her. Some broken fingers and a broken wrist."

Ahnah had been a fighter. Bexley said she'd never yield to him. At least...at least she'd fought to the bitter end.

Bexley stood far enough away that she didn't have visual access to the scene, but she'd refused to wait downtown.

"Agent? Agent, are you okay?" Dorn asked. Ty's vision blurred; spots formed before his eyes. Could he do this?

Rain leaked into his poncho, and rivulets dripped into his eyes from the hood.

As they walked up the boardwalk, the victim's hair came into view.

Red.

Ty's shoulders slumped, and he let out the breath he'd been holding. Turning back, he waved to Bexley to signal it wasn't Ahnah, but another fighter. A small measure of guilt nipped at him for feeling relief it wasn't Ahnah, because it was someone.

Tanned skin with little pink flowers tattooed down her right arm and neck and probably her back. Posed in a sitting position, her legs stretched out in front of her. One hand on her left thigh and her other arm out with the palm up, the note nailed into it.

His brain filed through the list of missing women with flower names and their pictures. He didn't recall seeing a red-head. Didn't mean the killer hadn't taken someone who hadn't been reported missing.

"Something's not right," Fiona said, and put her hand on Ty's arm, pausing midway on the boardwalk. "Her hair...it doesn't look right." A gust of wind swept across the frothy waters and blew her hair to the side and then completely off her head, revealing she wasn't a redhead at all.

Nor was she a brunette like Ahnah.

Blond. Pulled into a bun on top of her head.

The killer had put a wig on her just to toy with them again!

Fiona ran forward, whispering, "No," then startled and reeled backward. "Asa!"

Asa darted past Ty while he remained, his feet cemented to the wet wood.

He grabbed Fiona and held her face to his chest.

Ty forced his feet forward and rounded Asa, who was embracing Fiona.

The atmosphere tilted and he wobbled, then righted himself. His mouth opened to deny the horror, but he didn't have enough breath to speak, cry or mutter a prayer or even a curse. His lungs squeezed and his chest cracked with a sharp stabbing pain.

Her fingers were crooked on her left hand where they'd been

broken, and her hand was twisted at an odd angle where her wrist had been broken too.

How had he gotten to her? It didn't make sense.

"Oh, God in heaven. God. In. Heaven," Owen said as he approached, clutching Ty's arm.

Violet inhaled sharply and knelt, ignoring protocol.

She tipped their admin assistant's chin upward. "Camellia," she whispered. "Camellias are flowers. Pretty pink flowers."

Cami's once blue, sparkling eyes stared back, milky and hollow.

Dead.

Chapter Eighteen

"Someone cover her up," Ty whispered. No one moved. He shoved back the hood from his poncho. "I said someone cover her up! Cover her up!" No one needed to see her like this—exposed and exploited. "Please!" He went into child's pose, his head on the boardwalk. "I'm so sorry. I'm so sorry, Cam." Tears mingled with rain. He hadn't even known her name was Camellia or that it was a flower.

Cami had been their mama hen at twenty-six. Tough and hilarious and full of sass. Their Tinkerbelle—nicknamed by Fiona, and though it hadn't been a compliment at the time, it'd stuck.

"Somebody cover her up," he shouted. "I'll kill him. I will kill him. I swear I'll kill him."

Owen's heavy hand rested on his shoulder, and he peered

up through blurry eyes at his best friend. Owen didn't hide his tears. "We can't, Ty. Not yet. She might have—" his voice cracked "—she might have evidence to recover. Covering her up will compromise her."

The last thing she told him before she left for two weeks of vacation was she'd bring him back something fun. That was almost two weeks ago. She'd saved up time to take the whole enchilada at once, which he'd told her was dumb. Once vacation was burned, it was the rest of the year with nothing to look forward to.

She'd laughed and reminded him of Barbados. That one crazy time a hurricane hit. He only wished they were caught in one together now. This kind of storm wasn't one he was prepared for.

No wonder she hadn't texted him back when he dogged her hotel booking skills after seeing the beach house earlier in the week. She hadn't been on a beach ignoring him. She'd been in the clutches of a killer all this time.

"Why did she come here? How did he find her?" he asked with a hoarse voice, his throat raw and burning.

Fiona and Violet took the lead and examined her body, without moving her. Still felt intrusive and too personal. Too wrong.

"Tiberius," Fiona said, "there's a note you need to see."

"I can't look at her, Fi. It's wrong." Like this. In this way.

Violet backtracked and knelt in front of him. "Tiberius, she would want you to do your job. To find her killer. And when we do we'll make sure he pays."

She meant justice to the fullest extent of the law.

Ty wanted vengeance.

The killer had said he'd pick someone close to Ty. How had he known? Ty and Cami had kept that week a secret. Cami never once mentioned being in a hurricane.

Cami would want him to find this man. He stood and wiped his eyes, inching toward her. He read the note card nailed into her palm.

She tasted sweet as honey. Sassy and stubborn, but you know this. What will you tell her family? And what will you tell Bexley when it's Ahnah's turn? I'm running out of lighthouses. Maybe I'll put her on her sister's doorstep. I'm not done. You haven't suffered enough. Paid enough for your sins. I will not rest until you're destroyed. Secret's out now, though, isn't it?

"What secret?" Owen asked.

Ty's hands shook, and he formed them into tight fists as he processed as quickly as he could. "I think he's been tracking me for a very long time. At least two years. He said in the last letter that I cared about her, and I thought he meant Ahnah. But he's had Cami too, and that's who he actually meant."

"Why?" Fiona asked as the ME approached.

"Because Cami had gone through a hard time with her boyfriend—remember, Asa? You about did a beatdown on him, then helped her get straightened out?"

"I remember," he said in a raspy tone.

"We were just talking and I mentioned she could come to Barbados with me. Take a week. Come out a day or two after me. Just us."

"And she did," Asa said. "You think the killer knows you were in Barbados with her?"

"I know he knows. I don't know if he was targeting flower names and chose Cami. Or maybe it was icing on the cake, either way. He knew we were close. Nothing super romantic. It heated up a little but...we were cool when we got back."

"She was in that hurricane with you," Violet said.

He nodded. "Never said a word. We didn't want rumors flying, and it was that one time. She must have told him or posted something. I don't know how he found Ahnah or how he lured Cami here. It makes no sense."

Dried blood crusted her lip and chin, and he closed his eyes. "She fought him."

"I'd expect no less," Asa said. "I should have pressed her about where she was going. She was secretive, and I didn't want her to think I was pushing into her personal life." The vein running along his brow protruded, and his face had turned crimson. "I should have—"

"This is on me, Asa. Not you." This monster had somehow connected with Cami and enticed her. Then he'd captured her. Made her his flower. In his plan to get Ty, she was a pawn. "He's always ten to twenty steps ahead. I—we—can't catch him. How am I going to live knowing I couldn't bring Cami or her family any justice?" He spun on his heel and stalked down the boardwalk, the wind whipping and blowing his tie into his face. He leaned over the railing and vomited.

Asheville, North Carolina
Family of Glory gated community
Thursday, September 6
3:10 p.m.

The mountain road narrowed as it wended upward with sharp curves that turned Ty green. It'd been a minute since he'd driven these roads barreling straight into his past. A place he never expected to return to. He was quickly learning no one truly escaped their past; it clung to his frame like days-old sweat. Or maybe only those who didn't deal with it never escaped. Was it possible to go back and face it like a headwind so that he could truly be free?

After they'd left the scene this morning, Asa had shouldered the responsibility to inform Cami's parents and sister of her death while Ty and Owen prepared to fly to Asheville, rent a vehicle and visit the Family of Glory. Asa had blamed himself for not being more intrusive in her life. Cami was beautiful inside and out, but she often picked the wrong men. She'd been hurt and abused before, stemming clear back to grade school and a pervert uncle. But she'd risen above it and had been a part of the SCU family.

Selah was combing through Cami's social media accounts. Most of the team steered clear of social media accounts for privacy, but Cami was a social media junkie and a fan of dating sites and apps. She and Ty had gone through some of hers in Barbados as she repeatedly swiped left and he reminded her that dating apps rarely worked in favor of the woman. Cam was a Southern woman through and through. Kind and courteous and stubborn as a goose. Selah was scouring those dating sites too. It had to be how the killer found Cami. Like an unseen enemy hunting for information, finding and poking at it, hoping for a weak spot in the wall so he could slip his way in and dismantle everything piece by piece.

"Why didn't you tell me about Barbados?" Owen asked. "Seems like you been keepin' more secrets from me than tellin' 'em to me."

"It was a spur-of-the-moment idea, and I honestly didn't think she'd take me up on it. I was probably half-drunk when I asked. She needed a break and wanted to work on her art for the next show." Cami had done several art shows and was gifted. "It was one night that got a little out of control. She didn't want to make a big thing of it, and I knew how you felt about interoffice relationships. We returned and stayed close, never crossing a line like that again." But it was enough that it's why the killer chose her over Violet—if he was hunting among Ty's closest friends.

Or he was afraid of Violet.

Or he was coming for her and everyone all in good time.

Ty wasn't sure he could handle another move. He'd been unraveling since his first day in North Carolina, and he was down to a frayed thread about to snap into a dark free fall.

Their team had been fractured.

Fiona and Violet had gone to the ME's office in Raleigh to be present for the autopsy. Cami's family wanted to fly in, but with the hurricane coming and her body already identified, there was nothing they could do. Once the procedure was finished, they'd send her home and arrangements would be made. Dense forest flanked the mountain roads and his ears filled with uncomfortable pressure.

"You should have told me," Owen said.

"I know." Ty tapped his heart with his fist.

Owen arched an eyebrow. "She was smart. She didn't have a single open bloom. That girl took the fight to the grave. He had to have infiltrated an app to meet her. How does a guy like that slip in like a phantom?"

"Cami was the best, but she was insecure," Ty said. "He caught a whiff of it and told her what she wanted to hear, proved he wasn't a catfish. She was wise to catfishers. Who knows how long they'd been talking. He was grooming her and planning this. He's cleverer than I originally thought. It's like he's omnipresent and omnipotent. How do we fight that?"

"He's neither of those. He's flesh and blood. A man. He can be hurt."

"Are you pulling *Rocky IV* lines at a time like this, O?"

Owen lifted a shoulder. "They fit."

"I've taught you well." He sighed. "I do want to hurt him, though. I want him to pay with his life for this." His grip tightened on the wheel, like the emotion tightening around his ribs. The road narrowed on the curve, and then the wooded, gated community sprang into view. Upscale and posh. No one would know the atrocities that took place in this community, led by a reptile with good looks and a silver tongue.

"He doesn't have to talk to us, but I can't promise I won't lose it if he refuses." Ty approached the gates, which were open during daytime hours. As he drove past them, his mouth turned dry and his palms damp. Houses were tucked into the woods, some with longer winding drives.

But Rand Granger had the Prophet's house. Eight thousand square feet of his own private kingdom. "One more unfortunate bomb, O. Rand is racist. You won't find African Americans in the Family."

"Okay," Owen murmured.

"I don't carry those beliefs with me. I don't—"

"Ty," Owen said, and laid a hand on his shoulder. "I know you. I know how you feel, and I'm not going to change my view of you because your dad is a bigot. But if you think my presence will hinder his willingness to talk to you, I can stay in the car."

"Absolutely not. We're doing our jobs. He'll talk. Just not to you. He probably won't even acknowledge you're in the room, and I'm... I'm sorry." His heritage, his past, was nothing he could remotely be proud of, and this was another factor in why Josiah should never know his family.

"I appreciate that. I do. But I been dealin' with his kind a long time."

"I never felt or believed like he does. Not ever." He needed his ride-or-die to know that. Because Rand Granger was a pathetic excuse of a human being, but he could be shrewd and unkind. Owen needed to go in knowing the deal so he wouldn't be blindsided.

At the top of the hill, Rand's house was nestled into the mountains. It was as obnoxious as his father. Ty parked by the fountain in the circular drive behind a Land Rover and an F-350. A group of young children chased each other around the trees, laughing. The poor kids had no idea they were being manipulated and deceived by the ones they loved most. They paused as he and Owen closed the SUV doors, drawing their attention. Outsiders. But Ty was a half-brother to many if not all of them. He shook his head as they walked up the porch steps. His home growing up looked more resort than residential with its A-line windows running ceiling to floor.

Ty rapped on the door, his pulse on the uptick.

A girl about sixteen greeted them with a chubby baby with dark hair and big brown eyes on her hip. He held his bottle in one hand and a pacifier in the other. Was this girl another of Rand's wives? Was this baby his half-brother too?

"May I help you?" she asked as her gaze shifted between the two of them, lingering a little longer on—and seeming leerier of—Owen.

"We need to speak with the Prophet. It's urgent," Ty said.

"The Prophet is in prayer, sir. He can't be interrupted during communion with God." That's when he noticed her eyes. Green in color and shape, matching his own. A sister, not a wife.

"I'm Special Agent—" Did he say his last name? Did he even want to? "Granger, and this is Special Agent Barkley."

"Granger? That's my last name." She smiled. "He could be a while, if you don't mind waiting."

A figure approached and Ty cocked his head, studying the dark-haired man with eyes equally as dark. Surely not. He couldn't hold back a smile. "Lysander?"

The man paused in his approach and squinted.

Wasn't it his younger brother? He'd only been fourteen when Ty had left that night. Upon further inspection, he decided, yes. It was. He looked more like their mother than he and Garrick did. He'd filled out and become a handsome man. Ty's gullet cinched. "It's me. Tiberius."

His eyes widened, and he closed the distance between them. "Laurie, you may return to daycare duty. I'll handle this."

"Yes, sir."

Lysander ruffled her hair, then stretched out his arms, and the baby reached for him. He scooped him up and kissed his forehead.

"I've got Alex."

"Yes, sir." She darted from the open door.

Ty stared at the baby.

"Not your brother. Your nephew." Lysander smiled.

"You're married."

"I am."

"Good for you. I guess that means Garrick married?" He might be asking questions too soon, but the only way for Lysander to have a wife would mean Garrick had one.

A small divot formed across his brow. "He was. What brings you here after all these years? And why does Garrick's marriage matter?" He glanced at Owen, but refrained from speaking to him. Guess he'd adopted Rand's view, or maybe he was simply stunned to see Ty on his doorstep. The fact Lysander was talking to him suggested he wasn't as opposed to Ty as Rand was.

"I need to talk to the Prophet. Laurie says he's in prayer." As if he actually prayed, and if he did, and there was a God, Rand wasn't talking to Him. "Official business." He showed his credentials. "This is Agent Barkley, my colleague and friend."

Lysander nodded and extended his hand to Owen. "Nice to meet you."

Owen shook Lysander's hand. Maybe he had more Mama in him than his father. But here he was, still a believer, and Ty couldn't let himself forget that.

"What is the official business? We haven't had anything nefarious go on here, Tiberius."

Bunk. But that told him Lysander was as fully immersed in the Family as he'd always been.

"I need to know who's been disfellowshipped, or left of their own accord, in the past decade. Also, is Garrick around?"

Lysander bent over, picked up the pacifier Alex had dropped, and pocketed it. "Today? No. He travels a lot. Our real estate company has gone global now. Father had to buy a new plane, but Garrick's travels are mostly in-state. He's running the coastal properties. Why?"

"Just curious."

"Tiberius, you were never a good liar. If you explain why you want to know, I might be—"

"What is going on?" Rand Granger's deep baritone registered, causing a dull thump in Ty's chest before his looming frame appeared next to Lysander, filling the remaining space with his once-intimidating physique. Rand had really aged in the past decade. His formerly straight shoulders now stooped and the lines around his eyes, mouth and neck had deepened and multiplied, but his sharp green eyes hadn't dimmed, and they were narrowed and trained on Ty. "I asked a question."

Lysander stepped aside with apology splayed across his face. "I'll let the Prophet be alone with you, Agent." Ty extended his hand, and when Lysander shook it, his eyes widened. Ty had palmed his business card and left it with his brother in case he wanted to reach out.

"Agent Granger, I've already told you that you can't have access to the list. You've wasted your time coming here."

"Women are dying. My friend has died. I'm not leaving this place until you speak with me." He had no legal grounds, and Rand could easily call the police to have him escorted off the property. But Rand heaved a sigh and frowned at Lysander as he opened the door wider.

"Fine. But I'll only speak with you," he said.

"You will—"

Owen's throat clearing paused his words. "I'll be out here." He leaned in. "This is about Cami," he whispered. "Whatever we have to do for her."

Ty nodded and entered the house. For as many children running around as there were, the home was immaculate. Guess that's what dozens of wives got you. Rand's gait was rigid and his mouth silent as they walked the length of the first floor to his office located in the back of the house, where he had an incredible view of the mountains. As a child, Ty had loved to visit his father's office and pretend he was a mountain climber.

Rand eased into his massive office chair, and Ty caught a whiff of his pipe tobacco and a hint of lemon left behind from a good dusting. Rand stared at him and for a brief moment, Ty recognized a flash of regret and a fatherly perusal. "You had such potential. You know I had been praying and felt you would become the next Prophet, not Garrick."

Ty reared his head back. "I never wanted that."

"It wasn't about what you wanted but what God wanted. I was going to throw a party and surprise you with the calling. Then Garrick discovered what you'd done to Bexley—his bride-to-be—and I knew it would be impossible then. Public scandal. I had no choice but to disfellowship you. I've been disappointed in you since then. I actually thought when you called you might be begging for forgiveness, which is within my power to grant."

Rand had been angry that Ty hadn't wanted to return into his good graces, and not giving him the list was punishment. If Ty could attempt to find common ground, soften him up, Rand might give him what he wanted. "Why did you allow Garrick to have Bexley's hand? You knew I loved her and wanted to marry her. That's bothered me all these years and may be why I never returned for your forgiveness. I thought you didn't care about me like you cared about Garrick." Ty had learned from the master that a lie would sell better if it held a kernel of truth.

Rand's expression softened, exactly as Ty had hoped. "I always loved you, Tiberius. But I didn't think Bexley Hemmingway was the right match for you. She was from a good family, but I thought she filled your heart with rebelliousness. Like coming to me about the little sister. I know that was her influence. She had too much influence over you, and I'd been contemplating what to do about the two of you when Garrick asked for her hand. I saw it as a sign from God you were to carry

out the office of Prophet after I went to be in paradise. You
need a clear head with no female influence to be a good leader."

How did he not recognize his own insanity?

Ty's jaw hardened, but reasoning or arguing with a lunatic
wasn't going to fix the past, mend the future or get him what he
needed now. The list. "I suppose Garrick's been reinstated now."

He hit a few keys on his computer, and the printer whirred.
"You know nothing. God has excommunicated Garrick from
the prophetic office. Dalen will take my place."

What? Ty had dozens of swirling questions. Rand wouldn't
answer him. No point asking. But he wanted to know what
Garrick had done. Had his sadism escalated?

Rand swiped the two-page list from the printer. "I'll give
you this. But it's all I'm giving you. If you change your mind,
you'd be the first FBI agent in the Family."

Oh, he'd love that. A federal agent in his pocket when allegations of child abuse came knocking. No thanks. Ty accepted
the list. "Thank you for this." He pretty much wanted to burn
the rest of this place to the ground.

"Tiberius, what kind of evidence do you have that someone
from this Family is murdering those innocent girls?"

"Someone embedded the Family's logo on their tattoos." No
point hiding it from Rand. He wouldn't go to the press with
damaging information about the Family.

Rand frowned. "That only proves someone knows how to
tattoo our logo. It doesn't prove it's someone who was once a
part of the Family. You've considered that, haven't you?"

No. He hadn't. Someone wanted him to believe that this
killer was also the Fire & Ice Killer. But he might not be. The
logo was there leading them to the Family, but Rand was correct. What if the killer was toying with him yet again and leading him down a path he wanted Ty to take?

Puppet strings.

Maybe he wanted him to come here and face his past simply to force him to do something he'd vowed never to do again.

Who would know this about him?

He marched outside and stepped inside the SUV. "I got the list."

"Well, it's something." Owen buckled up. "Cami's cell phone provider turned over her texts and calls along with all the dates and time stamps. Selah's been combing them from the past year, but hasn't found anything tying Cami to our killer. She was communicating with this guy through an app or phone service that doesn't store information on their servers at all or for very long. He was smart and she fell for it. With all her past experience with men and her knowledge from working with the SCU, she knew how to vet a dude. He was clever enough to gain her trust. He probably used her personal past to his advantage, telling her exactly what she wanted or needed to hear to drop her guard."

Ty had come to the same conclusion. Their killer had talked to Skipper on WhatsApp and he probably talked to Cami that way, but wouldn't that have been a red flag? "He had to be a sweet liar." He was yanking Ty's chains too. Why did Ty believe everything written in those notes to him was true? This killer was a liar, manipulating Ty and the team, and he was over it.

"You learn anything else inside there?" Owen asked.

Ty pushed the ignition button and glanced in his rearview mirror as a car pulled in behind them. "Hold up," he mumbled. The driver's door opened and a tall man with thick dark hair and sunglasses strutted out. "I thought he was out of town."

"Who?"

"My brother Garrick."

Chapter Nineteen

Ty darted out of the SUV, ready to confront his older brother. He'd bulked up since the last Ty had seen him, smirking at his disfellowship and the fact he'd been escorted off the property. He'd traded in jeans for a flashy, expensive suit and a watch that cost more than Ty's vehicle. Garrick had followed in Rand's footsteps with his taste for the finer things in life. Garrick paused, surprised at Ty's presence.

"I was told you were out of town," Ty said.

"And now I'm not." Garrick approached him. "Why is the long-forgotten favored one here? Are you a prodigal?"

The animosity hadn't mellowed over the years. "You live under a rock? Haven't you heard about the lighthouse murders?"

Garrick checked his watch. "What does that have to do with the Family, Tiberius?"

"I think the killer may have ties to the Family."

"You'd love to believe that, wouldn't you? Take down the Family as a vendetta? No one presently in or formerly from our community has had anything to do with murders over two hundred miles away." That was a long way to live and be separated from the victims, but this particular UNSUB had zero fear of getting caught. Could it be Garrick? Ty leaned toward no. He didn't have much artistic ability either. Their killer did.

But almost eighteen years had passed. Plenty of time to hone a craft, to work in a tattoo shop, gaining the knowledge and experience before setting out for his master fantasy. Not to mention they'd found prostitutes who had been tattooed in the Charlotte and Raleigh areas.

"I'm told you handle the Prophet's coastal properties."

Garrick's beam was smug. "You think I'm doing this? How have you made it this long in the FBI being so stupid? I handle more than Father's coastal properties, and I suppose it's a good thing. Hear a hurricane's coming to the Outer Banks. Seems to me you don't have a lot of time before everything takes a hit, including you."

His phone dinged and he checked it, but his eyes didn't track like one's did when reading lines. He muttered something and then pocketed the cell. "Is this revenge for asking for Bexley's hand in marriage? Your sweet precious Bex. She was nothing but a hot piece of tail and you know it. The real sweet spot would have been marrying the sister. All young and ripe..."

Ty balled his fist but remained level-headed. "How did you even know Bexley and I were sleeping together? Did you know before you asked to marry her?" Did he put it in motion to make sure Ty was disfellowshipped and Garrick retained standing as the upcoming Prophet after Rand's death? The last thing he would have wanted was for Ty to be named as the new Prophet and get everything Garrick wanted.

Had Ty been a puppet even then?

His blood froze.

"You look like you've seen a ghost, Tiberius." Garrick grinned. "Of course I knew you were sleeping with Bexley. Just like I knew when I went in, shocked and devastated, about her being deflowered, Father would take her from you. I couldn't care less about that skank."

Owen stepped out of the car and nonchalantly walked up. He must have heard the conversation and decided to intervene before it escalated. Smart move. Ty was unraveling faster than a sweater stuck on a hook.

Garrick took one peek at Owen and laughed. "Gotcha a bodyguard now? How's it going, *boy*?"

Ty thrust himself into Garrick's personal space, grabbing him by the collar, but Owen yanked him back. "Don't give this slug the time of day. He's not worth it."

Garrick laughed and brushed back his dark hair blowing in his eyes. "Go find a killer somewhere else, Tiberius. You're barking up the wrong tree here."

"Well, you didn't get what you wanted. I left and you still aren't taking Rand's place. I take satisfaction in that."

Garrick didn't even bat an eye. Why? Why wouldn't he be angry about it? Garrick loved power and authority and privilege.

"I wouldn't be feeling satisfied just yet, Agent."

What exactly did that mean?

"Bexley never went through with the consummation, so I'm feeling pretty satisfied," Ty blurted, then suddenly realized his mistake. How would he know that if Bexley was dead?

Garrick folded his arms over his chest and blinked a few times. "No, he didn't get to plant his babies in the woman you loved. But I take pleasure in knowing you didn't get her either. Do you miss her? I don't. Do miss little Ahnah, though. The way she lapped up the mud on my boots. If only she were still alive. I'd be all over that. But that's what happens to girls who run away."

Blood whooshed in Ty's ears.

"Y'all have a nice day and don't come back. Or I'll have the police escort you off the property. Your badge doesn't scare me, Tiberius."

When Garrick reached the porch, Ty hollered, "It's not my badge you should be afraid of!"

Owen gripped his shoulders. "Again, he's not worth it. Let's go. He's trying to get under your skin and it's working." Ty didn't budge. "Tiberius, *let's go.*"

Finally, Ty acquiesced and clambered into the passenger side. He had no business driving while this distracted and angry.

"He knows they're alive. He's doing it, and he's all but taunting me to try and stop him. I should have suspected him first-go. Question is, is he also the Fire & Ice Killer?"

"I don't know what he is, Ty. Other than a wicked man. But, yeah. I think he knows they're alive. Whether or not he took Ahnah or has plans to take Bexley is another story. And without proof, we can't search the home or his room or car or anything. All we have is his condescending tone and suspicion." Owen buckled his seat belt and pressed the ignition button.

Ty scrolled to his mother's name on his phone and pressed Call. He had questions.

She answered on the first ring. "Tiberius, have you seen a hurricane is heading for the Outer Banks? You don't plan to be there when it hits, do you?"

"Mama, you know I do. I've always wanted to go out by drowning." He rolled his eyes. "Sorry. I'm having a bad day."

"Why?"

"I saw Rand."

The line remained silent. Finally she asked, "Why?"

He told her what he could regarding the case. "How can Dalen be the Prophet? I thought only first wives could have heirs, and you're the first wife." Could Rand have been lying to protect Garrick? Did Garrick have plans to eliminate Dalen and usurp the office? Something wasn't jiving.

"Tiberius, I am not the first wife. Nor was I ever the 'first' first wife. It's not about who he married first. It's about who he chooses to be first. There was one before me—before I ever came into the Family. Mother Lorna. She had a son. He was in line to be the Prophet. But he had some…problems, and Rand said he had to do what Abraham did to Hagar and Ishmael. He sent them away. I became his next choice."

"What kind of problems?"

"Well, for one, he kept carving the Family's logo into squirrels and cats. Or that's what I heard from your father. It was difficult for him to send them away but it had to be done."

The killer had been putting the logo on unsuspecting women.

"How old was he when he had to leave?"

"I don't know. Fifteen or sixteen? Rand had other wives before her and me—they just didn't get the title 'first wife.' The first wife bears the next Prophet. Could be Dalen's mom was made the first wife."

He'd never questioned that before. You didn't question anything in the Family.

"Mother Mae told me that the boy was pretty angry about leaving and losing the office of Prophet. He loved the Family. Couldn't believe anyone would want to leave. And he was furious with your father. Vowed no one would take the Prophet's place but himself, but he was only a teenager blowing off steam."

Ty wasn't so sure.

"What was his name?"

"I don't remember. Mother Mae would know, or Rand. Disfellowshipped members aren't allowed to be spoken about. You know this."

Rand would never cough up the name, and Mother Mae was dead.

Could some tossed-out first son be out there coming for Ty, and was anyone else who might take the position be in danger too? When he said he was after those close to him, would he assume Ty was close to his brothers?

And who was this man?

Bexley paced the deck outside the room she'd been staying in since she'd come to Ty and his team about the killer's threats. All day she'd been contemplating if that was the wrong decision and if the killer would call her to tell her Ahnah was dead.

God help her, she needed guidance, divine help. As it turned out, it had been a team member, a friend, Ty lost. And she hadn't seen him all day, hadn't been able to talk with him. Nerves had her on edge. What if he'd slipped up and mentioned her and Ahnah? Could Rand talk Ty into returning? Had he seen Garrick or any of the other men who'd given Ahnah a hard time?

Thunder startled her and she backed up, sitting in the Adirondack chair, listening to rain pummel the house. It'd been nonstop all day. Josiah had been sullen and irritated he was stuck here, but he'd played some video games and they'd ordered pizzas for dinner. The entire team had shown them kindness and compassion and had moved their murder board to a room in the ground level apartment so Josiah and she didn't have to see it every time they entered the kitchen.

A soft knock on her bedroom door drew her from the deck. She opened the door and Tiberius stood there, hair wet and curling around his temples, his scruff a full day's beard. "How you doing?" he asked as he rubbed the nape of his neck.

"I was about to ask you the same. Tiberius, I'm so sorry about your friend Cami."

He nodded once, and she welcomed him inside. "I was sitting outside thinking. Praying. Hoping. Wondering."

Tiberius followed her onto the screened-in private deck and sat on the swing. She sat next to him. "Wondering what?"

"How Ahnah is holding up. What the consequences will be of my choice to not push you away like the killer demanded I do. How it went at the Family."

"I wish I had an answer. You did the right thing by coming to us with the phone call. And things went about as I expected in Asheville. Dalen is next in line when Rand dies—but I don't know if that old man is ever going to die. I saw Garrick."

Bexley tensed. "And?"

"He hasn't changed. It's in the eyes."

Shifting, she scooted closer, facing him. "How are you feeling?" She couldn't begin to imagine the feelings banging around inside him.

"Don't analyze me, Bex."

"I'm not. I want to know."

"You want to know how I feel? Okay," he said, through an expelled breath. "I feel left out of my kid's life. Someone has it in for me and literally plotted out a plan to derail me better than in some kind of spy novel. My dad hates me and barely acknowledged my existence but would be willing for me to return because it benefits him—me being an agent. I probably have nine hundred half-siblings and the only person who actually feels like family to me is Owen. I'm hanging on by a thread, and I don't have it in me to find this guy. Which means Ahnah might die like Cami and those other victims and their blood is staining my hands. No matter how hard I try to wash it off, it's there. All their blood on my hands."

She took his hands in hers. Big, warm, a few calluses on his palms. "No one's blood is on your hands, Tiberius. That's what he wants you to believe. He wants to make you suffer—and he is. He's messing with your head."

"He's messing with my head. My life. People I care about. How will I ever look Cami's family in the eye?"

He held his palms open and she continued to gently caress

them. Lightning lit up the room and she caught his eyes, boring into hers and searching. For what?

He laced his fingers between hers. "I had a flood of memories there today. Many of them were about you. The time you threw dirt in my eyes before a race so you'd win. Or the time you jumped out of a tree and terrified me. I squeaked like a mouse and you made fun of me for weeks."

She laughed. "It was too easy to give you a hard time."

He inched closer. "I remember the first time I picked you flowers."

"Out of Mother Mae's garden."

Her body instinctively moved with his, bringing them together; she smelled mint on his breath, and goose bumps broke out on her skin. "I fell out of puppy love with you that day and into real love." He pulled her to him, sliding his hands into her hair as the rain fell in sheets. His nose bumped hers and his lips brushed against her mouth, feather-soft. "I remembered what you tasted like..." He let the thought linger, giving her the power to decide.

"I may have forgotten," she murmured and peered up from her lashes with a permissive smile.

Recognition dilated his pupils, and he deliberately explored her lips as they recaptured one another's taste. Encircling his neck, her fingers toyed with the hair curling above his collar. Memories washed over her like afternoon sunshine and sweet tea. Their breath mingled and his hands got lost in her mess of curls.

"I've missed you," he whispered against her lips. "Missed your smell, missed...*you*. I wish things could have been different."

She did too, but before she could agree, his mouth was on hers again, devouring. Like stepping into the ocean. Unpredictable but beautiful. She wasn't afraid to let the current draw her out and under. She was fully accepting of drowning in this luscious, heady moment. A place where monsters didn't exist, pain was banned and hope soared. The passion was unbridled and the only thing in this moment that wasn't broken.

But unrestraint had once been their downfall.

As if Tiberius had read her thoughts, he brought the crashing waves to a small lapping at the shore, not abrupt but a gradual glorious fade. Framing her face, he rested his brow on hers, his breath shallow. "I'm not sorry for that."

Was she? No, but it had complicated a civil relationship. Did he want more? Did she? What would that mean?

Finally, he moved away and leaned back on the swing. "When are we going to tell Josiah?"

Their son never strayed far from Tiberius's thoughts.

"I almost told him. But you showed up. We can take him somewhere. Just the three of us. Although Drew doesn't think it's wise. He backed up my original idea."

Lightning skewered through the sky. Bex flinched.

Ty leaned his elbows on his knees. "Drew isn't his dad. *When* we tell him, we need a game plan about spending time with me in Memphis. He's almost eighteen and I know it'll be his choice, but I'm hoping he'll want to know me. We need to rip off the Band-Aid and tell him where we came from, and why he can never have anything to do with them. He's a smart kid. He'll get it. Let me psychoanalyze you. You've been project- ing your greatest fears onto him."

He was right. She feared losing Josiah to the Family. Feared she'd made a mistake and he'd hate her for withholding him from Tiberius. What if she lost them all—Ahnah, Josiah and Tiberius?

Ty hadn't come to Bex's room for a make-out session, and now he was puzzled in new ways. Did he have feelings for her? Yes. Was he mad at her for her epic past blunder? Absolutely.

How could a man want to kiss and kill a woman at the same time? Maybe he was a psycho in disguise.

"You're right, Tiberius. I am afraid. But his right to know is greater than my fears."

"We'll figure out what to tell him and when. I'll back you up as being a good mom. You are. Even if he's been nothing but a punk, when we're playing video games I glimpse the young man he truly is and that's a testament to you."

"You can be quite charming when you want to be, Tiberius." She playfully elbowed him in the arm.

"I suppose." He eyed her mouth. "You got better at kissing. You have a lot practice?" The idea of Bexley kissing men—plural—unsettled him.

She raised an eyebrow. "If I answer that, you'll have to return the favor."

Smart cookie.

"I'll be transparent, Bex. I've had a lot of practice kissing. It started as a way to bump you out of my system. It didn't work. I purposely chose women who weren't looking to settle down. No feelings involved. Just a person to pass time with and keep from being alone." Nothing had ever been right after he thought he'd lost her for good. Was a second chance even possible? Did he want that? Did she?

Bexley rubbed her thumb with her index finger. "I've dated less than ten men. Only *dated*. I thought I could move on and forge a new life but I couldn't. Every time I look into our son's eyes, I see you, and I guess... I couldn't commit that piece of my heart to anyone else. Didn't seem fair."

"Nothing about this has been fair. Let's sleep on it. In separate rooms. I'm pretty tired, and tomorrow I'm running down that list that Rand gave us. Asa and Fiona are driving out of the hurricane zone and flying to Memphis in the morning to work Cami's case on that end. Talk to friends and family. Visit her gym and go through her past art shows, interviews. Anything that might lead us to this guy."

"I have appointments. With the hurricane, some of my clients are presenting anxiety, and want to talk through it. I also need to pack up a few more things. I'll go during the day, change up my routine and be careful."

"Okay. I'd feel better if you'd share your location with me. Until it's safe."

She pulled out her phone and shared her location. "I should go to bed."

"Me too. Or I might kiss you again." He couldn't remember the last time he'd showed this much restraint. He followed her into the bedroom. His emotions were out of whack. At the door she rose on tiptoe and kissed his cheek.

"Good night, Tiberius." She touched her lips. "I'm not sorry either."

Before it was all said and done, they might both be sorry.

Chapter Twenty

Kipos Island
Friday, September 7
1:54 a.m.

"Up, up, up, my garden girls." He clapped his hands, then pressed the remote button as his favorite musical score, Saint-Saëns's *Danse Macabre Op. 40*, began to play. Absolute sheer brilliance! Gorgeous staccato strings. Oh, death had come at midnight with his fiddle! He air-bowed and glided among his hanging baskets, ignoring that a few were empty.

Now Camellia's was void too. She'd been the feistiest of flowers and he wished he could have kept her longer—see how long until she surrendered. But letting her go at the perfect time had been worth it to see Agent Granger's knees buckle, his team's cries.

He imagined himself fiddling Granger's death. With every bow, Granger's time shortened. The Artist held his life in his hands. He'd been in charge from infiltrating the agent's team members and settling on the easiest score—Cami. A stage-five clinger, it hadn't been hard to jump through her security hoops. He'd been everything she'd wanted and then some.

But who would fill his sassy camellia's place? He'd rather liked the challenge she'd presented. A feisty flower would only suit taking her place.

Tonight wouldn't be focused on all the empty baskets needing to be filled with new garden girls. No, he was elated! He'd gotten everything he'd wanted. Tiberius Granger and his team had followed the crumbs he'd laid out like Hansel and Gretel, and he had reaped the benefits. Right there under Granger's nose yet again, and still he had no clue who he was looking upon. The power the Artist wielded. But the agent had felt the power. Felt his own helplessness.

And it had been euphoric.

"Dance, my girls. Bloom, my flowers." He watched their bodies take form, lovely and enticing. "Ah, you are beautiful." Perfection and grace. His blood pumped hot and hard and fast through his veins as he watched their long, slender arms arc above their heads, up on their toes, their calf muscles protruding.

But the beauty he'd created surpassed the beauty of their born flesh. The lines perfect, the shading... He kissed the tips of his fingers. Superb. Vibrant colors.

Waltzing between the cages, he continued to bow his invisible strings, taking pleasure in his pretty dancing flowers. Unspeakable joy, not only in his hunt and the ripe plucking, but in the truth that they were made for him to remake. To bring him glory.

He ached with anticipation as the crescendo began. "Faster. Faster. Faster! Keep with the time. Keep with the time!"

Throwing his head back, he inhaled the fragrance of the garden, the scent of his girls and the glory of his supremacy. And as the piece slowed, he dropped to the floor, spent, his heart beating out of his chest and his thoughts trailing back to Agent Granger. He was going to destroy him.

Blue Harbor
SCU beach house
Friday, September 7
7:55 a.m.

Storms normally lulled Ty into slumber, but not last night. He tossed and turned to the tune of dread and impending doom. And when the power went out at two a.m., it mirrored this entire investigation. Powerless and in darkness. Like a huge vortex he'd been sucked into with nothing to secure him from whirling into utter chaos.

He had to get ahead of this storm, and the killer's storm brewing.

Thankfully at five a.m. the power returned, but it was nothing short of a prelude to what was coming. Ty trudged to the second floor and the scent of fresh coffee.

Bexley sipped her cup at the table. "Last night was rough and today doesn't look any better."

Asa and Fiona were already gone. Ty heard the shower running when he'd walked past Owen's room. Where was Violet? Wasn't like her to not be up and working before dawn.

"I watched the five o' clock news, Tiberius. Hurricane Jodie's moving up the Georgia coast and not slowing, just sticking around long enough to cause serious damage. Governor's declared a state of emergency. Tens of thousands are without power and people are evacuating in droves. They're predicting a cat 3 to hit us within twenty-four hours."

Not the news Ty wanted to hear. Would Cami have lived longer if the hurricane wasn't expediting the killer's plans? Ty might have found her given a few more days—a week.

Jodie would derail the investigation. Businesses would close and many people would leave the island until the weather cleared. At some point they'd probably close the bridge—or it would flood first—and once that was done, they'd be stranded on the island. No way out. No control.

"Bexley, you and Josiah can't stay on the island. Nothing can be done anyway. If people evacuate, we lose potential witnesses or anyone we need to interview. Local authorities will be dealing with other things. He might be crazy enough to evacuate the women he's still holding—if he's holding them on the island."

"I can't leave her."

They all needed to evacuate, but if she refused he couldn't leave her here alone. "Reconsider or at least let me send Josiah with Owen and the rest of the team. They'll secure a hotel outside the danger zone and return as soon as it's safe. And in a week if she's still not been found, I'll stay. If I have to quit my job and do this alone, I won't leave until we find her, find all of them." Ty couldn't walk away, and he had a strong suspicion this UNSUB wouldn't let him leave. He had an agenda for Ty, and he wasn't the type to let it wash out to sea. The question was, could Ty endure it? Could he get a jump on this guy? Turn the tables and make him his puppet for once?

His phone rang.

Asa.

He slid the bar across his phone and answered.

"You know a Levi Devlin?"

"Levi Devlin..." Wasn't ringing a bell.

"He was on the list of disfellowshipped men leaving within the past ten years, arrested on drug charges and in prison, so I had Selah do a check on the rest of the Family."

"I don't know a Levi. I know a Matt Devlin, though."

"Matthew Levi Devlin. Goes by Levi now. Left Asheville—I'm assuming the Family—and moved to Raleigh. Two counts of sexual assault. Did some time and is an over-the-road truck driver now."

"Hey, I'm putting you on Speaker. When Bex was sixteen, Matt had a thing for her."

"He bullied me and pushed me against a tree and groped me." She instinctively folded her arms over her chest.

"I put my fist in his face and we went to Rand. He was reprimanded and…come to think of it, his family moved. Never saw him again."

Bexley gave him a knowing look. "He hated Tiberius. Because of me, I think."

"Did their leaving have anything to do with you taking his behavior to your dad? If your dad forced them out of the community, he might blame you for any downward spiral in his life."

"Maybe. He had to receive ten lashes. That was standard punishment, but Rand rarely enforced it unless he thought the man was a threat to him."

Asa grunted. "I'm sending over his photo. We're looking for him. If his runs are anywhere near here, and during the times of our victims' disappearances, we might have something. Selah's working on this mystery brother you told us about. The one from the first 'first wife' who cut the emblems into the squirrels. But she has quite a few men with *Granger* for a last name to sift through, and that's with it narrowed down to North Carolina. She's cross-referencing the ones she does find with criminal records. I guess the portrait artist hasn't returned to work early and provided a sketch for the Smoothy character at the Inky Octopus?"

"Nope. If he doesn't send it tomorrow like the other guy said he would, I'll follow up." Ty's phone dinged, and he stared at Matthew Levi Devlin. "That's him, only older and scruffier. I could see Cami being into him. She had a bad-boy type." His words carried regret.

Ty removed Asa from speakerphone. "Violet in charge while you're gone?"

"Yes. She's objective and has a level head."

"I get it."

"Ty, the hurricane has less than twenty-four hours to landfall if it doesn't pick up speed—and they're predicting it will. The team is going to evacuate before they close the bridge. That includes you."

"Yeah, I hear ya," he mumbled. "Talk to you later." He ended the call. Bexley took her coffee and headed to her room. Violet came up the stairs.

"Hey," he said. "I hear you're in charge."

Violet strode to the fridge and removed a carton of organic strawberries and blueberries. "Asa needed to go to Memphis. Too much guilt eating at him. Besides, he and Fiona have a good working rhythm."

"And?"

"And I know things Asa doesn't. For one, how to keep you in line," she teased, and he barely caught it. "What's Bexley going to do about the hurricane?" She popped a blueberry in her mouth. Ty stole a strawberry from her bowl.

"She's going to hunker down like most. Asa said we'll have to evacuate." He snagged another strawberry, and she held up the paring knife she'd been using to slice away the green tops.

"Take one more bite of my breakfast..." The corners of her lips twitched. "Have you told him you won't be evacuating?"

"How do you—"

"You have a son, and you love that woman even if she did tear out your heart and stomp on it with steel toes. If she doesn't go, you won't go."

"Nice imagery, Vi." Ty wasn't so sure he loved Bexley, but that kiss had brought out deep feelings. Feelings he didn't have time to act on.

She finished slicing the stems off the small carton of strawberries. "You should tell him. If you don't, he's not going to take insubordination well. We all know what Asa is like when he shows his big bear claws."

Ty sighed. "You're right—about telling him I have a son. He's going to be mad I kept it from him."

"Probably." Violet stuck a spoon in her bowl of fresh fruit. "Before I lose my chance, I'm taking advantage of the fact people are mostly indoors today, and plan to interview more family and friends of the missing women. Catherine Overly is our newest missing woman, and I want to focus on her. Asa combed her condo, but I haven't."

"I can go with you."

"Okay."

He climbed to the third floor, where Owen sat in a little alcove with his laptop, phone and papers in hand. "Selah called," he said. "Cami had receipts from gas stations and a few food places to prove she was on her way to the Outer Banks. And specifically here, Ty. She bought a loaded tea at a little shop here in Blue Harbor, right on the main strip. Tea Totalers."

"When?"

"Ten days ago, Saturday. Around one o'clock. Seems like she made the drive, got into town and had time to kill—" He cringed. "After one o'clock, nothing tangible to track her. No phone location. Nothing."

Winds were at almost fifty miles an hour, but the property management had arrived earlier and hurricane prepped. Thunder roared.

"He told Violet to make sure and keep up with the weather, to vacate before it was too late. And we both know she adheres to rules better since John."

Ty huffed. "The old Violet would have said, 'Pound sand, we're staying.'"

Owen chuckled and pointed to his notes. "Cami had no hotel or condo reservations. She told her parents and her sister she was going to Florida—a lie. One he probably manipulated her into telling."

"Where would she have stayed? With him. But where?"

"Selah and I have already checked from here to Hatteras to Nags Head. I've narrowed down island homes that are more secluded, like the house Patrick Swain owns. There are four private islands that have had a home or homes built on them, and twelve of those homes might fit the bill. I'm looking into the private homeowners and the companies. The locations are far enough out for complete privacy but not so far you couldn't park at a boat landing or marina and ride out there. We're going to have to split up since we don't have Asa or Fiona with us if we want to search properties and continue our interviews with families before we can't."

Ty nodded. "He could leave them to die in a hurricane. And if it's bad enough, the hurricane could destroy everything, wash homes out to sea and ultimately decimate our investigation." A gale struck the house. Ty's heart pounded.

"I can work the properties that might fit the bill and the private islands for now if you want to cover the last two women who went missing. Not all of them had flower names or we aren't sure if they are flower names. I'm not a botanist. Violet is covering Catherine Overly's place and working through the victimology."

Asa always preferred they work in pairs or even trios, but time was slipping through their fingers. They'd all be fine alone.

Owen tucked his ink pen behind his ear and shuffled through a few papers, handing two of them to Ty. "We aren't going to be able to physically go to the private islands, only the secluded properties we can drive to. Fishing boats aren't even running." He stood. "I mean it. It's dangerous, Ty. No one will rent you a boat anyway. No one is that crazy."

Ty kept his remarks to himself. "I hear ya."

Owen shot him a warning glance. "You hear me. Fine. *Listen.*"

"I'm going to shower." He walked out of the alcove and to his room. Thirty minutes later he was dressed—not for rainy weather but work. Some days he wished his job didn't require suits and ties.

He grabbed his phone and saw a missed call.

Unknown number.

Chapter Twenty-One

Blue Harbor
SCU beach house
Friday, September 7
9:02 a.m.

Thunder shook the beach house. The sky had darkened like an evil beast who'd been woken from slumber. One wicked battle at a time. Ty's phone rang again as he grabbed the hot-pink umbrella with purple unicorns that had been left by a pre-schooler, no doubt, but it would do in a pinch. This time he answered it. "This is Agent Granger," he said.

"It's me."

"Lysander?" Ty had given him his card with hopes he might be in touch, but he hadn't been holding his breath. "Is that you?"

"Yeah," he whispered, as if trying to keep his conversation discreet. If he lived in the main house with his wife and son, then ears were everywhere.

Emotion clogged his throat. He'd always tried to look out for his little brother and wished he could have taken him with him, but Rand would never have allowed it.

"It's good to hear from you, but if Rand finds out, you could be in serious hot water."

Lysander sighed. "I know. After you left, I overheard some of the conversation between Father and Garrick. Truth is, Tiberius, I've wanted to reach out over the years, but…it would have been a sin against the Prophet, and that's a risk I'd never take—until now."

"What's changed now?"

"I need to ask you something. Will you tell me the truth?" His voice was soft, hesitant and yet urgent.

"I will." He was the only one who would.

"Garrick and Father had a conversation about the crimes. Garrick told Father that Bexley and Ahnah are alive, that you helped make them appear to be dead. That they didn't drown. Is that true?"

"What did Father say to that?"

"Just that Garrick was mistaken and must have seen someone similar. But is it true? What he said?"

Ty was at a crossroads here. The news hadn't fed a list of the missing women to the public, so the knowledge that Ahnah and Bexley were alive hadn't spread yet. "No. It's not true. I didn't help anyone escape. I wish I had." He hated lying through half truths, but if Lysander believed they were alive, he might tell Bexley and Ahnah's father. He had to protect them. And Josiah.

"Why would he say that?"

"I don't know for sure." Why would it benefit Garrick to tell Rand? How long had he been sitting on this information? Long enough to put a plan in motion? "Hey, do you remember Matt Devlin?" He would have been six years older than Lysander, but he was mean enough he might remember him.

"Vaguely. Why?"

"I was wondering if his name ever came up that you heard of? He got into trouble, and then his family left the community. Would you know anything about that?"

"No. I remember him eyeing Bexley often. And that you punched him in the face for it and broke his nose."

"How did Dalen become Rand's successor? Could you tell me that?"

The line hung with silence.

"Lysander? You still there?"

"Yeah. I'm still here. Look, Dalen isn't taking Father's office. Father is protecting Garrick. Look, some ugly things have gone down here. Garrick got into trouble. Families talked amongst themselves, and the rumors reached Father's ears, so he had to give Garrick penance. He named Dalen as his successor and made his mother the first wife. You should know that he never intended to keep that decision in place. He was waiting on the talk to die down."

"How did Dalen take that—or did he know?"

"Well…he had an affair with Garrick's wife and left the Family, taking her with him. Threatened to bring the whole thing down, but that was a little over a year ago."

Dalen left? He wasn't on the list Rand gave him. Who else had he omitted from it? And why?

Dalen's stealing of Garrick's wife seemed like revenge enough. If Dalen was the UNSUB, tattooing women with the Family's logo would be another way to disgrace them and implicate them in the murders later. Maybe that's why he never retaliated in other ways. But it didn't explain his personal beef with Ty—if it was Dalen. Unless Garrick had fed him some kind of bogus junk about Tiberius to help him join the *let's hate Ty* club. But what could he have said to sway Dalen into a grudge like this? "Do I know this woman?"

"No. She made friends with Garrick on his business trips and joined the Family."

"Does she have a name?" He'd like to talk with her. She might know things, or she might not realize she knew things. This could be a break for him, and if she left Garrick, she would have no reason to refrain from answering questions about him. In fact, she might be all too happy to spill the tea.

"Carrie. Why?"

"This has been helpful, Lysander. Thank you." And yet Ty was lying. His entire job was focused on finding truth, letting truth bring justice, and he was concealing it like a common criminal. Hiding under all the lies and half truths. "But I have one more question. Have you heard any buzz about a son and mother disfellowshipped because he was carving the logo in animals and causing disturbances within the family? He'd be older."

The line was quiet. "No, but I could find out. Why?"

"He might be killing women in the Outer Banks."

Lysander hummed. "I'll try to find a way to secure the information without looking sketchy and text you if I get it."

"Great. This means a lot."

After he ended the call, feeling like a jerk, something niggled in his chest.

Carrie. The name sounded familiar. As if he'd seen it recently. He replaced the umbrella back in the metal can and retrieved the list of missing women from Blue Harbor and the surrounding areas, scanning the names.

His chest constricted. He had seen it and remembered because the spelling was unique. Not *C-a-r-r-i-e* but *C-a-r-r-i*.

Carri Evans.

Missing ten months ago from Kill Devil Hills. Her car had been found empty at a Food Lion, and there had been no video footage of the parking lot. She'd vanished.

Retrieving his cell phone from his pocket, he Googled the name in connection with a flower.

His search popped.

Carri could be short for carrion.

The corpse flower.

Kill Devil Hills, North Carolina
Friday, September 7
9:45 a.m.

Rain had mercilessly continued and slicked down the windows like tears, matching the ones on Mrs. Evans's cheeks. After Ty conveyed the new information in the group text, Selah sent him an address for Mrs. Evans in Kill Devil Hills, where Carri grew up.

Mrs. Evans lived in a two-story cedar-planked house on the beach. Sand dunes rose like mountains on either side of the home, and her private boardwalk was only steps from the semi-private beach.

Could Carri leaving Garrick have triggered his plan? On his hunt for his wife who'd left with Dalen, did he discover Ahnah and Bexley? Did his revenge plot take shape then?

Mrs. Evans sipped tea from a tiny china cup with red blooms. Her haircut was more for comfort than style and was streaked with gray, matching her weary eyes. "I was suspicious of the Family of Glory. I know a cult and commune when I see it, but Carri had been obsessed with Garrick. She met him when she was a server at Jimmy Jo's Bar and Grill." She handed Ty a photo of the woman. Average height, slender. Long, dark hair and dark eyes. Pretty smile.

"She's very lovely." Presently, they had no way to know if she was deceased. No evidence she'd been tattooed in flowers that were known to smell like rotting flesh, though beautiful.

Mrs. Evans went on to share the best about her daughter.

Kind and sweet to everyone. She lit up a room. If he had a dollar for how many times he heard that exact phrase… It might be somewhat true, but in his line of work, he discovered far more secrets about the "lights in rooms." Dark secrets. But he let a grieving mother grieve and think of her baby girl as a perfect human being with no dark parts, no ill behavior.

"Did you mention that he belonged to a cult?"

"I tried. But he was a smooth talker. Even I got caught up in him for a moment with the way he discussed the Family, and even the uglier sides—I'd seen them in the news a couple of times. I wasn't in love with him, though, and wasn't as enamored as Carri."

If anyone was a carrion flower, it was Garrick.

"After he had her in his grips, he isolated her from me and her friends and eventually took her to Asheville to his big fancy home. I had no contact with her for three years. Then she called me and said she was coming back to the Outer Banks Never said much about her time there. I met her for lunch at the Blue Marlin in Blue Harbor. I tried to coax her into telling me about her time in the Family, but she said things weren't as they seemed and that was it. We never talked about it again."

Mrs. Evans shrugged. "Two weeks later she vanished again from the grocery store. That was over ten months ago now. I assumed she'd had a change of heart and gone back, but I reported her missing anyway about four days later."

Had local law enforcement talked with Garrick? If Carri had left the Family with Dalen…had Dalen done something to her? Why didn't he report her missing? Did she think she was in the arms of a lover only to discover she'd been trapped into the arms of a madman who wanted revenge on Garrick and the Family?

"You think that flower killer person has her, don't you?" Mrs. Evans wiped her nose. "Because she's named Carrion and we call her Carri for short. I know it's a flower. But that's not what I named her after. He has to know that. She has to have told him it was my maiden name. Sharla Carrion. My husband and I divorced, but I kept his last name. It was easier."

"I'm not sure where Carri is, but we're doing everything in our power to find the person who might have taken her." A gust of wind knocked over something outside, and the clanging startled Mrs. Evans.

"I wonder if hunkering down and waiting out the hurricane is smart," she said. "What will you be doing?"

That was the million-dollar question. "I have family here, so…" Family that didn't even know about him. "If you think of anything, please call me." He stood and dreaded heading out in the downpour. The wind alone was fierce. News said it could get up to seventy miles per hour before landfall and then…then it was going to be unbelievable. He hunched forward, pushing against the gales to the vehicle. He'd been pushing against dark gales since this case had begun. But he wasn't giving in or backing down.

As he opened the car door, the wind assumed control, and it flew from his grip. He ducked inside, soaking, and put some grit into shutting the door. Once inside he called Owen.

He answered. "What's up?"

"Just left Carri Evans's mom." Glancing upward, he frowned. Rain pummeled the roof, making it hard to hear but he relayed the conversation to Owen. "Why wouldn't Dalen—if she was still with him when she left the Family—not report her missing? Why didn't Carri tell her mother about Dalen? What happened to make her want to leave without a trace? Is she in the clutches of our killer?"

"I firmly believe this killer is someone from the Family. While coming after you is personal, it feels like a shot at your father too, even if he did write you off. Maybe he talked of you fondly after you left. Showed remorse and regret, and it infuriated someone. Maybe they feared you returning to the fold and usurping their upcoming power."

"For every question we have, we accumulate more questions instead of answers." A streak of white-hot light flashed through the gunmetal-gray sky, and the car rocked. "We don't have much time left, O," he whispered. "And we don't have what we need." Any moment the text would come from Asa.

Evacuate.

"I know. It's getting nastier by the hour. I checked two houses and got zip. No way to check the private islands. Have you seen that water? Pass."

But women being held captive might be out there in an abandoned home. Their lives were in danger from their killer and a hurricane. There had to be a way to fight through the storm to rescue them. On the other hand, if they were wrong, Ty would be sailing straight into his grave.

Chapter Twenty-Two

Blue Harbor
Bexley Hemmingway's house
Friday, September 7
11:02 a.m.

Bexley had rushed home around eight a.m., leaving Josiah at
the SCU beach house. With this weather, she didn't expect
anything more dangerous than the hurricane, and Drew was
only minutes away. He could check on him or swing by and
pick him up if needed. No point in waking a sleeping bear, and
after his stormy mood last night when she'd informed him that
he was evacuating with the rest of the SCU team, she knew
he needed space.

She understood his desire to remain; it was her desire too.

For the past three hours, she'd worked on hurricane-proofing
her home. The windows had been boarded, and she'd filled the
bathtub with water. Battery-operated lanterns and other sources
of light had been scattered in each room. She'd brought in the

garbage can, patio furniture and small gas grill as well as put the generator in place.

Several of her neighbors had already left to go inland, but others were weathering it and making last-ditch efforts at buying groceries and supplies.

A tornado had touched down in Nags Head during the wee hours of the morning, doing a nasty bit of damage but with no fatalities. Storm damage alone in Charleston had felled trees and power lines, leaving widespread power outages in over a hundred thousand buildings.

Now Jodie was coming for them.

Meteorologist Tom Stanley was live on Channel 3 in his rain gear and helmet at the shores of Ocracoke, hollering into a microphone, his image blurred from the rivulets of rainwater running down the video camera lens. The cameraman wiped them, but it did no good.

"Folks, it's a challenge to stand out here. You can see how much strength I'm putting into keeping upright."

"Then use that brain and get out of there, you idiot." Why weather people thought they had to be some kind of storm junkie hero was beyond her. Viewers didn't need him putting his life at risk when all they had to do was look out their windows. "Tom, don't be a hero. Go back to the station," she mumbled, as she rubbed the tension tightening her neck muscles.

The lights blinked.

No. Not yet!

"Even if you've ridden out storms before, this one is different. Don't risk your life on riding out this monster," Tom said. "Heed the evacuation orders, folks. It's not only Hurricane Jodie with deadly winds, but flooding from storm surges you and your families need to consider. You only have two hours before surge floods are going to be too dangerous to cross. That's an estimate. It could be sooner."

With a boom of thunder, the lights flickered once more, and then the house went silent. Her breath caught in her throat. "Great," she muttered. Did she power up the generator now? She only had so much gasoline. No, this was insane. Leaving Ahnah, who wasn't safe, to be safe herself felt wrong on every level, but she was no help to her sister or her son if she was dead.

She had to go too. The window of opportunity was closing. Grabbing her phone, she called Josiah to let him know she would be joining them. All she had left was to pack a bag and she'd be on her way.

His phone went to voice mail. He was either still sleeping or ignoring her.

Great.

Growling and slamming her phone onto the counter, she stomped to her bedroom to pack a bag for evacuation. She opened the door, gasped and stumbled backward.

"You look surprised to see me, Bexley." He was kicked back on her bed dressed to the nines, and his expensive cologne permeated her room. How had he gotten inside? How long had he been inside, and why was he on her bed as if he owned the space?

"What—what are you doing in my house? How did you get in?" How could it be?

"I do whatever I want. I wanted in. I got in." His vile grin pierced her very core.

She backed farther into the hall and glanced toward the front door.

"I wouldn't make a mad dash. I know that's what you're thinking." He lazily swung his legs over the side of the bed. "I've come to get to you. That's why I'm here. It's time."

Bexley clutched her chest. "I'm not going anywhere with you."

"See, Bex," he said as he stalked toward her, "that's where you're wrong."

She needed a weapon, but her bat was by her bedside. He followed her gaze and chuckled. "You don't need that. Besides, you're a swing and a miss."

She turned to dart down the hall when his words froze her into place. "I have Josiah, Bexley. If you want him, you'll come with me willingly. Obediently." She pivoted as he stood in the hall by her room. She peered into his eyes, dark, cold and wicked.

"He's with the FBI in their beach house," she said. "I know you couldn't have breached it." He was bluffing and she now regretted assuming Josiah would be okay alone for a few hours. Once again, she might have made a costly choice.

He laid a hand on his chest. "Bex, I didn't have to breach it. He came to me willingly. He trusts me. And why shouldn't he? I've built quite the rapport with him."

She wanted to shout *liar!* But he wasn't lying. Things clicked into place. He'd pretended to be Abe, and built a friendship with her son. He was the source fueling Josiah's recent hatefulness and rebellion. He'd been filling his impressionable mind with carefully crafted lies. "I don't understand why you're doing any of this."

"You will."

"Do you have Ahnah?"

"Why do you ask questions you already know the answer to?" He held out his hand. "Put your hand in mine and come of your own accord."

If she ran, he'd catch her. If he didn't, he'd kill Josiah and Ahnah. But if she went with him, she was as good as dead too.

Why couldn't any of her choices be easy or clear?

She stared at his perfectly manicured hands, shock thrumming along her nerves, and placed her trembling hand into his.

Blue Harbor
SCU beach house
Friday, September 7
12:01 p.m.

"Look, I know the situation's grim and no one wants to stop the investigation," Asa said, "but it's dangerous. As soon as it passes, we'll fly back and pick up where we left off. But I'm saying it's time to go. Period. End of story."

Ty threw his head back and silently screamed at the direct order. His gaze bounced from Vi to Owen, both wearing sympathetic expressions.

"Why's it so quiet on that end?" Asa asked.

"Asa," Ty said, through a half groan, half sigh. "I can't leave, and it's not because I'm bent on finding this killer."

Violet twirled her index finger for him to get on with it and reveal the truth he'd been keeping from his SAC.

"Then what is it?"

"Bexley's son…"

"He's yours?" Asa asked reverently.

"Yes. I can't leave without him. Bexley won't go, but she is allowing me to take him. However, he's not making it easy, and if she doesn't change her mind, I can't leave her."

Asa blew out a long breath. "Team can't stay. Anyone going with us needs to be ready within the hour. Do what you gotta do. But don't do anything stupid, Tiberius. I mean it."

"I'll call her now. I'll make it happen. Have all of us together and ready on time." Even if he had to hogtie her.

"Be careful, Tiberius," Fiona said, from the other end of the line.

"I can stay," Violet said. "I'm not afraid."

"Well, John will be," Ty said. "You aren't only thinking about yourself anymore. He has a little girl—you have a little girl now. Go before it grows any worse." He turned to Owen and met his steely dark eyes.

Owen tapped his chest with his fist twice. "Ride-or-die, bruh. I'm staying. We can all drive out together."

"Call when you're safe," Asa said, and ended the connection. "You should go with Violet. If it hits faster than expected, you'll be out of the danger zone."

Owen didn't budge. "What, no *Top Gun* song to hum?"

"Now is not the time, O. You need to vacate the premises."

Owen stared him down. "I'm not going anywhere."

Violet left them in their standoff, and he called Bexley's phone to inform her that he was on his way with Josiah to pick her up.

Her phone went straight to voice mail. Where would she be that she couldn't answer her phone? He went downstairs and knocked on the room Josiah had been staying in. "Sorry to wake you, dude, but we have to go."

No answer. Bexley had mentioned he slept like the dead. Ty opened the door, but Josiah was gone. His gaming system was on his bed and the covers thrown off and crumpled on the floor. Didn't appear to be a struggle.

He clicked on Bexley's icon on his phone's location-sharing app, but it said *Unable to show location*. His heart went into arrhythmia as he raced back to the second floor.

"What is it?" Violet asked, wearing a black raincoat and pulling her rolling suitcase behind her.

"Bexley isn't answering her phone. I can't see her location." Where would she be? Why would her phone be off? "Josiah is gone. Did you see him leave? Did anyone see him leave?"

"No. But he's on ground level. We haven't been gone that long."

"Well, he's gone so it doesn't matter how long it's been!" he bellowed. He sighed. "I'm sorry."

No signs of anything broken. Windows were boarded. Josiah must have walked right out the door of his own volition. But with whom and to where?

"I understand. You want me to stay? I will," she said.

He shook his head. "We got this. Get out of Dodge." His phone rang. Selah. He answered. "What do you have?" He put her on Speaker.

"I narrowed down the Grangers who would be in their midfifties now. I have three names but only one fits. Gabriel Granger. Nothing on him until he turned seventeen—which would be after he left the Family of Glory. He got into some misdemeanor trouble until his thirties. That's when things turned serious. He's currently in prison for abducting a woman in Greensboro and holding her for three days. It's ugly. Torture. Sexual assault. My guess is that wasn't his first victim, just the one that got him caught. She escaped from a cellar and found a car driving down a lone highway. Flagged it down. I'm sending over a file with news articles and his photo. He looks like you—like your father. But he's not our guy. He's been in prison all this time."

"Thanks, Selah." He hung up. "How is my entire family insane and I'm not?"

"Your sanity is debatable." Violet smirked and Owen chuckled.

"Real funny. Time's running out. Get to steppin'." Ty all but shoved her to the door. When she'd left, he turned to Owen. "Let's go. Maybe Josiah went home and her phone died. Power's out all over. No point worrying until there's something to worry about, right?"

Owen nodded. "Right."

But they both knew that was a lie. They had a lot to worry about. Ty grabbed the keys, and they ran into the fierce wind and rain. Roads were already flooding in areas, and the sea churned like a furious leviathan ready to snatch and drown its prey. The car rocked, and he gripped the wheel to steady them on the road. Once they arrived at Bexley's, they parked and raced to the porch. Her phone must have died—her car was here.

Ty knocked but no one answered.

He turned the knob and it opened; hairs rose on his neck. The power was out and the house was eerily quiet. Not even a whisper. Only the howling wind and whipping rain beating the snot out of the roof.

"Bex? Josiah?" he called as he entered the kitchen, smelling the scent of coffee and cinnamon. No one answered, and his pulse quickened. Where were they? Why was the door unlocked?

"I don't like this," Owen said. "You take the east side while I go west. Clear the place."

Ty unholstered his Glock and inched through the dark house. A cold chill bubbled along his skin as he moved to Josiah's room. The door was open. He entered and cleared it, then moved to the bathroom, clearing it as well, then her office.

Ty's phone dinged with a text, but he ignored it.

"Ty," Owen called, and the tone in his voice sent Ty's world to a screeching halt.

A note card had been stuck to Bex's bedroom door with a knife.

I've killed. I've stolen almost everyone you care about. I'm not done. You can't stop me.

Ty read it once, then twice. Ahnah. Cami. Now he had Bexley and Josiah. This freak of nature hadn't left the island and was using the hurricane to his advantage. They never expected anyone but their own desperate selves to be out in this nightmare weather. It had been an oversight. A potentially deadly one. "I can't leave now." How was he going to fight a hurricane and this killer at the same time? He slumped on Bexley's bed and cradled his head in his hands, a temptation to pray entering his thoughts. Because nothing he'd attempted so far had proven successful. He'd believed in no one but himself, and he was spent, stretched as far as one man could be stretched, feeling it in every beat of his heart and in every breath. A deep aching pressure that wouldn't release. Like being enclosed in a tomb alive with little air.

He had no peace.

No hope.

No help.

Panic set in, shivering through his veins until he trembled. A dam of tears burst and he was powerless to stop them. "He has them. He's going to kill them and I'm going to be too late. Josiah will never know I was his father. Never know…never know that I loved him more than myself. How am I supposed to do this? He's won. He's ended my life without killing me."

"No. You're struck down, friend. But not destroyed. You're hard-pressed but not crushed." Owen sat beside him on the edge of Bexley's perfectly made bed. "We're not going to leave. We're going to clear our heads and find them." He tapped his fist to his heart as he said, "Together."

"I can't let you stay. If the hurricane doesn't kill us, he might. You go—"

"Tiberius, stop. If the tables were turned, would you leave me?"

"No," he whispered. "You know I wouldn't."

"Then why are you pushing me to do what your own stubborn self wouldn't do?" He leaned over and gripped the back of Ty's neck, bringing his brow to Owen's. "We are in this together." His grip tightened to deliver his resolute message. Ty might not have a single brother he could trust, but he had Owen. Like some divine blessing—if he believed in those things.

Ty nodded against his brow and then pulled back, wiping his

face and standing. "I'm going to check Josiah's room. Maybe the killer left a note there too."

"I'll call Asa, take the heat for us both."

"Thank you," Ty murmured, and tapped his chest as he left the room, knees like twigs about to snap in half.

His phone dinged a second time as a reminder he'd received an earlier text.

He gripped the wall. Ty wasn't ready to see photos, or a video, of his dead son and the woman he'd never gotten over. This would break him. He decided to take a chance. "God, if You're listening…" That was it, the only words he could muster. Right now, he had come to the end of himself. Bexley had been right. He'd been disappointed in his own ineptness. He'd fooled himself, and the reality terrified him.

He hesitated opening the text, his finger hovering over the unknown number, but he bit the bullet and tapped the text.

A sudden wave of relief enveloped him. The text was from the portrait guy from the Inky Octopus in Wilmington. He'd drawn the sketch of Smoothy, who had tattooed the Family's logo secretly on three of the victims.

His relief was short-lived. The hits kept coming regardless of his internal pleas for a reprieve.

He'd known the truth, but had been in denial, hoping shared blood would have meant at the very least civility.

But there was no question. No doubt of who this face belonged to.

Garrick Granger.

Chapter Twenty-Three

Blue Harbor
Bexley Hemmingway's home
Friday, September 7
12:42 p.m.

Garrick had been a sociopath since childhood. This sick flower girl fetish was something already percolating in his twisted brain, and he'd used his traveling as a cover for working in a tattoo shop, where he could hone his craft after practicing on prostitutes. He'd loved painting on blank canvases. What better canvas than flesh. To tattoo his creation and embed the logo would feed his narcissistic tendencies. It would be like owning those women unbeknownst to them, and maybe later he went back to make them his—permanently.

When he'd spotted Ahnah—previously thinking she was dead—he hatched a new sick idea. He must have spent more than a year stewing, plotting and planning with incredible patience.

Every move he'd made was meticulous and thought-out.

Even Skipper's confession and tangling the law up in Patrick Swain's business. Ty wasn't sure what he gained by that, but at some point, it would be clear—when Garrick decided to make it clear. And he would. He wouldn't be able to stop himself from revealing it. He'd want to lord it over Ty.

Nothing in the house indicated a struggle. He must have subdued Josiah from the beach house and used that to coax Bexley into leaving with him from here. She'd do anything for Ahnah and Josiah. Ty strode into Josiah's room. A total disaster.

Ty noticed Josiah's laptop. He'd forgotten it, then when he remembered last night, griped he'd needed it. Bexley was going to bring it back to the beach house for him. It might have something on it to help him. He opened it and it woke. Passcode. Ty growled and entered Josiah's birthday. Nothing. He looked around Josiah's room covered in *Call of Duty* merch. He typed in *Call of Duty*, and it opened up to a chat on Discord. The one he'd seen before.

Ty perched on the edge of Josiah's bed. The sheets smelled like fabric softener and teenage boy musk.

Abe: Meet up tomorrow. Your mom is crazy. The storm isn't that bad and I have a shelter. Get away from that witch. She never really looks out for you, you know this. I'll pick you up at the beach house. SCU will be gone right?

Josiah: Yeah. They usually leave early. See you at nine at the end of the street just in case.

Abe: I'll be there. No one has your back like me. Remember that. When no one has been there for you, I have. You're like a little brother to me. Or...a son.

A son?
Abe wasn't a teenager.

Bexley had never met him—giving Josiah space to be independent. She didn't monitor his activity online at seventeen, and the truth slashed through Ty like hot, jagged metal.

Abe wasn't a gaming friend. He was Garrick. When he'd seen Ahnah, he'd stalked her—too clever to approach her. He'd seen Bexley and he'd seen Josiah and done the math. He'd know she never consummated her marriage, so the only possible father of her son was Tiberius. Garrick began grooming him online. Ty quickly scrolled through message after message, proving his theory correct. Garrick befriended him. Became a good listener and built trust, preying on his deep need for a father in his life, someone who could give him advice and guidance.

And when he had what he wanted, when he knew Josiah fully trusted him, he began planting seeds of doubt about Bexley and his father—Ty. Grooming 101. The seeds became bolder; he grew more forthright in what he said until he had Josiah hating his mother and Ty. Only Garrick had never mentioned Ty by name. Only trash talk about a dad who didn't love him or want him, who wouldn't be there for him. No one would be there like good ole Abe, aka Garrick.

Ty rushed into the hall, listening to Owen talk to Asa from Bexley's bedroom. As he entered the living room, a shadow caught his eye on the porch. He pulled his gun and yanked open the door.

This time the shadow didn't run.

"Don't shoot me!"

Milo Brandywine. Bexley's client. "What are you doing here in this weather? Don't you know the eye is making landfall within hours?"

"I... I look out for Miss Hemmingway. She's real special, you know." Milo's dark eyes met his, and he rubbed his hands on his wet jeans. He was drenched head to toe.

"How long have you been here?" And why was he here? "Have you been peeping on her recently? Was it you I chased?

Did you steal the box of mementos from her closet and the photo and blanket?" Ty was ready to pummel him, except he had bigger fish to fry than some punk stalking Bexley.

"I didn't steal them. I—I wanted to be a part of the family. I didn't take any mementos. I took the photo and the blanket."

Then who stole the memorabilia? "Did you hurt her? Take Josiah?"

He shot his hands up in surrender. "Dude, no way! I came by to see if she needed help hurricane-proofing the house."

Ty's eyes narrowed as he stepped closer to Milo.

"Honest! I have boards and water and stuff in my truck. But when I got here, she was leaving."

"With who?" Ty demanded.

"I don't know. I didn't see his face. I was crouched behind the bushes, and it's raining pretty good if you can't tell."

"I don't need a smart mouth." He did need the truth. If Milo came to help, why not just knock on the door? "Why did you hide? Was he holding a gun to her head?"

"No. Nothing like that. Seemed like she knew him. It's just…" His face turned red. "Miss Hemmingway said I couldn't help anymore so I was going to do it without her knowing."

And how was he going to accomplish that without her hearing or seeing him? He wasn't being completely honest, but now was not the time to read him the riot act or debate his motives. Time wasn't on their side.

"He wore a suit. I saw that."

"Is it this guy?" He opened his phone to the sketch Smoothy had sent of Garrick.

"I don't know. A suit stood out. That's why I remember his clothes."

"Where did he walk her to?"

"Down the street a bit. To his car." Milo's eyes filled with moisture. "Was he a bad man? Did I mess up again? My dad was a bad man, and I didn't help my mom. But… I thought they knew each other. She walked right beside him like it was all good."

Join the Men Who Failed Bexley Hemmingway Club. No wonder the kid needed therapy.

"Did you get the make and model of the car?"

He pulled something from his back pocket. A soggy piece of paper, the ink smudged. This kid wrote down plate numbers. "This is excellent work, Milo." He must have followed them to the car, and the weather kept Milo from being spotted.

He could hug this kid. Stalking had indeed paid off. Maybe Ty was getting a leg up. Maybe... He glanced up. No. It wasn't divine help. It was nothing but a break, a coincidence.

He called Selah and gave her the plates to run. "I need this yesterday, Selah. You understand."

"I hear ya, Ty." Her keyboard clacked over the line. "Asa says you're not coming back, and Owen's being a stubborn but good friend sticking it out with you. Don't be stupid, though, okay?"

"Selah, *stupid* is my middle name. You know this."

Owen opened the door. "What's going on?"

"This is Milo. Milo saw Garrick take Bexley."

"How does he know it's Garrick?"

Owen and Ty kept their eyes on the kid, who hadn't bothered to leave. When this was over—if everything turned out okay—he'd have some kind of talk with him about stalking. "I know it's Garrick, aka Smoothy, from the tattoo studio. The artist sent me the portrait. I know who was in the car. I just want another layer of proof to put a nail in his coffin."

"Got it," Selah said.

Ty put the phone next to his and Owen's ears.

Here it comes.

"The car is registered to..."

"To?" Ty asked, drawing out the word. "Garrick Granger."

"No," Selah said. "Dalen Granger."

Chapter Twenty-Four

"What?" No. That couldn't be right. The portrait of Smoothy was Garrick, not Dalen. Garrick had left the embedded logo on customers. Not Dalen. "Are you sure?"

"I'm sure," Selah said.

He leaned against the door, the wind blowing rain on his face. "Are they in this together, O? Is Dalen setting up Garrick to take the fall? Or has Dalen been behind this from the beginning?"

"I don't know, man."

"Thanks, Selah." He ended the call.

"I know where he took her, Agent Granger," Milo said. "I followed them."

"Well, why didn't you lead with that?" he hollered, and Milo flinched. "Sorry. I'm worried about her is all."

"Where did he take her?" Owen asked.

"To a marina. They got on a big speedboat, and I couldn't follow. So I thought I'd come back and see what was left to be done to prep the house. My place is already done, and I want Miss Hemmingway to be safe. She said she wasn't leaving."

Ty noticed the tailgate of his truck down and materials inside. Seemed maybe he was telling the truth. Or he was using the hurricane proofing to simply skulk around her and her property. One crisis at a time. "Where is it? The marina?"

He gave them directions. "Milo, everything you've done is great, but you can't show up at Miss Hemmingway's without permission even to help with chores and stuff. It's stalking, bud. And that's illegal. Am I getting through?"

"Sure."

Pretty certain he wasn't. But now was not the time. "Go on home or evacuate the island. It's getting worse. I'll find her." He had no idea how, but for once Ty was a step ahead. No way Garrick or Dalen would know about Milo. If they did, he'd be dead.

Unless Milo was also a part of this. Was it his job to infiltrate Bexley's life? Was his story even real? Had he been groomed like Josiah? His story had been flimsy.

This could be another elaborate part of the game. A trap.

He stormed back into the house, Owen on his heels. Both of them dripped water onto the floors as they moved to Josiah's room and to the computer. "He might have mentioned his place in a chat with him. He's been grooming him, Owen. Goes back a solid year. I have no idea what he's made that child believe, but it's been nothing but antagonistic words toward Bex and the father he doesn't know. He's using him as a pawn."

"We'll figure it out." Owen scrolled through his phone. "I can use the boat landing address and see what's around. I'm thinking an island. Maybe one I've already flagged."

Ty didn't find anything in the chat about an island, and he kicked a shirt lying on the floor. Time was running out. He glanced down at Josiah's sketchbook. The shirt had concealed it, but now it was open, and he picked it up.

Landscapes. A portrait of Tiberius. He flipped until a sketch caught his eye of an island surrounded by marshy land and a monstrous house right smack-dab in the middle. The place didn't seem conjured from his imagination, and every other drawing was a real location.

He showed Owen the sketch.

Owen studied it. "I know where that is. 'Bout twenty miles south of Patrick Swain's place, and the marina is only ten minutes away."

Ty tossed the sketch pad and punched the wall, feeling his knuckles crunch and burn. "We can't make it twenty miles with a hurricane barreling down on us, and it's out in the middle of the water. We'll all die."

"They made it twenty miles," Owen countered. "The hurricane hasn't progressed much more since then. We can make it. We can do it. But it's going to take some faith in something greater than ourselves."

Ty didn't buck him. He was on a teetering seesaw at the moment.

Owen laid a hand on Ty's shoulder. "I don't say anything to you about faith and religion and God, and that's my mistake. I know you got jacked by your family. All your life was about being controlled and manipulated in the name of God to benefit them. You've been hurt. Betrayed. But that's a cult, brother. That has nothing to do with a very real God."

"Owen, now is not the time to preach me a sermon. Bexley and my son are on some godforsaken island and we may not be able to rescue them." Anxiety tightened his lungs and shot acid into his throat like a fire-breathing dragon.

"It's not godforsaken. No place is godforsaken, Tiberius. I'm not preaching. I'm telling you the truth. We need divine intervention here. Or we ain't gettin' 'em back."

Owen was right about one thing. They couldn't man a boat alone in a hurricane. If God was real and wanted to climb in a boat with them during the storm of his life, he wasn't going to say no. Not today. "Who's going to give us a boat?"

"Use your imagination." He smirked, then got serious. "It's time to go." He tapped his chest with his fist, and Ty mimicked it.

"This is a suicide mission, O."

"Ride or die."

He'd rather ride.

But he was probably going to die.

Blue Harbor Marina
Friday, September 7
1:10 p.m.

Debris, trees and a kid's bike hurtled across the road. "It's like we're in the *Twister* movie," Ty said, gripping the wheel to keep them steady. Trees and power lines littered the ground. Sand from the dunes swept across the road in twirling tornados, pecking the windshield like pebbles.

"Well, we don't have cows yet," Owen said.

"There are wild horses though."

"If a horse flies by, Ty, I might tap out."

According to his GPS, Blue Harbor Marina was only five minutes away. Tornadoes had been spotted out at sea.

"You rethinking this?" Ty asked as he put some muscle into keeping them in the right lane.

"I'm not thinking at all." Owen smirked, but his eyes mimicked the same dreadful anticipation bordering on fear that Ty felt.

Their destination was on the right, and they approached a parking lot, empty except for the one dark blue sedan registered to Dalen Granger. Slipping into ponchos was a mechanical response to the devastating weather. They wouldn't protect them from this storm.

Boats slammed against the waves as they scouted the marina for a boat with keys they could borrow. *Borrow* sounded better than *steal*. After all, they were federal agents. Stealing was frowned upon.

"We need something big and fast if we plan to make it to the island alive," Ty hollered against the whipping wind, his clothes sticking to his body like a second skin and rain slicking down his hair and running into his eyes. This was what it had come to—pilfering like bandits and pirating boats in the name of justice.

They hunched forward, working to hold their ground against the wind at their front, and fighting through the stinging rain pelting their faces and blurring their vision. "Remember that true story movie with George Clooney about that boat in a hurricane?"

"No," Owen yelled.

"Okay, good."

Ty boarded a charter boat and climbed into the cockpit. He tried a console underneath the radio. Then he hurried back to the stern, waving his arms and signaling to Owen. "Yes!" he hollered.

Owen rushed down the slip and skidded to a halt. "Are you kidding me right now?" He pointed to the name painted on the back of the boat.

Sea Flower.

"Maybe it's a sign!" He could care less if it had an ominous vibe going. The boat came with keys. "Cut the ropes and come on!"

"A sign from who?" Owen retrieved his knife from his pants pocket. He sliced the ropes, then jumped on board and ducked into the cockpit with Ty.

"I'll take a sign from anyone or anything. The stars. Even God."

Owen ran his hand over his face, clearing drops of water. "I think we're gonna need a bigger boat."

The charter rocked, and Ty grimaced from the nausea. "Ha ha."

Ty turned the key, and the boat hummed to life; Owen tossed him a life vest and began securing his own. "Just FYI, it's been a hot minute since I manned a boat." Ty slipped on his orange vest and buckled it, pulling the strap tight.

Owen sat in the chair next to him and shook his head. "Why did I need to know that?"

"You didn't."

Ty's attempt to be funny fell flat as a wave crashed against the boat, tossing them.

"Hey, maybe this is like riding a bike." He'd maneuvered them out into the water. "Where to?"

"South. Go south!" Owen groaned. "I'm gonna be sick." His skin turned sallow.

"Hold your breakfast." Ty powered ahead, the waves clobbering the boat.

Twenty miles. Twenty miles was doable.

He hoped.

They powered through the dark, choppy waters. His stomach jackknifed as he lost his sea legs. Next to him, Owen gripped the rail, bouncing uncontrollably and pursing his lips.

Farther out, a cluster of small islands surrounded by marshy land came into blurred view. In the center of the small islands surrounded by forest and foliage stood a large mustard-yellow home on stilts with shaker siding and a large turret with windows. Was that where he was holding all these women? Like Rapunzel?

"Look! That must be the boat he brought Bexley over on." Approaching a private dock, Ty eased off the gas, unsure if they'd be able to dock this boat. The storm was increasing in force dramatically. But another boat had been docked. She was here. They were all here.

Marshland covered most of the area. "He must dock here and take a canoe through the narrow channels. No other way to approach the home."

But now a majority of the water had been sucked out from a reverse storm surge. Instead of the wind pushing water inland, the force of the fierce winds had resulted in pushing water outward, leaving sand, mud and debris to trek across.

"What do we do?" Owen asked.

"Let me dock this thing and we'll figure it out." Did they take a chance on walking through this marshland up to the island house? If the eye made landfall soon, the sound could return the water with destructive force, leaving them powerless.

He cut the boat engine and threw out a rope, working to attach it to the wooden beams.

"Leave it already! It's not worth it. Guy's insurance will cover it." Owen motioned him to follow, and Ty leaped from the boat onto the dock. The wind was coming from the north at their backs. This wouldn't be an easy trek. Leaving on their life vests, they began the battle, and Ty gripped Owen as they fought to stay upright.

"This is crazy!" Owen said through a nervous laugh.

"We'll look back on it with fond memories." Bits of marsh grass and sand pelted Ty's face and neck. He kept his head down and hunched, protecting his eyes the best he could manage.

Owen sank to his knees and growled. Ty pulled him from the sludge acting as quicksand. They only had about ten yards to go to reach the house but it felt impossible. Like miles.

Pushing through the gunk, they dodged flying trees. Forced to the ground by the gales, they clawed their way toward the house. Mud and sand slipped under Ty's nails and sailed up his nose and into his mouth. He squinted and continued the trek. A maze of boardwalks was up ahead.

His leg muscles spasmed and bits of shell sliced into his palms. From the wounds and traces of marsh debris on her body, Ty imagined Cami running from this place, slipping into the dark water and attempting an escape. The same grit and nettles digging into her feet and slashing at her skin. Fear fueling her to risk the torture that would come if she failed and enduring it with hopes the team would come to her rescue.

Ty had let her down.

He could redeem his lost efforts. He'd bring Garrick or Dalen or both of them to justice, give Cami's family closure and hope they could all forge ahead into some kind of new normal, but the office would never be the same without her. Their lives would never be the same.

Bexley, Josiah, Ahnah. The other women trapped. They kept him moving, but exhaustion overwhelmed his body and he couldn't catch his breath. He needed renewed strength. Not his own strength but something far greater and powerful—more powerful than this hurricane—to allow him to continue. Owen was right.

Lightning pierced the black sky, and the next peal of thunder rattled Ty's chest.

"You know I must love you something fierce, bruh, to willingly fight a storm for you," Owen yelled.

"You had the chance to back out!" Ty hollered as rain blew down his throat, choking him with sand. He coughed and crawled as the storm battered and beat them down.

Blood ran down Owen's cheeks and cuts littered his hands, but he pushed onward, never leaving Ty's side. Ty owed him. He would buy him coffee for a year or pay for his fancy suits to be dry-cleaned until he retired.

"And leave you to your own devices? Not a chance."

"Almost to the boardwalk. We can do this," Ty said.

"Ty!" Owen pointed upward, and Ty strained to see against the downpour, shielding his eyes.

Above, a funnel began shooting down over the water.

"Tornado!"

Chapter Twenty-Five

Kipos Island
Friday, September 7
2:02 p.m.

The tornadic waterspout widened, and headwinds held them at bay. Branches, driftwood and planks ripped from nails soared like flying monkeys through the atmosphere.

"We ain't gonna make it," Ty hollered, but Owen hung on to him with a secure grip.

"Yes, we are! Muster some faith!"

The funnel began moving right for them, the water angrily churning and roaring. If the tornado hit the house, it would result in complete destruction, but Ty would not back down now.

Forcing himself to pitch forward, fighting the torrential storm and winds, he pressed on with Owen at his side, neither of them willing to give up. As they inched toward the maze of boardwalks leading out to more marshland and one to the house, a portion of railing ripped from the nails with a crack and came hurtling in their direction. Ty dove onto Owen, the end of the railing clipping his hip with a sharp, stabbing pain.

Owen laid a wet hand on Ty's head and ruffled it. "Close one." He pointed at the funnel cloud. "Look! It's changing direction. Thank God!"

Ty winced but looked on, stunned. That thing should have barreled straight into their path. But tornados were unpredictable. That's all it was—unpredictability. "Almost there now, bruh."

"I see why you hate hurricanes," Owen said. "Don't ask me to go on any water trips for a long, long time."

"Fair enough. Also, I kinda wanna sing 'Waterfalls,' but it feels a little inappropriate."

"Nor does it make sense, but when has that ever stopped you?" he hollered.

Today. Every muscle burned and ached from working to maintain an upright position, not to mention the weight of his waterlogged clothing.

"Asa can never, ever know about this."

"I'll take it to the grave." Owen laughed, then coughed again.

Once they finally made it to the boardwalk, they toppled over the railing. Lightning flashed and flickered.

"Not to make light here, O, but this weather reminds me of the moment before Gozer made its entrance in *Ghostbusters*. Just sayin'."

Owen shook his head. "Maybe quit sayin'."

The house loomed before them. Massive with windows from floor to ceiling and two sets of stairs leading to a main door at the second level.

Something about this house felt familiar. Had he been here before? Seen it before?

He shook himself out of the disjointed thoughts. Garrick was holding women hostage and he traveled often, which meant he probably had a state-of-the-art security system.

No lights on inside.

If things worked in their favor, the power would be out, meaning no access to the security system.

"You take the first level, clear it. I'll go up those stairs and clear level two. Then meet me at the second floor, and we can do the top together."

Owen clasped the back of Ty's neck. "I'm praying for ya, brother."

"If I pray too, will He hear me?"

Squinting, Owen smiled. "Yeah. He'll hear you."

Ty wondered if He already had—they'd made it this far. Somehow the impossible had become possible, and it couldn't be attributed to adrenaline. And neither could the tornado turning at the last second. But divine intervention? Nah. That would mean... No. No, he wasn't going there.

Now they had a whole other kind of hurricane to battle.

Owen went under the house to the back door while Ty crept up the slippery wooden stairs to the second-floor patio under the middle of the turret, where a door beckoned him to enter. Sidling into a corner between the window and the glass door, he peered inside.

No lights. No noise. Didn't appear to have any power. Nerves throbbing, he reached for the doorknob and twisted. The door opened. Guess he didn't expect someone to show up in a hurricane.

Or he did and wanted Ty to walk right into his trap.

Blood whooshed in his ears as he drew his Glock and slipped inside, dripping on the tile flooring. No hiding he was here. He'd leave wet, muddy footprints all over this house. So much for an element of surprise.

Crouching and surveying the dark surroundings, he concocted his plan. Start with what he could see and then clear room by room before moving upstairs. The home was masculine, done in earthy coastal tones. Tasteful and expensive. He caught a faint whiff of lemon and pine-scented cleaner. Not a speck of dust. Who did the cleaning? Would he risk a cleaning crew? Where were the women being held, and where were Bexley and Josiah?

Ty surveyed the open living concept, spotting a hallway that flanked the living room. Which way to go? Right or left?

He listened. Complete silence. Why wasn't Garrick using a generator? Was he planning on evacuating? It was too late for that now.

Keeping low, his breath shallow, Ty crept down the hall on the left, finding two bedrooms and a bathroom. Clear. He hurtled down the right hallway and found one more bedroom and bath and a theater room with only two chairs. Clear.

On his way back into the living area, he noticed a bookshelf that jutted too far out from the wall.

Odd.

Where was O? He should have cleared the ground level by now and made his way up the stairs into the living area on this floor. Inching closer to the wall, Ty noticed the crack.

A false front.

Carefully, he opened the hidden door and slipped through, his gun poised, ready for confrontation.

Silence.

Before him stretched three glossy black doors on his right and four on the left.

He cracked open the first door on the left. Pungent scents of ink permeated the stale air, and tattoo equipment rested in the corner, but the room was vacant. Definitely the correct house.

Moving to the right, he checked the opposite room. Empty except for a twin bed with expensive sheets. A chain had been anchored to the wall. He cleared each empty identical room.

Last two doors.

He chose the one on the left and entered.

Ty's lungs deflated and he lowered his weapon. What was going on? His heart hammered against his ribs and his mouth dropped open as he tried to grasp what he was seeing.

Garrick sat in a chair, staring right at him with dark, vacant eyes.

His throat had been slit from ear to ear, but the left side near the ear was shallower as if someone had hesitated—or toyed with him before ripping through his flesh and veins. Blood stained his unbuttoned white dress shirt and pooled dark and sticky on the concrete floor. Bound to the chair with thin ropes, Garrick had prominent swelling along his jaw and dried crusty blood caked along his split lip; burn marks and shallow cuts riddled his torso where he'd been brutally tortured.

If Garrick was dead, where was Dalen? Did he kill Garrick with plans to pin this on him?

Cracking the door, he peered down the hall. Coast was clear. He darted to the last room.

Empty.

Where were Bexley and Josiah? Where were the women he'd been keeping in these rooms?

He had two options for where to go next—one was a dead end, but this place was full of secrets. Ty approached the dead end and felt along the wall until he found a small button under the chair rail. He pushed, and a door opened for him.

Dozens upon dozens of flowers arranged in pots filled the room, their sweet fragrance permeating his senses. The fountain in the middle must be a grand focal point, though the water wasn't flowing during the power outage. But what struck him with an alarming force were the seven huge birdcages circling the room.

Occupied cages.

Women in several stages of flower tattoos sat with their knees drawn up and their heads resting on them. No one moved. No one spoke.

This was how Cami had spent her last weeks on earth. Caged, confined and controlled by the will of a madman.

"I'm federal agent Tiberius Granger. I'm getting you out of here." He'd figure out the logistics later. No one was leaving this house or island. The earlier tornado had veered away from the home, sparing them, but that didn't mean another one—a larger one—couldn't pop out of the sky at any moment.

A woman raised her head at his presence, and then, one by one, all gazes were on him. Hollow eyes with a sliver of hope glimmering.

None of those eyes belonged to Ahnah, Bexley or Josiah.

Three cages were empty.

Where were they?

Chapter Twenty-Six

Kipos Island
Friday, September 7
3:12 p.m.

How was he going to unlock the cages? He could shoot off the lock, but that might bring Dalen. The entire house shook, creaked and groaned. Fear crept into his muscles, pulsing and gyrating, but he focused, forcing himself to remain calm. "Does he have a key? Does anyone know where it is?"

A blonde woman with almost her entire body covered in flowers sniffed. "It's in the drawer over there. By his recliner. With the remote."

What exactly did that remote do? He rushed to the table and pulled open the slender drawer. Inside was a remote control and a single key on a piece of twine. He grabbed it and headed back to her.

"What's your name?"

He'd burned the photos of the missing women into his memory. She had purple irises tattooed across her body. "Are you Iris Benington?"

She nodded.

"It's okay now. I'm Tiberius," he said soothingly. "He isn't going to hurt you anymore. We're going to help you."

"Thank you. I—I don't know how long I've been here."

"Over ten months, ma'am. I'm so sorry."

"Ten months…my mom. She had cancer when I was taken. Stage four breast cancer." Tears bloomed in her eyes. "Do you know… Is she…?"

A lump formed in Ty's throat as he recalled Violet's visit to the family. "Let's focus on getting out of here, okay?" His heart smashed into bits; Iris's mother passed away four months ago.

The lock clicked, and he opened the cage.

She reached her arm through, out into the open. To freedom. But then withdrew.

"It's okay, Iris. You don't have to stay in this prison anymore."

As Iris stepped from the cage, others perked up and began asking questions.

"Have you heard from my mom and dad?"

"How are we going to get out of here?"

"Help me!"

Tiberius moved to the next cage, the woman covering her breasts with one arm, the other hanging limp at an odd angle. When she made eye contact, he immediately recognized her.

Catherine Overly.

"Hi, Catherine. Let's get you home."

Sobs erupted. "I'm so sorry. I should have never—"

Ty touched her hand. "None of this is your fault. You did nothing wrong."

Panes of glass cracking and shattering drew his attention. Must be an outer window. He had to move faster. Find his family. Find Owen. Subdue Dalen and at this point ride it out in the safest part of the home possible.

He quickly unlocked her cage.

"Okay, all we need is—"

"Love?" a deep male voice asked.

Ty froze, light-headed, and discreetly pocketed the key.

"You'll need more than *love* to save you."

"Dalen." He pivoted and scrunched his eyebrows, confusion short-circuiting his thoughts.

Ty's hands tingled like pins and needles, and his heart lurched into his throat. He'd been under Ty's nose exactly like Ty suspected, like Violet had said. Inserting himself into the investigation and into their lives.

Dark, familiar eyes met his, although they no longer resembled those of a human being but a maniac locked into a dark fantasy, malevolent and drunk with power. In his left hand, he held a gun.

"Lysander," he breathed.

Lysander looked more cover model than monster. He'd been a good kid, helping Mom in the garden and drawing. Often coming to Ty for help with shading or angles. He'd only been fourteen when Ty left. What was this all about?

"You have a wife and a kid."

"Do I?" He cocked his head. "Do you know how many babies are floating around that house? A lot. You like this house?" He motioned around with his arm as if Ty was here to hang out for a barbecue. "It's a design I found in your room."

That's why it seemed familiar. Ty had sketched the design over twenty years ago.

"Not the garden, though. That's all my creative license." His gaze landed on Iris Benington frozen outside of her cage and Catherine up on her feet, her good hand on the unlocked door to freedom.

"I see you've met most of my garden girls."

"Where are Ahnah and Bexley and Josiah?"

"Drop your gun and slide it toward me." He pointed his own

gun at one of his victims, then at the two who'd been freed. "Back inside now."

The women returned to their prisons. "Tiberius, I'll ask one more time politely, and then people are going to bleed. Would you be so kind as to drop your weapon and slide it over here?"

Lysander had already murdered too many and was capable of anything. Ty acquiesced, then raised his hands in surrender. "Where are they?"

The corners of Lysander's lips quirked. "All in good time."

"We don't have time. If your deranged brain hasn't figured it out by now, we're in the middle of a hurricane, and it's only growing stronger." Where was Owen? He should have made it to the second floor and to the open secret door leading to this room.

"I have enough time to do whatever I want, Tiberius. I brought you here. I have not only the upper hand but the only hand. Speaking of hands, I'd say sorry about breaking Cami's if I were. I'm not. What a piece of tail. Right? I know you had a taste of that in Barbados. Cami told me her whole life story. It's pathetic."

Ty ground his teeth but stood firm, refusing to bite the dangling bait and revealing no emotion. Lysander wanted emotion. Wanted to see Ty's suffering over the loss of Cami, wanted him to beg for his life and the lives of those he cared about. Wanted him to plead for mercy to spare these women.

They both knew he wouldn't spare a soul.

His brother had been clear he planned to destroy Tiberius. The only way to succeed was to take away Bexley and his son. He'd been outmatched and outwitted since the get-go. Now they were face-to-face and almost on equal footing. Ty didn't have a gun anymore, but he had Owen—an element of surprise if Lysander believed Ty came alone.

Where was O?

Could Ty overpower his baby brother?

"She was feisty. Didn't matter how much punishment I doled out, she kicked against the goads. It should do your heart good knowing she believed you'd come for her—that the team would come. She was aware of the press conference. Knew you were on the island searching. I imagine the knowledge that you were so close gave her hope and kept her fighting. In the end, you failed her. I made sure she knew that before I shoved the Xanax down her throat. Take comfort, though. I didn't let her die alone. I sat with her as she grew sleepy, and the last thing she heard was my voice telling her this was your fault. Taking her was consequence of your sin."

His sin? "What did I do to you? What sin did I commit? You were only a boy when I left."

His dark eyes grew black as night as he stepped closer, the gun trained on Ty's face. "You were going to take away the one thing I loved most in the world."

"Mom left a year before, Lysander. I didn't take our mom."

"No, you took Ahnah."

Ahnah.

This was revenge over Ahnah? How? "Lysander, I didn't take Ahnah. I was booted out with guards and gates. You were there. You saw it with your own eyes."

Lysander bared his teeth. "I overheard you and Bexley plotting to leave the Family with Ahnah. You were going to condemn her for eternity and leave me without her. I couldn't let that happen."

Jagged pieces of the past began to fit, but only the edges. "What did you do?" Had he been scheming even then?

"What needed to be done. I saw you bedding Bexley on more than one occasion, and I was going to be loyal to you because after you married her, I could ask for Ahnah and be betrothed until she turned sixteen and could marry me. I'd already been working on a plan for Garrick to marry so we could be free to marry as well, but you ruined it. I had to readjust. And I did. Garrick was easy to manipulate. All I had to do was feed him breadcrumbs and make him believe it was his idea to go to Father with what you'd done—and what you were planning to do."

Rand had known he was leaving the Family all along. That's why he disfellowshipped him. It would be easier to save face than have his congregation know his favorite son had left of his own free will. Otherwise, he would have forgiven him the indiscretion.

"Things didn't go according to plan, though, did they? Bexley ran anyway with Ahnah," Ty said.

"And all these years I thought she was dead."

"So did I, Lysander. I had nothing to do with that." Why was it still his fault?

"No, but you planted the idea in her to leave and to take Ahnah."

"Do you know the things Garrick did to Ahnah? She wasn't safe. If you loved her, wouldn't you want to protect her?"

"I was handling things!" Lysander bellowed. "Delicately," he added with more control. "He was the Lord's anointed, but he was still flesh and blood, and men have accidents."

He'd been planning to murder Garrick and make it look like an accident. Then Ty could ask for Bexley's hand, Ahnah would be free from Garrick's wickedness, and Lysander could be with Ahnah. Except Ahnah and Lysander had only been kids.

"Well, slitting him from ear to ear doesn't exactly look like an accident. But it does put you in position to take office after Rand dies. You going to kill him too?"

His eyes widened as if he didn't expect Ty to know Garrick was dead. "Why would I want someone else's kingdom when I can build my own? I simply need Father's company to fund it."

He wanted his own place where he could do whatever he wanted with whomever he wanted. The dots connected. Lysander had seen Skipper dump the body of Jenny Davis and used the ammunition to force Skipper into confessing in order to implicate businessman and rival land developer Patrick Swain. His own property was a short distance away. That was the ulterior motive, the puppet strings. Ty had done exactly what Lysander had wanted him to do. "You want Patrick Swain's land for this new kingdom." Lysander would rule here, and his followers would have property not far away, set up exactly like Rand arranged his own empire in the mountains.

Roaring sounded overhead. The glass ceiling was underneath solar panels—blocking out the view of the women from airplanes and drones. He could roll the panels away or keep them in place; either way, sunlight entered, growing his flowers and plants. Standing here, they could be impaled by shards at any second if the winds tore away the panels.

"Of course I want it. And guess who's selling it to me now that I've shown him what I can do if he doesn't cooperate?" He bowed as if he'd been applauded for a perfect performance.

"In scouting prime property, you stumbled upon Ahnah. You said it was Garrick's job—that he often traveled—but you lied. Like you lied about being married and having a son. I wouldn't suspect you."

It had worked.

"But Ahnah wasn't into you. Bexley had made it clear what the Family was—a cult that specialized in degrading women— and that made you angry. It was my fault, Bexley's, and even Garrick's that she didn't believe anymore. This is how you exact your revenge, even on Ahnah for rejecting you. No one rejects you. These women, like Cami, came here with you willingly."

Lysander still believed the doctrine of the Family, but he would add his own teachings and rules, which justified his sick need for collecting women. That sickness had nothing to do with his revenge plot, but he'd used it to his advantage to bring Tiberius to the island.

"Where are Ahnah, Bexley and Josiah? Where have you locked them away? Other hidden rooms?"

Lysander's nostrils flared, and a vein pulsed at his temple. "I gave these deflowered sluts a chance at rebirth. To give them back their purity that they willingly gave me and men before me. I offered them an open door to say no, but they said yes."

That's why they were in cages and Ahnah wasn't. She hadn't said yes. Hadn't come willingly. She could have been dead for the past week, her body buried in the marsh.

"They belong to me now. Purified and one flesh."

Ty gawked. "What happened to you? This...this isn't you."

Lysander laughed, hard and cold.

The monster raging on the outside demanded attention. Horrific tugging and tearing deafened them as a portion of the solar roof was wrested from the house and a pane of glass shattered to the tile, spraying the room. Women shrieked and glass dotted Ty's cheeks, leaving stings. He touched his face. His fingers were smeared with blood. Wind howled and swept through the room, rattling the cages as the women begged for help, for freedom.

"Lysander, we have to leave this room or all of us, including you, will die."

"You are going to die. You're right in saying that, you selfish vain fool." His mouth spread into a wicked grin. "And the beauty is, I'm not the one who's going to kill you. I will enjoy the show." He turned toward the hallway. "It's okay, bud. Come on in. Meet your dad."

Chapter Twenty-Seven

Tiberius's knees turned to rubber as he forced himself to look at the open doorway. A shadow appeared, and then his son walked into the room, eyes hardened and jaw set.

Until he saw the women.

His eyes widened and his mouth formed a perfect O. Then he turned to Lysander. "Why are these women in here, Lysander?"

A new wave of terror engulfed Ty. Josiah knew Ty's brother's true identity. What else did he know? How long had he known?

Lysander remained calm, pointing the gun at Tiberius. "These women are here of their own volition. They live here, and they're paid to dance for me. Like dancers for kings in the past. Look at them, son. Wouldn't you want them to dance for you?" He waggled his brows.

"Do not call him *son!*"

"Why not? I've been the father he's never had."

Josiah shoved his hands in his pockets. "Like strippers?"

"Yes, like strippers."

Josiah frowned. "But women died, and they believe Ahnah was taken by whoever took these women."

"I don't have Ahnah. You've had free rein of the home. Have you seen her? No. Would I actually leave you here alone if I had abducted her? Abducted anyone? I didn't kidnap these women. They didn't want their lives. They had reasons to run from family," he said calmly, lies oozing like silk from his tongue. Lies that made sense to a vulnerable, groomed teenage boy.

But that explained how he brought Bexley here without Josiah knowing. He'd left him on his own, and that too had built trust. It was in Josiah's eyes. He was swallowing down Lysander's trumped-up story like it was sugar.

Rain and debris littered the solarium. Above, the glass panes and solar panels that remained convulsed. The eye of the hurricane was approaching like a freight train barreling off its rails.

Josiah flinched and edged toward the wall and away from the open ceiling. "And the dead women?"

"Pill poppers and, to my regret, I did supply them. Unfortunately, they overdosed, and I left them at the lighthouses to be found. Not everyone would approve of our arrangement here."

"He's lying, Josiah. He's a murderer. He has Ahnah and your mother. He kidnapped her while you were alone here this morning. These women have families and lives and homes, and he's been messing with your head."

Lysander sighed and skirted a puddle of water. "Josiah, I do not have your mother or your aunt. Did you see me bring her back? No. You saw me bring in supplies. Ahnah hated your mom, and she probably left of her own accord for a new life. Your mother has never loved you. Women's hearts are fickle. Remember Bree?"

Josiah nodded.

"She toyed with you, and then she crushed you by dating David. I was there for that. Who was at your last pinball competition at the arcade?"

"You."

"Because your mom had to take care of other fickle women. They've always been her priority. You know that. Look." He pointed to the open cage where Catherine Overly sat. "Door's wide open and she hasn't left or denied what I've said."

She was too afraid to speak. He held power over them, and Ty was defenseless while Lysander held a gun.

"I didn't kill anyone. Men like me enjoy the pleasure of women. I haven't done anything to them they didn't ask me to do. I have never forced myself on them. But this man...he abandoned you."

"No!" Ty insisted. "I never knew you existed."

"But he did, Josiah. He came to the Outer Banks because the sheriff believed the islands housed a serial killer. Your mom reported Ahnah missing, and he believes I have her. Again, I do not. Let me ask you, in all the time he's been here, been in your home, played video games with you, has he once revealed he's your father?"

"No." Josiah snapped his head in Ty's direction. "Is that true? Did you know this whole time? When we played video games and talked about art? Did you know you were my father?"

Ty's tongue stuck to the dry roof of his mouth, and he nodded.

Josiah's nostrils flared and he backed up next to Lysander, allowing his uncle to drape an arm around his shoulders.

"We were going to tell you after we found Ahnah."

"Lie!" Josiah boomed. "You've known all this time. My mom lied about you."

"She's a liar," Lysander singsonged. "She'd rather you be miserable than tell you the truth. What kind of mom is that?"

Josiah shouted exactly what kind of woman she was. Lysander had gotten into his head, filling him with lies, and he'd swallowed them down until they rooted in his heart. Ty could not undo a year's worth of grooming in five minutes, and they needed to find a safer place where glass couldn't slice them open.

Lysander had become what Josiah needed—an excellent cult leader if ever there was one.

Ty's son was loyal to a psychopath.

"Josiah," Ty pleaded. "I love you."

"You have a funny way of showing it," Josiah said, the venom in his voice tearing through Ty. But he did love this boy more than he'd loved anyone. All lanky arms and green eyes and unruly hair.

Josiah's hands balled into fists. "You don't even know me."

Ty stretched out his arms for him. "I want to."

Lysander tsked him. "Now, when you're caught, you're trying to backpedal. If you wanted to know him, you'd have told him. Bexley would have told him years ago."

"Your family isn't criminal," Josiah shouted. "She lied. Your father is a pastor of a big church. Lysander told me everything this morning and why he approached me with a different name. Because he didn't know what kind of lies Mom or you told me about my family."

"No," Ty said. "None of that is true."

"Remember what you said about your father?" Lysander patted Josiah's shoulder. "How you wished he was dead, that you could be the one to look him in the eye and blow him off the planet? Now's your chance. You know in wartimes, warriors would bring their captives back, and their sons would run them through with a sword to bring them into manhood. It's biblical. God allows it in wartime. God called David a man of war. Approved of the slaughters, sanctioned them. Men. Women. Children and even babies. Oh yes. And animals."

"This isn't war." Ty held out his hands again. "You don't want to do this. I know you're angry and we have a lot to talk about, but this is murder, not war."

"The written word says an eye for an eye," Lysander said.

Josiah's eyes darkened, and a bolt of panic shot through Tiberius. No longer did he look like Ty but like Lysander. Most of his family was unstable. Had he passed on some kind of broken gene to him?

Lysander offered the gun to Josiah.

"Don't do it, son."

"Don't call me *son*. I am not your son." He accepted the weapon and aimed it at Tiberius, but his hand shook, and the wind howled as more solar panels ripped away. One of the women shrieked when a shard of glass fell onto her cage.

"I—I…" Josiah was unsure. He was not a murderer. He wouldn't do it. Couldn't. No matter how angry he was at Ty. But it wasn't Josiah who had Ty's attention.

It was Lysander.

Jaw working, he'd cast a glance in Josiah's direction. "Do it, Josiah. He'll wash away with the storm, and we'll be a family. I'll take you to meet your grandfather, who will love and adore you. You can live here with me on this island once I establish my own following, but you'll like Asheville too. We have to spend some time there until then, but you'll never want for anything."

"I don't know," Josiah said through trembling lips.

"What don't you know?" Lysander said, gritting his teeth.

Josiah wasn't acquiescing. The profile. Narcissist with a god complex. Untouchable. Invincible. Punishing those who didn't obey his commands. If Josiah didn't comply, Lysander would kill him.

And force Ty to watch.

Josiah wasn't a killer, but if he wanted to live, he had to obey Lysander's order. To save his son, Tiberius had to go against every fiber of his being. This confused, brainwashed boy who desperately wanted a father's love had Ty's love but didn't believe it.

And Ty needed to build on that lie, unravel his son to the

core in order to force his hand. Deep down Josiah had a moral compass and knew murder was wrong.

Ty was in a war created by an enemy that lived on lies and kicked weak areas searching for a way in, a way to manipulate thoughts and appeal to desires until he turned it into reality. Lysander and Patrick Swain both provided services to change fantasies into realities. Patrick for money and Lysander for souls.

Tiberius inhaled deeply, pushing back a dam of tears and a wall of nausea. He was on the precipice of mentally and emotionally ripping his child apart, but Josiah could be mended. The chip in his shell, the brokenness, wouldn't be wasted. He'd bear the scars, but he'd live to tell his story. Bexley would see to it he had counseling and the truth that his father had to wound him to rescue him.

"We're probably all going to die anyway." Ty gave him a reason to justify pulling the trigger. "I'll tell you the truth. Yes, I knew this entire time. Lysander's right. And when this case is over—if we live through it—I'm returning to my life in Memphis. I like it. I do what I want. I get dating action without anyone in the way. I'm free."

Josiah's eyes narrowed and grew moist. "Free from me?"

"Free from every nuisance and interruption. I didn't know Bexley was pregnant at the time, but I've had a good seventeen years. Distraction-free." Vomit hit the back of Ty's throat, and he balled his agony in fists to hide the truth. He often had to tamp down emotion and reaction when interviewing serial killers. He was practiced. But nothing had prepared him for this performance. This wasn't a killer. It was his kid.

Josiah's lips tightened and his jaw tweaked. The vein running along his brow popped in angry purple against red splotchy skin. Ty was accomplishing his dreaded mission.

"I mean, you're a cool kid, I guess, but I'm not cut out to be a father..."

Josiah hadn't ever handled a real gun, which was far different from a controller to a video game. He might not hit a major artery. Ty only needed to push him over the edge.

Almost there.

Once Josiah did the deed, Owen would rescue them all. Ty was counting on it. Owen would protect them. Care for them as if they were his own family. But where was he?

"You don't...you don't want me?" His voice choked. "You don't love me?"

Ty broke. Exactly what Lysander wanted. This was destruction at its finest. The nail in his coffin, but he couldn't lie. He could only punctuate what Josiah already believed about him as a father. A deception Lysander had sneakily ingrained in him, using his insecurity and circumstances to manipulate, twist and bend truth. He had a dim view of Ty already and no reason to trust him.

He didn't know him.

Here came the hammer. "Do I want you? Do I love you?" *Yes. Yes. Yes!* "What do you think?" he asked nonchalantly, hoping Josiah would believe Ty's tears were nothing more than rivulets of rain.

A snap of fury flashed in Josiah's eyes, and his hand rose. The gun fired, and a bullet ripped through Tiberius's chest.

Chapter Twenty-Eight

Bexley hadn't seen Josiah since she'd arrived. Lysander had bound and gagged her, keeping her in a room behind the primary bedroom closet. What if he didn't have her son at all and this was a trap to lure Tiberius? She'd seen the note he'd nailed into her bedroom door.

The false wall shifted and she huddled in the corner, but behind the panel appeared Agent Barkley, filthy and blood-stained with fresh drops of blood dripping onto the floor. He removed her gag.

"Thank God, I found you."

"My family? Tiberius?"

"I haven't seen them. But I was hit by debris. Knocked me out a few minutes, maybe more. We need to move. Now." He untied her hands and feet and helped her out of the closet. "Do you know where Garrick or Dalen might be?"

Bexley frowned. "No. Are they here too?"

"Who took you?" Owen asked.

"Lysander Granger. He has Ahnah and Josiah. I don't know where, though. He brought me straight to this room."

"He's keeping you separated from each other for a purpose. I don't know why. Ty's supposed to be on the second floor. Come on."

Whatever Lysander's reasons, they would be deadly.

Bexley followed Owen down the stairs to the second floor. In the living area, a bookshelf concealing a door was open, revealing a hallway.

A gun fired.

Owen pushed her against the wall and put a finger to his mouth, then raised his hand to signal her to stay put. He dashed down the hall, out of view. Fear and adrenaline pumped in unison. Her son or Ahnah or Ty could be dead. She couldn't stay, and darted into the hall after Owen.

"Drop your weapon!" Owen shouted.

What was this place? Tattooed women were naked in cages.

Josiah stood holding a gun and crying while Tiberius lay bleeding on the ground, unmoving and pale. Deathly pale.

A thundering sound erupted, sending a hiccup into her heart as the winds ripped away a portion of the side of the house, blowing it out to sea. The churning waters beyond began to gather and flow right for the house.

Storm surge!

"Don't shoot him," Tiberius said, but it was faint. "Don't shoot my son, O."

Owen trained the gun on Josiah. "Drop the weapon, man. You." He pointed the gun at Lysander. "On your knees, hands behind your back. Do it!"

Water hit with an iron fist, crashing into the side of the house and flooding into the solarium. Pieces of roofing, insulation and glass clattered to the tile.

Screams erupted.

Josiah gripped the gun. "I thought you said she wasn't here?"

Lysander dropped to his knees, hands behind his back and a glint in his eye.

Owen commanded Josiah to drop the gun one last time. "Don't make me fire this weapon."

Josiah dropped the gun, and Owen kept his trained on Lysander. Bexley raced to Josiah and hugged him, then shoved the gun he'd dropped in her waistband and knelt beside Tiberius as water continued to flood the room.

"You're going to drown. I need to move you. Can you get up? Can you walk?" Water rushed over his legs, and she grabbed him under his arms, trying to drag him, but he cried out and she halted.

"He needs pressure applied to his wound." A woman opened her cage and stepped out. "I'm a nurse. I can help him."

"Key...in my pocket," Tiberius said. "Get Josiah help. I'm sorry. I didn't mean anything I said. I love you, Bex."

Bexley took the key. "I love you too. Whatever you did, it saved our son. Now stay alive to be with us."

With a half grin, he touched her face. "I think love lingers even when we don't."

"Don't talk like that." She grasped the key and darted for the women, but the rushing water was too powerful and kept surging through the gaping hole in the side of the house. Roaring and thunder hindered her hearing. She fell and went under, inhaling water and flailing until she felt the metal cage and grabbed on to steady herself.

"Josiah, get your dad out of here," Owen hollered. "There's a secret room on the third floor. Last door at the end of the hall. You." He pointed to the two women outside their cages while keeping his gun on Lysander. "Go with him. Get in the room behind the closet. It's the safest place in the house with the flooding. We have to take our chances. God help you! Go!"

The two women, covering themselves, clung to one another, falling and clambering to escape the rushing water.

"Bexley, you don't have the strength to handle the water. Go with Ty and your son. I'll free the women and send them up. And bring up this dirtbag too, unfortunately." Lysander still knelt as water rose to his waist and his hair matted to his cheeks, a smile in his eyes.

Josiah struggled to help Tiberius stand. Bexley threw the key to Owen. As he caught it, Lysander rose up and aimed another gun at Owen. "This is my kingdom! I control it. No one is going to ruin my plans. Not you. Not him. Not this hurricane." He cursed and fired the gun Ty had slid across the floor earlier. He must have found it during the commotion.

Owen jerked backward, taking a hit to his shoulder, and returned fire. The bullet hit Lysander's leg and he buckled.

The roaring intensified, and a gale blew another pane of glass from the roof. Bexley screamed as a jagged shard ripped through Lysander. With a horrifying scream, he fell into surging water that swallowed him up.

Tiberius couldn't stand, but he had to fight for his family. He had no strength of his own, and the dizziness was overwhelming. He couldn't stop the tremors. He was bleeding out and going into shock.

Help me stand.

A thought, maybe a prayer.

He clutched Josiah as he worked to stand, but water pushed against him and his son.

Help me stand.

A definitive prayer.

He rose to his feet, and they fought against the powerful flow toward the hallway. "I lied to keep you alive. You understand?" He needed Josiah to know the truth before he couldn't tell him himself. He had more words but no strength to share them. Every second it became harder to breathe.

Water funneled in faster than they could move. The women

left in cages screeched and gripped the bars. "Owen. Owen! Stop. You can't. You can't." The water raged too fast. He'd be swept out and drowned if he tried to rescue the remaining women. But they were doomed to die without rescue. He shook off Josiah and Bexley. "Get Josiah to higher ground. I have to help O."

He pushed into the swirling water, furniture and debris floating away. He didn't feel the agony anymore. Numb but cold now. So cold.

He fell into the water, and it dragged him toward the rip in the side of the house.

"Tiberius!" Bexley hollered.

A firm hand grabbed him by the waist and hauled him upright. "What are you doing?" Owen screamed over the roaring. "Get out of here."

"You can't do it alone. You won't make it. We both know it."

"So we both die? Because you surely will. Listen to me." Owen framed his face, water and blood running down his cheeks and seeping through his shirt where he'd been hit in the shoulder. "I was supposed to be a preacher, and I didn't do it. But I preached to you when it counted. I'm okay with that. Your boy needs you."

"You're talking out of your head." Ty's lungs squeezed and his throat tightened. "Let's go."

"No. Take your family to safety. I'll get these women out. I promise." He tapped his chest with his fist.

Ty shook his head. He hadn't promised to get himself out. O knew in order to rescue them he wouldn't be able to rescue himself. "No."

"Yes. Live in light, brother."

Ty grabbed his arm to hold him in place but he was too weak. And Owen, bloody and bruised and beaten, was still stronger. Ty's wet grasp was slippery, and his fingers couldn't hold on.

Owen shoved him backward. "Josiah, help your daddy. Go. I got this."

But he didn't. The water tugged him, insatiable.

"Owen." Ty's heart stuttered.

Josiah and Bexley wrangled him, forcing him to put distance between himself and his best friend.

Owen unlocked the first cage closest to him and struggled to help the woman find her footing, but she made it. The other two women had already entered the hallway, but Ty needed to watch. Needed to make sure Owen made it to safety.

The house convulsed.

Iris Benington touched his shoulder again. "You're going to die if you don't let me help you."

The water sucked Owen under but he surfaced and unlocked another cage. "Go, hon! Go!"

Engulfed in the sea, he struggled but clutched another cage, setting free another captive and pushing her toward cover.

Pieces of solar panel and glass were ripped from above. Flood waters continued to rise. Up or down. It was a toss-up which was safer, but either way, they needed to go somewhere fast. Yet Ty balked.

One last cage.

Owen clung to it with one hand while unlocking it with the other. Susan Mayer swept out, but he snagged her before she could be carried away.

He did it.

Owen did it.

Ty allowed the nurse and Bexley to aid him through the water into the hallway, which was engulfed in about three feet of water and rising.

Movement in Ty's peripheral had him turning toward the huge opening in the house.

Lysander.

He hadn't been swept out. He'd managed to grip one of the

bolted-down cages closest to the wall and hang on somehow. He pushed himself up, bloody and drenched, still gripping the gun. His guttural scream pierced the atmosphere as he aimed the gun at Ty.

The world shifted and stilled.

Owen released the cage that was holding him from being dragged away and gripped Lysander around the waist; the gun fired and missed Ty.

But nothing anchored Owen or Lysander, and Ty gaped in horror as his brother by choice was swept out to sea with a madman.

Chapter Twenty-Nine

Ty's brain wouldn't process what he'd witnessed.

Voices were muffled. He was moving but he didn't feel it. Not even when he tripped and fell on the stairs toward the third floor.

"Get that on him. Use it to apply pressure."

The sounds of clothes being yanked off hangers registered.

"We need a phone. Call someone!"

"Dad! Dad, I'm sorry!"

"Stay with me. I love you. I need you."

Owen. Owen was gone. "Why did Owen do that, Bex?" A sob escaped his lips.

Iris held his wrist. "I have a palpable pulse, which means for now his blood pressure is decent, but it's growing faint. Looks like a small-caliber wound." She felt around his back. "I don't feel an exit wound. It's lodged."

"What does that mean?" Bexley asked.

Iris frowned. "The bullet could be lodged in his aorta. He could have a small hemothorax."

"And if that's the case?"

Iris shook her head. "We might have a few hours."

Ty might have a few hours but Owen had none. "Why would he do that for me? Why? Why?" Owen should have let him help him. They could have worked together like they always had. They could have saved those women together.

But deep down he knew that wasn't true. Ty didn't have the strength to save anyone.

He couldn't even save himself.

Owen knew it too.

And Owen had chosen to lay down his life to save Tiberius.

Bexley wept as Iris worked on Tiberius. Women who'd been held captive for months huddled together draped in the shirts and suit coats of their captor, but that was all they had to help give them back their dignity.

Josiah cried on her shoulder, apologizing for everything he'd ever done and said. He was going to need to see Drew to work through the trauma. All of them needed mental health care.

But where was Ahnah?

Josiah said Lysander told him she left them, but she couldn't believe that. Their lives had not grown that far apart.

She leaned her head on Tiberius's for a moment. He was quiet. Too quiet. The only sound was the terrifying destruction happening all around them. More roofing had been ripped away and crashing continued, but so far they were safe here. They had found jugs of water in the room, flashlights, a lantern and packages of snack crackers and granola bars plus blankets and a first aid kit, which Iris had used on Tiberius to pack his wound as they prayed the hurricane would pass quickly or Tiberius wasn't going to make it.

As she shifted against the wall, she heard a noise. Like a mouse squeaking. "Do you hear that?" she asked.

Everyone froze, listening.

She heard it again. A squeak. She turned, placing her hand on the wall. "It's coming from behind here." Getting on her knees, she held a flashlight in one hand and ran the other along the wall and felt it give. "It's another false wall!" She pressed until it opened and shined the light inside.

Gasping, she clutched her chest.

"Ahnah!"

She scrambled inside. Her sister was draped in a blanket and her mouth was gagged with a silk tie. Her hands were tied with another behind her back. Bexley pulled out the gag. "Ahnah!"

"Bex." Tears flooded her cheeks. "Bex!"

Bexley hugged her until she thought she might never let go. Lysander had separated them. For Josiah to play his part in Lysander's sick plan, he couldn't let him discover Bexley or Ahnah, and they'd been a wall apart for hours. She untied her and helped her into the bigger room, where they huddled.

"What's happening?" Ahnah asked, looking at the women. "Who are they?"

"You haven't been in the cages?" Bexley asked.

Ahnah shook her head. "No." She draped herself on Bexley. "How did he find you?"

"He came into a bar I was in one night. At first, I didn't recognize him, but then he spoke to me. He was shocked and I was shocked. I tried to pretend he was mistaken about who I was, but he knew. Told me it was okay, that he wouldn't tell a soul, and I believed him because he had never hurt me. We'd been friends. He didn't want me to tell you because you'd think he was trying to force me back in the Family. He told me he'd left and owned his own real estate company." She did a double take. "Tiberius?"

"He's been shot," Bexley offered, too exhausted to tell the story right now.

"Lysander shot him?"

"Long story." Bex smoothed Josiah's hair and tenderly smiled. Josiah hugged Ahnah and held her hand.

"How did he get you here?" Tiberius whispered, his face pale and his lips pasty white.

"I came on my own. We'd been talking awhile, and he invited me out. So I came. We... Anyway, after, he put me in a room with a bed and chained me to the wall. He forced me to take these little yellow pills that knocked me out. He became someone I didn't know."

"Well, you're safe now." Bexley kissed her and leaned on Tiberius. "Everyone is safe." If they could weather the hurricane. It could go on for hours—hours they didn't have. And without power, they had no way to know when the worst had passed. She had no phone.

Ahnah reached over and clasped Ty's hand. "It's good to see you. I'm so sorry about the death of your friend Cami."

Tiberius's cheeks were sallow and the light behind his eyes dim, but he smiled at Ahnah, then frowned. Bexley touched his cheek. "What is it? What can I do?"

"Hand me the gun," he whispered, raspy and strained.

"What? Why?" she said as she handed it over.

Tiberius pointed to Ahnah's shoulder where the blanket had fallen away, revealing her skin. "Because she shouldn't know about Cami...and she doesn't have a single tattoo."

Chapter Thirty

Nags Head, North Carolina
Outer Banks Hospital
Monday, September 10
8:20 a.m.

"Hey," Asa said, as Ty opened his eyes. "How you feelin'?"

"What day is it?"

"Monday."

"I feel like I got shot. And… I can't really remember much."
He'd passed out after Bexley handed him the gun, and when
he'd woken, he was being airlifted to the hospital. He knew
there'd been surgery and sedation for pain. In his few moments
of consciousness, a hand had held his, squeezing.

Bexley.

She loved him. He loved her. They were gonna have to do
something about that.

"After the hurricane passed—seven hours of it—Bexley called
the sheriff's office from a burner phone she found in Lysander's

desk drawer, and they airlifted all y'all to the hospital, where you were rushed into surgery. Bullet was trapped in your aorta, but the surgeon removed it. Said it was unbelievable you made it as long as you did and no irreparable damage had been done. Iris Benington's fast work helped. Once the storm cleared, we flew in. Arrived yesterday."

"Ahnah?"

Asa ran his tongue along his top teeth. "Bexley held her at gunpoint when you passed out."

That couldn't have been easy for her.

"Then Ahnah went straight to the sheriff's office for questioning. She said she reconnected with Lysander at the bar. Like she told you. She didn't tell Bexley because of the Family and because she'd make her cut ties like Bexley had cut ties with you. She continued with her story that he kept her elsewhere and hadn't tattooed her—no idea why or what he was planning."

"You believe that?"

"No. After getting nowhere, I sent in Violet."

Ty smirked. "Nice. She jeeper-creeper it?"

Asa lifted his eyebrows and gave him a what-do-you-think expression. "Until she had her blubbering and spilling it all."

"I love that scary woman."

Asa nodded. "Turns out the way they reconnected is true. But for a solid year he did to her what he did to Josiah, preying on the void in her life, her hurt and regrets about her parents and leaving them. He convinced her they could run their own Family together and seek revenge on everyone who tore them apart and ruined their lives."

Ty closed his eyes, thinking of that sweet little girl who loved flowers and drawing.

Asa continued. "Lysander knew Garrick was tattooing art in Wilmington and inking the stereograms on women. She didn't know how he knew, but let's face it—the guy had ways. Lysander confronted Garrick. He didn't deny it but told Lysander how much fun it was to paint on fresh skin and to leave his permanent mark. Ahnah said when she was a child, he had often made her undress from the waist down to paint on her back. Said other girls were forced to as well. Lysander also knew this."

Ty hadn't. But then, he'd suspected Ahnah hadn't admitted every way Garrick had tortured her. They'd had the profile right about Lysander, but it also fit Garrick.

"Ahnah befriended Lily and Amy-Rose, and later it was her idea to get the tats, knowing Garrick would be the artist and leave the emblem. But she said she pretended to be sick and backed out but encouraged them to go anyway. They did."

Garrick would have seen her and recognized her. She couldn't go. She'd lied to them about where she'd received her tattoo. "Lysander knew that we'd find them and that it would send us straight to Garrick. Did Ahnah also know Dahlia?"

"Yes, but she never mentioned her to Bexley, because knowing too many of the victims would be suspect."

"Ahnah joined the other girls for the dark fantasies at Patrick Swain's for a setup. Point the finger at Patrick, keep you chasing wind and strong-arm Patrick to sell his property to Lysander, which worked. We still haven't found Jenny Davis's body and probably never will. That's all Dare County Sheriff's job. Skipper and Patrick haven't been charged with anything."

Without a body, they probably never would be.

"Ahnah also copped to taking the mementos and photos from Bexley's closet to give Lysander more personal information. She also confessed to knocking out Owen and pulling that fire alarm at the pizza place. They'd worn disguises. Our blond guy with the beard—Lysander."

Ty assumed as much.

"She then went to the garden and saw everything transpire. Knew she was in trouble and hid when Owen and Bexley arrived in the hall leading to the solarium, then ran upstairs and hid herself in the other room. Used Lysander's ties to loosely tie herself up and covered herself with a blanket to appear she'd been locked up naked like the others."

"But the blanket fell when she reached out, and she made the mistake of mentioning Cami." Ty paused. "She killed Garrick, didn't she?"

Asa nodded. "Revenge for what he did to her."

That explained the hesitation marks on his throat. If Lysander had killed him, the slice would have been deep and quick.

"They were going to pin all the murders on him."

"But she jumped the gun," Ty said. "I knew Lysander was surprised to hear that."

"They had ways to pin it on Dalen if that didn't work, and to cast suspicion on Patrick."

"Where's my son? What's going to happen to him?" He'd committed a crime. Yes, Ty had incited him, but it had been his choice, his impulsive choice.

"He's with his mom. CID questioned him, and we talked with the district attorney. He doesn't want to press charges, but Josiah has to go into mandatory counseling, which will do him good. We pulled a few strings like you know we can."

Relief washed over him. "Good. That's good. Thank you."

"Was Lysander also the Fire & Ice Killer? Was Patrick Swain?"

"Swain was in the locations mentioned during the time frame of the killings, but his receipts and alibis all check out. As far as Lysander, nothing matches. He used the Fire & Ice Killer to add to your guilt and run you on his own fun wild-goose chase as well as to provide another option if his plan to frame his other brothers didn't work."

"He played me good."

"No. You got the upper hand with Milo. He wasn't able to see his plan through on his own terms."

Maybe not. But no one won this one. Everyone had lost something. "Dalen involved?"

Asa shook his head. "He reported his car stolen two weeks ago. He didn't report Carri missing because she left him prior to that."

"She wasn't in the cages."

"I know. She's still missing. My best guess is Garrick found her, killed her himself. Or maybe Lysander did. We'll probably never know, but the other survivors are now with their families and gave testimony to everything Lysander did. Cami's funeral is next week," he whispered.

Now to face the other elephant in the room. "And Owen?"

Asa shook his head. "They found him not far from the house. I've notified his mother and sister. We had his body flown in to Greenwood, and arrangements are being made."

When Ty's tears came, he didn't try to hide them. "I'm so sorry. I'll resign first thing when we arrive in Memphis. Their deaths are on me."

"No," Asa said softly. "We saw Lysander that first day in the coffee shop. He came in purposely to be close to us. Dropped his phone, and I picked it up, not giving him much more than a glance. One of the girls said he had them on camera on his phone, and the house was a smart house with all the bells and whistles. Sheriff said they found cameras in what remains. What if they'd been on camera and I'd have paid more attention? I could have stopped it. Fi could have. This is not on you."

"Not on you either."

"We can pin it on Fi, then," Asa teased, wiping moisture from his eyes. "She has it coming for thinking he was hotter than Orlando Bloom." He chuckled and then sobered. "Cami's life was snuffed out, Ty. She was conned and killed. But she would not want you to blame yourself. You know that. And Owen… Owen wasn't killed because of you. He laid down his life *for* you."

He had.

Owen had been the brother he'd always wanted. They'd spent weekends together, competed in a softball league together, and played office pranks for sheer merriment. He knew Ty better than anyone and never judged him—never preached.

Until the end, when he believed it had mattered most.

Now he was gone, and Ty was alone.

"I didn't ask for that. I didn't ask him to do that!" His nose ran and he covered his face, his entire body breaking down and grieving.

"No. You didn't. He wanted you to live, Ty. And in order for you to live, he had to die. He chose to die for you. His love saved you. And if you quit—the team, life—you'll have wasted his sacrifice. Don't do that."

Bexley's words returned to his memory.

I don't believe anything in our life is wasted. This shell is chipped and broken. Been tossed by the waves. No control and yet it's here on this beach. It's not so far destroyed that I can't recognize what it's meant to be or find the beauty in it. I think the broken shells have stronger, richer stories than those I find that are in mint condition.

He'd been broken. Owen had been broken. Ty had not only his story to tell but Owen's. One of sacrificial love and bravery.

Oddly, a verse from the Bible came to mind. "No greater love than laying down a life for a brother," Ty murmured. "Lysander said I'd need more than love to save me. He was wrong. It was absolutely love that saved me."

Asa remained silent but nodded.

Owen had showed a greater love. A higher love. Because that's the only kind of love that could have given Owen the courage and peace to lay everything down for Tiberius. "Owen was gonna be a preacher. You know that?" he asked.

Asa shook his head. "I can see it, though."

"Asa?"

"Yeah?"

"I didn't make it to that island house by myself. Too many things clicked into place right when I needed them to. I believe in coincidence, but that was too many, and to push through that marsh in seventy- to eighty-mile-an-hour winds? Or stronger. Something...*someone* did that. And I think that same Someone gave Owen the bravery and the peace to let go. But how can I repay him? How can I look his mama in the eye knowing I lived and he died?"

"I think his mama is proud of him and that he'd returned to his faith roots, and you should tell her as much." Asa's eyes shimmered, and his hand enveloped Ty's. "If you know the truth, Ty...it's time to accept it and live in it. For yourself. And for O."

Ty wiped his nose with the back of his hand. "I don't know how to do that."

"Well, you got some friends who can help you."

Ty began by allowing Asa to pray, and as he did, a warm peace washed through him. Not like a storm surge or hurricane, though it had taken hurricane force to sweep away the lies he'd been steeped in. His past experiences, all horrific, had shaped his stubborn heart, leaving him robbed of true peace, desolate and lonely.

No, it wasn't a storm or hurricane drowning his heart, but a serene bubbling brook drenching his soul.

Asa left him, and soon Bexley knocked on the door. "Hi," she whispered as she entered.

"Hi," he returned, and scooted up in his bed.

"How are you feeling?" She sat where Asa had, smelling like flowers and something pure and clean.

"Weird." He told her what happened with Asa. "I don't feel much different. But... I legit have a peace I didn't before. And... Owen."

"It's grief, baby." She brushed his forehead with the back of her hand. "You grieve and also have hope. Your friends came through for Josiah. I told him the truth about us and our past, everything I should have. I asked for his forgiveness, because at times I did put helping broken women before my family. If I'd have done a better job, maybe Ahnah and Josiah wouldn't have fallen prey to Lysander."

"Bexley, you did the best you could with what you had at the time. Don't put this on you. Lysander learned from the master—Rand Granger. He kind of reminds me of Absalom. I wonder if he cut his hair and weighed it too."

She laid her head on his. "Probably. Narcissistic sicko. And for someone who hasn't claimed to be a believer, you sure know a lot about the Bible."

He grasped her hand and grinned. "How did Josiah take the truth?"

"He understood, I think. Things will have to change. I'm going to relinquish some control and take more time for him. Ahnah will be charged. She was a victim, but she also made her choices. As much harm as she did, I still don't want to see her go away. I want to go back, but we can't ever go back. Only move forward or stay stuck, and I'm sick of being in the same place."

"I don't want to go back either, Bex. I want to move forward. With you and Josiah. I love you."

She gently kissed his lips. "I love you too. We're gonna figure this out."

He kissed her hand. "I want us to be a family."

"I do too," she whispered, and lay beside him. All he was missing was his son, who poked his head inside.

"Can I come in?" he asked hesitantly.

"Of course you can, son." *Son*—a word he didn't know he'd love so much. "You never have to ask to be near me."

And the truth of drawing near to God rang true. He didn't have to ask. He only had to draw. Funny how the word *draw* meant "to be close" and also "art." It had been his son's art that had ultimately drawn him to the Father. To the Architect of his life.

Ty had laid down his stubby pencil, with an eraser eroded from working so hard to blot out mistakes in his life. But it had left streaks and smudges, never truly giving him that fresh blank canvas. And, at times, the paper of life had ripped and crumpled.

Now he had a fresh, clean canvas, one he didn't have to attempt to sketch on his own. This surrender wasn't giving permission for someone to control his life. It was surrendering to a freedom he'd never experienced, or wanted, until now.

He'd finally scaled the wall he'd been climbing his whole life. He could unpack his belongings and lay down roots.

Because, finally, he'd found home.

Epilogue

One month later

Ty sneaked from the small room behind the baptistry of Asa and Fiona's church and peeked into the sanctuary filled with family and friends. Bex and Josiah sat in the fourth row on the bride's side. A week after Ty had been released from the hospital, they'd packed and moved to Memphis.

He rubbed his gold band on his left ring finger. Two weeks ago, they'd been married in this very church, with just their immediate family and his SCU family in attendance. Owen's mama had prayed over them at the ceremony, and Ty put her heart at ease—Owen may not have preached to the masses, but he'd shared the truth with him. And it had changed his life forever.

Josiah had been his best man. After their long conversations and counseling, their relationship was growing, and they were bonding. They even teased each other a little now.

Remember that time I shot you?

Remember that time I made you shoot me?

Bexley didn't find it funny, but Josiah was like Ty in using humor to deflect big feelings, heavy subjects and conflict. He was finishing up his senior year homeschooling, and then would go on to community college to stick close and make up for lost time.

Ty and Bex had discussed adding to the family. Maybe he'd do alright with another son. He'd name him Owen. But if they had a little baby girl, he'd be equally happy. And they'd name her Camellia. Call her Tink. His eyes watered, and he ducked back inside, tiptoeing down the hall to the bridal suite and knocking.

"Let me in, Fi Fi McGee."

"I hate it when you call me that," she hollered, but she opened the door, and his breath caught.

"I know." He tossed her a mischievous smirk. "You look amazing." She wore a simple, silky white gown that flowed to the floor and a pearl headband.

"Thanks."

Ty thumbed toward the sanctuary. "Luke Rathbone is out there. Asa just rubbing it in that he won you or what?"

His remark garnered him a reprimanding glare.

Violet, wearing a long, dark green dress, poked her body in front of Fiona's. "Why are you in here?"

"You look stunning. Until you open your mouth. You got a gun under that skirt?"

Violet smirked and drew her dress up to reveal an ankle holster.

"Seriously?" Fiona asked. "Who do you think you're going to need to shoot during the ceremony?"

"Tiberius. When he opens his fat pie hole during the 'speak now or forever hold your peace' portion of the ceremony." She narrowed her gaze. "You know I'll do it too."

"I've been shot enough in this life. I'll hold my peace." For once he had peace to hold.

Selah popped her head over Violet's shoulder, her eyes watery. "Nice bow tie," she said. "He'd love it."

It was black with one brown and one white fist-bumping each other. "Yeah. I thought he would. We'd be doing a lot of joking today—at y'all's expense of course—and fist-bumping."

Fiona framed his face with her hands. "Joke all you want." She kissed him on the mouth. "At Asa's expense."

He tossed her a crooked grin. "I edited all the Lee Brice songs out of the playlist for the reception. Just so you know. We will be doing the conga and maybe 'The Banana Boat Song.' 'Day-O,'" he sang.

His song choices incited groans all around.

"It's almost time. Go away," Fiona jested.

"Saw John and Stella out there," he said to Violet. "She's wearing a frilly dress and a plastic holster and sheriff's badge."

Violet grinned. "Girls can be sheriffs. They can be whatever they want. When they want."

"Yeah. Yeah. I'm going." He shuffled down the hall as Asa exited the groomsmen's room.

"It's time."

"You nervous?" Ty asked.

Asa beamed. "No way. I love that woman, and I can't say 'I do' fast enough."

"I said it faster."

"Whatever. Come on."

Ty followed Asa through the door to the stage, and they took their places. Asa, then Ty, and beside Ty a large portrait of Owen. They were both supposed to have been Asa's best men. Together.

He slowly reached out and fist-bumped the canvas showcasing Owen's infectious smile—a mischievous gleam that was all Owen Barkley.

Agent.

Friend.

Sometimes ladies' man.

Preacher.

Brother.

And Ty looked on as Asa and Fiona said, "I do."

★ ★ ★ ★ ★

*Read on for a sneak peek at Jessica R. Patch's
next thriller from Love Inspired Trade,
coming in 2025!*

Prologue

Her eyes are vacant orbs that pierce my soul and chill my bones. The kind of chill that can only be warmed by immersion in scalding water. The kind that leaves a paralyzed shiver in its wake.

I stand with one clammy hand on the railing and the other pressed on the pain that constricts my chest. Am I having a heart attack? This must be what a heart attack feels like. Tight and heavy with shocks that ripple like electricity along my left arm, leaving me stunned with my pulse out of rhythm.

My hand slides along the wrought iron and my knees feel languid and weak. One push is all it would take to send me to my death.

I know she's thinking about it.

Her gaze swings from me to my hand to the stairs and to the concrete flooring below.

"What do you think you saw?" she asks through a narrowed gaze. "Whatever you think it was—it wasn't. You shouldn't even be awake this time of night. Have you taken your pills?

The doctor said you can't skip them. If you do, you could hallucinate."

"I—I didn't hallucinate what I witnessed just now. I didn't." But I hadn't taken my pills tonight, and I can't remember if I took them last night. My days have been running together lately. However, my eyes didn't conjure up the atrocity I walked into five minutes ago.

She steps into my personal space, predatory like a lioness. She's hungry to pounce, but she's careful, calculated. I am her prey, and I don't understand how we've gotten here.

That's a lie.

I do know.

I know exactly how we've gotten here.

"You're sick," she says in a gentle but mocking tone. "You've been sick a very long time. You know this. You've been hospitalized four times in six years." Her lips turn down as if she feels sorry for me. She doesn't. She has no pity or compassion because she feels nothing. Her heart is a black abyss.

"Let me help you back to bed. Give you your meds and some water. You'll feel better in the morning."

I don't want to take my pills. I'm fine without them. I've been having more good days than bad days. They make me tired and foggy. She eyes me, holding my gaze. She's not going to back down.

But I know what I saw. The horror was real, and the terror that races cold through my blood proves I saw it with my own two eyes.

And I have no idea what to do but to allow her to gently yet firmly guide me to my bedroom like a naive child. I've tried a million different things. Interruptions. Distractions. I thought distance would solve it.

It didn't. Things actually grew worse.

"Okay. You're right. I—I'm not thinking clearly. What would I do without you?" I fake a smile, and she returns it in an equally saccharine measure. She helps me into bed, and I slide between the soft sheets as she picks up the brown prescription bottle and empties two trazadone pills into her palm, then holds them out to me.

I willingly accept them, and she hands me the water. I drink and swallow.

"Good." She pats my head like I'm a good little puppy who didn't piddle on the floor. "You'll feel much better now. You'll see more clearly in the morning."

No, I wouldn't.

"Good night, Mother," she says.

"Good night," I murmur. After she leaves the room, I spit out the pills. I'm seeing more clearly than I ever did on these things.

And I know what I saw.

I slip my diary out from between the mattress and box spring and grab my pen from the nightstand. I've been chronicling her behavior for years. No one has believed me. According to her, it's nothing but a diatribe from a broken woman.

But I know the truth.

I fear this will be my last entry. But I fear every entry might be my last.

She's tried to kill me before.

Chapter One

Chicago, Illinois

Charlotte Kane closed her eyes and inhaled the years of other people's lives. But she wanted something new in her own life. Shiny and sparkly.

The greasy-haired guy—with jeans that showed way too much of his checkered boxers—cleared his throat, tucked a cheap cigarette between his thin lips and gawked.

"I don't have a light, if that's what you want." Charlotte folded her arms over her chest, knowing full well that wasn't what he wanted at all. "Besides, you can't smoke in the shop." Not that it mattered. In less than an hour, every antique and trinket would be on the truck outside and shipped to auction.

"I'm looking for the old guy. I got my own lighter." He pulled it from his pocket and shook it like a pendulum.

"He's in the back. On the phone."

Mr. Moving Guy muttered a curse and took his almost-nine-bucks-a-pack habit outside along with his scowl and droopy pants.

Mr. Sobolewski, her boss, was retiring, and his children didn't want a musty building full of junk. Which put Charlotte out of a job.

Junk.

Nothing in this shop was junk to her. She was surrounded by memories of the past, legacies proving people had been around. Lived. Loved. Or at the very least cooked. She picked up a wooden spoon and bowl, eyeing the man from her peripheral vision. He puffed away and pretended not to grope her with his gaze.

Every day she'd imagined these lives. Fairytale endings. Hope and love and light. Everything her life wasn't nor had ever been.

"Charlotte, you have big plans tonight?" Mr. Sobolewski asked, or, as she liked to call him, Sobo.

"If you count scouring the *Chicago Tribune* website for jobs a big plan, then yes."

"You're just now looking for a new job?" Sobo's bushy gray eyebrows came together in a V, and he shook his head. "You've known two months I'm packing it in."

"I'm kidding—well, I'm always looking." The next best thing that would catapult her into the life she'd always wanted to live might be in the *Tribune*. She read it daily. "I have a super awesome job lined up in two weeks. It'll be my pleasure to serve coffee too strong and eggs too runny to tired truckers and teens that are too strung out to go home—at least until their parents go to work." She sighed. "And since you're an old-timer, I'll clue you in…that was sarcasm."

Charlotte longed for the charmed life. She could barely afford a box of Lucky Charms, let alone a charmed life.

Mr. Sobolewski hooted and broke out in a full-minute-long coughing spell. She joined in the laughter, though truthfully, it wasn't all that funny.

But hey, she'd spent over six months saving up $2,000, which would cushion her for the next couple of weeks until she started her waitressing job—or found something new. Something better. Every time she started over, she could make herself over too. Be anyone she wanted to be. Maybe she'd cut her hair in a short bob and dye it black. Or red. She'd been a redhead before. Never black hair, though, and convenience store dye didn't cost much. She'd pick some up later.

"You've been a hard worker, Charlotte. I wish I could do more than this." Mr. Sobolewski handed her three hundred-dollar bills and smiled with lips as big as the Kielbasa sausages his wife brought them for lunch on Mondays. Perks of workin' with an old Polish guy.

She'd miss him—and the delicious artery-cloggers. She took the crisp bills and hugged the old man, holding back tears.

Time to move on. Maybe her own Richard Gere would waltz into the Flapjack House and order pancakes for breakfast and fall in love with her. She'd have her own Julia Roberts story without hooking for it. She had boundaries.

"Thanks, Sobo. I've learned a lot about history and antiques from you—and origami."

"I didn't teach you origami."

She hid her smile. "No? Guess that was some other guy."

"You know I didn't teach you that." His brows came together again, and she laughed.

"I do know. I just like your confused face. I have a notebook with how many times a day I roped you into making one."

"You do?"

"No." She gave him a playful punch. "But you did it again. Good times, Sobo. Good times."

"Take care, young lady." His eyes glistened. Maybe for her. Maybe because his livelihood was being set piece by piece on a truck. "Now get out of here." He shook his head and hurried across the floor, swiping at his eyes.

"Hey, where's he going? I need to know what to do with these mirrors."

Charlotte bit back her harsh remark. "Look, he's been here over forty years. What would you do if you hadn't had a cigarette all day, then opened the pack for your last one, only to see it was gone? Give the guy a minute."

He mumbled under his breath. Charlotte easily imagined the *pleasantries* she was being called. Wouldn't be the first time. Wouldn't be the last.

She pulled out her ancient iPhone to call her best friend, Tillie, to pick her up, but a car parked out front caught her eye. She stuffed her phone back in her pocket.

Her childhood social worker stepped out of the blue Taurus. Glenda.

Sleek in her tan pantsuit, she walked towards her, a tight smile on her face and weak wave of her hand. Over the years, lines had formed around her eyes, and her hair had turned grayer and was cut shorter.

Charlotte glanced towards the back room, then pushed the door open, listening to the rusty bell ding as she stepped outside onto the sidewalk. "What brings you here?"

"Call it an old habit."

Glenda wasn't family, but she was *much* better than the woman who'd incubated her. And occasionally, she checked in on Charlotte.

"When's the last time you saw Marilyn?"

Speaking of the woman who gave birth to her. Charlotte sighed. "Year ago maybe. She wanted money I didn't have."

"Are you heading out?"

"Yeah, it's my last day. Retirement. For Sobo. Not me."

Glenda's lips twitched. "I gathered that." She looked at the huge truck. The door rolled down with a clang. "Let me give you a ride."

Uh-oh. This sounded serious. "Is Tommy in trouble again?"

"He's twenty-eight, Charlotte. Not my problem if he is."

"I have to let Tillie know I don't need a ride."

Glenda picked up the mirror Sobo had given Charlotte earlier in the day and worked on shoving it into the back seat. Charlotte called Tillie and told her she'd fill her in on the unexpected visit from Glenda later. She climbed in the Taurus and buckled her seat belt.

"Why don't you get to your point, Glenda. I'm not a kid anymore. I've learned to expect and handle disappointments." She half smiled, but the years of rejection had lodged in her heart like a bee's stinger that couldn't be removed.

Glenda nodded and pulled a piece of paper from her deep handbag while keeping her eyes on the road. "You know I think Marilyn wanted to be a good mom. I do. She just couldn't break free from her habits and mental troubles."

Where was this going?

"When you went into the system the first time, she tried. She really did. It just didn't go the way she wanted."

The way *she* wanted?

And thank you, Glenda, for giving the woman another chance. Just long enough for no one else to want Charlotte. No one wanted six-year-old children—the age she'd been tossed back into the system…when Marilyn failed as a parent—a human being.

Couples wanted powdery newborns or chubby toddlers. Charlotte's life was a never-ending revolving door of four walls that kept her dry. Never could describe them as homes or families or safe places.

Glenda handed Charlotte a paper. "Her latest address."

Charlotte eyed the scribbles before looking at Glenda. "I don't want to see her."

Glenda sighed, and in those few seconds, the weight of her job revealed how tired she was. "You won't have to. She died of an overdose last night. I just got the news."

Charlotte was only surprised it'd taken this long for Marilyn to drop dead. Not a single tear surfaced. Nope, no waterworks for Marilyn Kane.

Glenda's face remained stoic as she stared up at the traffic light, waiting for it to turn green. "She might have something of interest to you."

Charlotte snorted. "Sorry, I'm not in the market for a crack pipe."

"I'm not talking about paraphernalia, Charlotte. What would it hurt to take a gander? You never know what you might find of importance." She patted her arm. "You're special, Charlotte. A real success in my eyes. Not everyone who cycles in and out of the system and lives with someone like Marilyn has a stable life."

Charlotte's life was far from anything she'd describe as successful. "Not sure you could call a woman with a GED, a meaningless job, and a low-income apartment winning. You're as delusional as our governor."

"You have a job and a home and some education, and you're scrappy and full of common sense—and no one can ever say you don't have wit." Glenda smirked. "You probably only have a few days before they haul off her meager belongings to the trash dump. Decide." She turned into Charlotte's apartment parking lot. "You may not be able to change your circumstances, but you can change *you*, Charlotte. Be anyone you want to be."

She'd been doing that for over a decade. "Thanks for the ride." She opened the door, and the smell of the dumpsters—her stellar view from the living room window—scrunched her nose.

Glenda cocked her head. "I'm here…if you need me. And Charlotte, remember that sometimes my job forces me to keep quiet about things. Things I wish I could share. Go to your mom's apartment. Okay?"

Charlotte pulled the mirror from the back seat and stared at

Glenda. Cryptic talk wasn't her thing. "Okay. I'll think about it. Thanks for the ride."

What was in Marilyn's Kane's apartment?

Don't miss this next thriller from Jessica R. Patch!

Copyright 2024 by Jessica R. Patch

Acknowledgments

It takes a village to make a book happen, and I had quite a lot of help from a myriad of people.

FBI Agent, Mr. Anonymous. Thank you for helping me with procedural information and answering endless questions. Any mistakes are mine alone.

Paul Perry, friend, tattoo artist, and owner of Pure 13 Tattoo shops in the Memphis area. Thank you for answering all kinds of fun questions about tattooing, tattooing equipment and how long it would take to do the necessary work, along with some wild stories I found fascinating. You rock.

Susan L. Tuttle, my brainstorming partner who helps keep me sane and not cross too many lines. Thank you!

Jodie Bailey, you are a closet meteorologist and know all things Outer Banks. Thank you for inviting me to the retreat and answering all my questions about geography and hurricanes and helping me create the fictional island of Blue Harbor. It was an honor to name this hurricane after you! Any stretches are on me.

Laura Ott, my friend and cook extraordinaire. Thank you for answering North Carolina questions. You helped me tremendously.

Luke Williamson, friend and Deputy Director for the Public Integrity Unit. Thank you for all the legal information. You always come through for me! If I stretched the law...have me arrested? Nah, just forgive me.

My Patch Pack, and specifically the winners, Renee Helton and Leslie McDonald, for naming the lipstick killer. I hope you enjoyed seeing your names in the book!

My launch team, for reading, reviewing and raving about the book. Your enthusiasm and passion to see these books out in the world warms my heart.

Bree Eichler, thank you for walking me through several medical scenarios that would be plausible. If I made any mistakes, it's on me!

Rachel Kent, my agent and friend and champion. Thank you for believing in me and these books even if they scare you a little!

Shana Asaro, rock star editor! Thank you for saying yes to these books and making them so much better than I originally wrote them. You stretch me in a good way.

The team at Harlequin, who brings these book babies to life with gorgeous covers and support. Thank you for your hard work and dedication.

My family, who supports me, likely because I terrify them and they know I can hide a body. For real, I love you all so much. I couldn't do this without your love and encouragement.

And finally, to my Lord and Savior. For Your glory and Your honor always.

Get 3 FREE REWARDS!

We'll send you 2 FREE Books plus a FREE Mystery Gift.

Essential Inspirational novels reflect traditional Christian values. Enjoy a mix of contemporary, Amish, historical, and suspenseful romantic stories.

FREE Value Over $40

YES! Please send me 2 FREE Essential Inspirational novels and my FREE mystery gift (gift is worth about $10 retail). After receiving them, if I don't wish to receive any more books, I can return the shipping statement marked "cancel." If I don't cancel, I will receive 2 brand-new novels every month and be billed just $24.98 in the U.S., or $30.48 each in Canada. That's a savings of at least 26% off the cover price. It's quite a bargain! Shipping and handling is just $1.00 per book in the U.S. and $1.50 per book in Canada.* I understand that accepting the 2 free books and gift places me under no obligation to buy anything. I can always return a shipment and cancel at any time. The free books and gift are mine to keep no matter what I decide.

Essential Inspirational (157/357 BPA G2DG)

Name (please print)

Address   Apt. #

City   State/Province   Zip/Postal Code

Email: Please check this box ☐ if you would like to receive newsletters and promotional emails from Harlequin Enterprises ULC and its affiliates. You can unsubscribe anytime.

Mail to the **Harlequin Reader Service:**
IN U.S.A.: P.O. Box 1341, Buffalo, NY 14240-8531
IN CANADA: P.O. Box 603, Fort Erie, Ontario L2A 5X3

Want to try 2 free books from another series? Call 1-800-873-8635 or visit www.ReaderService.com.

*Terms and prices subject to change without notice. Prices do not include sales taxes, which will be charged (if applicable) based on your state or country of residence. Canadian residents will be charged applicable taxes. Offer not valid in Quebec. This offer is limited to one order per household. Books received may not be as shown. Not valid for current subscribers to Essential Inspirational books. All orders subject to approval. Credit or debit balances in a customer's account(s) may be offset by any other outstanding balance owed by or to the customer. Please allow 4 to 6 weeks for delivery. Offer available while quantities last.

Your Privacy—Your information is being collected by Harlequin Enterprises ULC, operating as Harlequin Reader Service. For a complete summary of the information we collect, how we use this information and to whom it is disclosed, please visit our privacy notice located at corporate.harlequin.com/privacy-notice. From time to time we may also exchange your personal information with reputable third parties. If you wish to opt out of this sharing of your personal information, please visit readerservice.com/consumerschoice or call 1-800-873-8635. **Notice to California Residents**—Under California law, you have specific rights to control and access your data. For more information on these rights and how to exercise them, visit corporate.harlequin.com/california-privacy.

LIT24